WARRIORS

WINDS OF
CHANGE

WARRIORS

GRAPHIC NOVELS

Graystripe's Adventure
Ravenpaw's Path
SkyClan and the Stranger
A Shadow in RiverClan

Tigerstar and Sasha #1: Into the Woods
Tigerstar and Sasha #2: Escape from the Forest
Tigerstar and Sasha #3: Return to the Clans
The Rise of Scourge

WARRIORS
WINDS OF CHANGE

CREATED BY
ERIN HUNTER

WRITTEN BY
DAN JOLLEY

ART BY
JAMES L. BARRY

An Imprint of HarperCollins*Publishers*

Warriors: Winds of Change
Created by Erin Hunter
Written by Dan Jolley
Art by James L. Barry

HarperAlley is an imprint of HarperCollins Publishers.

Winds of Change
Text copyright © 2021 by Working Partners Limited
Art copyright © 2021 by HarperCollins Publishers
All rights reserved. Printed in Canada.
No part of this book may be used or reproduced in any manner whatsoever without written permission except in the
case of brief quotations embodied in critical articles and reviews. For information address HarperCollins Children's
Books, a division of HarperCollins Publishers, 195 Broadway, New York, NY 10007.
www.harpercollinschildrens.com
ISBN 978-0-06-304324-4 (hardcover) — ISBN 978-0-06-304323-7 (pbk)
21 22   TC   10 9 8 7 6 5 4
❖
First Edition

WARRIORS

WINDS OF
CHANGE

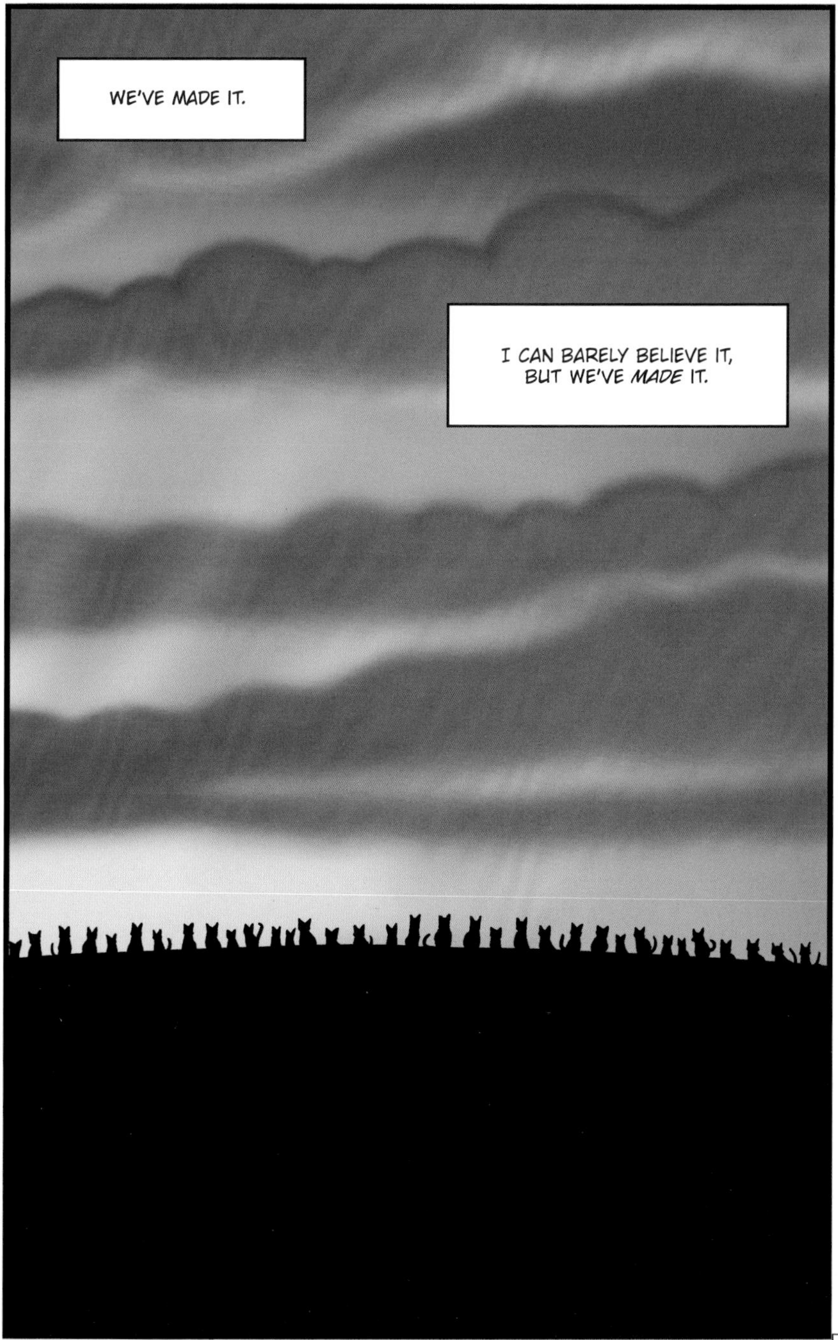
WE'VE MADE IT.
I CAN BARELY BELIEVE IT, BUT WE'VE *MADE* IT.

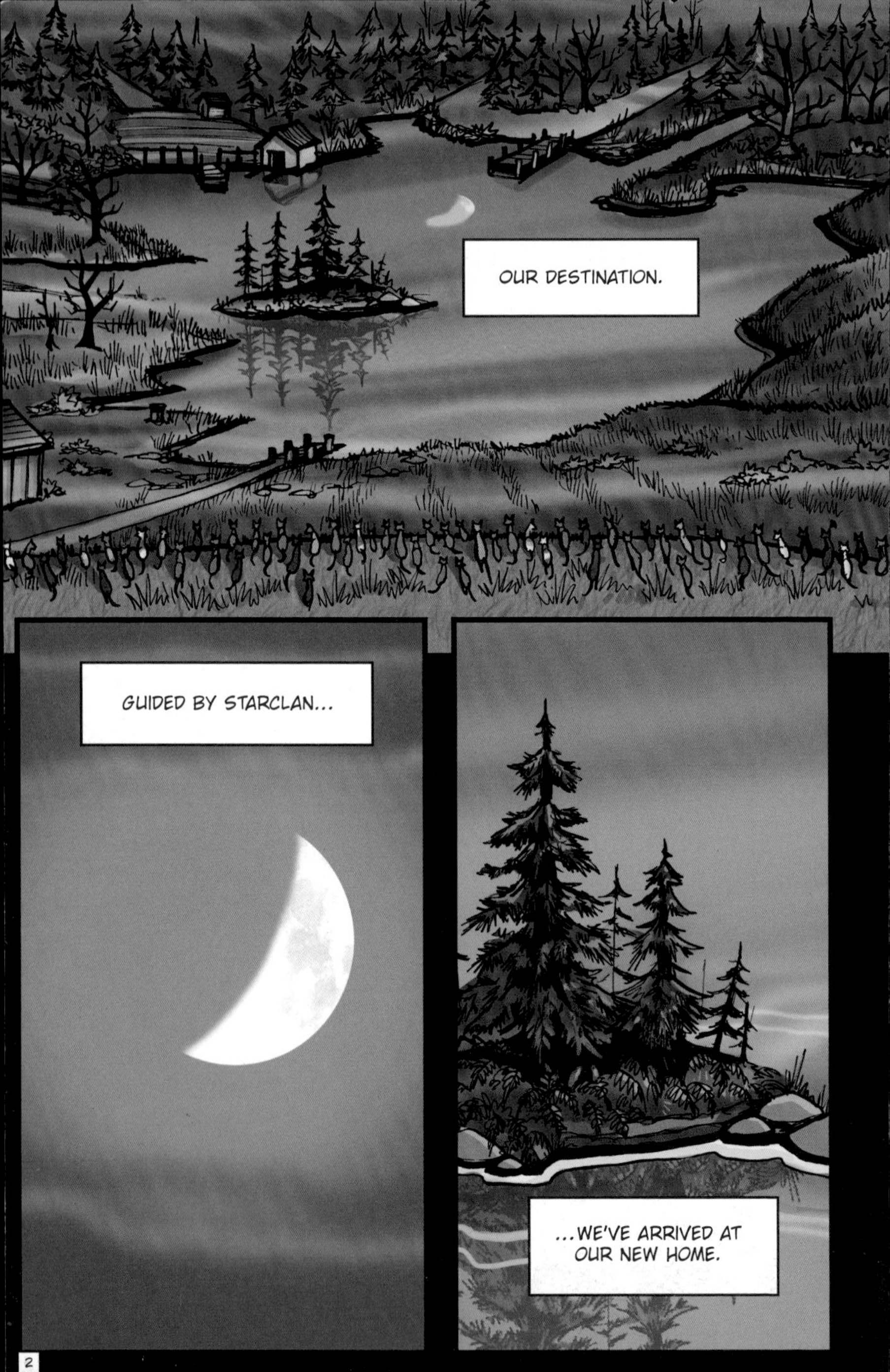
OUR DESTINATION.
GUIDED BY STARCLAN...
...WE'VE ARRIVED AT OUR NEW HOME.

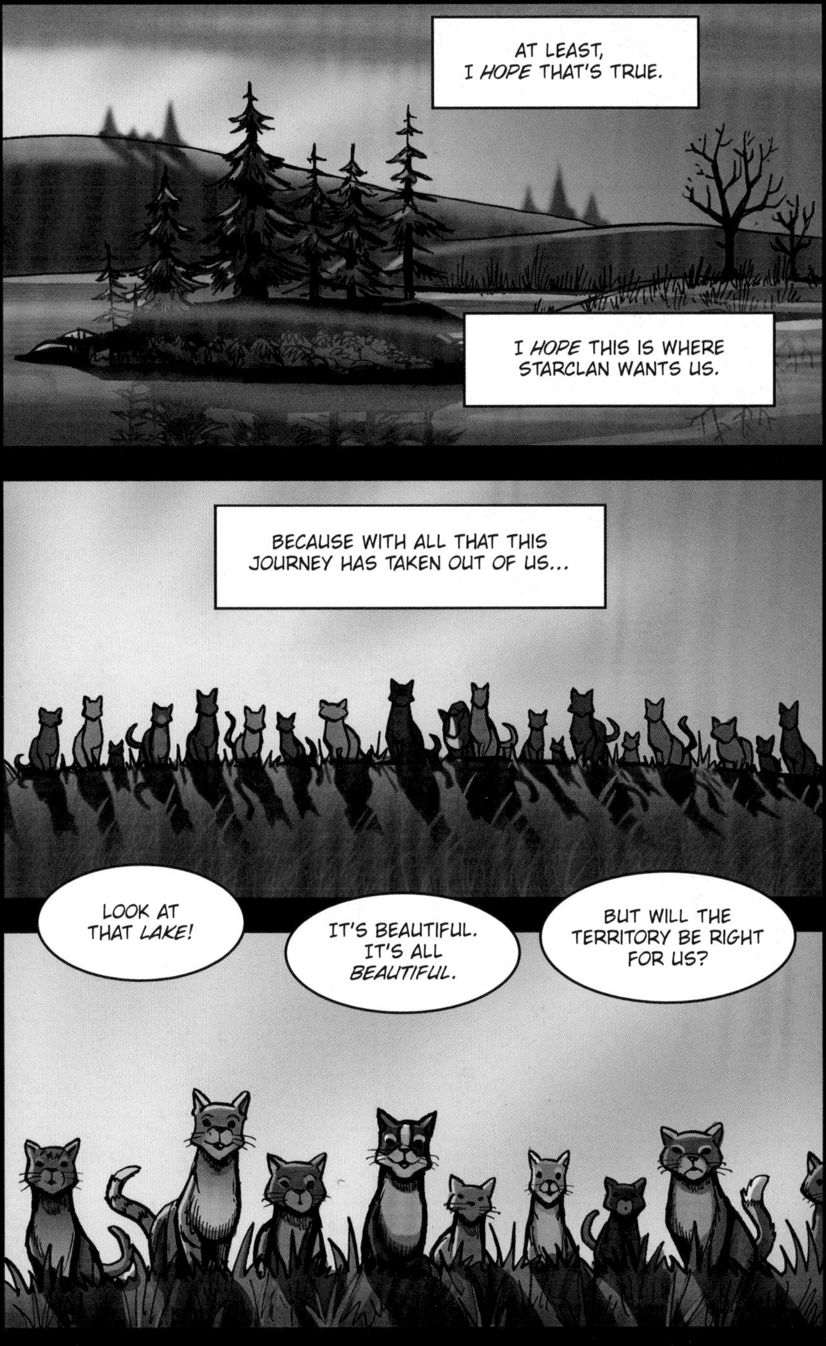
AT LEAST, I *HOPE* THAT'S TRUE.
I *HOPE* THIS IS WHERE STARCLAN WANTS US.
BECAUSE WITH ALL THAT THIS JOURNEY HAS TAKEN OUT OF US...
LOOK AT THAT *LAKE!*
IT'S BEAUTIFUL. IT'S ALL *BEAUTIFUL.*
BUT WILL THE TERRITORY BE RIGHT FOR US?

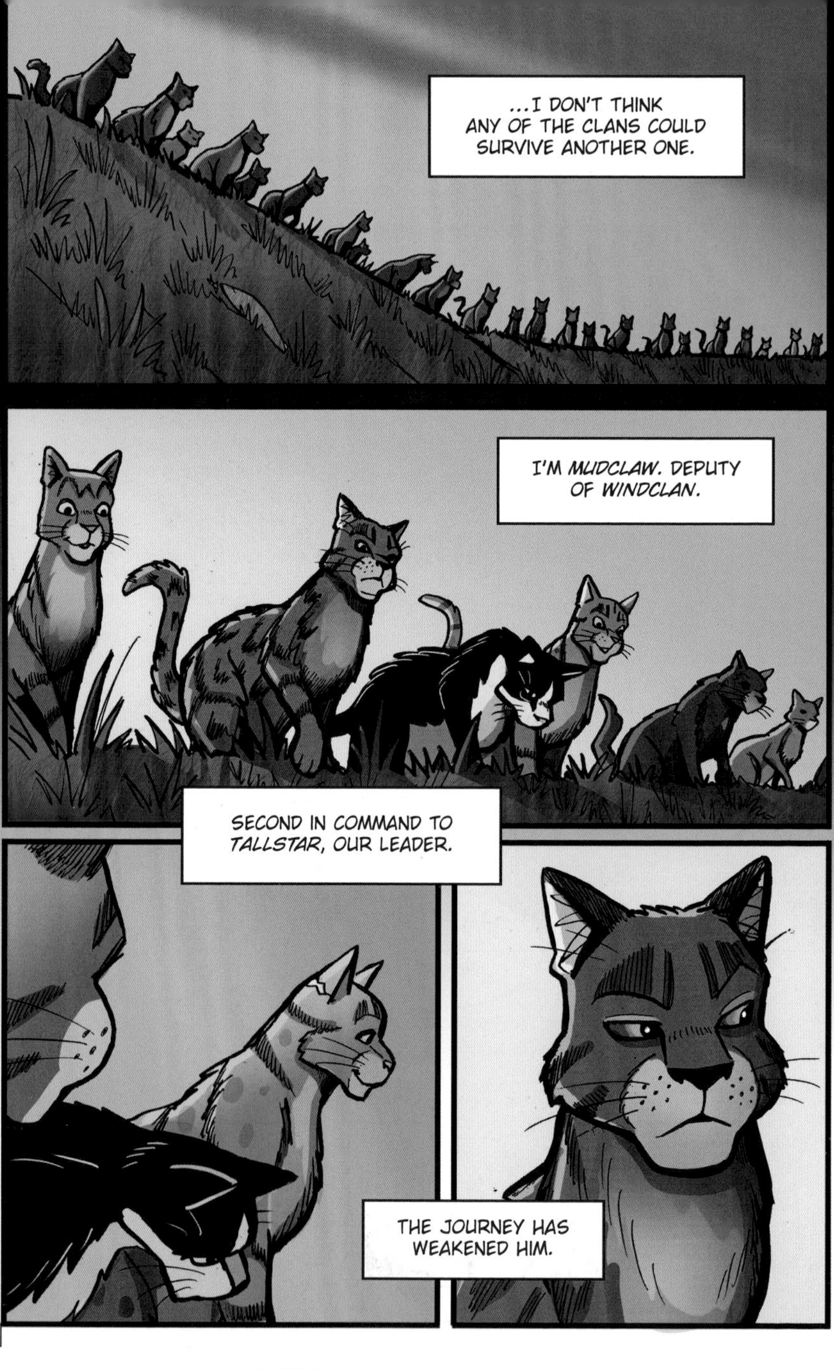
...I DON'T THINK ANY OF THE CLANS COULD SURVIVE ANOTHER ONE.
I'M *MUDCLAW*. DEPUTY OF *WINDCLAN*.
SECOND IN COMMAND TO *TALLSTAR*, OUR LEADER.
THE JOURNEY HAS WEAKENED HIM.

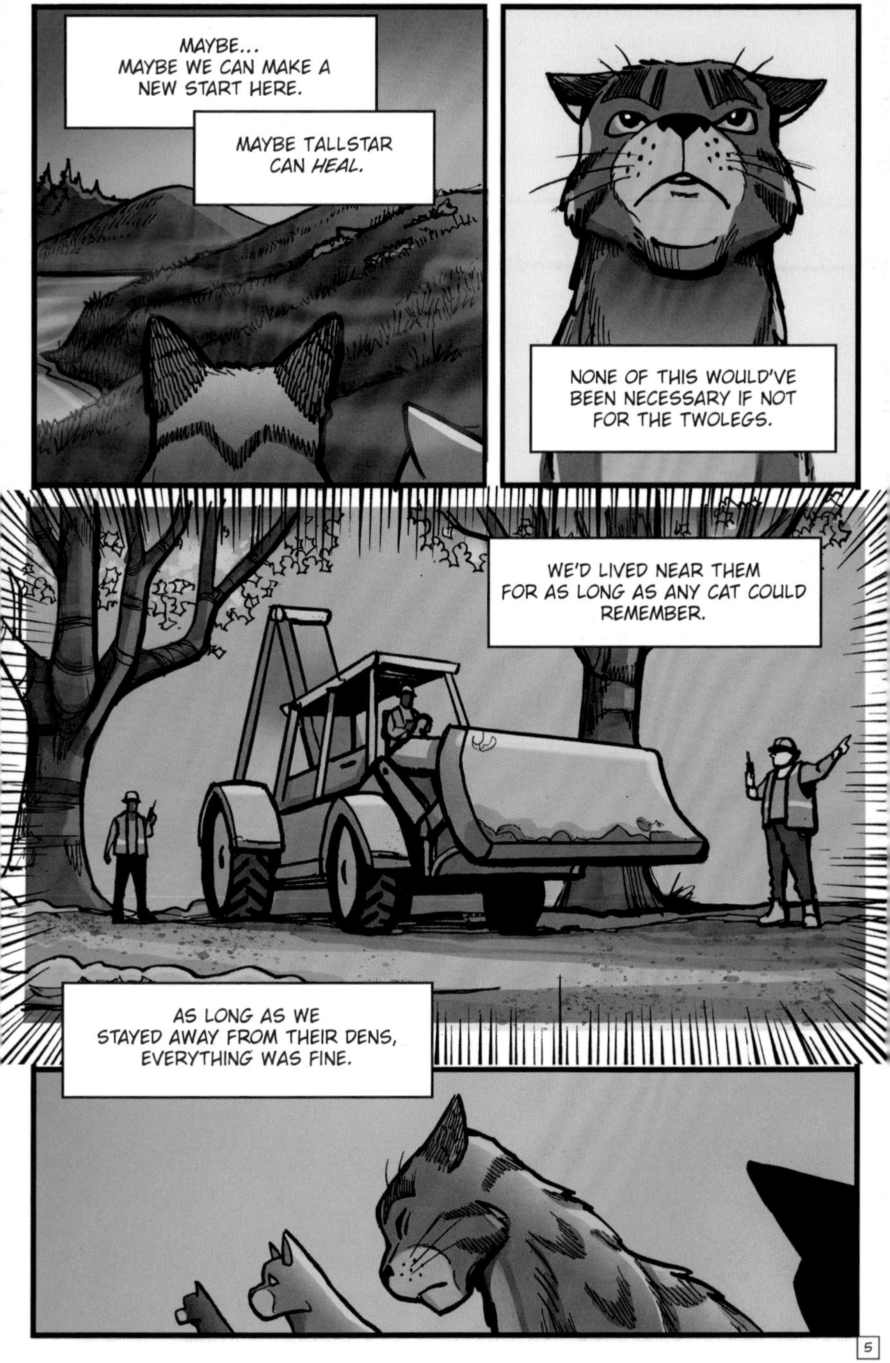
MAYBE... MAYBE WE CAN MAKE A NEW START HERE.
MAYBE TALLSTAR CAN *HEAL.*
NONE OF THIS WOULD'VE BEEN NECESSARY IF NOT FOR THE TWOLEGS.
WE'D LIVED NEAR THEM FOR AS LONG AS ANY CAT COULD REMEMBER.
AS LONG AS WE STAYED AWAY FROM THEIR DENS, EVERYTHING WAS FINE.

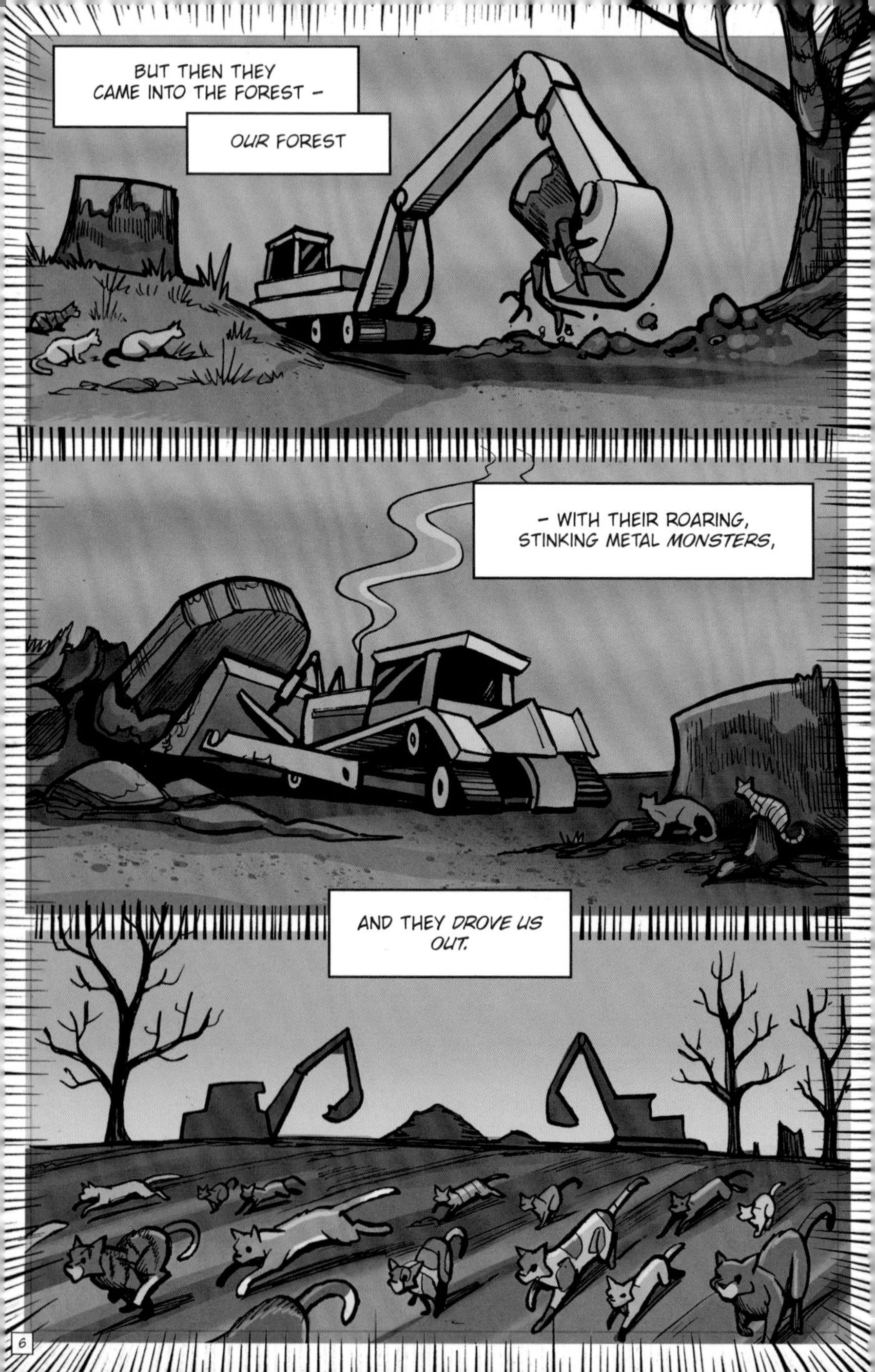
BUT THEN THEY CAME INTO THE FOREST –
OUR FOREST
– WITH THEIR ROARING, STINKING METAL *MONSTERS*,
AND THEY *DROVE US OUT.*

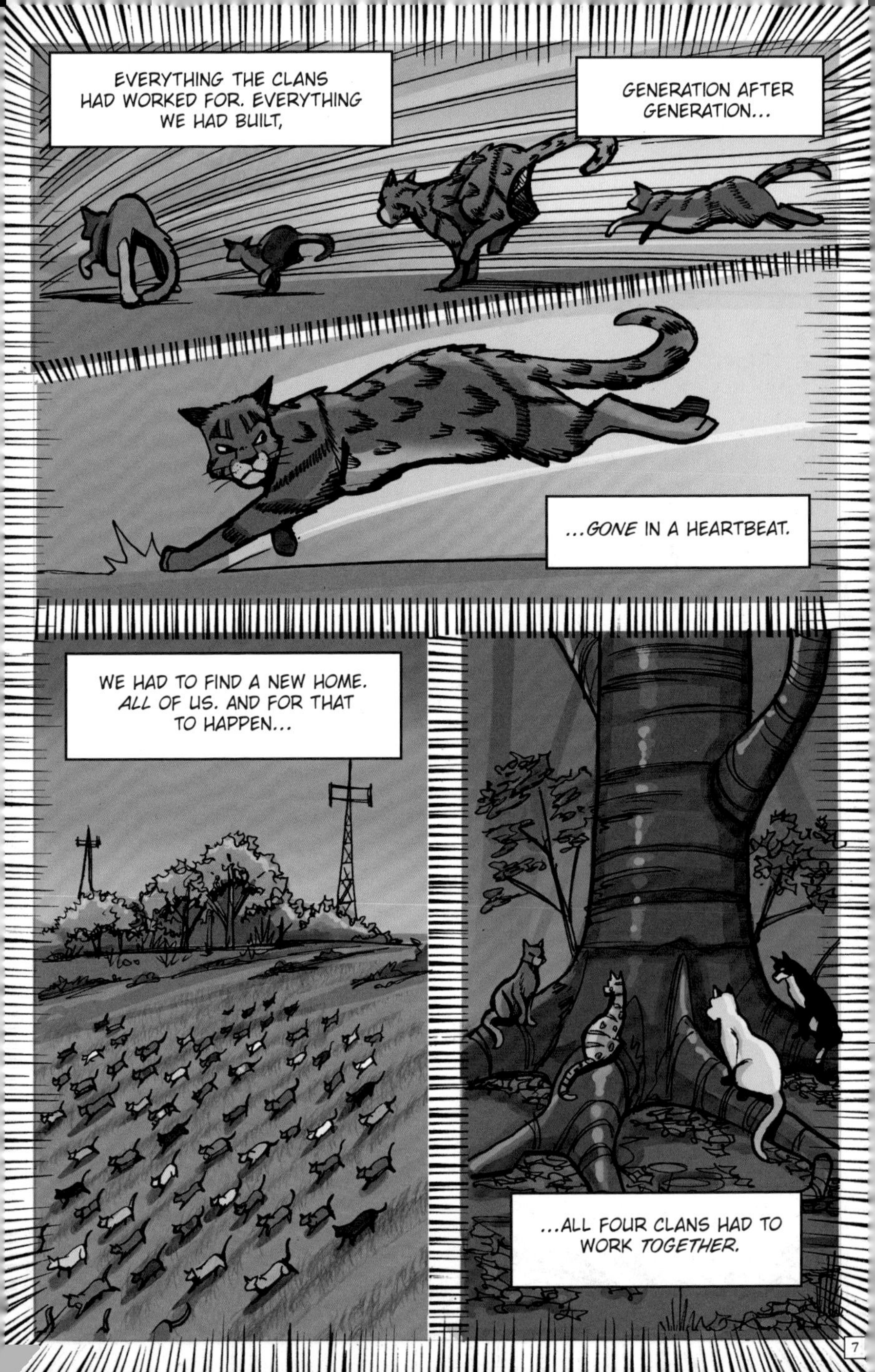
EVERYTHING THE CLANS HAD WORKED FOR. EVERYTHING WE HAD BUILT,
GENERATION AFTER GENERATION...
...GONE IN A HEARTBEAT.
WE HAD TO FIND A NEW HOME. ALL OF US. AND FOR THAT TO HAPPEN...
...ALL FOUR CLANS HAD TO WORK TOGETHER.

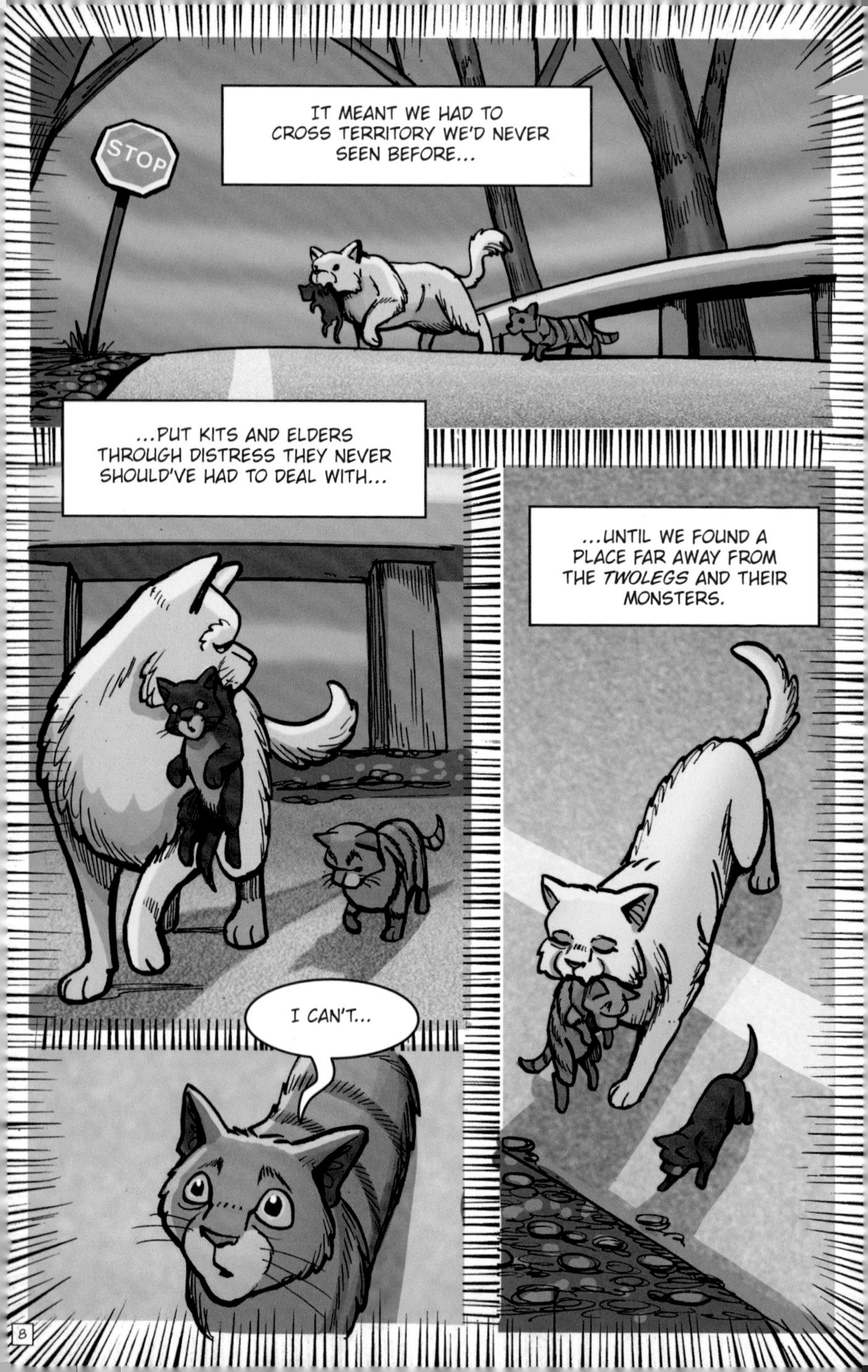
IT MEANT WE HAD TO CROSS TERRITORY WE'D NEVER SEEN BEFORE...
STOP
...PUT KITS AND ELDERS THROUGH DISTRESS THEY NEVER SHOULD'VE HAD TO DEAL WITH...
I CAN'T...
...UNTIL WE FOUND A PLACE FAR AWAY FROM THE *TWOLEGS* AND THEIR MONSTERS.

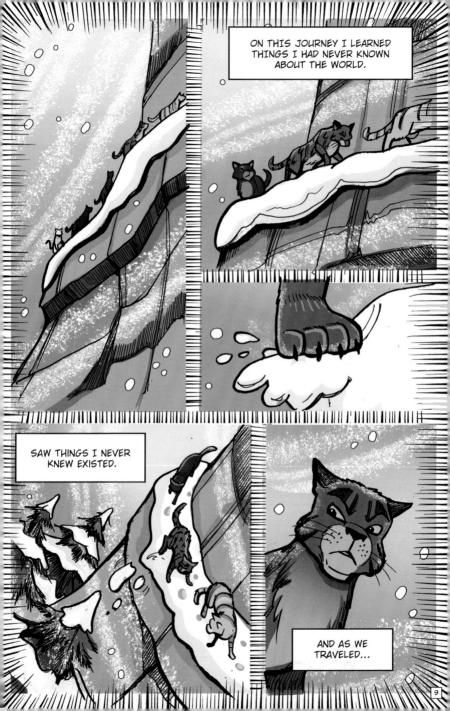

ON THIS JOURNEY I LEARNED THINGS I HAD NEVER KNOWN ABOUT THE WORLD.

SAW THINGS I NEVER KNEW EXISTED.

AND AS WE TRAVELED...

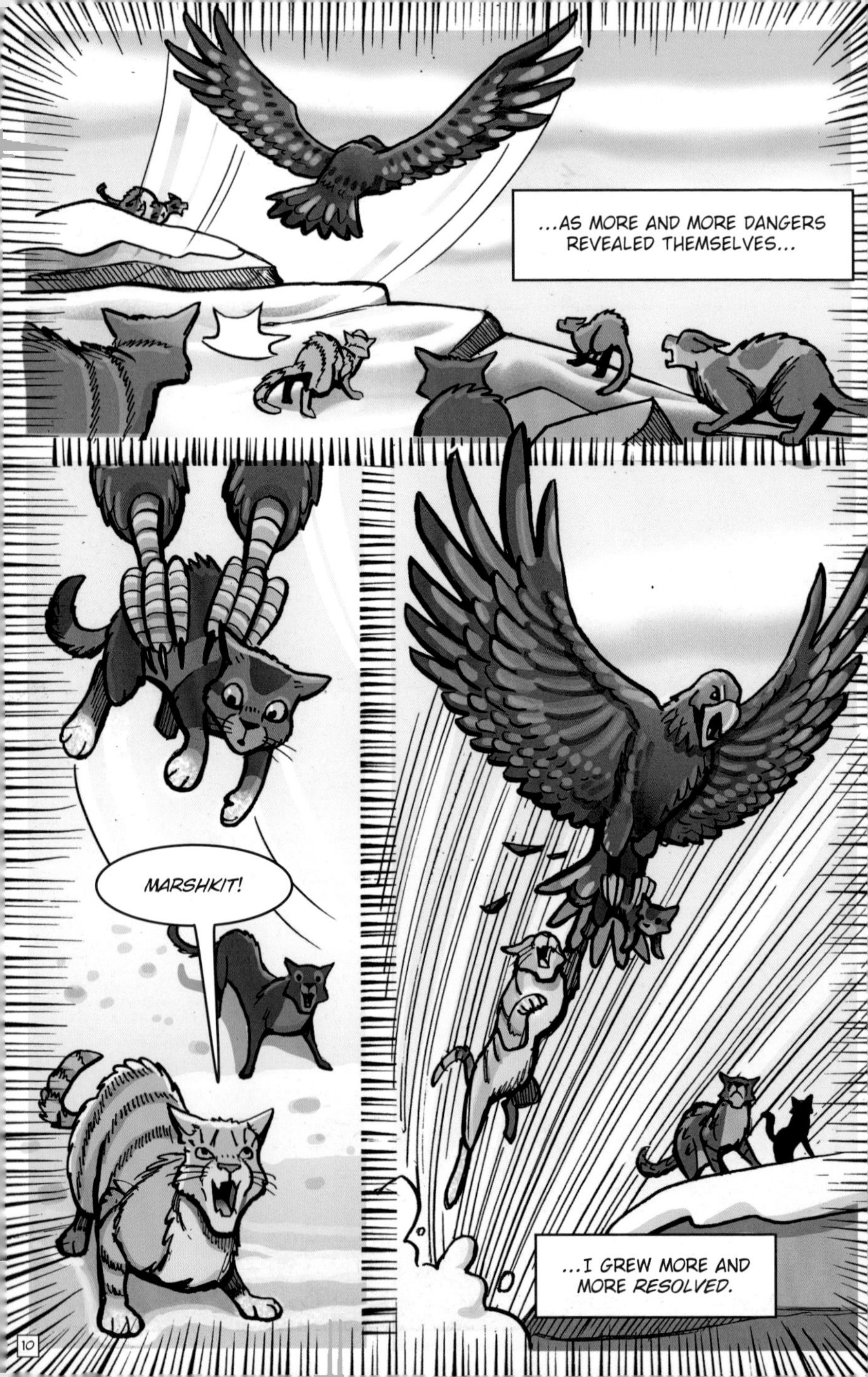
...AS MORE AND MORE DANGERS REVEALED THEMSELVES...
MARSHKIT!
...I GREW MORE AND MORE *RESOLVED.*

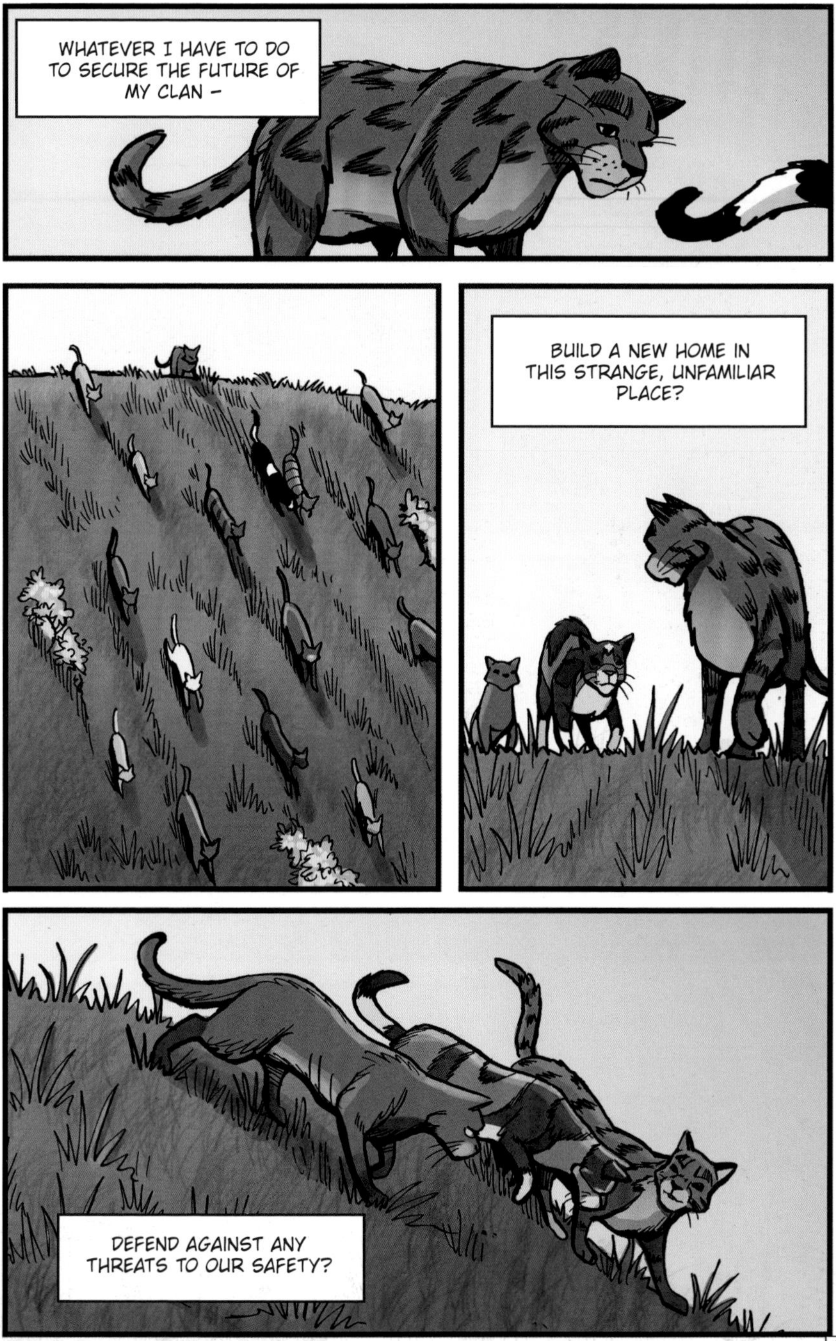
WHATEVER I HAVE TO DO TO SECURE THE FUTURE OF MY CLAN –
BUILD A NEW HOME IN THIS STRANGE, UNFAMILIAR PLACE?
DEFEND AGAINST ANY THREATS TO OUR SAFETY?

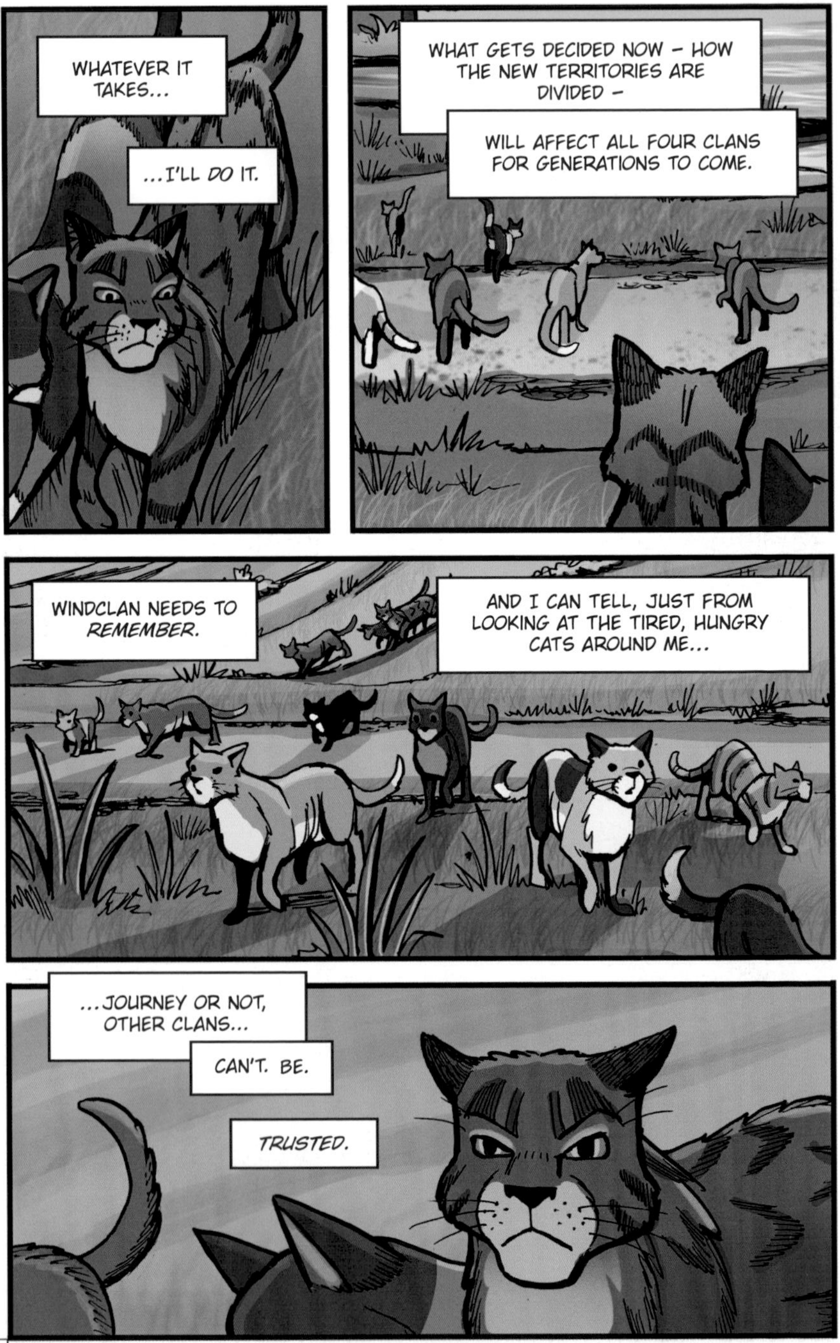
WHATEVER IT TAKES...
...I'LL *DO* IT.
WHAT GETS DECIDED NOW – HOW THE NEW TERRITORIES ARE DIVIDED –
WILL AFFECT ALL FOUR CLANS FOR GENERATIONS TO COME.
WINDCLAN NEEDS TO *REMEMBER.*
AND I CAN TELL, JUST FROM LOOKING AT THE TIRED, HUNGRY CATS AROUND ME...
...JOURNEY OR NOT, OTHER CLANS...
CAN'T. BE.
TRUSTED.

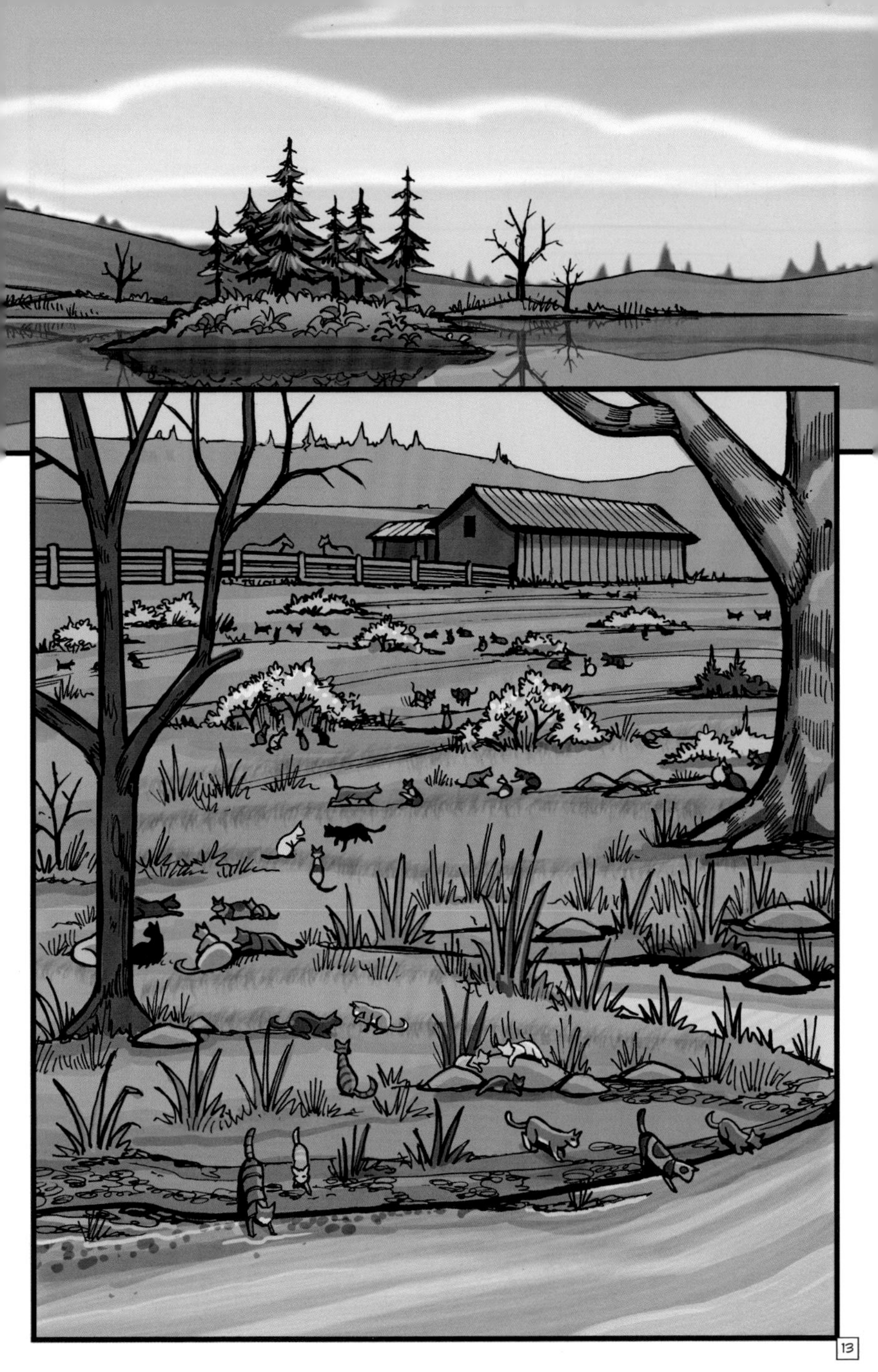

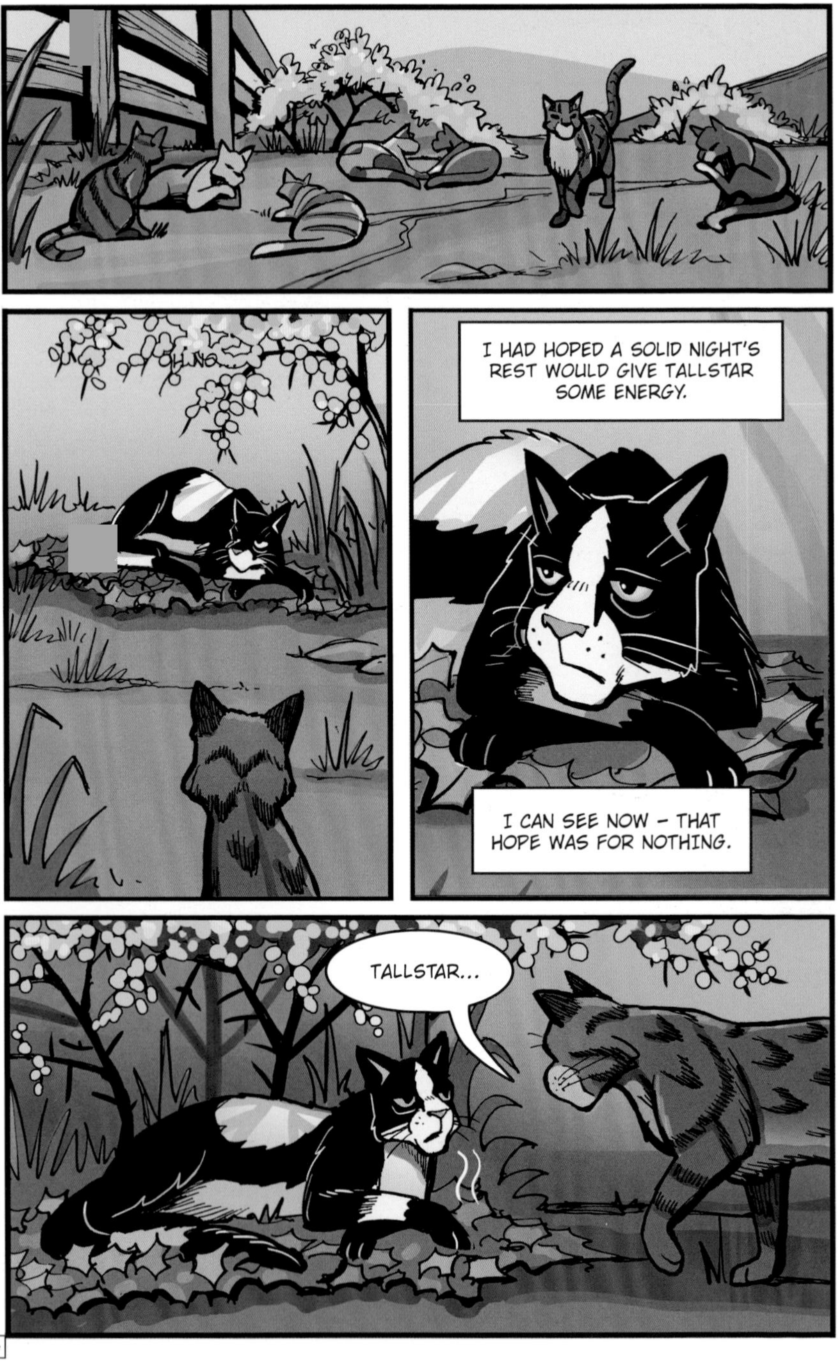
I HAD HOPED A SOLID NIGHT'S REST WOULD GIVE TALLSTAR SOME ENERGY.
I CAN SEE NOW – THAT HOPE WAS FOR NOTHING.
TALLSTAR...

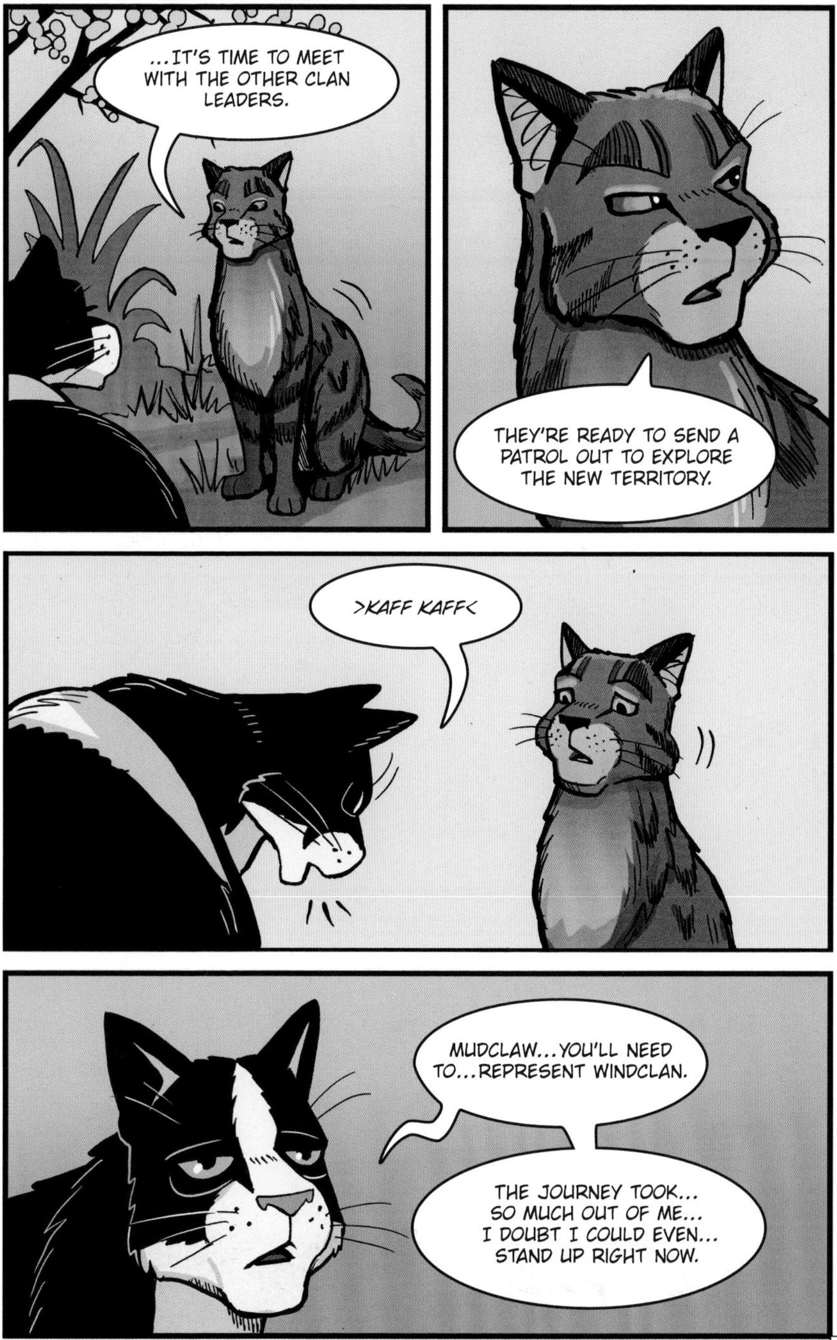
...IT'S TIME TO MEET WITH THE OTHER CLAN LEADERS.
THEY'RE READY TO SEND A PATROL OUT TO EXPLORE THE NEW TERRITORY.
>KAFF KAFF<
MUDCLAW...YOU'LL NEED TO...REPRESENT WINDCLAN.
THE JOURNEY TOOK... SO MUCH OUT OF ME... I DOUBT I COULD EVEN... STAND UP RIGHT NOW.

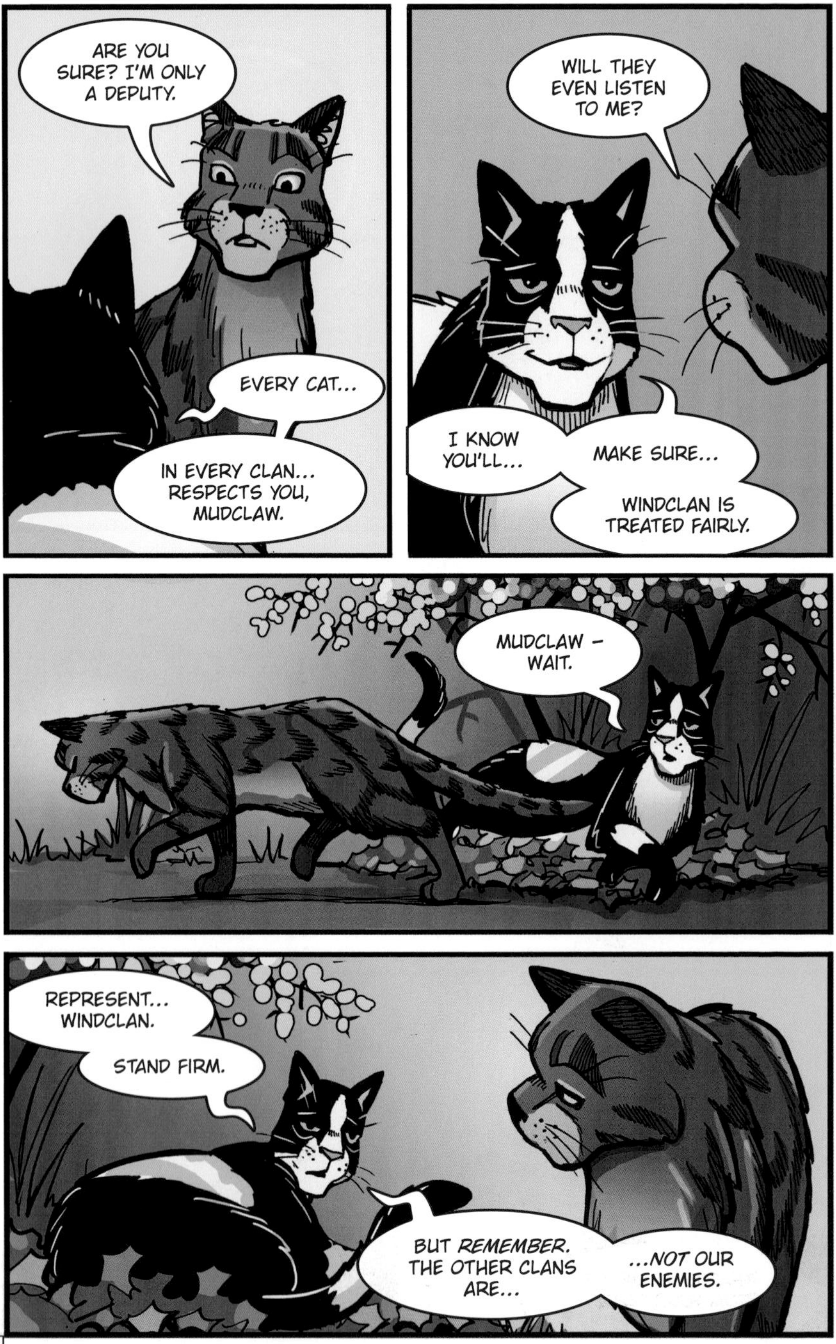
ARE YOU SURE? I'M ONLY A DEPUTY.
EVERY CAT...
IN EVERY CLAN... RESPECTS YOU, MUDCLAW.
WILL THEY EVEN LISTEN TO ME?
I KNOW YOU'LL...
MAKE SURE...
WINDCLAN IS TREATED FAIRLY.
MUDCLAW – WAIT.
REPRESENT... WINDCLAN.
STAND FIRM.
BUT *REMEMBER*. THE OTHER CLANS ARE...
...*NOT* OUR ENEMIES.

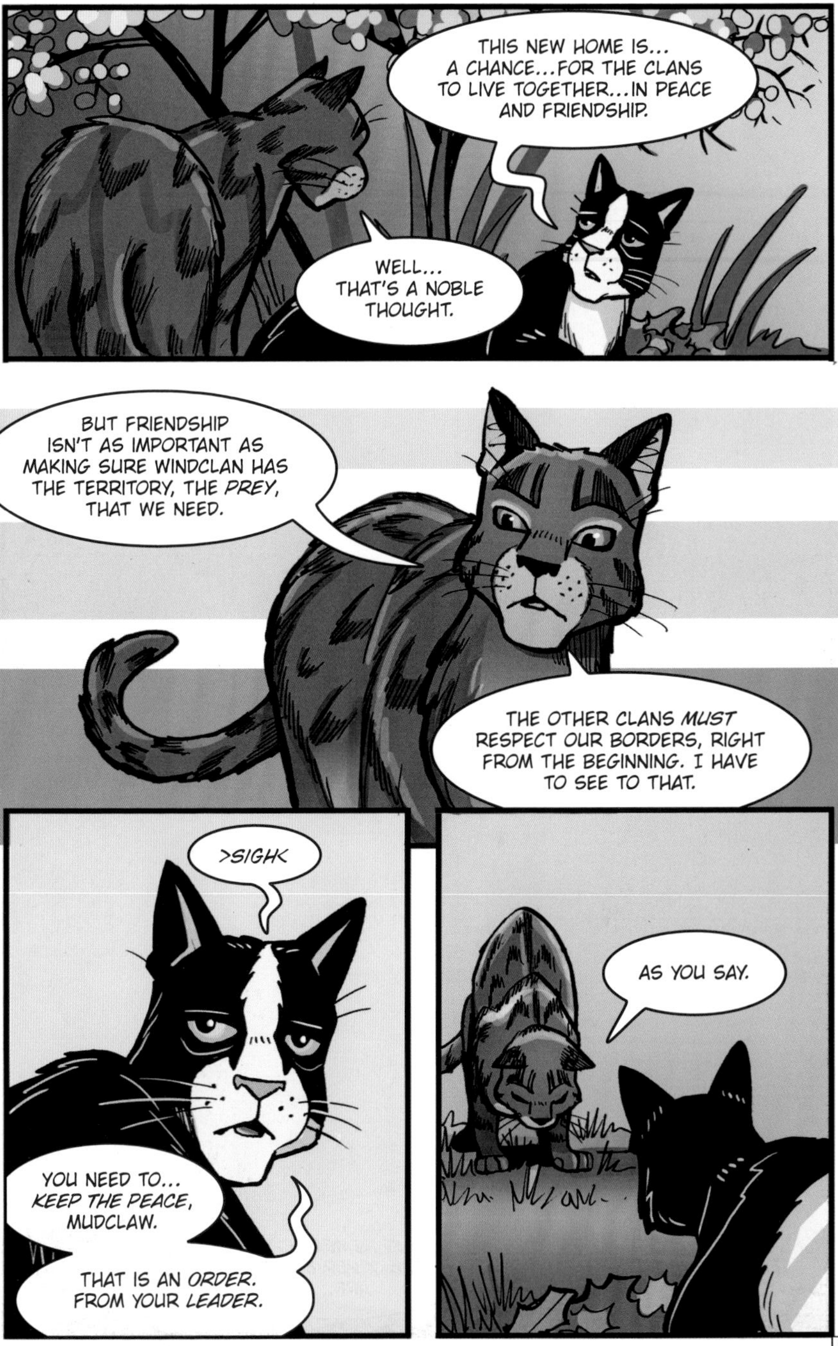
THIS NEW HOME IS... A CHANCE...FOR THE CLANS TO LIVE TOGETHER...IN PEACE AND FRIENDSHIP.
WELL... THAT'S A NOBLE THOUGHT.
BUT FRIENDSHIP ISN'T AS IMPORTANT AS MAKING SURE WINDCLAN HAS THE TERRITORY, THE *PREY*, THAT WE NEED.
THE OTHER CLANS *MUST* RESPECT OUR BORDERS, RIGHT FROM THE BEGINNING. I HAVE TO SEE TO THAT.
>SIGH<
YOU NEED TO... *KEEP THE PEACE*, MUDCLAW.
THAT IS AN *ORDER*. FROM YOUR *LEADER*.
AS YOU SAY.

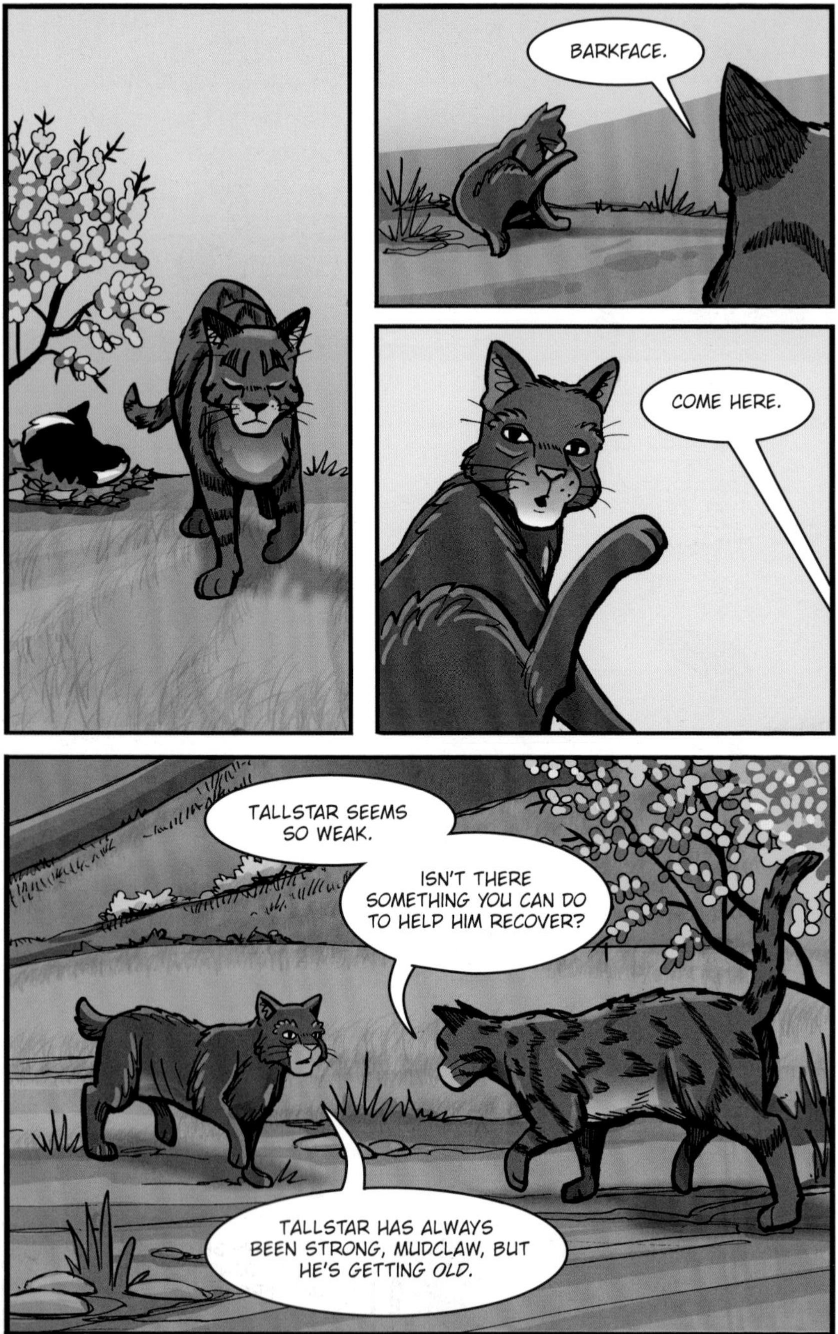
BARKFACE.
COME HERE.
TALLSTAR SEEMS SO WEAK.
ISN'T THERE SOMETHING YOU CAN DO TO HELP HIM RECOVER?
TALLSTAR HAS ALWAYS BEEN STRONG, MUDCLAW, BUT HE'S GETTING OLD.

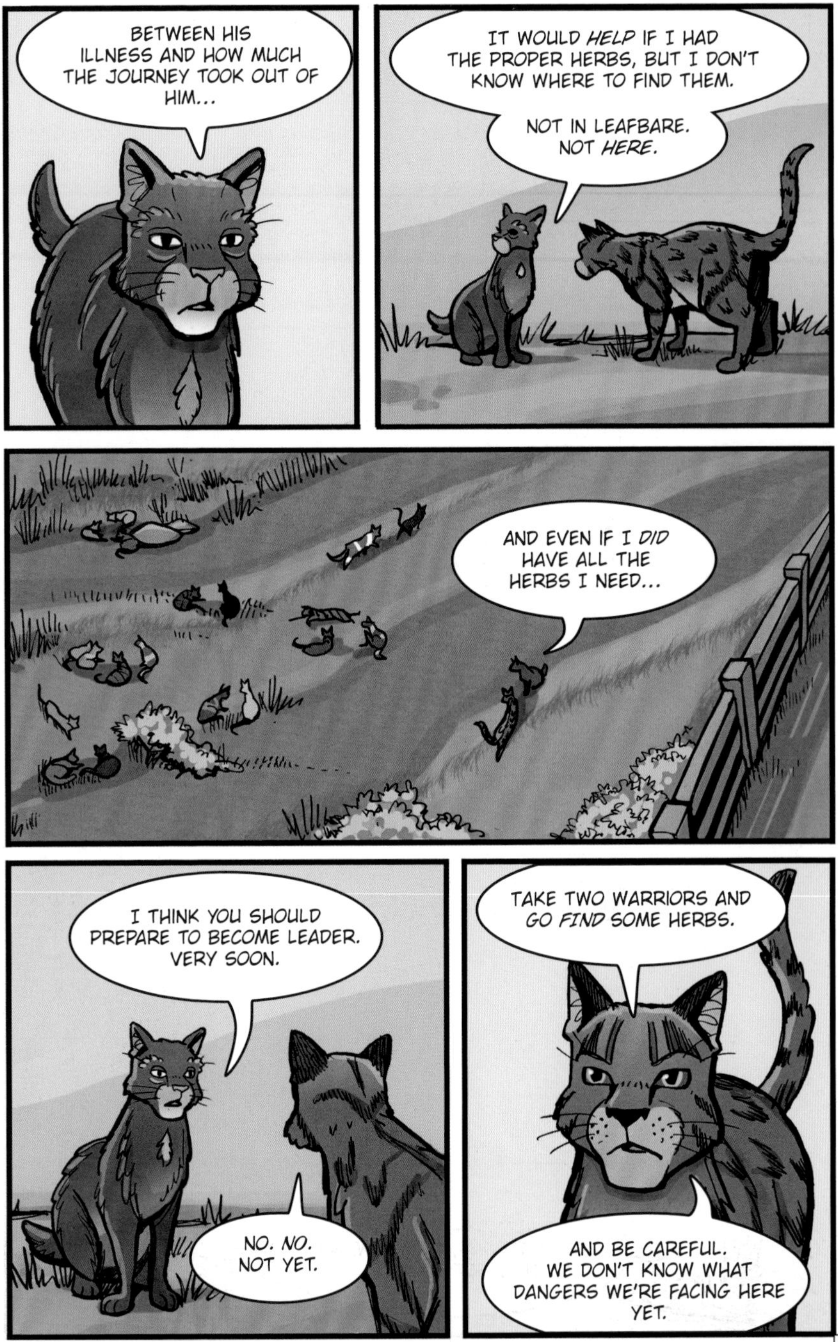

BETWEEN HIS ILLNESS AND HOW MUCH THE JOURNEY TOOK OUT OF HIM...
IT WOULD *HELP* IF I HAD THE PROPER HERBS, BUT I DON'T KNOW WHERE TO FIND THEM.
NOT IN LEAFBARE. NOT *HERE*.
AND EVEN IF I *DID* HAVE ALL THE HERBS I NEED...
I THINK YOU SHOULD PREPARE TO BECOME LEADER. VERY SOON.
NO. *NO*. NOT YET.
TAKE TWO WARRIORS AND GO *FIND* SOME HERBS.
AND BE CAREFUL. WE DON'T KNOW WHAT DANGERS WE'RE FACING HERE YET.

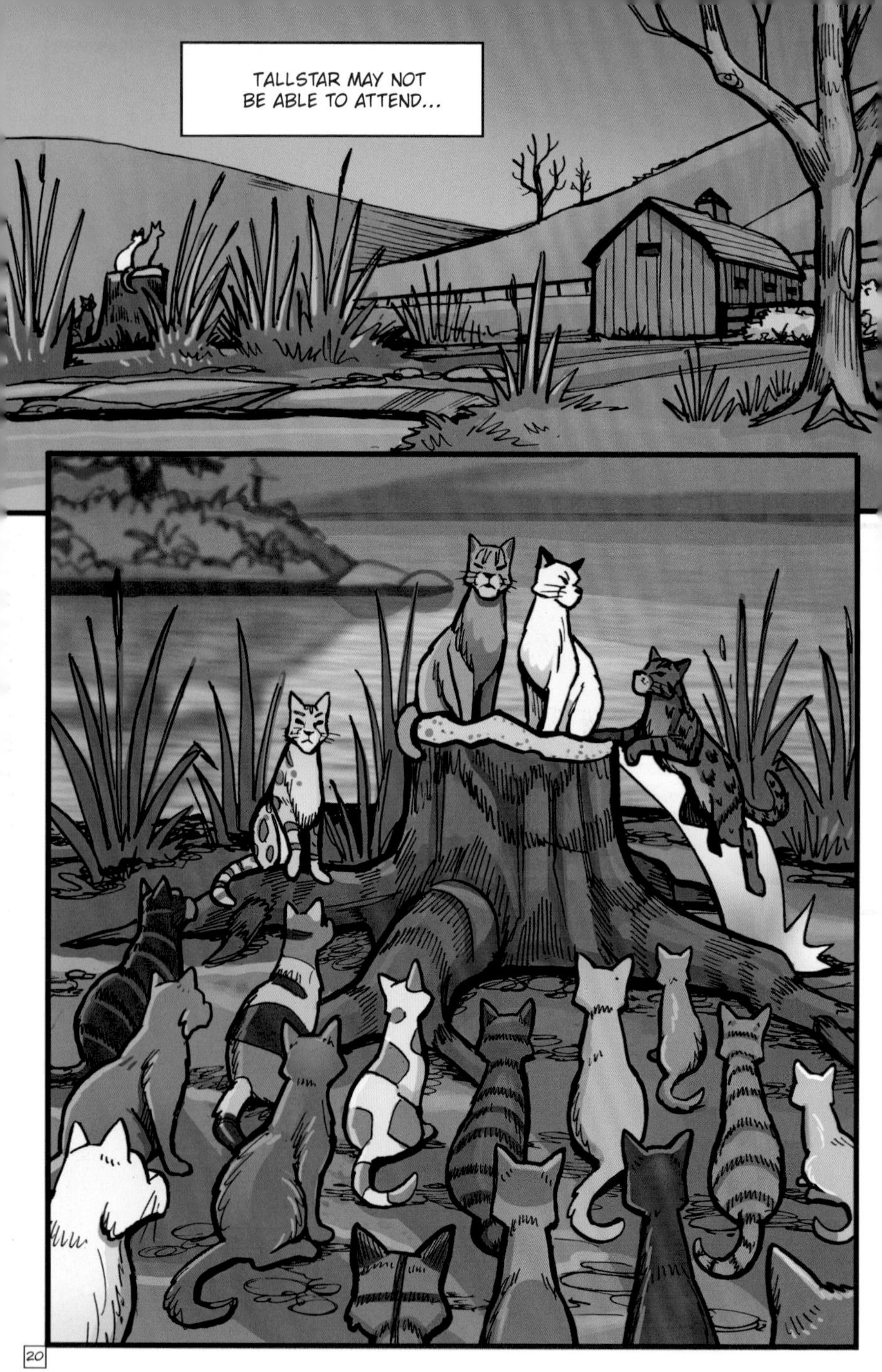
TALLSTAR MAY NOT BE ABLE TO ATTEND...

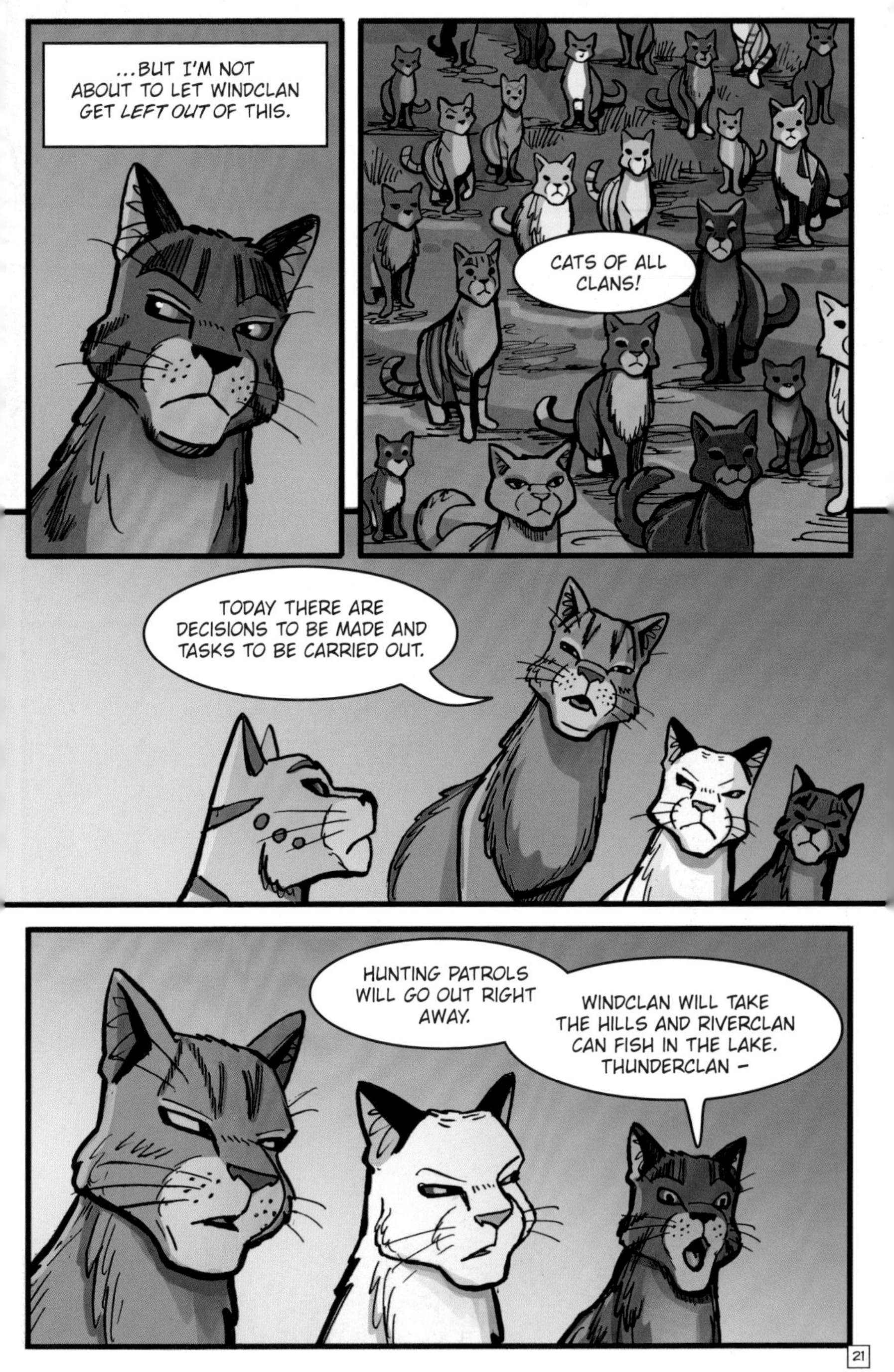
...BUT I'M NOT ABOUT TO LET WINDCLAN GET *LEFT OUT* OF THIS.
CATS OF ALL CLANS!
TODAY THERE ARE DECISIONS TO BE MADE AND TASKS TO BE CARRIED OUT.
HUNTING PATROLS WILL GO OUT RIGHT AWAY.
WINDCLAN WILL TAKE THE HILLS AND RIVERCLAN CAN FISH IN THE LAKE. THUNDERCLAN –

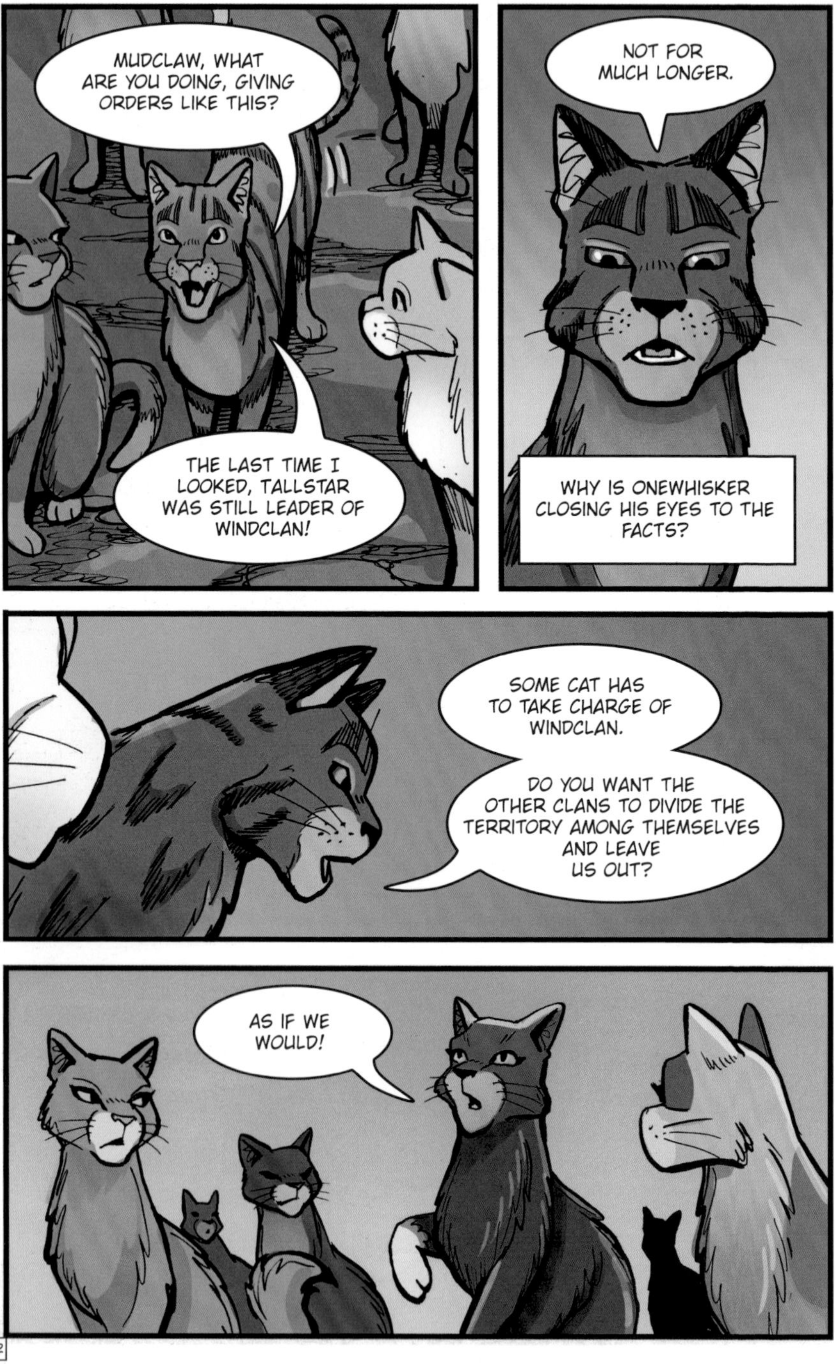
MUDCLAW, WHAT ARE YOU DOING, GIVING ORDERS LIKE THIS?
THE LAST TIME I LOOKED, TALLSTAR WAS STILL LEADER OF WINDCLAN!
NOT FOR MUCH LONGER.
WHY IS ONEWHISKER CLOSING HIS EYES TO THE FACTS?
SOME CAT HAS TO TAKE CHARGE OF WINDCLAN.
DO YOU WANT THE OTHER CLANS TO DIVIDE THE TERRITORY AMONG THEMSELVES AND LEAVE US OUT?
AS IF WE WOULD!

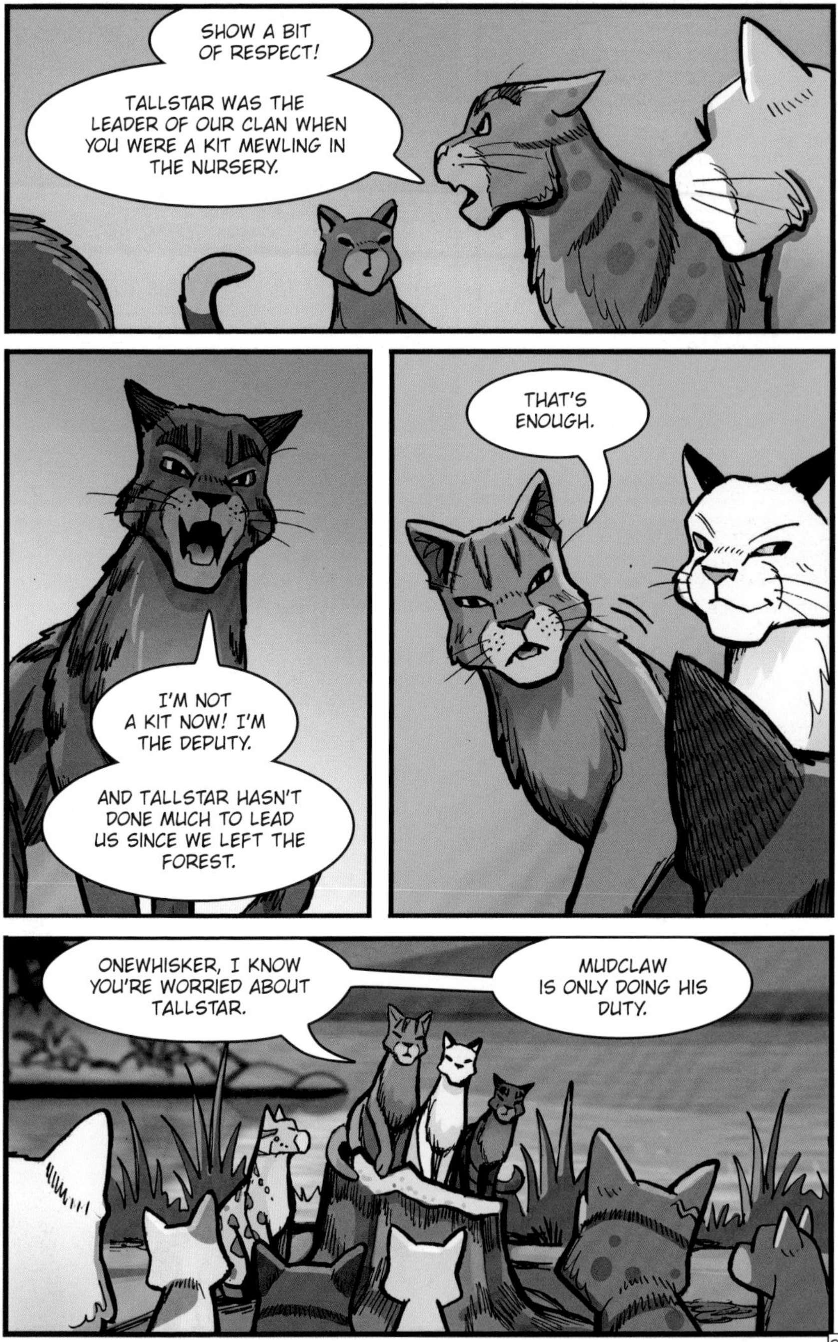
SHOW A BIT OF RESPECT!
TALLSTAR WAS THE LEADER OF OUR CLAN WHEN YOU WERE A KIT MEWLING IN THE NURSERY.
I'M NOT A KIT NOW! I'M THE DEPUTY.
AND TALLSTAR HASN'T DONE MUCH TO LEAD US SINCE WE LEFT THE FOREST.
THAT'S ENOUGH.
ONEWHISKER, I KNOW YOU'RE WORRIED ABOUT TALLSTAR.
MUDCLAW IS ONLY DOING HIS DUTY.

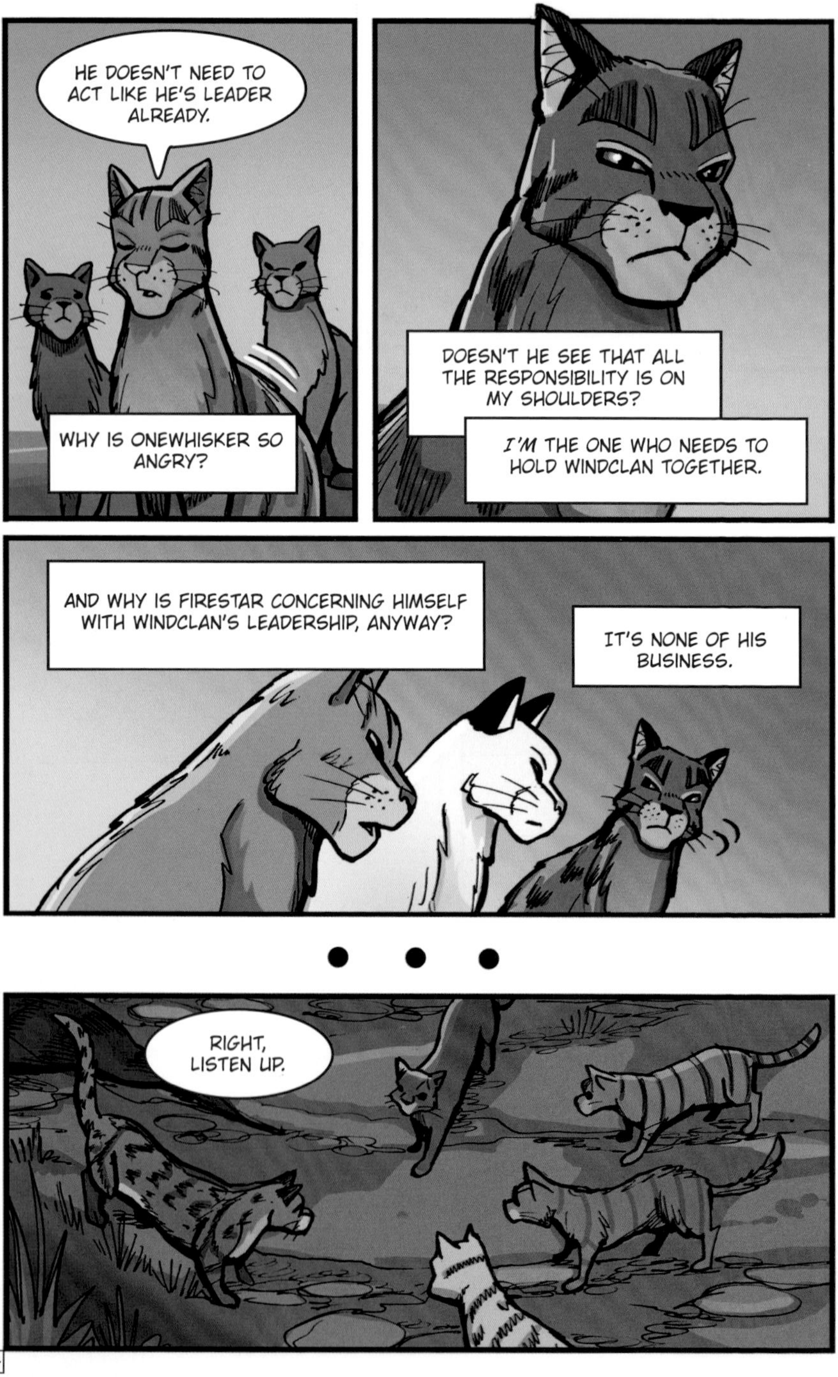
HE DOESN'T NEED TO ACT LIKE HE'S LEADER ALREADY.
WHY IS ONEWHISKER SO ANGRY?
DOESN'T HE SEE THAT ALL THE RESPONSIBILITY IS ON MY SHOULDERS?
I'M THE ONE WHO NEEDS TO HOLD WINDCLAN TOGETHER.
AND WHY IS FIRESTAR CONCERNING HIMSELF WITH WINDCLAN'S LEADERSHIP, ANYWAY?
IT'S NONE OF HIS BUSINESS.
RIGHT, LISTEN UP.

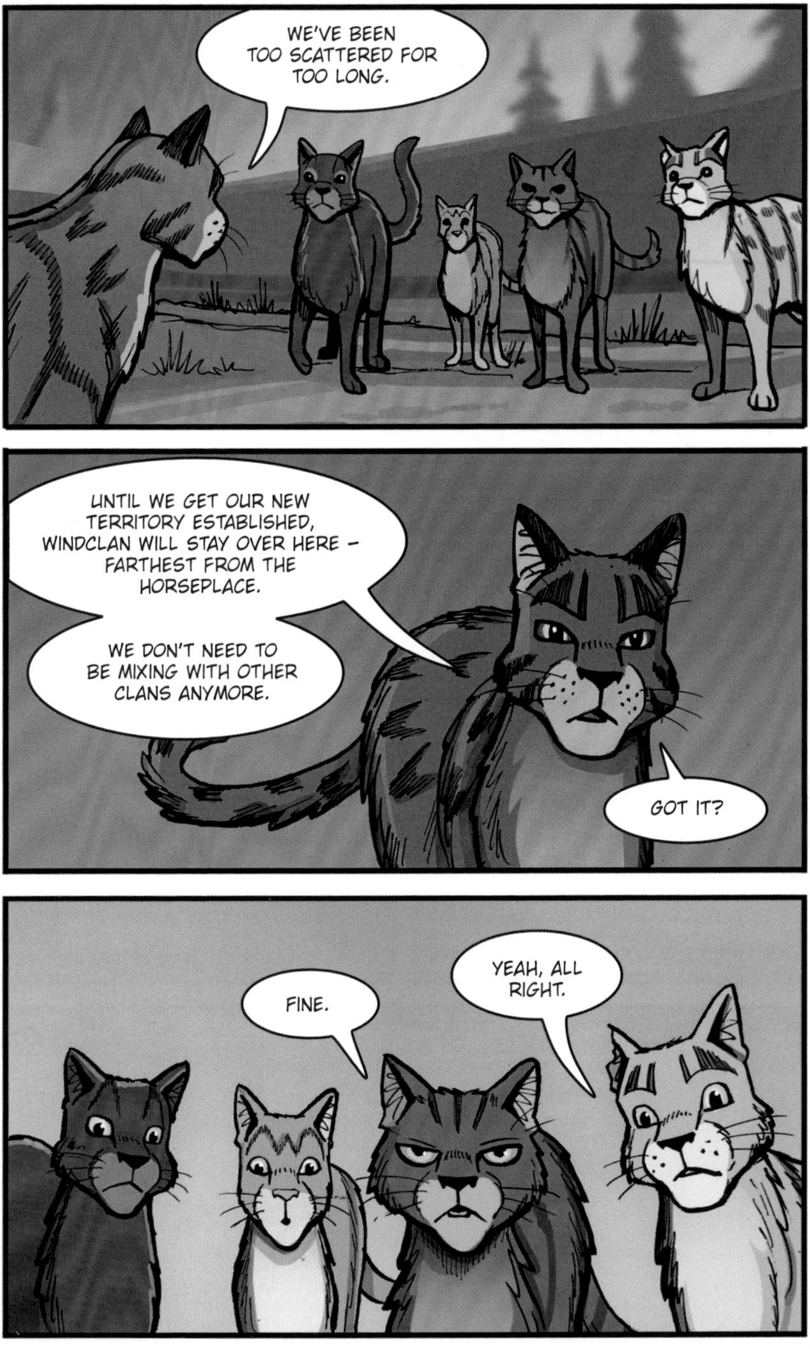
WE'VE BEEN TOO SCATTERED FOR TOO LONG.
UNTIL WE GET OUR NEW TERRITORY ESTABLISHED, WINDCLAN WILL STAY OVER HERE – FARTHEST FROM THE HORSEPLACE.
WE DON'T NEED TO BE MIXING WITH OTHER CLANS ANYMORE.
GOT IT?
FINE.
YEAH, ALL RIGHT.

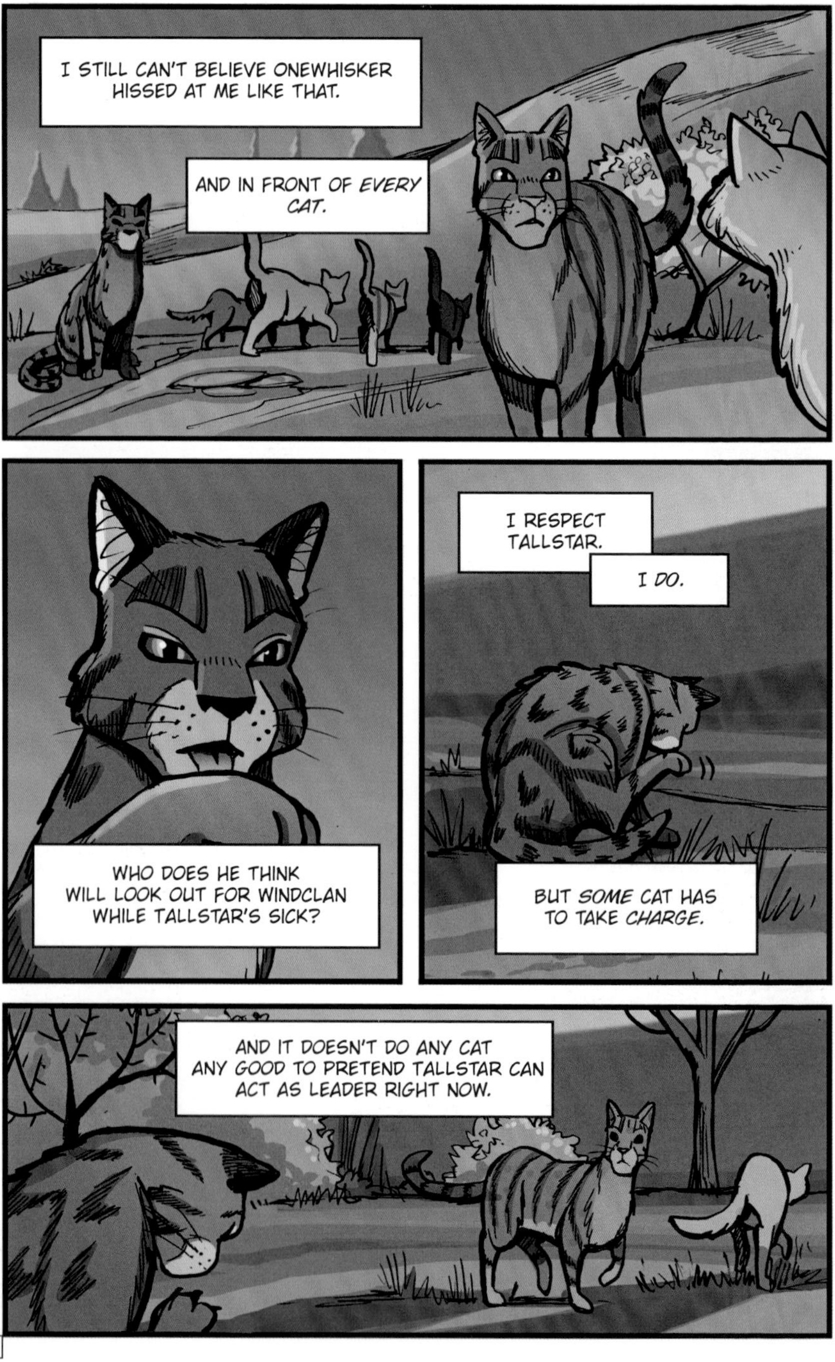
I STILL CAN'T BELIEVE ONEWHISKER HISSED AT ME LIKE THAT.
AND IN FRONT OF *EVERY* CAT.
WHO DOES HE THINK WILL LOOK OUT FOR WINDCLAN WHILE TALLSTAR'S SICK?
I RESPECT TALLSTAR.
I *DO*.
BUT *SOME* CAT HAS TO TAKE *CHARGE*.
AND IT DOESN'T DO ANY CAT ANY *GOOD* TO PRETEND TALLSTAR CAN ACT AS LEADER RIGHT NOW.

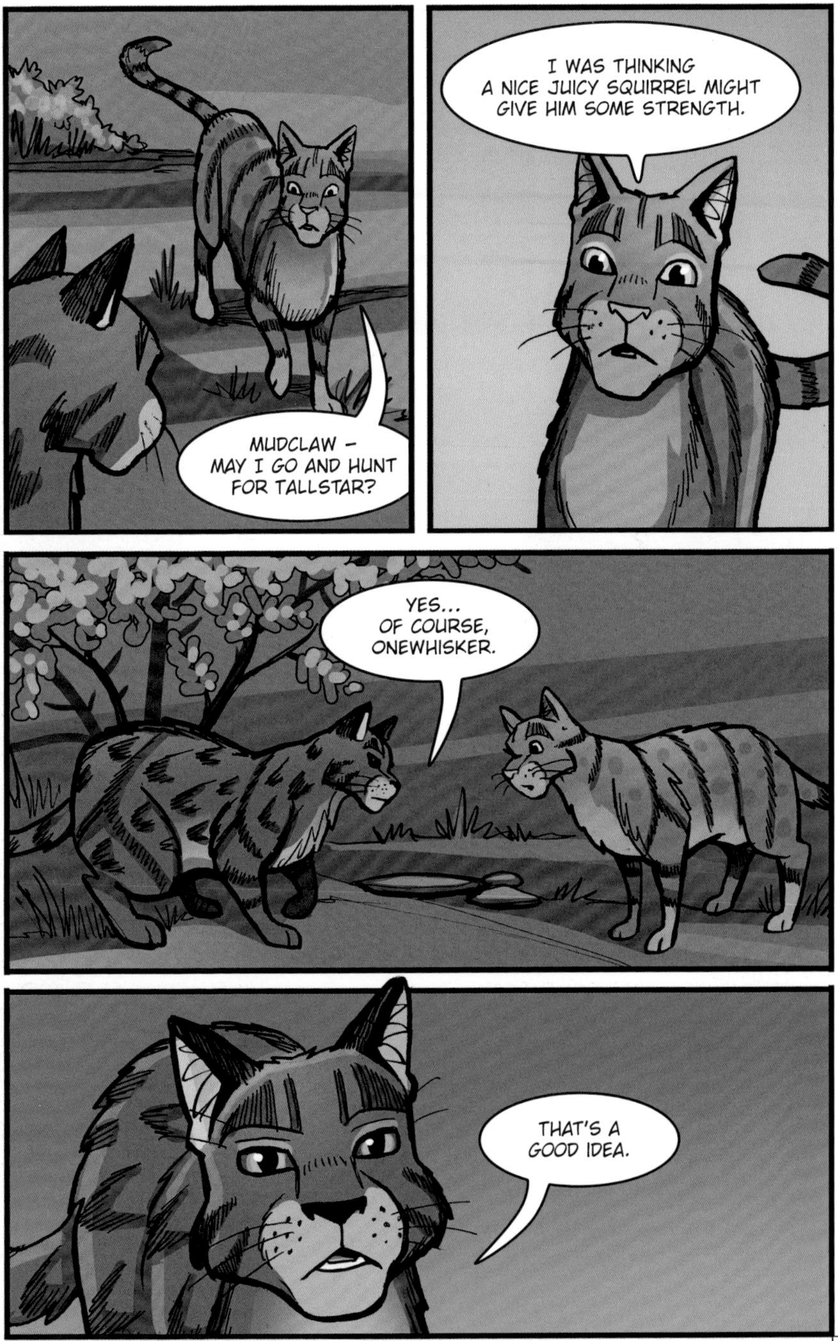
MUDCLAW – MAY I GO AND HUNT FOR TALLSTAR?
I WAS THINKING A NICE JUICY SQUIRREL MIGHT GIVE HIM SOME STRENGTH.
YES... OF COURSE, ONEWHISKER.
THAT'S A GOOD IDEA.

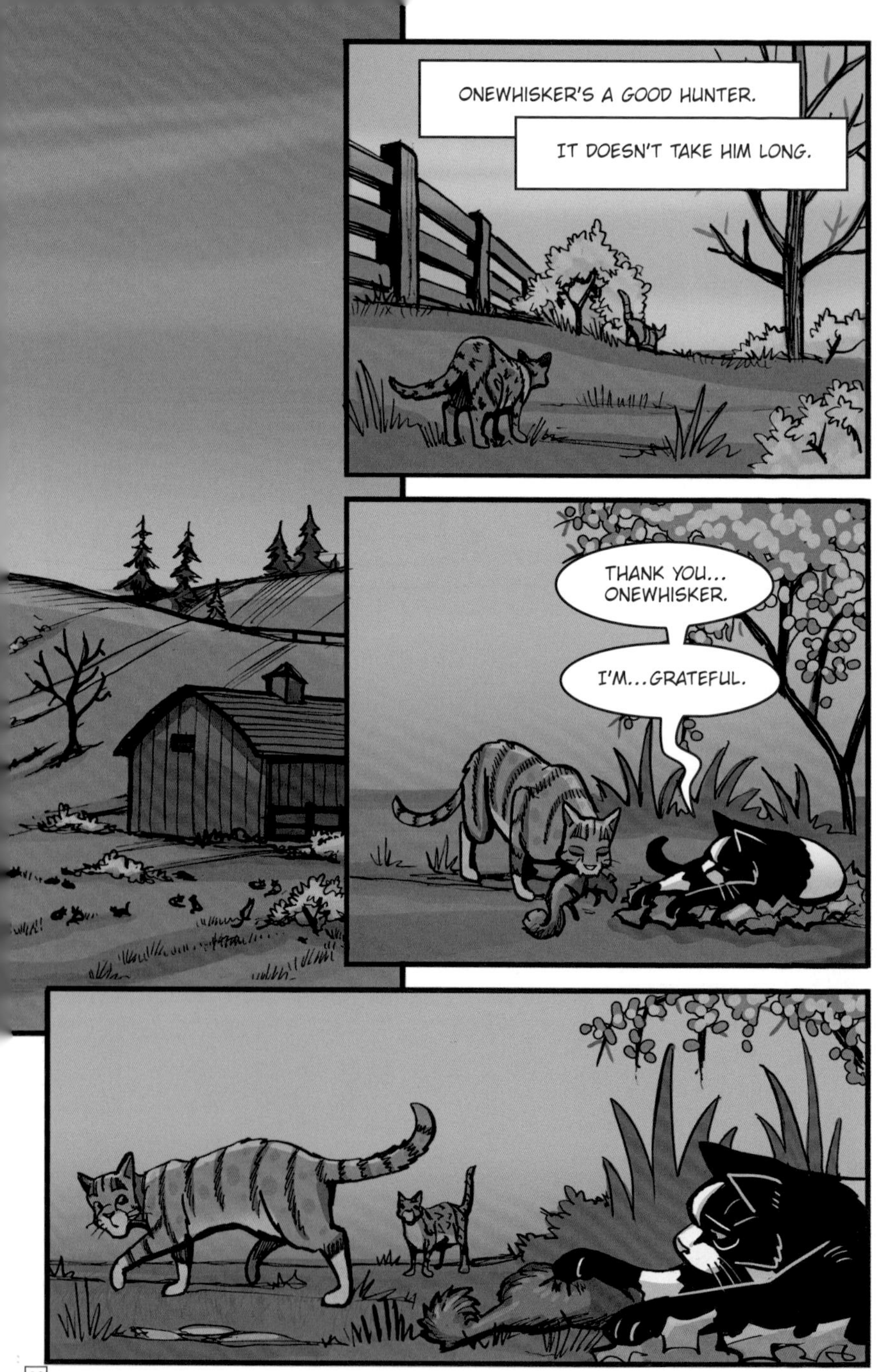
ONEWHISKER'S A GOOD HUNTER.
IT DOESN'T TAKE HIM LONG.
THANK YOU... ONEWHISKER.
I'M...GRATEFUL.

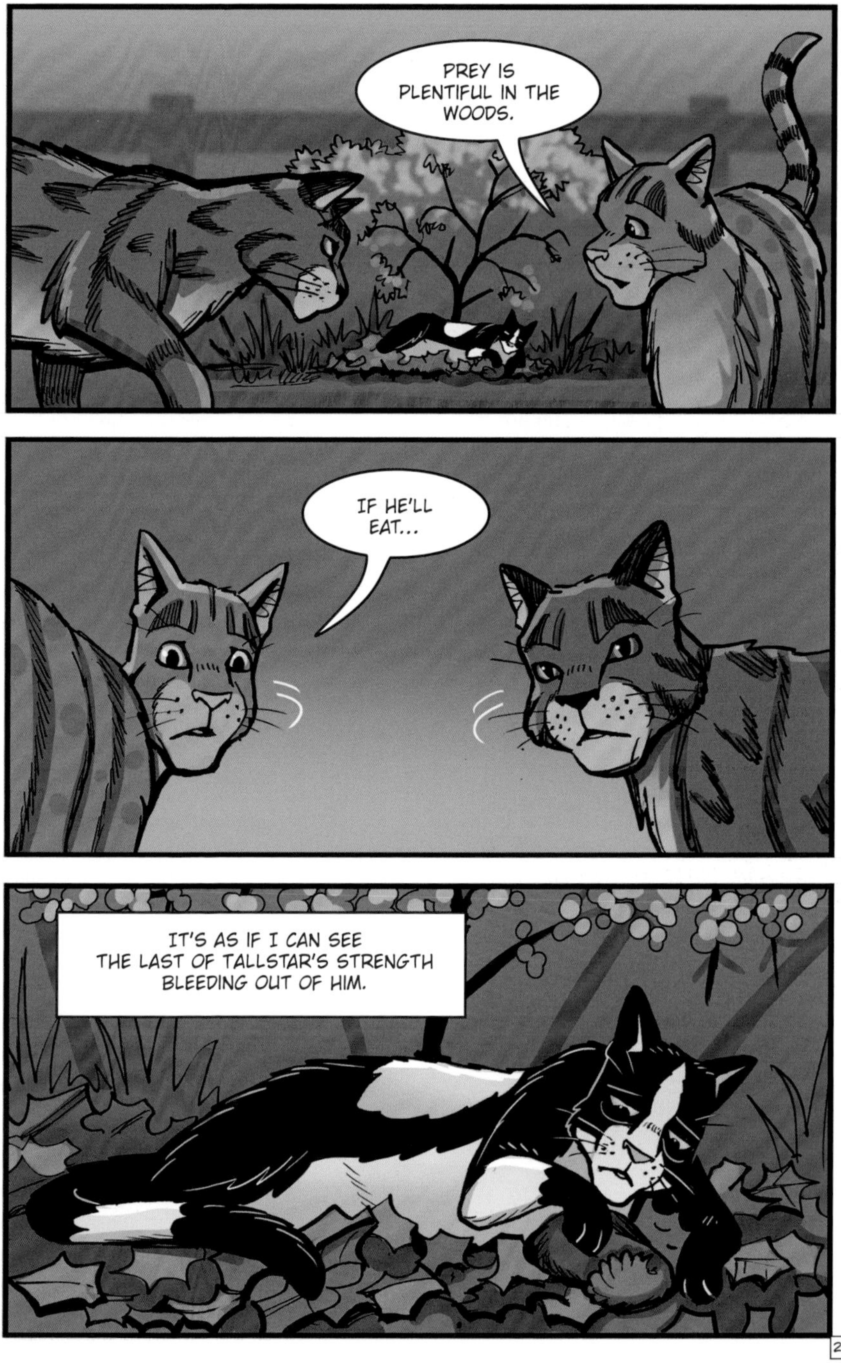
PREY IS PLENTIFUL IN THE WOODS.
IF HE'LL EAT...
IT'S AS IF I CAN SEE THE LAST OF TALLSTAR'S STRENGTH BLEEDING OUT OF HIM.

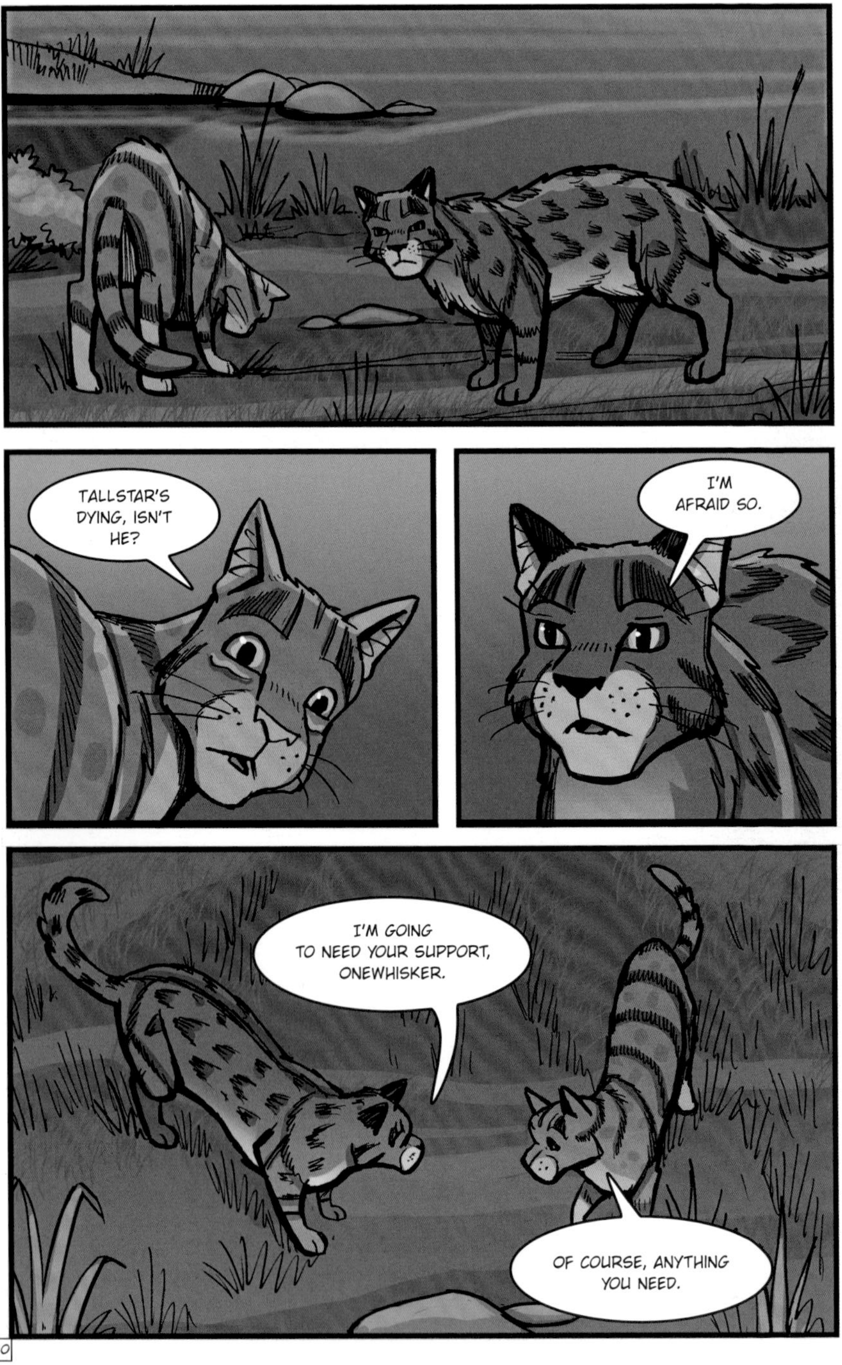
TALLSTAR'S DYING, ISN'T HE?
I'M AFRAID SO.
I'M GOING TO NEED YOUR SUPPORT, ONEWHISKER.
OF COURSE, ANYTHING YOU NEED.

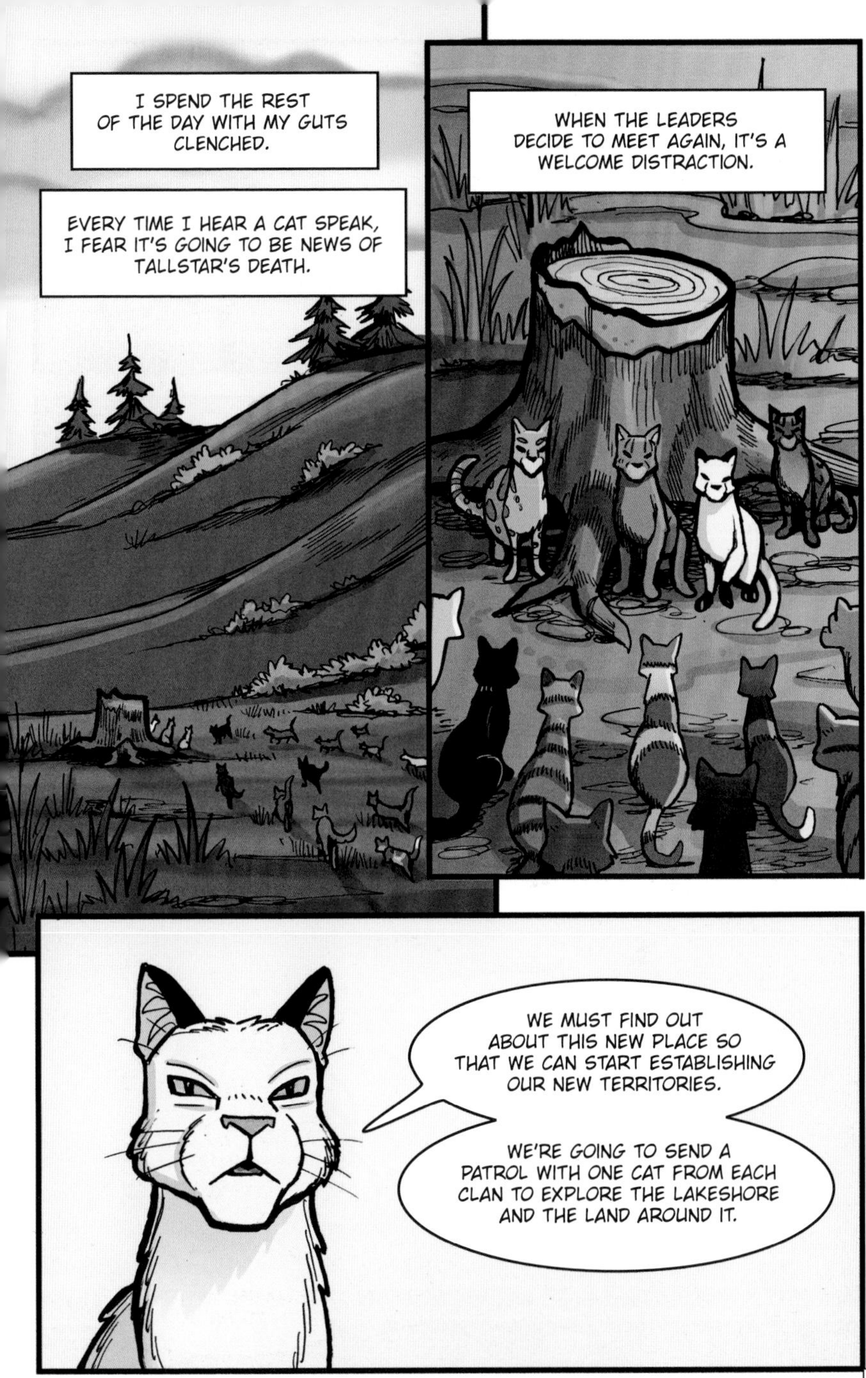
I SPEND THE REST OF THE DAY WITH MY GUTS CLENCHED.
EVERY TIME I HEAR A CAT SPEAK, I FEAR IT'S GOING TO BE NEWS OF TALLSTAR'S DEATH.
WHEN THE LEADERS DECIDE TO MEET AGAIN, IT'S A WELCOME DISTRACTION.
WE MUST FIND OUT ABOUT THIS NEW PLACE SO THAT WE CAN START ESTABLISHING OUR NEW TERRITORIES.
WE'RE GOING TO SEND A PATROL WITH ONE CAT FROM EACH CLAN TO EXPLORE THE LAKESHORE AND THE LAND AROUND IT.

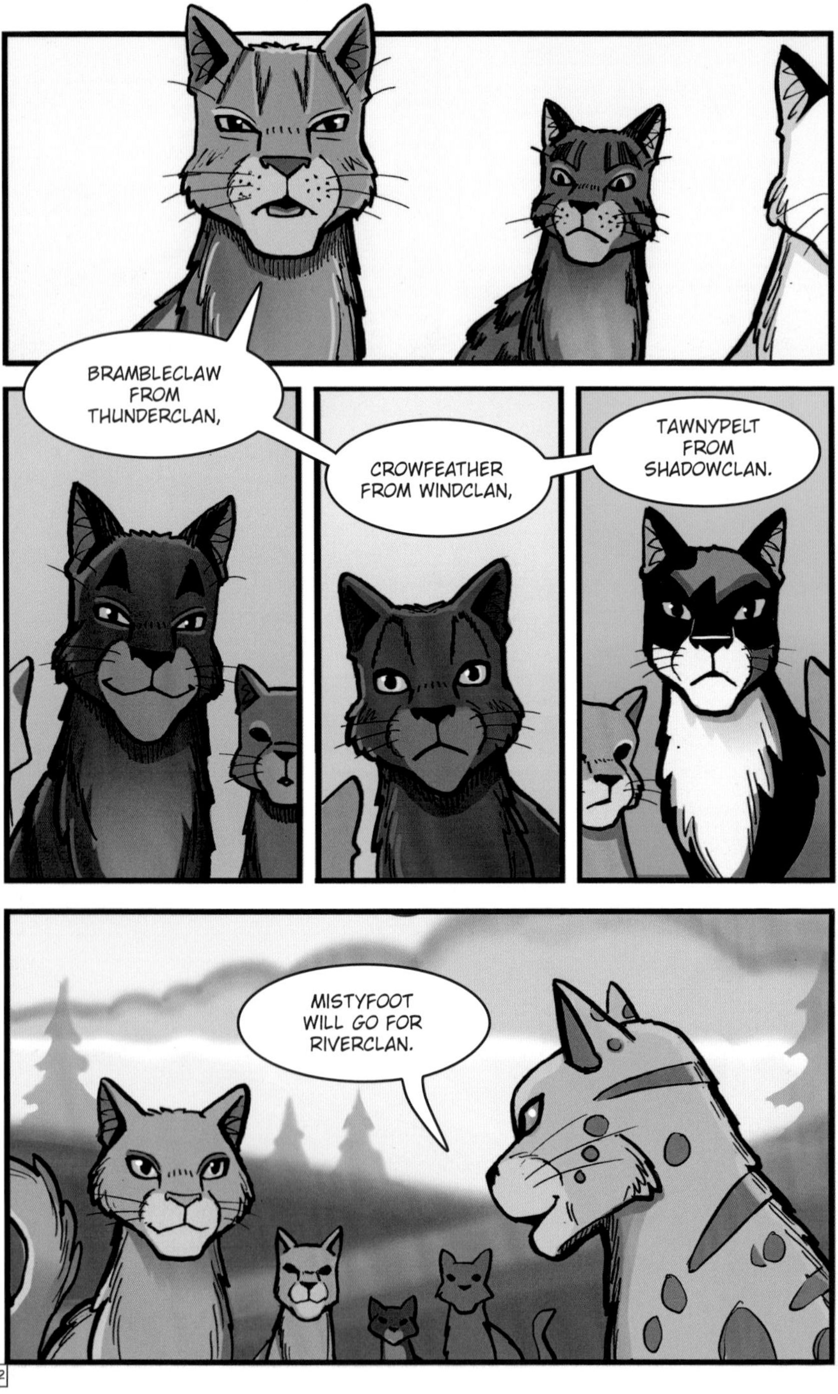
BRAMBLECLAW FROM THUNDERCLAN,
CROWFEATHER FROM WINDCLAN,
TAWNYPELT FROM SHADOWCLAN.
MISTYFOOT WILL GO FOR RIVERCLAN.

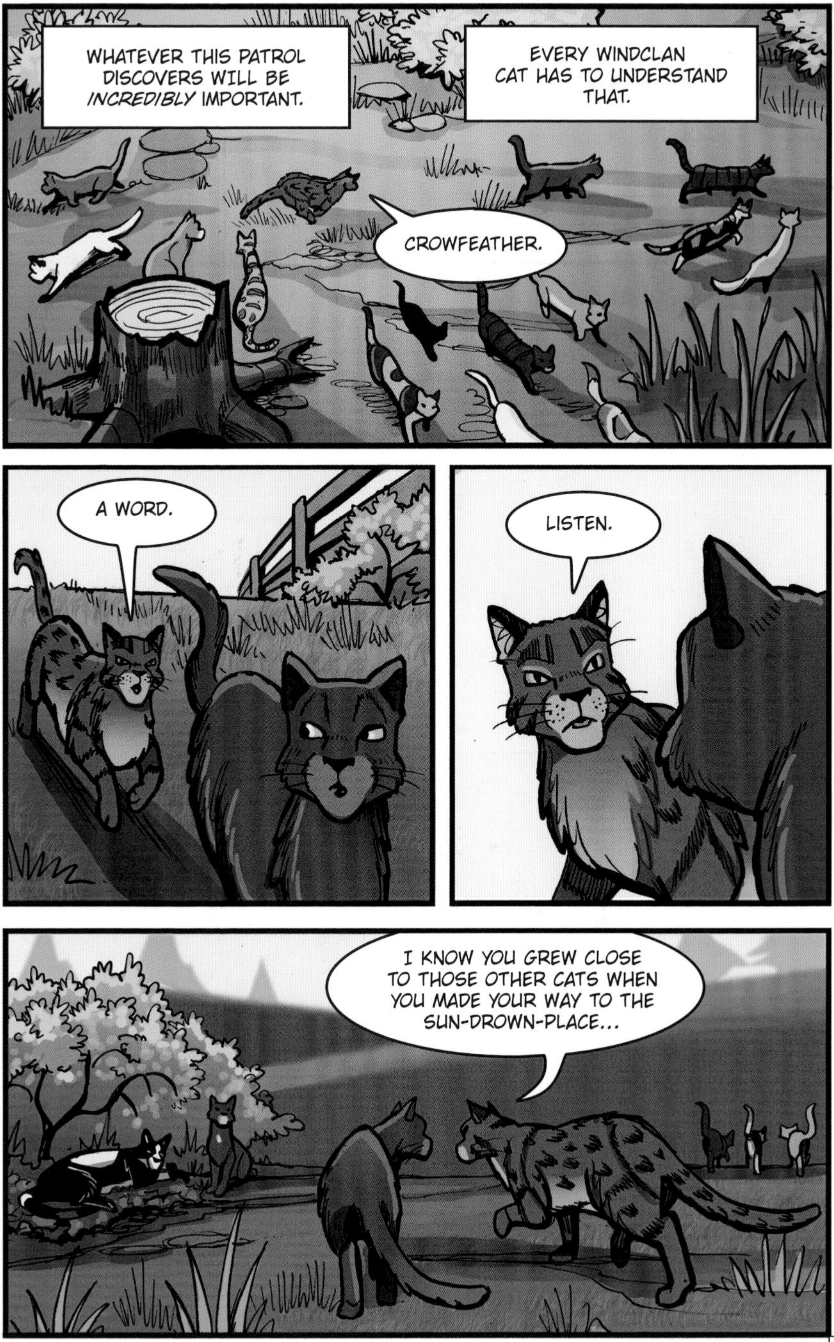
WHATEVER THIS PATROL DISCOVERS WILL BE *INCREDIBLY* IMPORTANT.
EVERY WINDCLAN CAT HAS TO UNDERSTAND THAT.
CROWFEATHER.
A WORD.
LISTEN.
I KNOW YOU GREW CLOSE TO THOSE OTHER CATS WHEN YOU MADE YOUR WAY TO THE SUN-DROWN-PLACE...

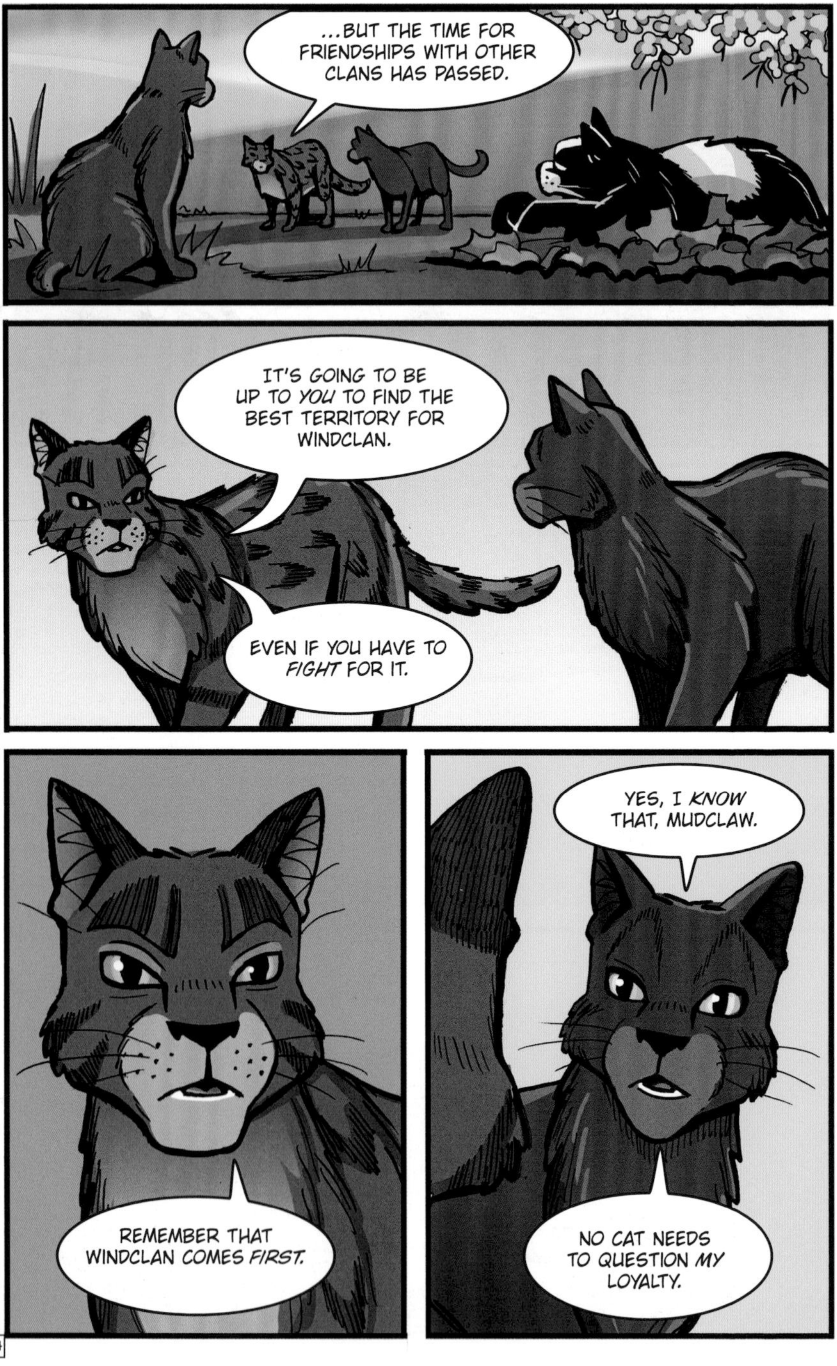
...BUT THE TIME FOR FRIENDSHIPS WITH OTHER CLANS HAS PASSED.
IT'S GOING TO BE UP TO *YOU* TO FIND THE BEST TERRITORY FOR WINDCLAN.
EVEN IF YOU HAVE TO *FIGHT* FOR IT.
REMEMBER THAT WINDCLAN COMES *FIRST.*
YES, I *KNOW* THAT, MUDCLAW.
NO CAT NEEDS TO QUESTION *MY* LOYALTY.

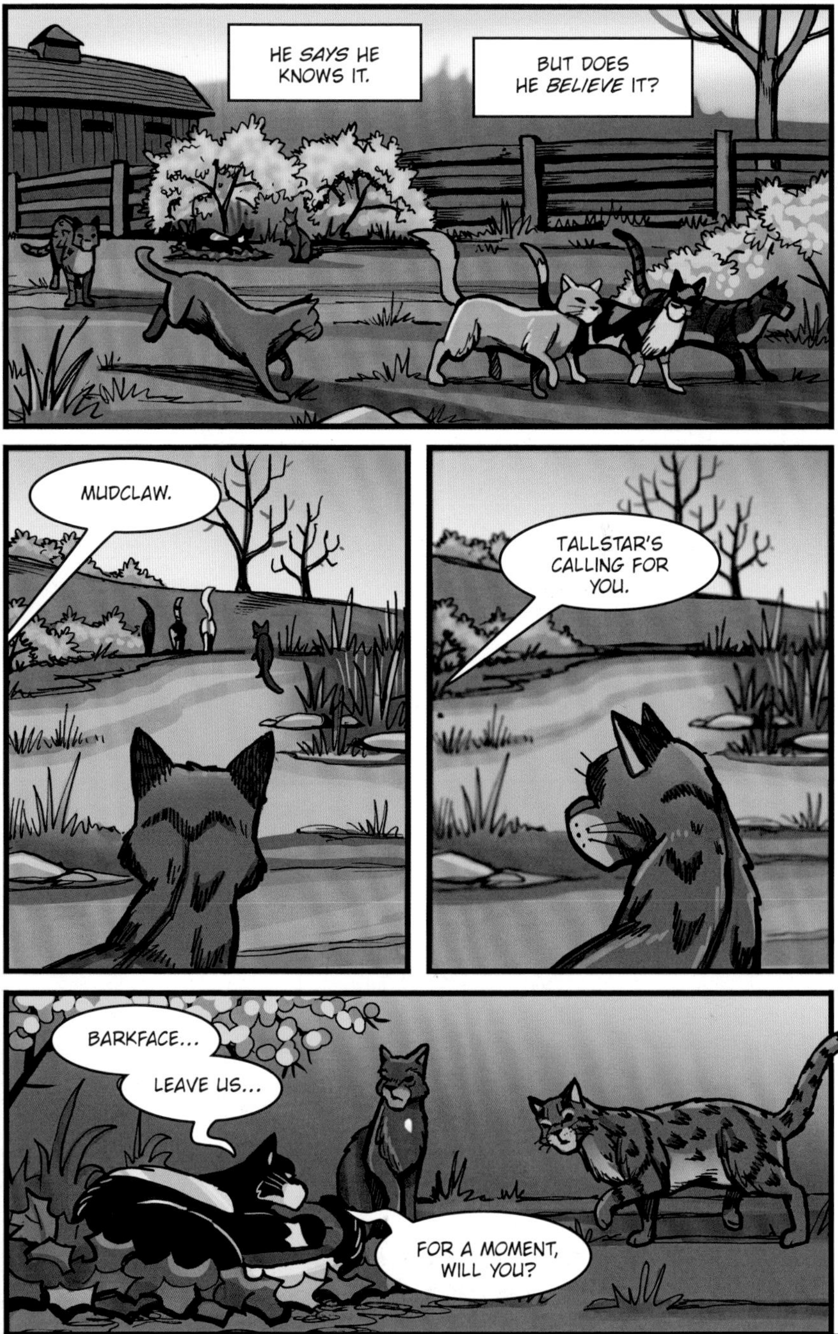
HE *SAYS* HE KNOWS IT.
BUT DOES HE *BELIEVE* IT?
MUDCLAW.
TALLSTAR'S CALLING FOR YOU.
BARKFACE...
LEAVE US...
FOR A MOMENT, WILL YOU?

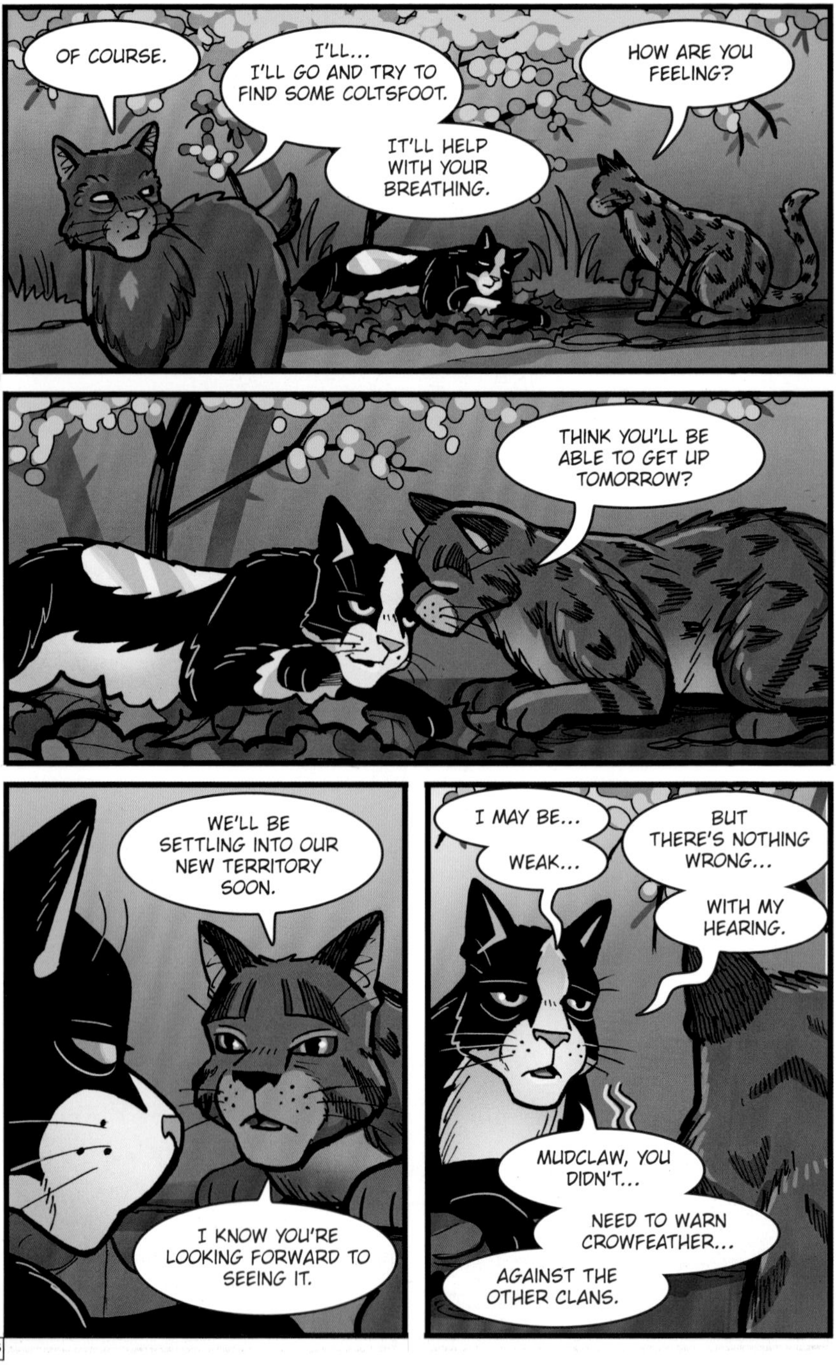
OF COURSE.
I'LL... I'LL GO AND TRY TO FIND SOME COLTSFOOT.
IT'LL HELP WITH YOUR BREATHING.
HOW ARE YOU FEELING?
THINK YOU'LL BE ABLE TO GET UP TOMORROW?
WE'LL BE SETTLING INTO OUR NEW TERRITORY SOON.
I KNOW YOU'RE LOOKING FORWARD TO SEEING IT.
I MAY BE...
WEAK...
BUT THERE'S NOTHING WRONG...
WITH MY HEARING.
MUDCLAW, YOU DIDN'T...
NEED TO WARN CROWFEATHER...
AGAINST THE OTHER CLANS.

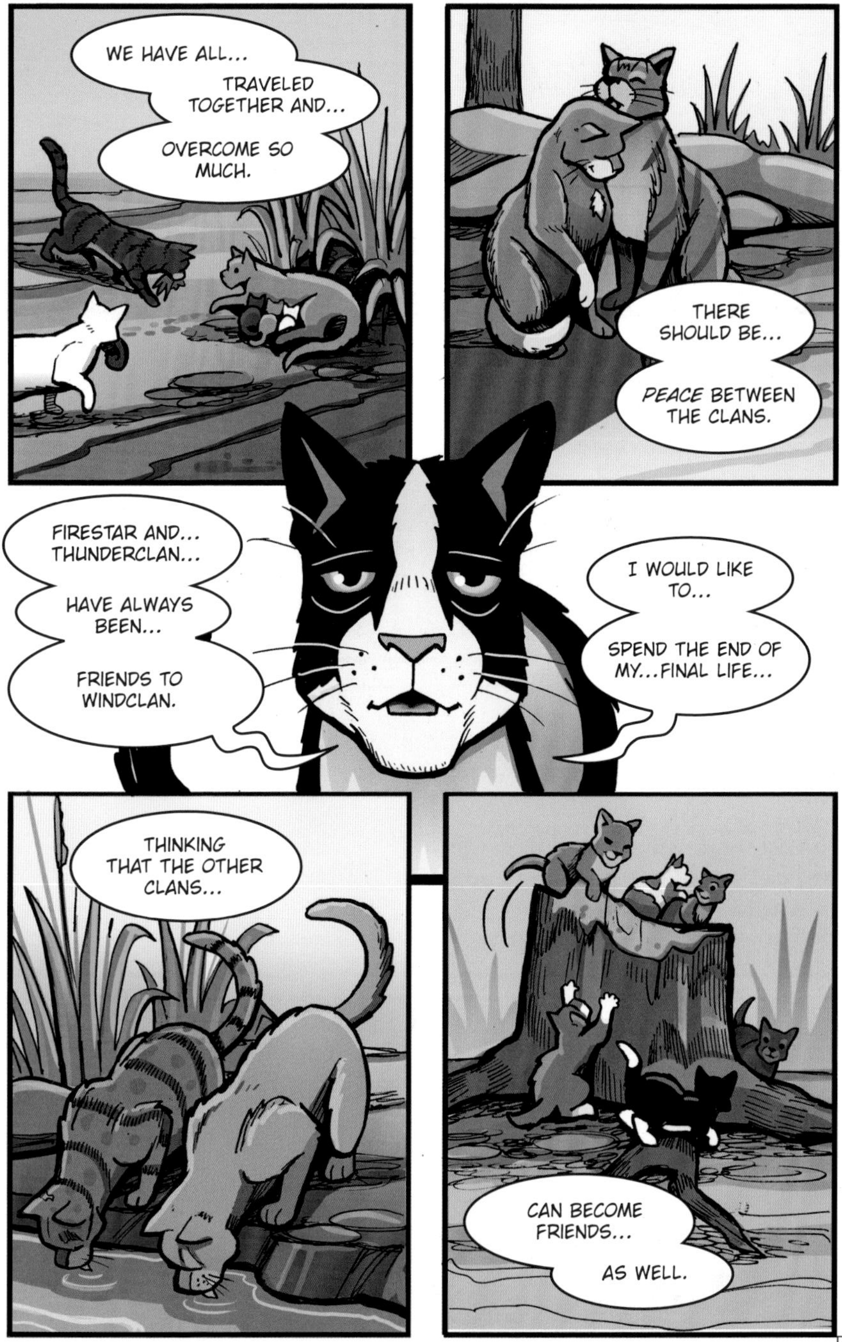
WE HAVE ALL...
TRAVELED TOGETHER AND...
OVERCOME SO MUCH.
THERE SHOULD BE...
PEACE BETWEEN THE CLANS.
FIRESTAR AND... THUNDERCLAN...
HAVE ALWAYS BEEN...
FRIENDS TO WINDCLAN.
I WOULD LIKE TO...
SPEND THE END OF MY...FINAL LIFE...
THINKING THAT THE OTHER CLANS...
CAN BECOME FRIENDS...
AS WELL.

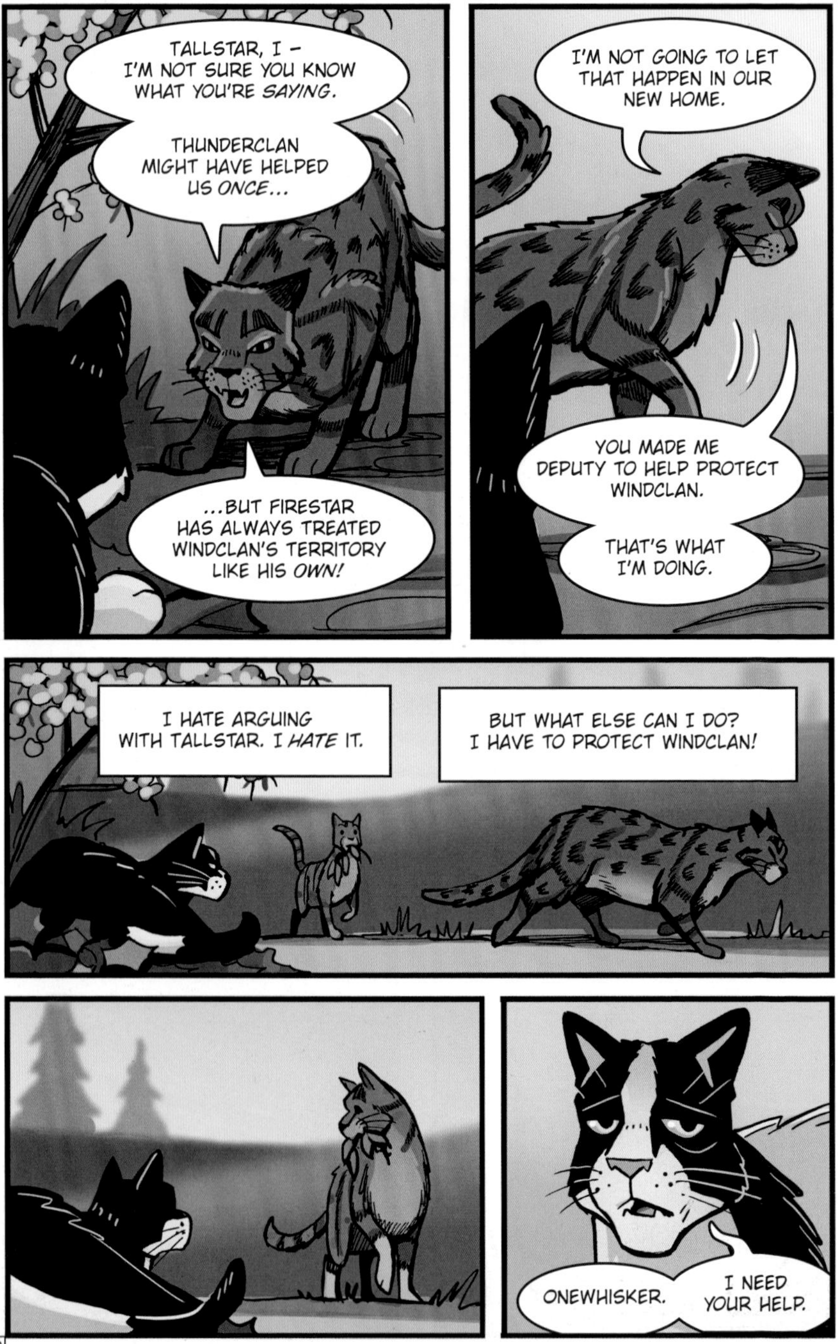
TALLSTAR, I – I'M NOT SURE YOU KNOW WHAT YOU'RE *SAYING*.
THUNDERCLAN MIGHT HAVE HELPED US *ONCE*...
...BUT FIRESTAR HAS ALWAYS TREATED WINDCLAN'S TERRITORY LIKE HIS *OWN!*
I'M NOT GOING TO LET THAT HAPPEN IN OUR NEW HOME.
YOU MADE ME DEPUTY TO HELP PROTECT WINDCLAN.
THAT'S WHAT I'M DOING.
I HATE ARGUING WITH TALLSTAR. I *HATE* IT.
BUT WHAT ELSE CAN I DO? I HAVE TO PROTECT WINDCLAN!
ONEWHISKER.
I NEED YOUR HELP.

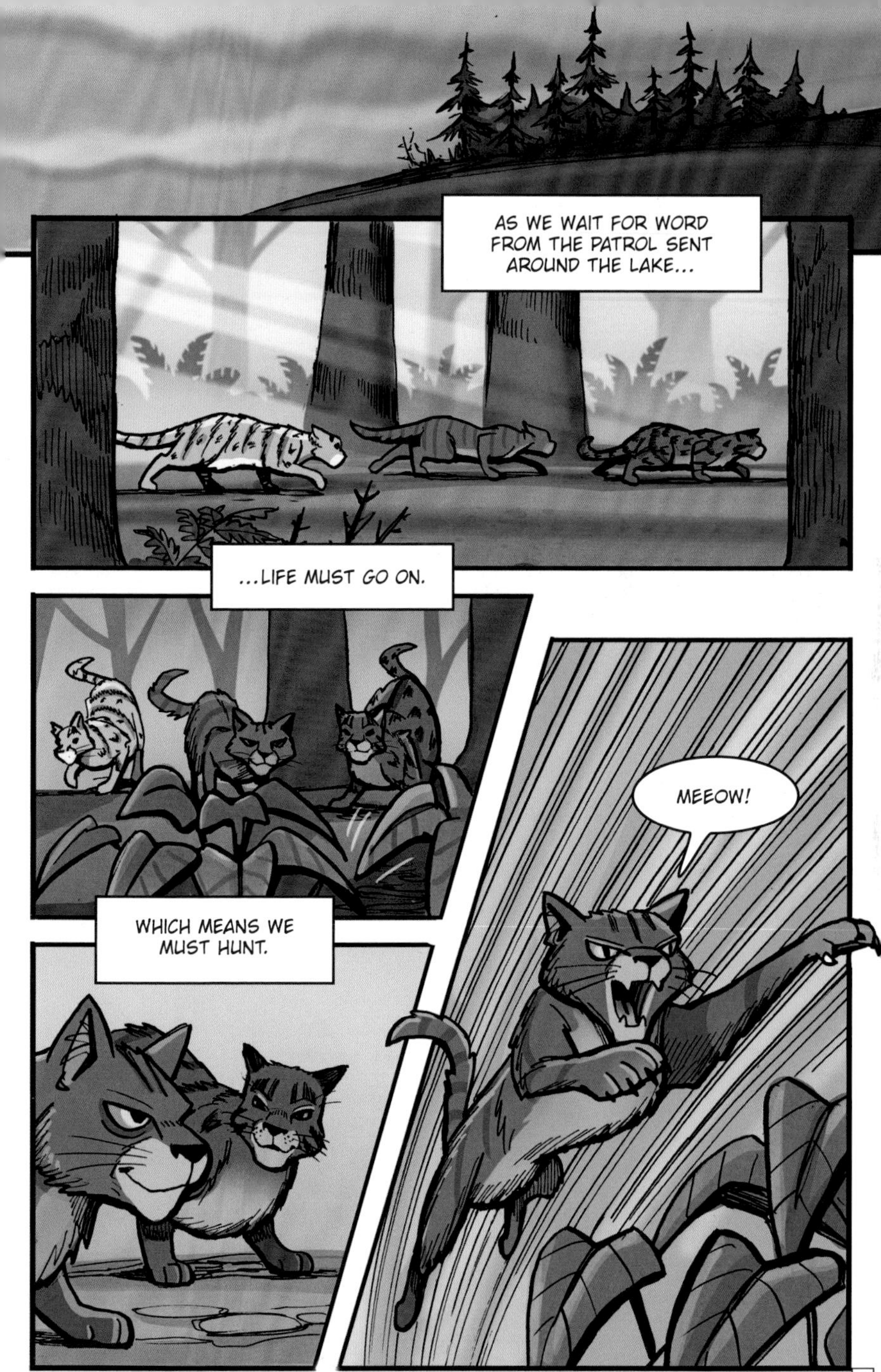
AS WE WAIT FOR WORD FROM THE PATROL SENT AROUND THE LAKE...
...LIFE MUST GO ON.
WHICH MEANS WE MUST HUNT.
MEEOW!

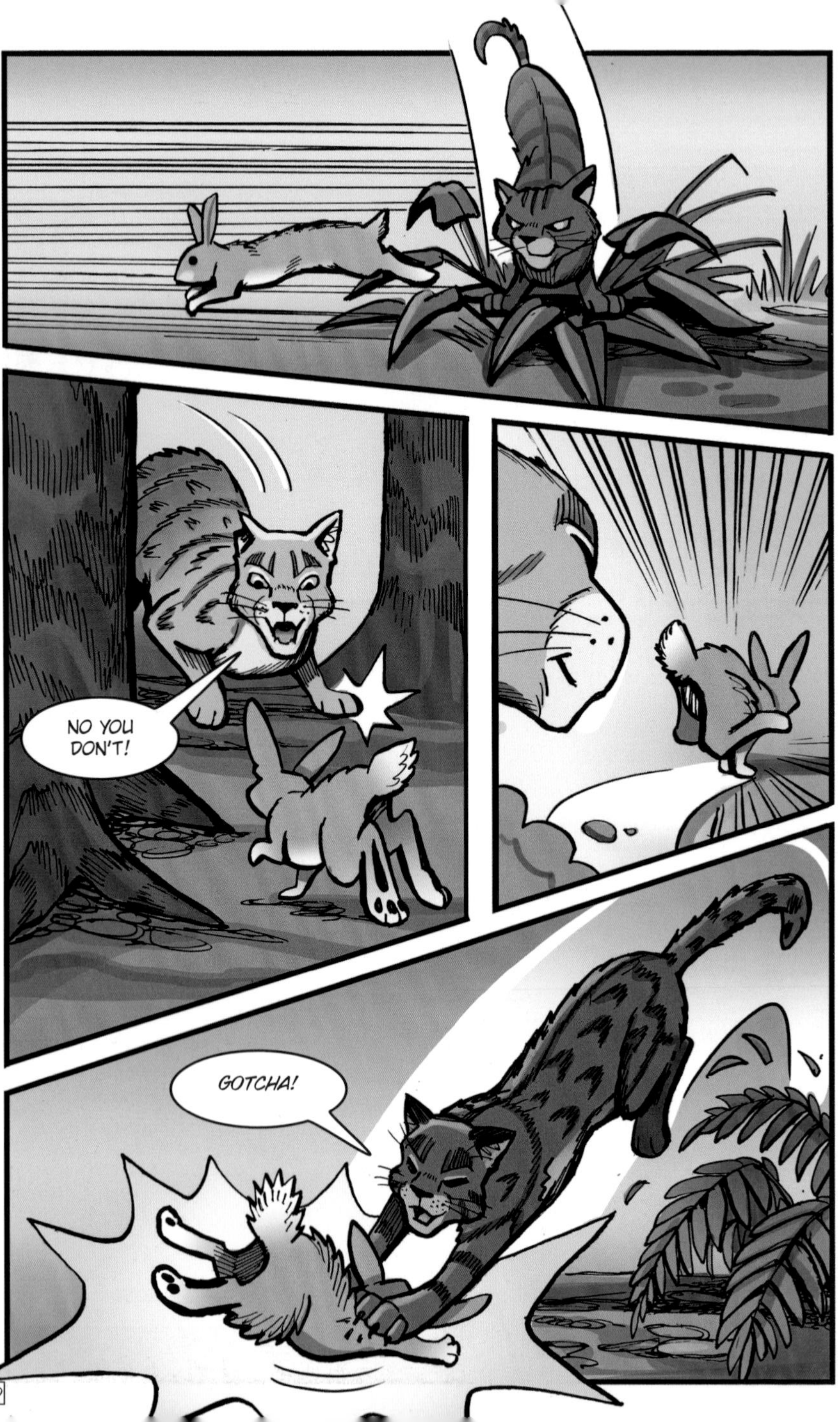
NO YOU DON'T!
GOTCHA!

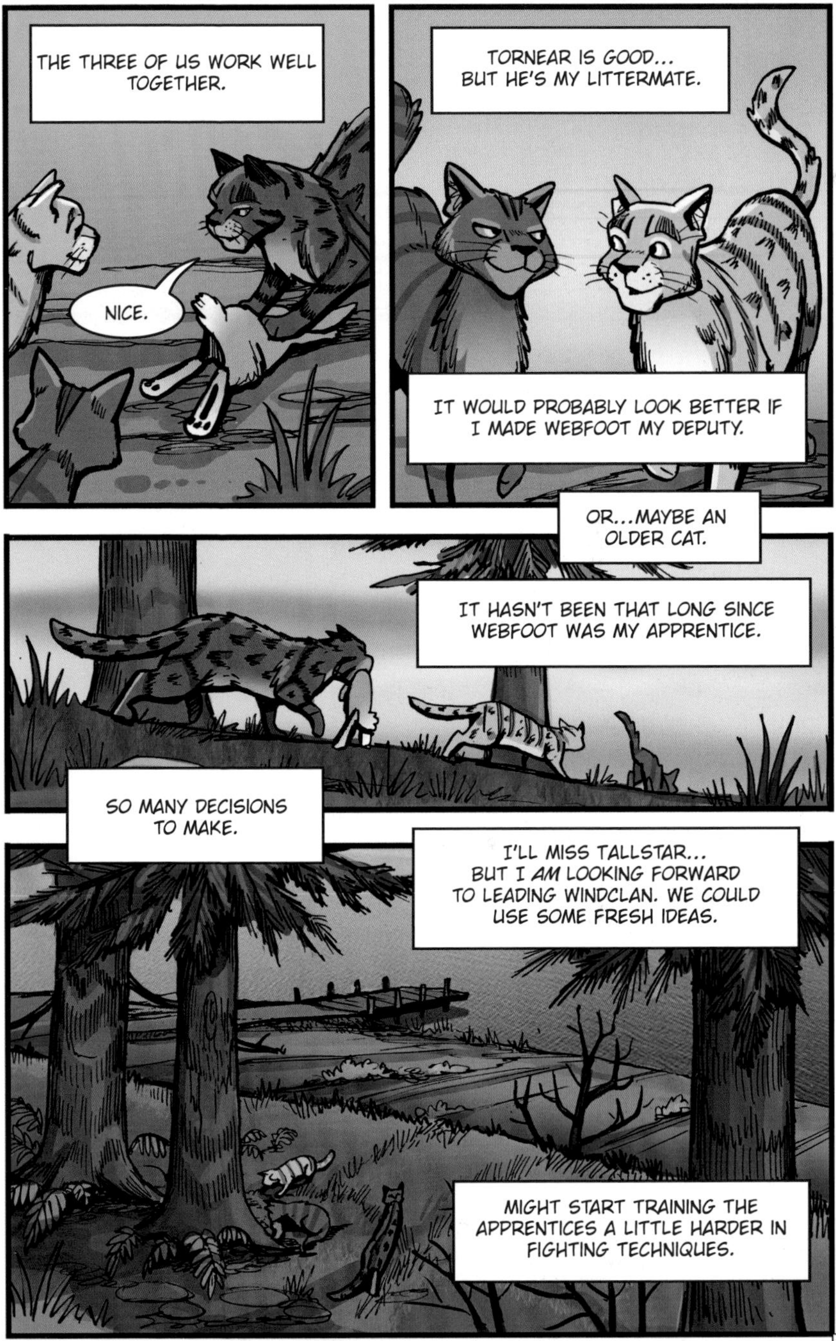
THE THREE OF US WORK WELL TOGETHER.
NICE.
TORNEAR IS GOOD... BUT HE'S MY LITTERMATE.
IT WOULD PROBABLY LOOK BETTER IF I MADE WEBFOOT MY DEPUTY.
OR...MAYBE AN OLDER CAT.
IT HASN'T BEEN THAT LONG SINCE WEBFOOT WAS MY APPRENTICE.
SO MANY DECISIONS TO MAKE.
I'LL MISS TALLSTAR... BUT I *AM* LOOKING FORWARD TO LEADING WINDCLAN. WE COULD USE SOME FRESH IDEAS.
MIGHT START TRAINING THE APPRENTICES A LITTLE HARDER IN FIGHTING TECHNIQUES.

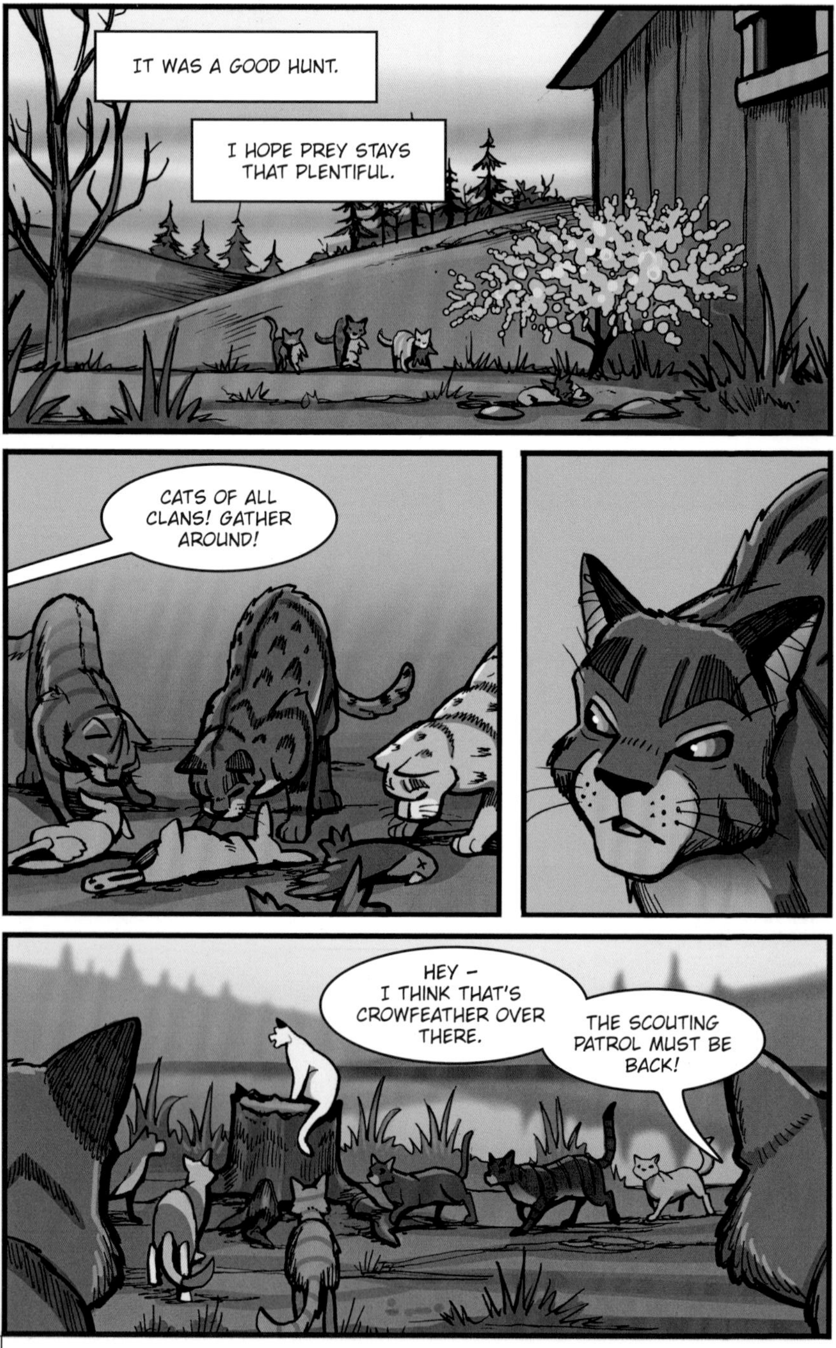
IT WAS A GOOD HUNT.
I HOPE PREY STAYS THAT PLENTIFUL.
CATS OF ALL CLANS! GATHER AROUND!
HEY – I THINK THAT'S CROWFEATHER OVER THERE.
THE SCOUTING PATROL MUST BE BACK!

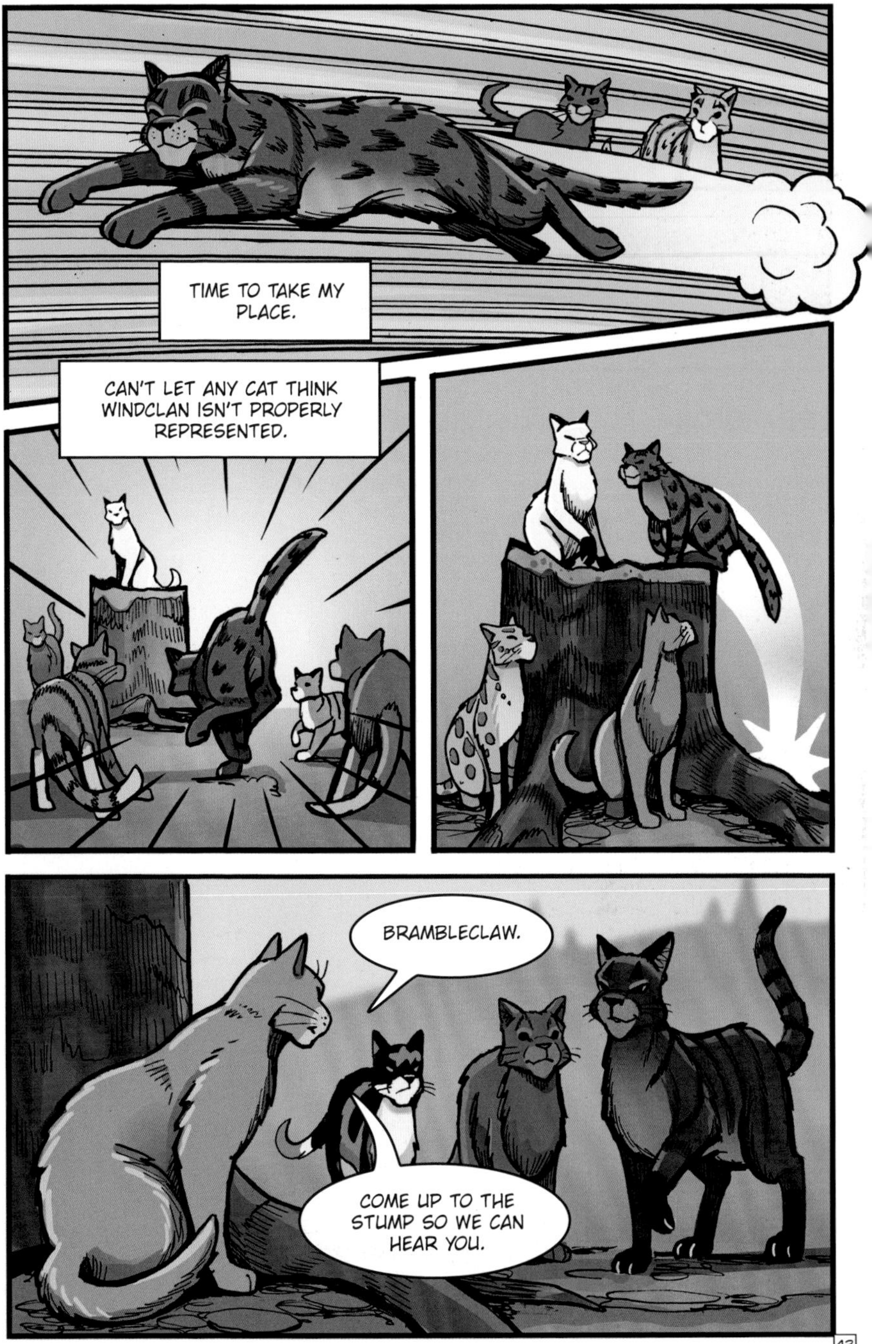
TIME TO TAKE MY PLACE.
CAN'T LET ANY CAT THINK WINDCLAN ISN'T PROPERLY REPRESENTED.
BRAMBLECLAW.
COME UP TO THE STUMP SO WE CAN HEAR YOU.

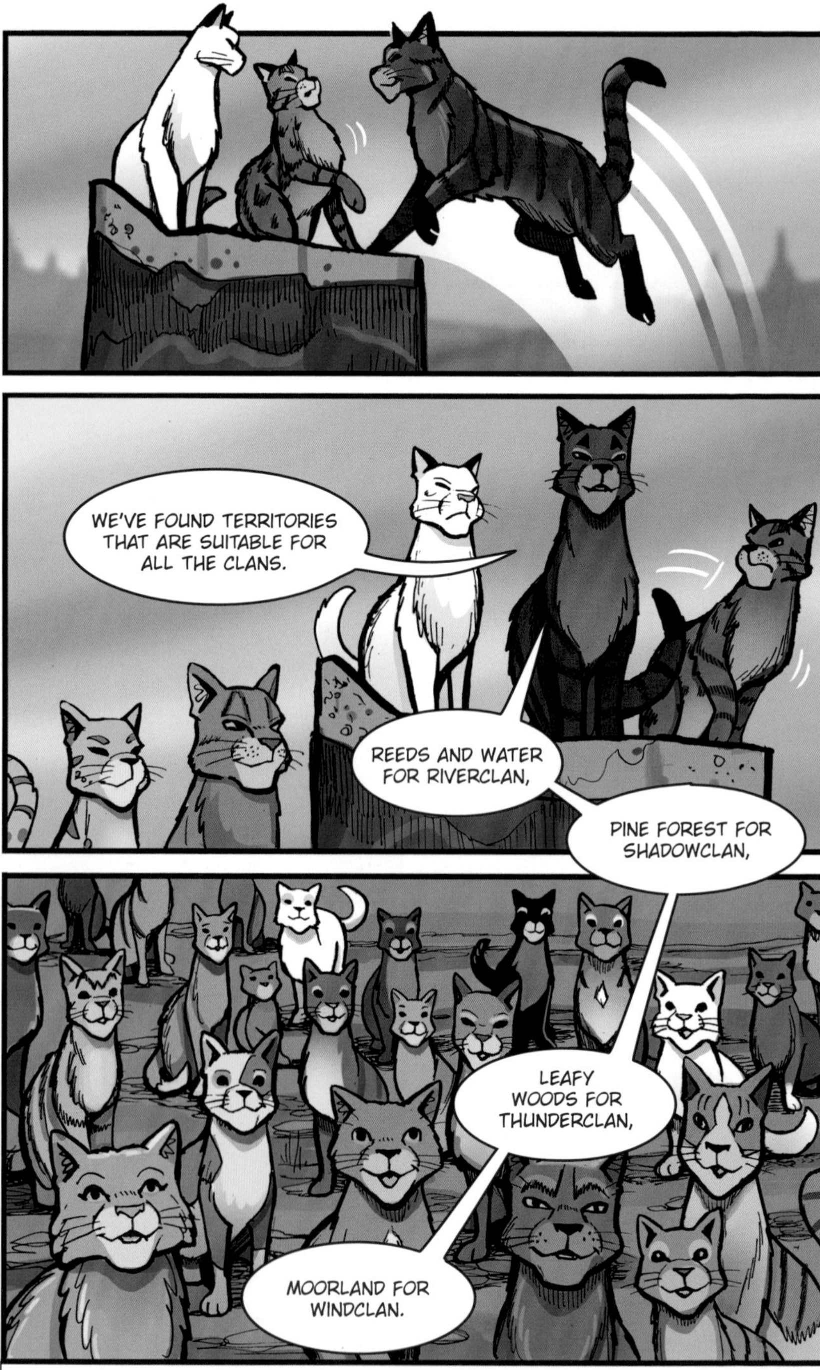
WE'VE FOUND TERRITORIES THAT ARE SUITABLE FOR ALL THE CLANS.
REEDS AND WATER FOR RIVERCLAN,
PINE FOREST FOR SHADOWCLAN,
LEAFY WOODS FOR THUNDERCLAN,
MOORLAND FOR WINDCLAN.

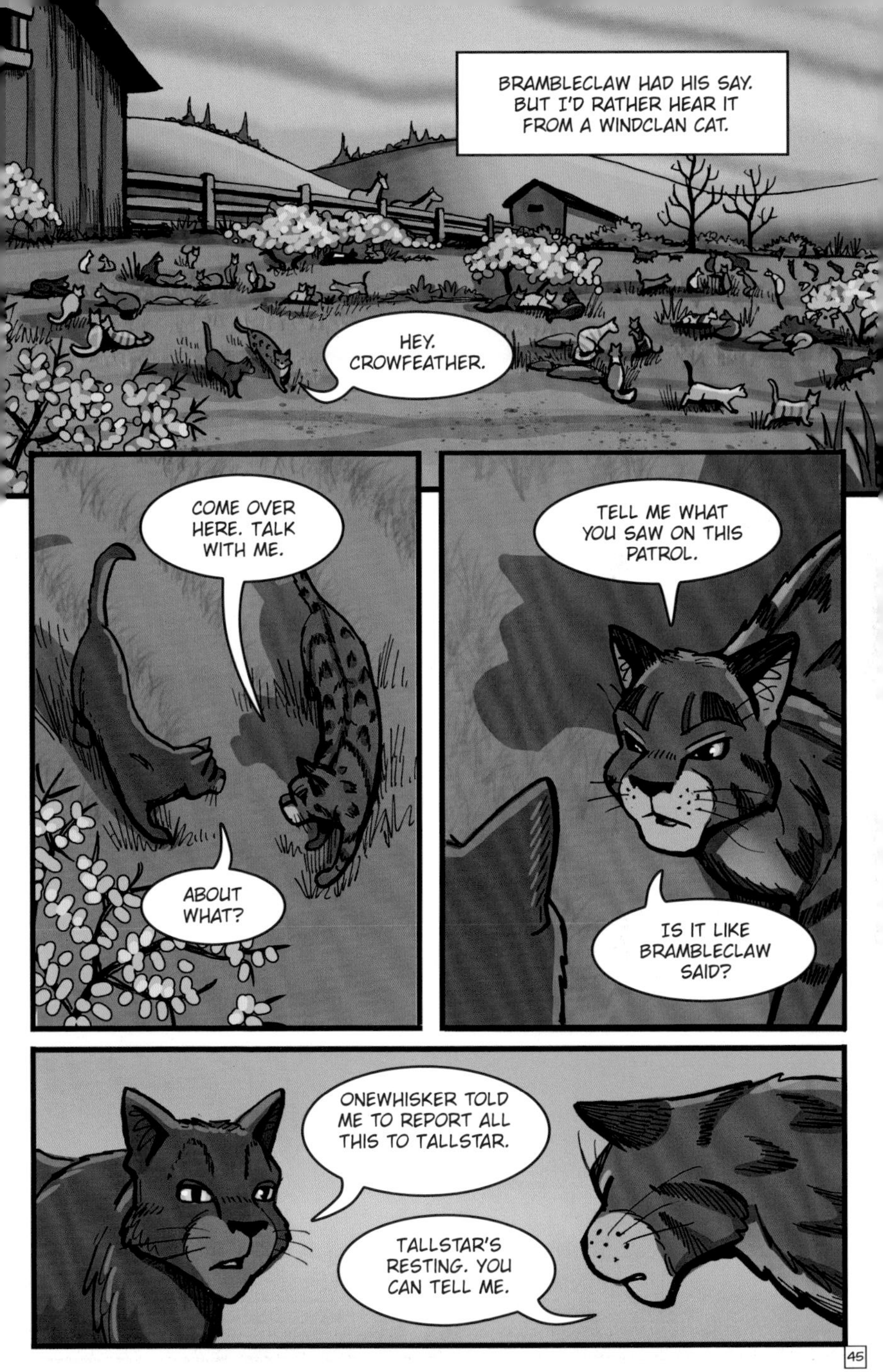
BRAMBLECLAW HAD HIS SAY. BUT I'D RATHER HEAR IT FROM A WINDCLAN CAT.
HEY. CROWFEATHER.
COME OVER HERE. TALK WITH ME.
ABOUT WHAT?
TELL ME WHAT YOU SAW ON THIS PATROL.
IS IT LIKE BRAMBLECLAW SAID?
ONEWHISKER TOLD ME TO REPORT ALL THIS TO TALLSTAR.
TALLSTAR'S RESTING. YOU CAN TELL ME.

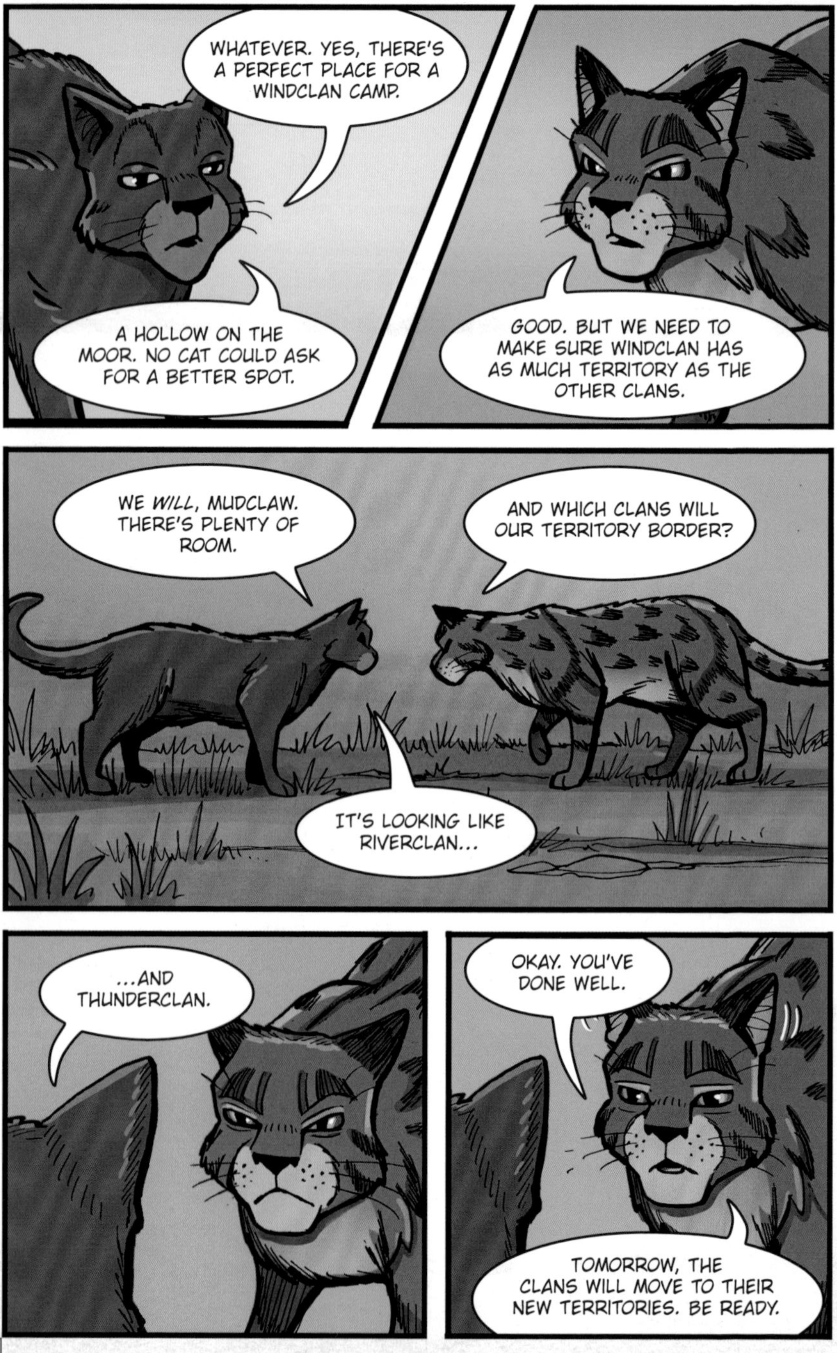
WHATEVER. YES, THERE'S A PERFECT PLACE FOR A WINDCLAN CAMP.
A HOLLOW ON THE MOOR. NO CAT COULD ASK FOR A BETTER SPOT.
GOOD. BUT WE NEED TO MAKE SURE WINDCLAN HAS AS MUCH TERRITORY AS THE OTHER CLANS.
WE *WILL*, MUDCLAW. THERE'S PLENTY OF ROOM.
AND WHICH CLANS WILL OUR TERRITORY BORDER?
IT'S LOOKING LIKE RIVERCLAN...
...AND THUNDERCLAN.
OKAY. YOU'VE DONE WELL.
TOMORROW, THE CLANS WILL MOVE TO THEIR NEW TERRITORIES. BE READY.

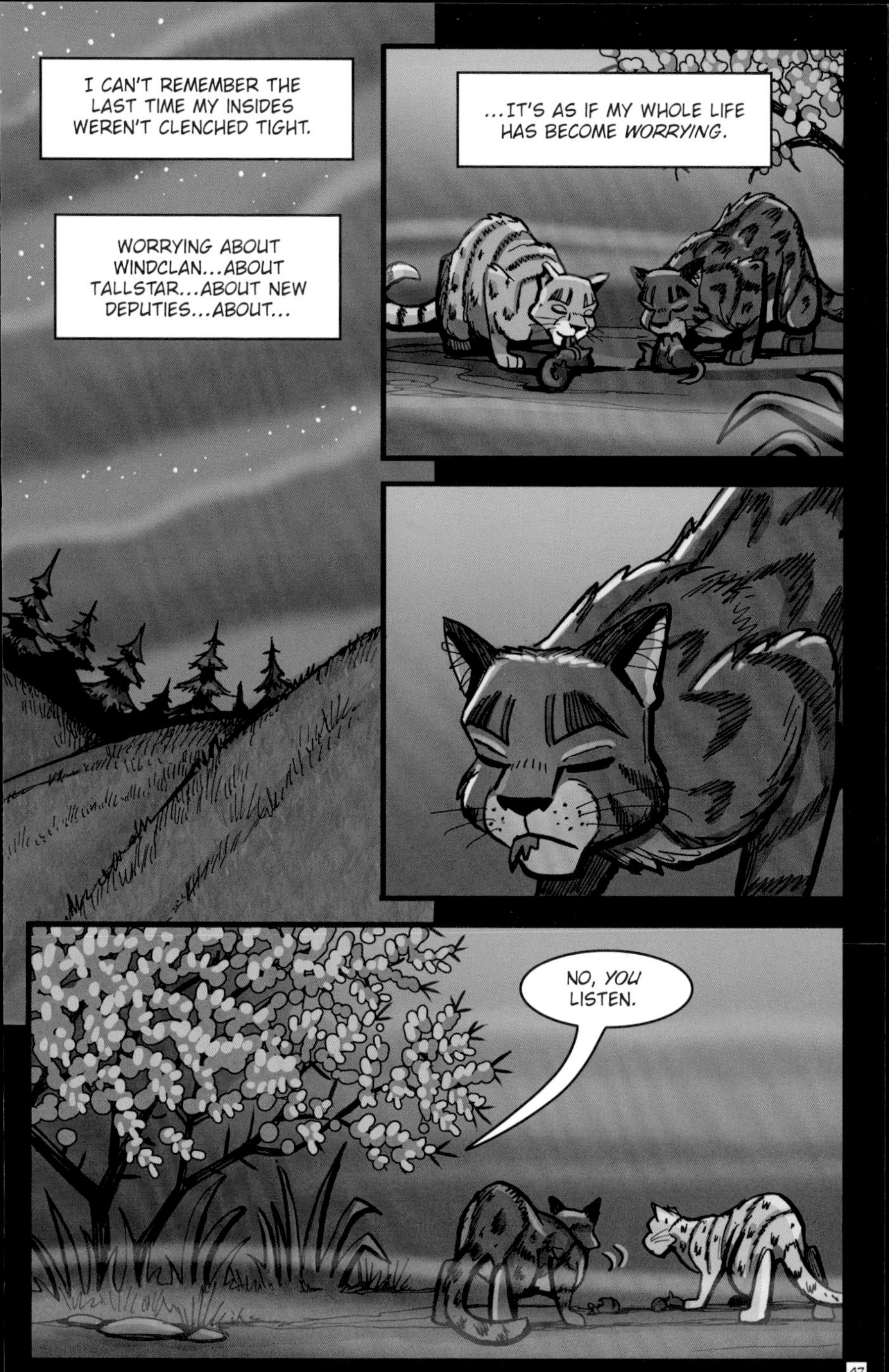
I CAN'T REMEMBER THE LAST TIME MY INSIDES WEREN'T CLENCHED TIGHT.
...IT'S AS IF MY WHOLE LIFE HAS BECOME *WORRYING*.
WORRYING ABOUT WINDCLAN...ABOUT TALLSTAR...ABOUT NEW DEPUTIES...ABOUT...
NO, *YOU* LISTEN.

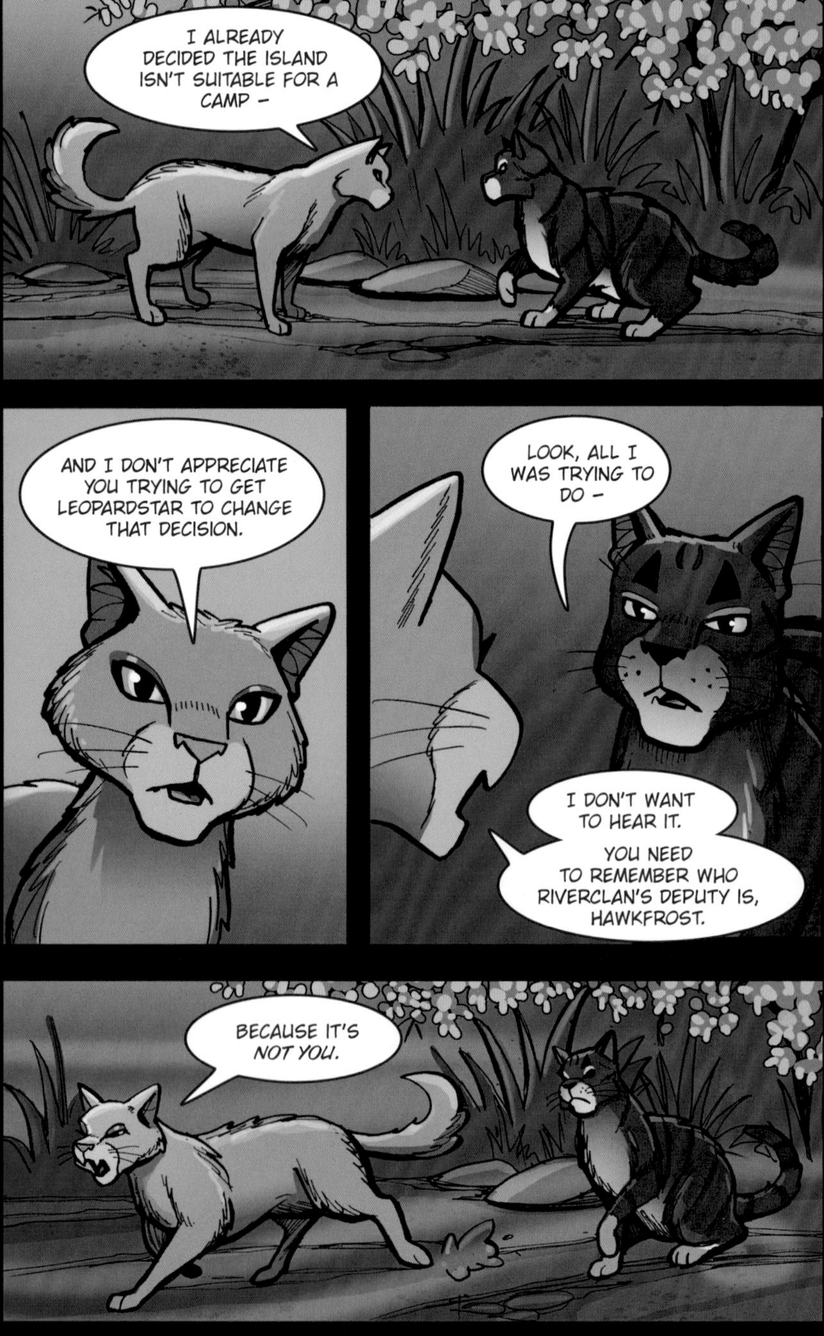
I ALREADY DECIDED THE ISLAND ISN'T SUITABLE FOR A CAMP –
AND I DON'T APPRECIATE YOU TRYING TO GET LEOPARDSTAR TO CHANGE THAT DECISION.
LOOK, ALL I WAS TRYING TO DO –
I DON'T WANT TO HEAR IT.
YOU NEED TO REMEMBER WHO RIVERCLAN'S DEPUTY IS, HAWKFROST.
BECAUSE IT'S *NOT YOU.*

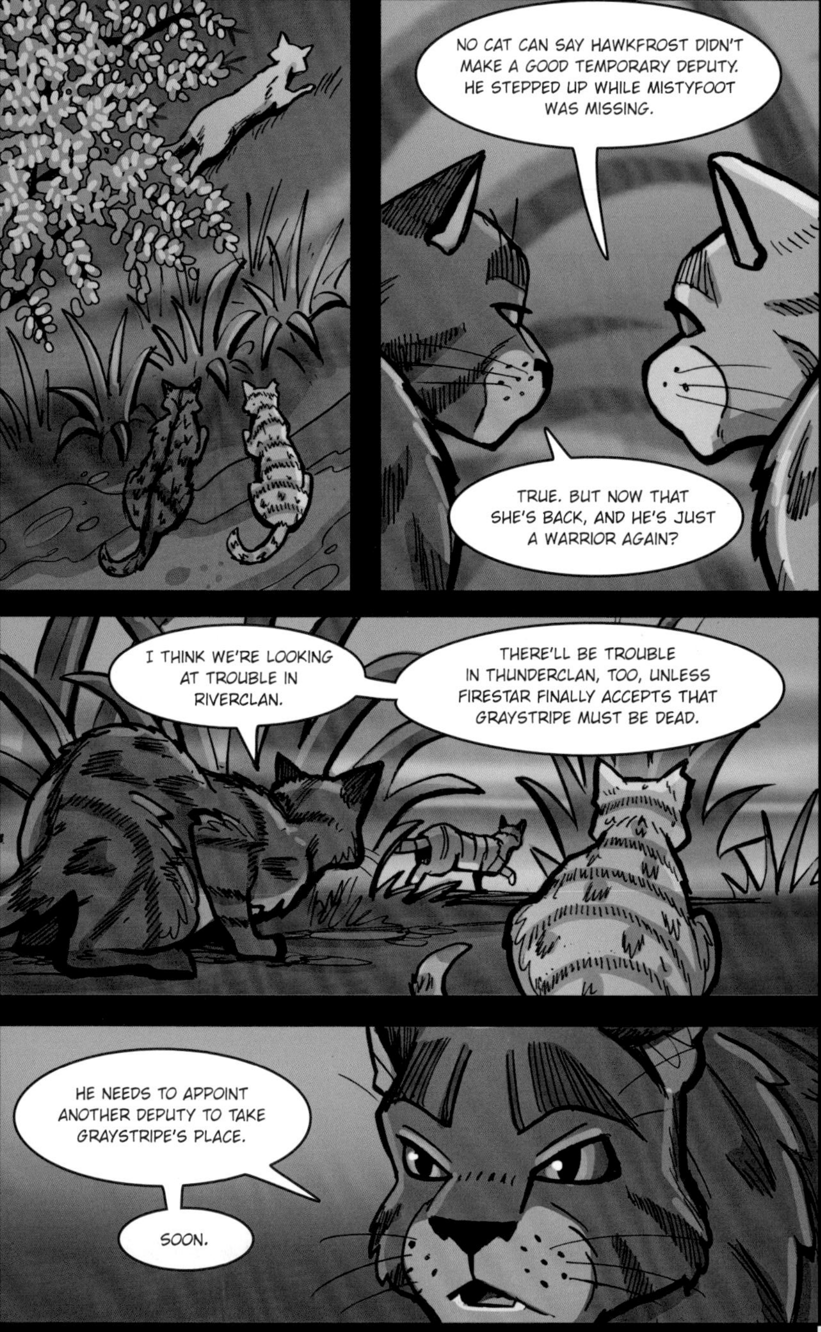
NO CAT CAN SAY HAWKFROST DIDN'T MAKE A GOOD TEMPORARY DEPUTY. HE STEPPED UP WHILE MISTYFOOT WAS MISSING.
TRUE. BUT NOW THAT SHE'S BACK, AND HE'S JUST A WARRIOR AGAIN?
I THINK WE'RE LOOKING AT TROUBLE IN RIVERCLAN.
THERE'LL BE TROUBLE IN THUNDERCLAN, TOO, UNLESS FIRESTAR FINALLY ACCEPTS THAT GRAYSTRIPE MUST BE DEAD.
HE NEEDS TO APPOINT ANOTHER DEPUTY TO TAKE GRAYSTRIPE'S PLACE.
SOON.

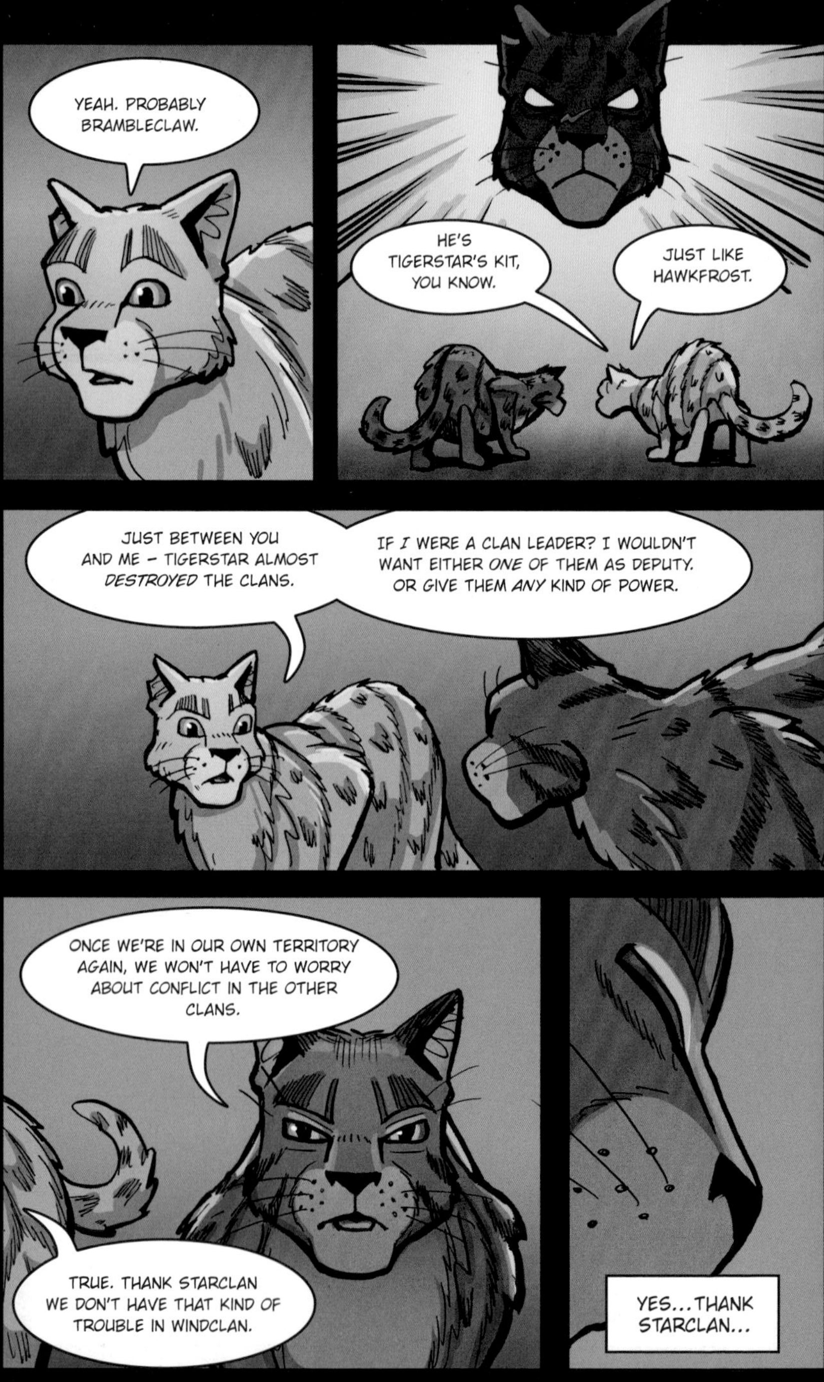
YEAH. PROBABLY BRAMBLECLAW.
HE'S TIGERSTAR'S KIT, YOU KNOW.
JUST LIKE HAWKFROST.
JUST BETWEEN YOU AND ME – TIGERSTAR ALMOST *DESTROYED* THE CLANS.
IF *I* WERE A CLAN LEADER? I WOULDN'T WANT EITHER *ONE* OF THEM AS DEPUTY. OR GIVE THEM *ANY* KIND OF POWER.
ONCE WE'RE IN OUR OWN TERRITORY AGAIN, WE WON'T HAVE TO WORRY ABOUT CONFLICT IN THE OTHER CLANS.
TRUE. THANK STARCLAN WE DON'T HAVE THAT KIND OF TROUBLE IN WINDCLAN.
YES...THANK STARCLAN...

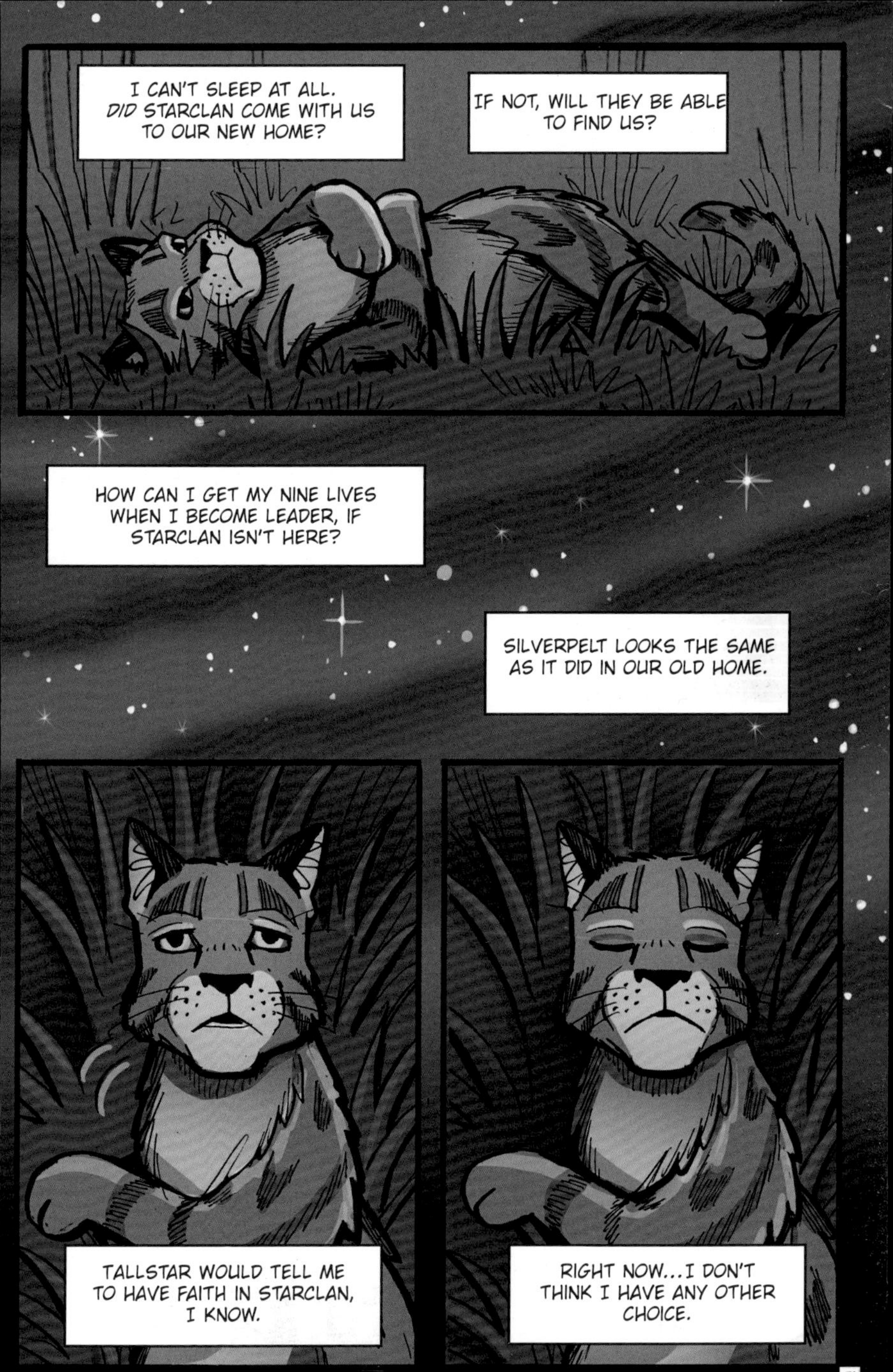
I CAN'T SLEEP AT ALL. *DID* STARCLAN COME WITH US TO OUR NEW HOME?
IF NOT, WILL THEY BE ABLE TO FIND US?
HOW CAN I GET MY NINE LIVES WHEN I BECOME LEADER, IF STARCLAN ISN'T HERE?
SILVERPELT LOOKS THE SAME AS IT DID IN OUR OLD HOME.
TALLSTAR WOULD TELL ME TO HAVE FAITH IN STARCLAN, I KNOW.
RIGHT NOW...I DON'T THINK I HAVE ANY OTHER CHOICE.

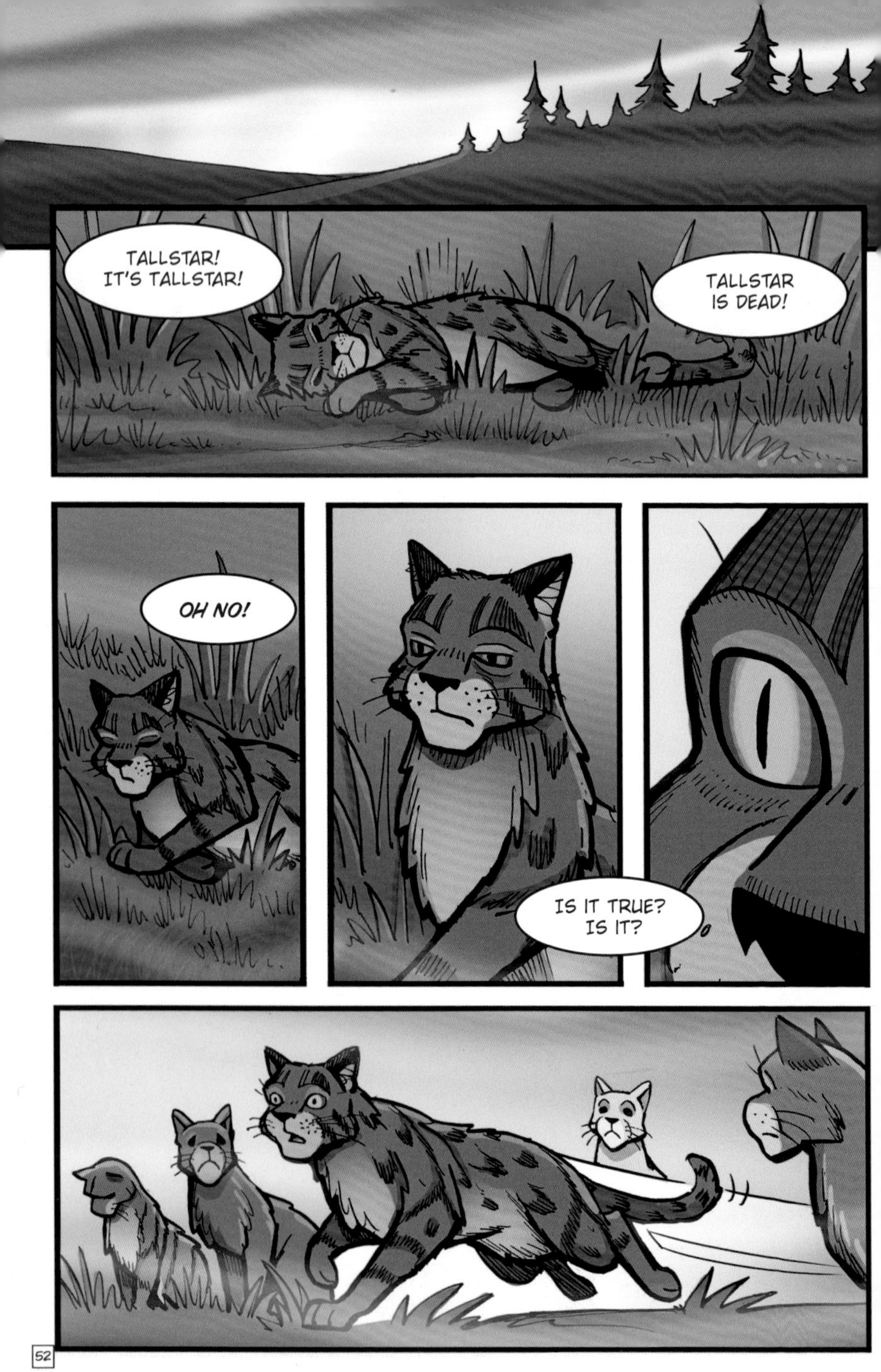

TALLSTAR! IT'S TALLSTAR!
TALLSTAR IS DEAD!
OH NO!
IS IT TRUE? IS IT?

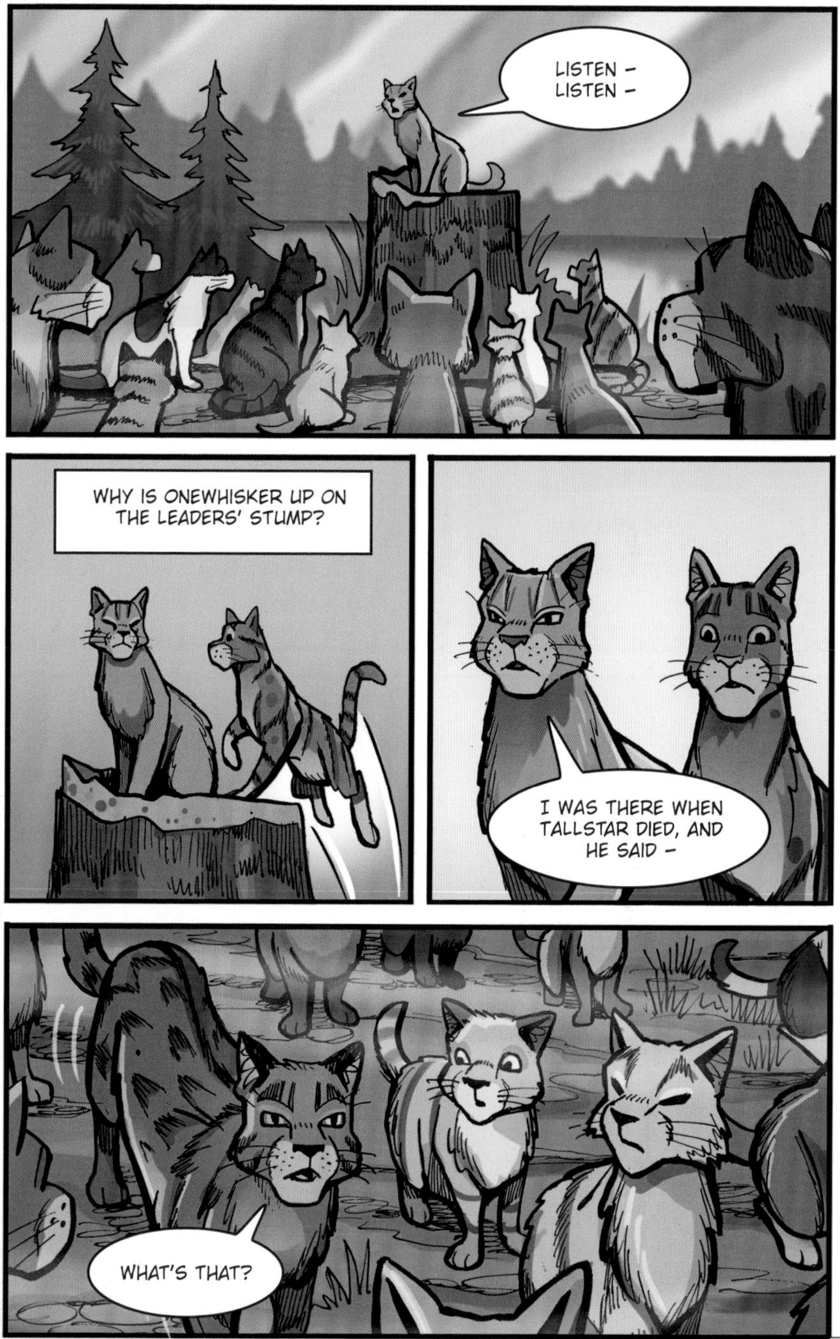
LISTEN –
LISTEN –
WHY IS ONEWHISKER UP ON THE LEADERS' STUMP?
I WAS THERE WHEN TALLSTAR DIED, AND HE SAID –
WHAT'S THAT?

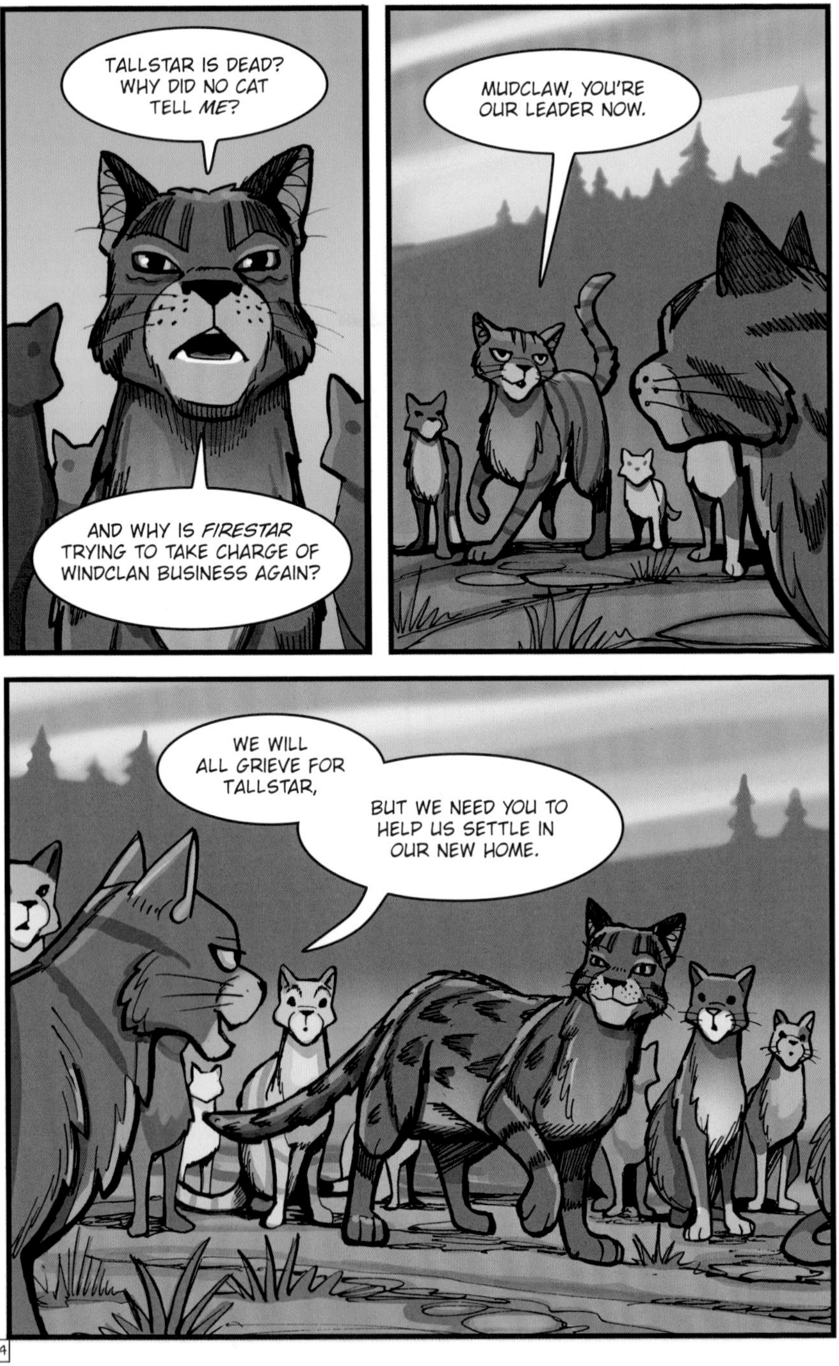
TALLSTAR IS DEAD? WHY DID NO CAT TELL *ME*?
AND WHY IS *FIRESTAR* TRYING TO TAKE CHARGE OF WINDCLAN BUSINESS AGAIN?
MUDCLAW, YOU'RE OUR LEADER NOW.
WE WILL ALL GRIEVE FOR TALLSTAR,
BUT WE NEED YOU TO HELP US SETTLE IN OUR NEW HOME.

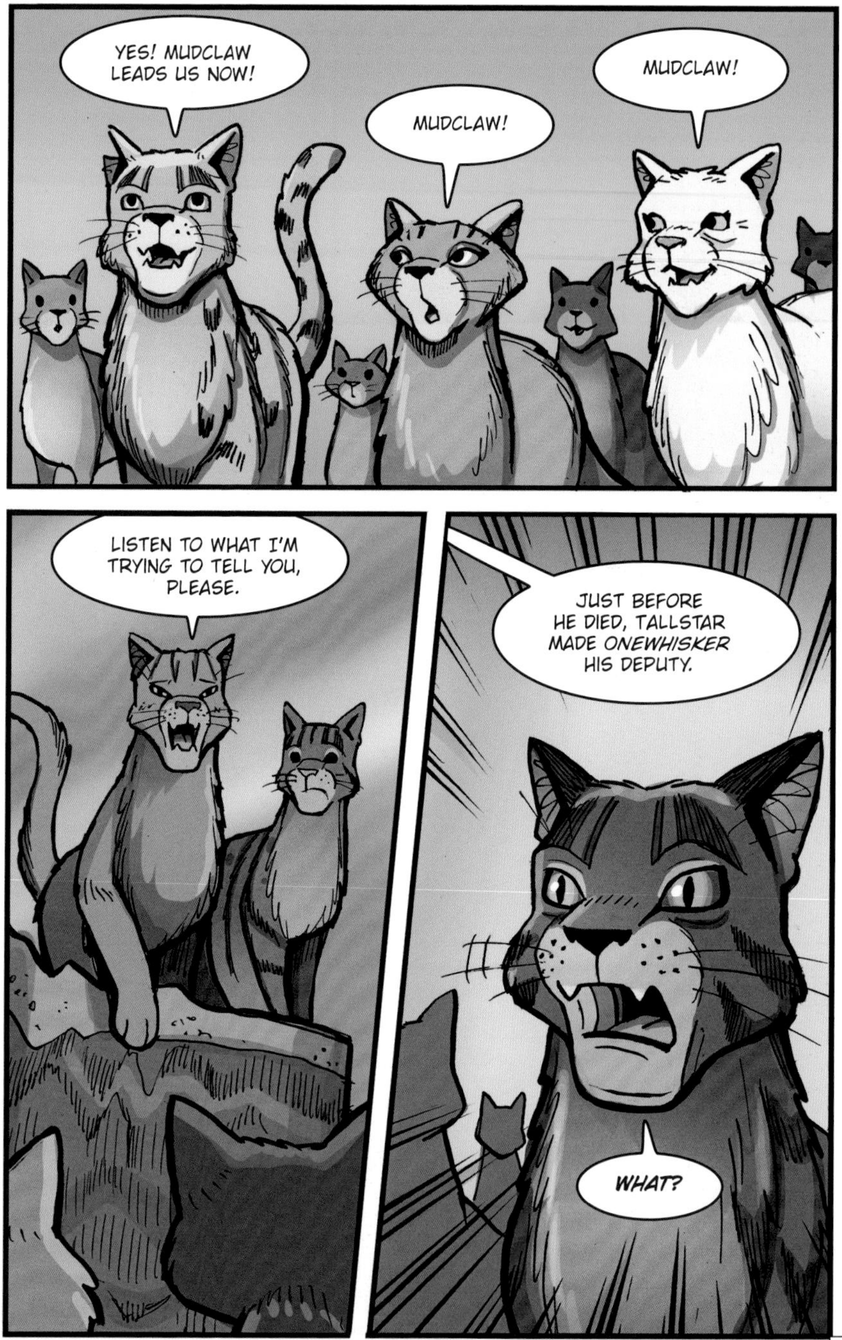
YES! MUDCLAW LEADS US NOW!
MUDCLAW!
MUDCLAW!
LISTEN TO WHAT I'M TRYING TO TELL YOU, PLEASE.
JUST BEFORE HE DIED, TALLSTAR MADE ONEWHISKER HIS DEPUTY.
WHAT?

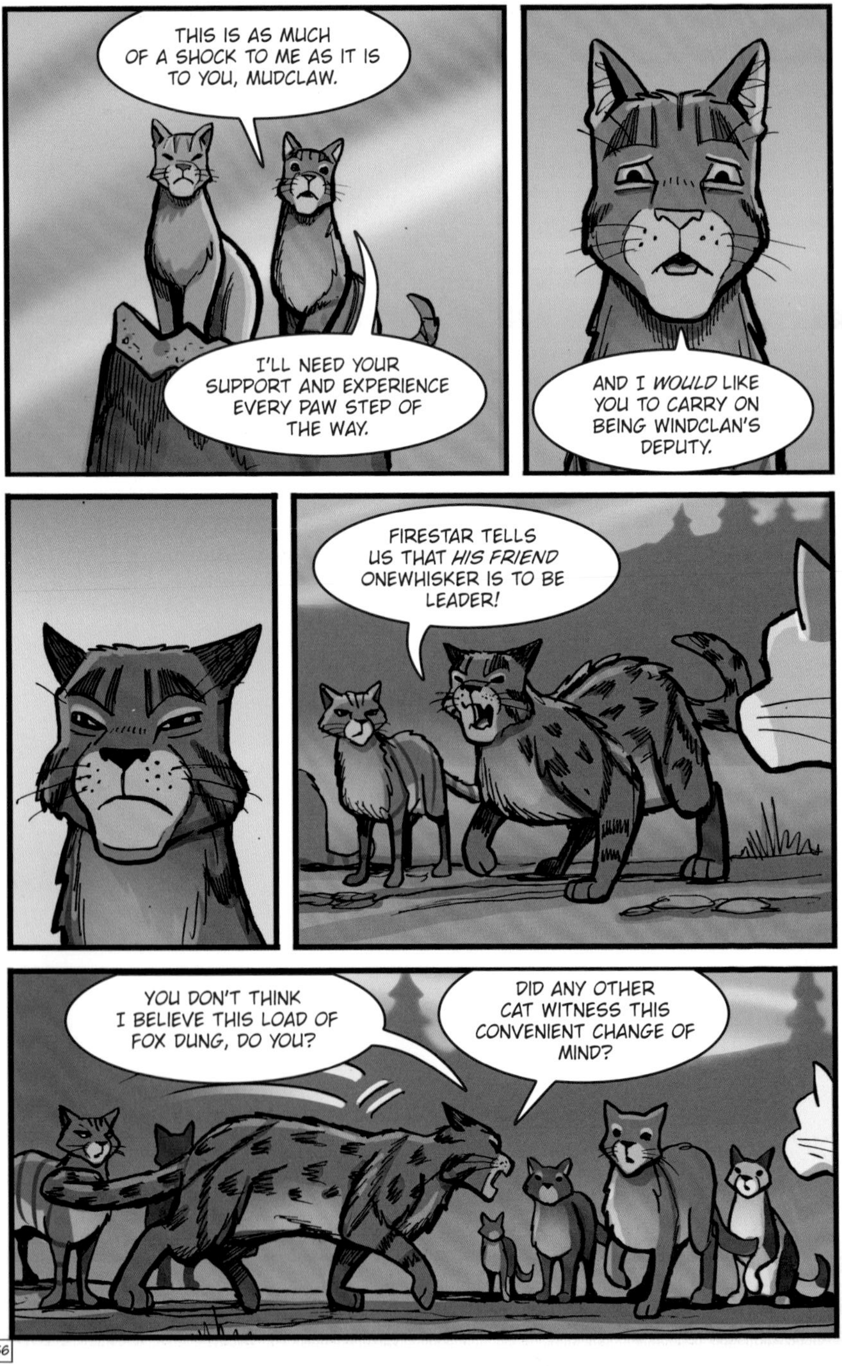
THIS IS AS MUCH OF A SHOCK TO ME AS IT IS TO YOU, MUDCLAW.
I'LL NEED YOUR SUPPORT AND EXPERIENCE EVERY PAW STEP OF THE WAY.
AND I *WOULD* LIKE YOU TO CARRY ON BEING WINDCLAN'S DEPUTY.
FIRESTAR TELLS US THAT *HIS FRIEND* ONEWHISKER IS TO BE LEADER!
YOU DON'T THINK I BELIEVE THIS LOAD OF FOX DUNG, DO YOU?
DID ANY OTHER CAT WITNESS THIS CONVENIENT CHANGE OF MIND?

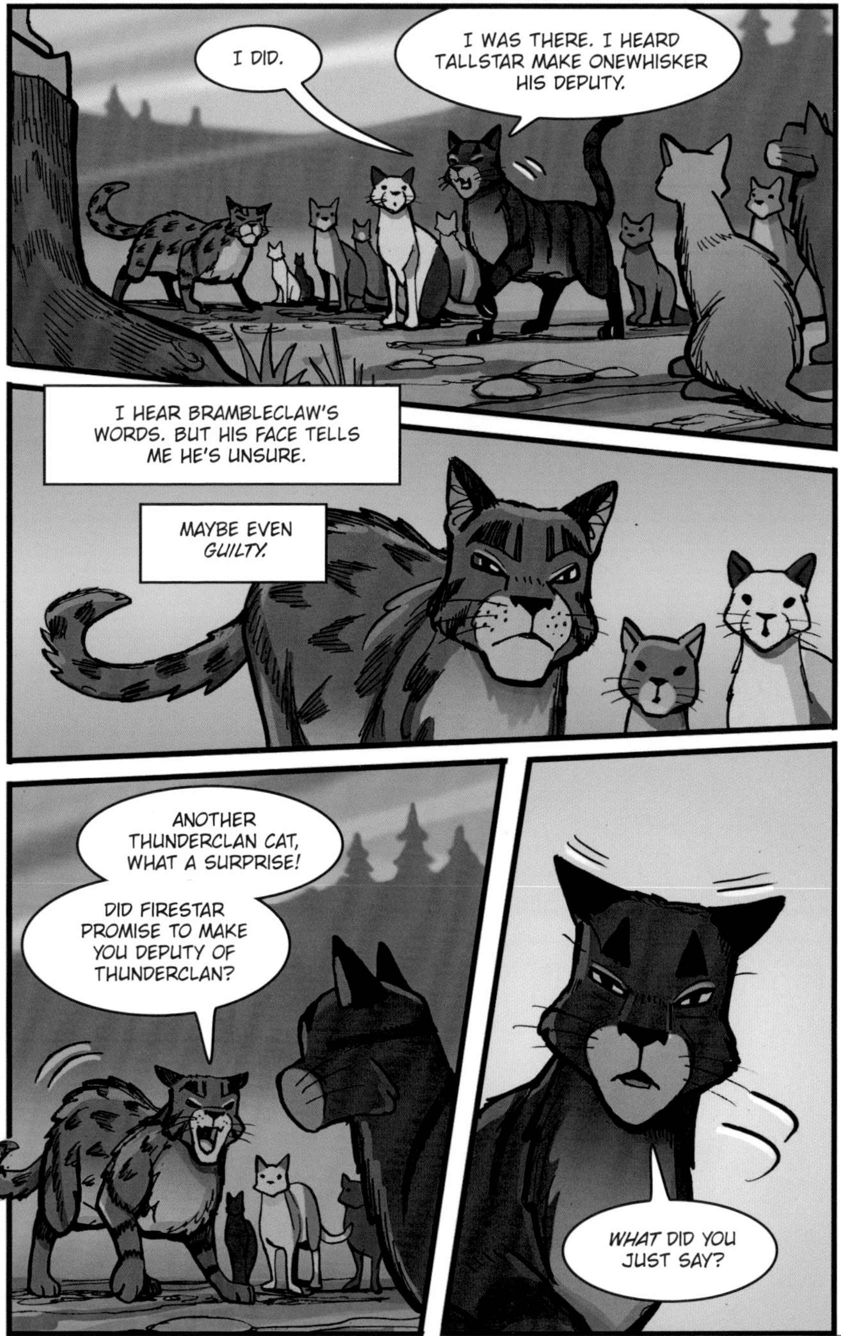
I DID.
I WAS THERE. I HEARD TALLSTAR MAKE ONEWHISKER HIS DEPUTY.
I HEAR BRAMBLECLAW'S WORDS. BUT HIS FACE TELLS ME HE'S UNSURE.
MAYBE EVEN *GUILTY.*
ANOTHER THUNDERCLAN CAT, WHAT A SURPRISE!
DID FIRESTAR PROMISE TO MAKE YOU DEPUTY OF THUNDERCLAN?
WHAT DID YOU JUST SAY?

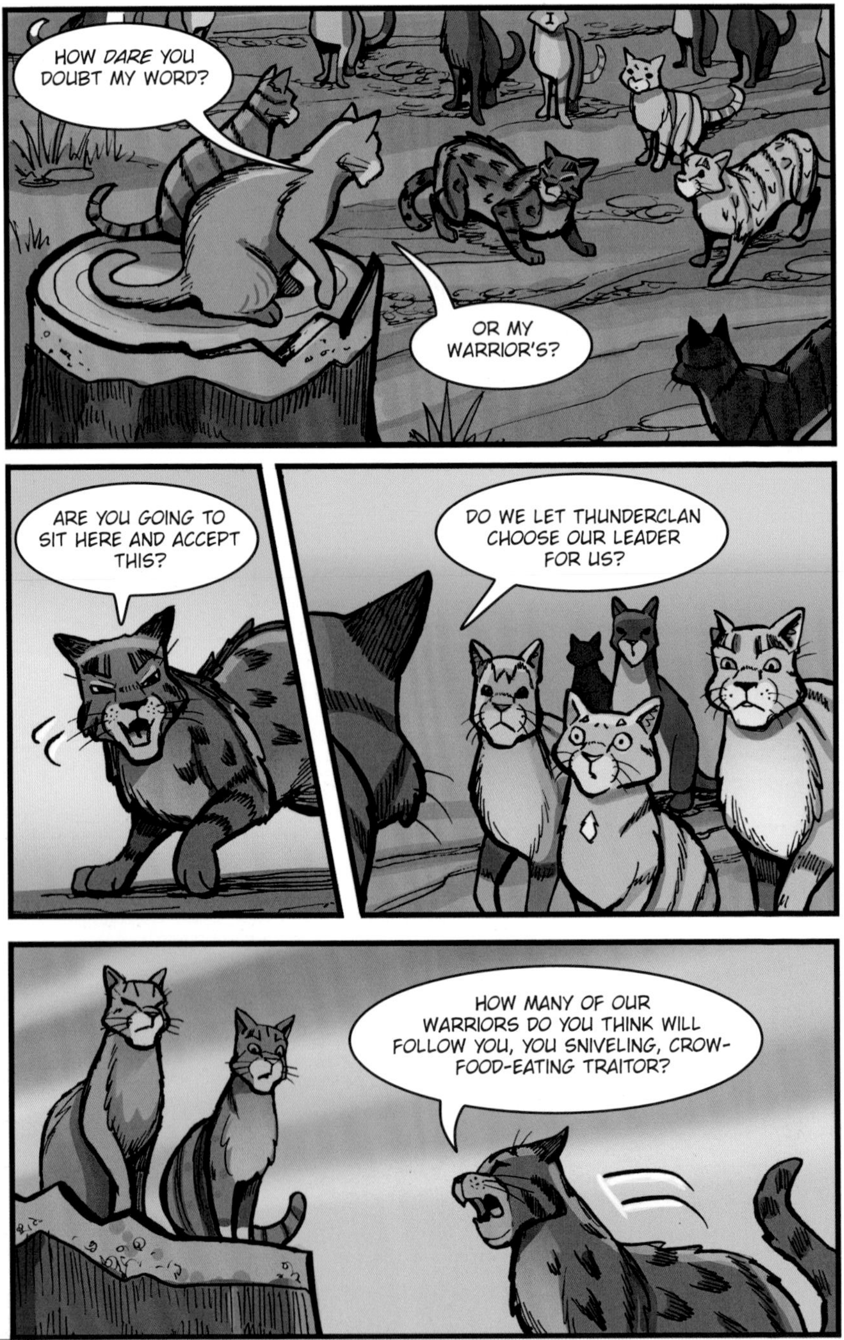
HOW *DARE* YOU DOUBT MY WORD?
OR MY WARRIOR'S?
ARE YOU GOING TO SIT HERE AND ACCEPT THIS?
DO WE LET THUNDERCLAN CHOOSE OUR LEADER FOR US?
HOW MANY OF OUR WARRIORS DO YOU THINK WILL FOLLOW YOU, YOU SNIVELING, CROW-FOOD-EATING TRAITOR?

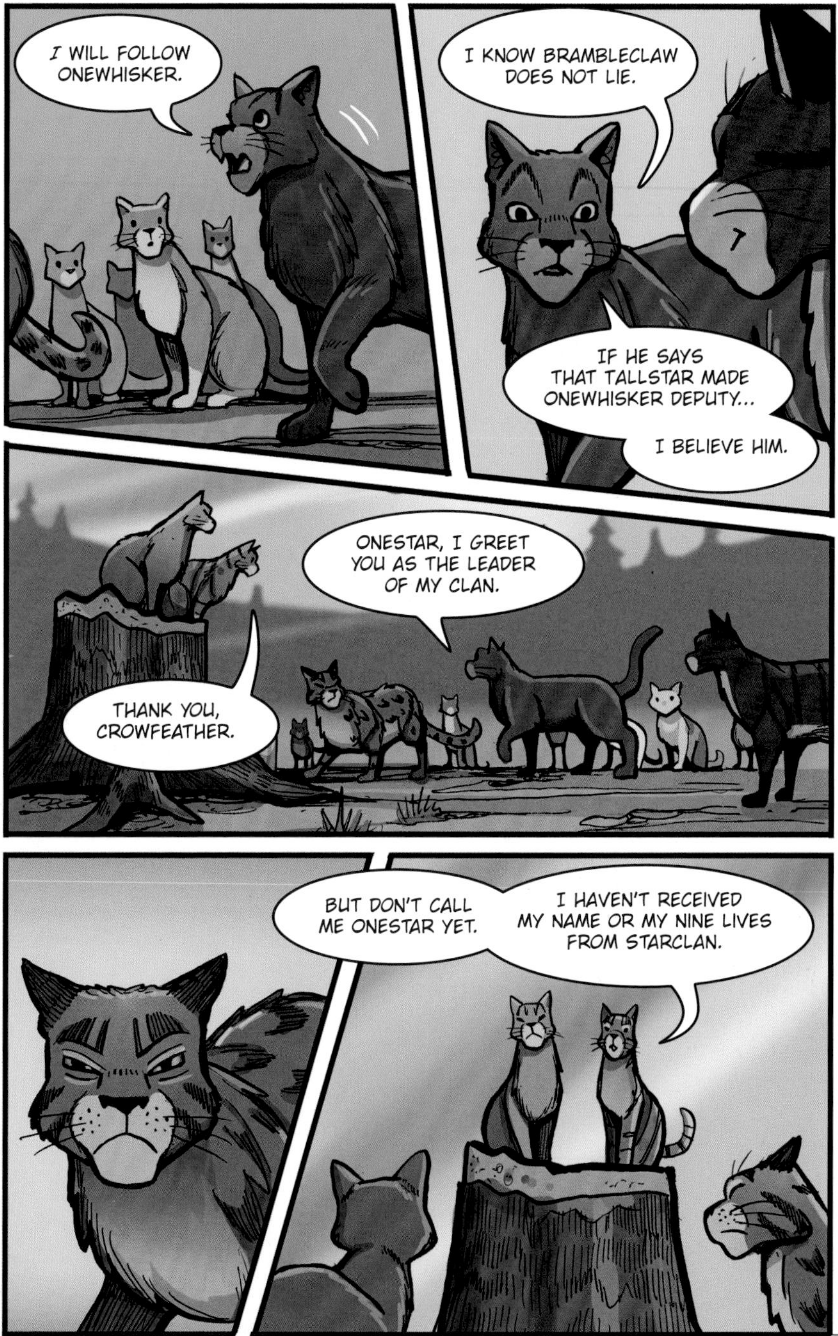
I WILL FOLLOW ONEWHISKER.
I KNOW BRAMBLECLAW DOES NOT LIE.
IF HE SAYS THAT TALLSTAR MADE ONEWHISKER DEPUTY...
I BELIEVE HIM.
ONESTAR, I GREET YOU AS THE LEADER OF MY CLAN.
THANK YOU, CROWFEATHER.
BUT DON'T CALL ME ONESTAR YET.
I HAVEN'T RECEIVED MY NAME OR MY NINE LIVES FROM STARCLAN.

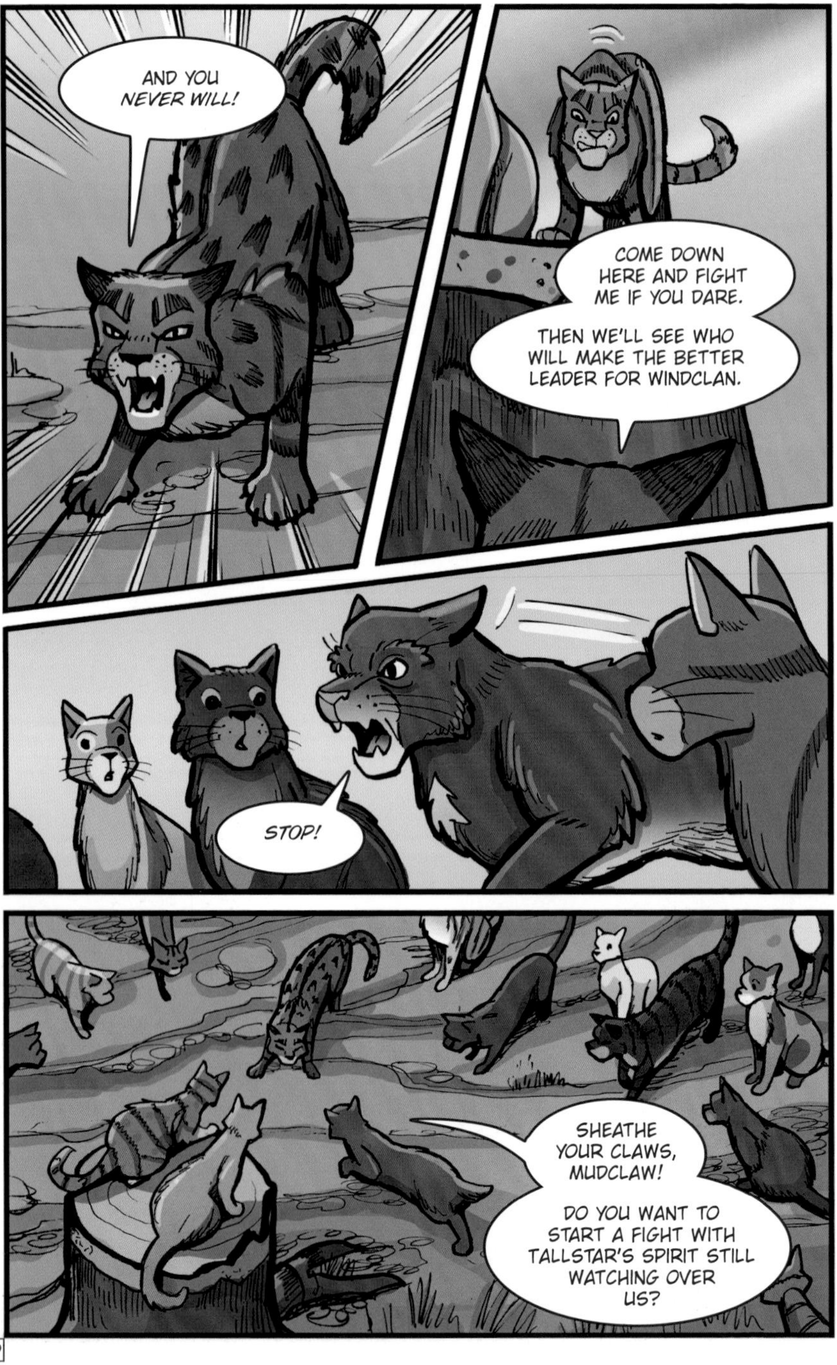
AND YOU NEVER WILL!
COME DOWN HERE AND FIGHT ME IF YOU DARE.
THEN WE'LL SEE WHO WILL MAKE THE BETTER LEADER FOR WINDCLAN.
STOP!
SHEATHE YOUR CLAWS, MUDCLAW!
DO YOU WANT TO START A FIGHT WITH TALLSTAR'S SPIRIT STILL WATCHING OVER US?

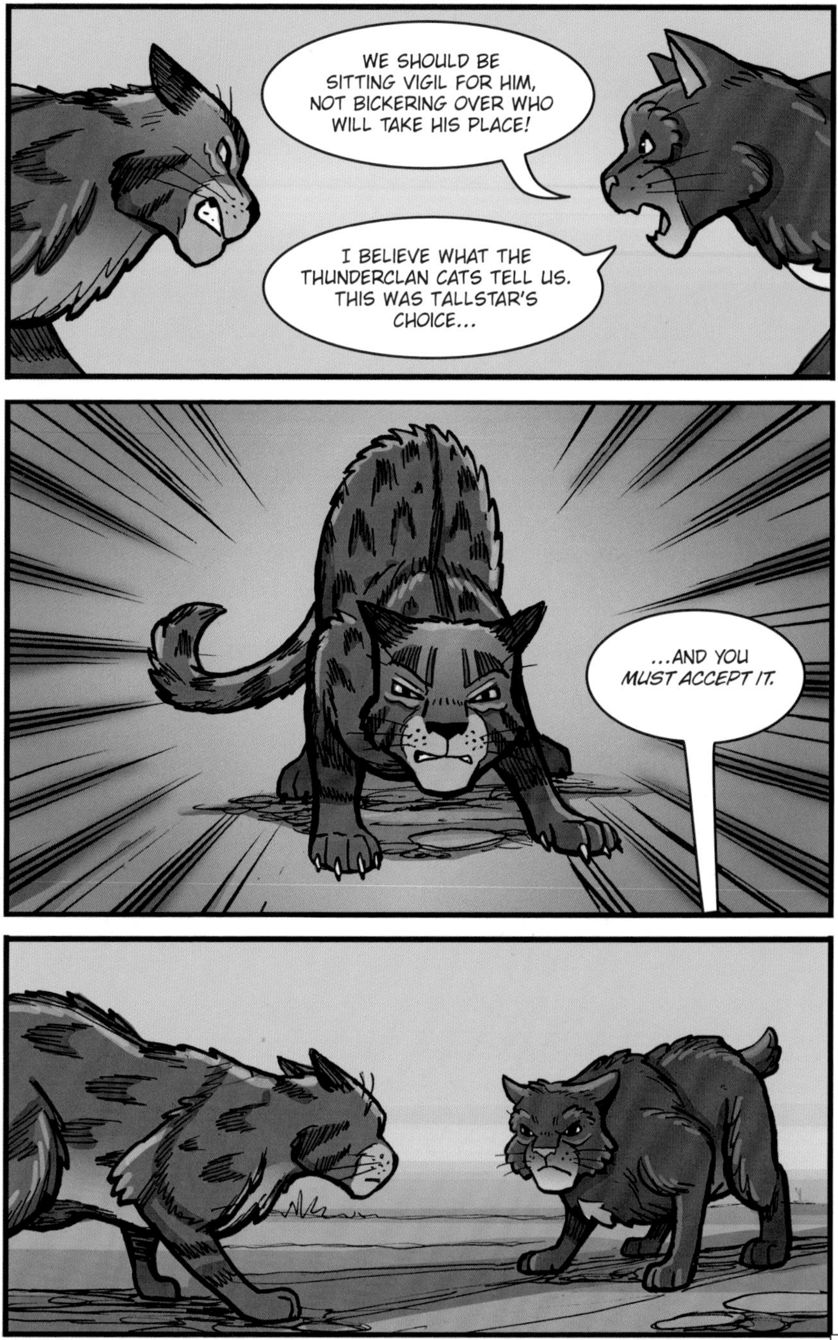
WE SHOULD BE SITTING VIGIL FOR HIM, NOT BICKERING OVER WHO WILL TAKE HIS PLACE!
I BELIEVE WHAT THE THUNDERCLAN CATS TELL US. THIS WAS TALLSTAR'S CHOICE...
...AND YOU *MUST ACCEPT IT.*

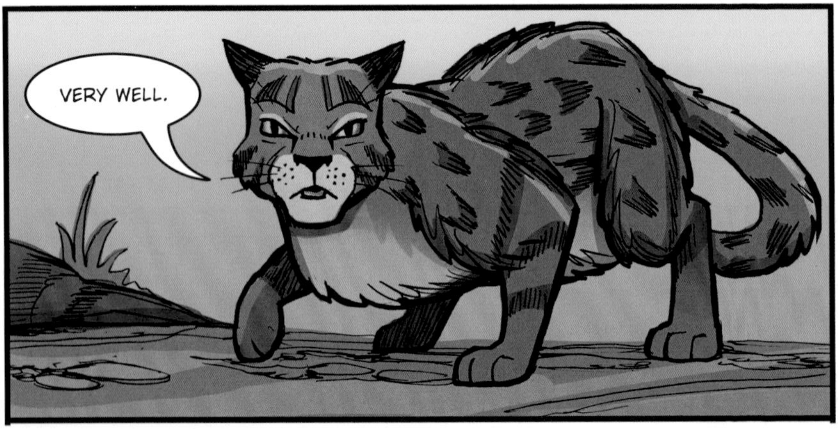
VERY WELL.

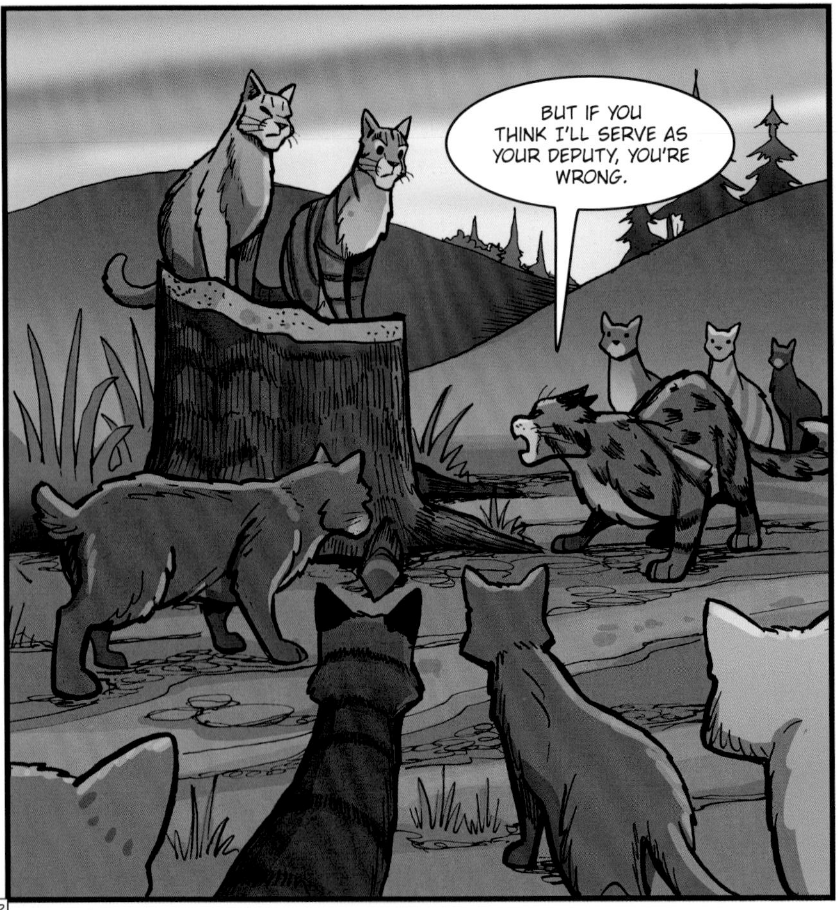
BUT IF YOU THINK I'LL SERVE AS YOUR DEPUTY, YOU'RE WRONG.

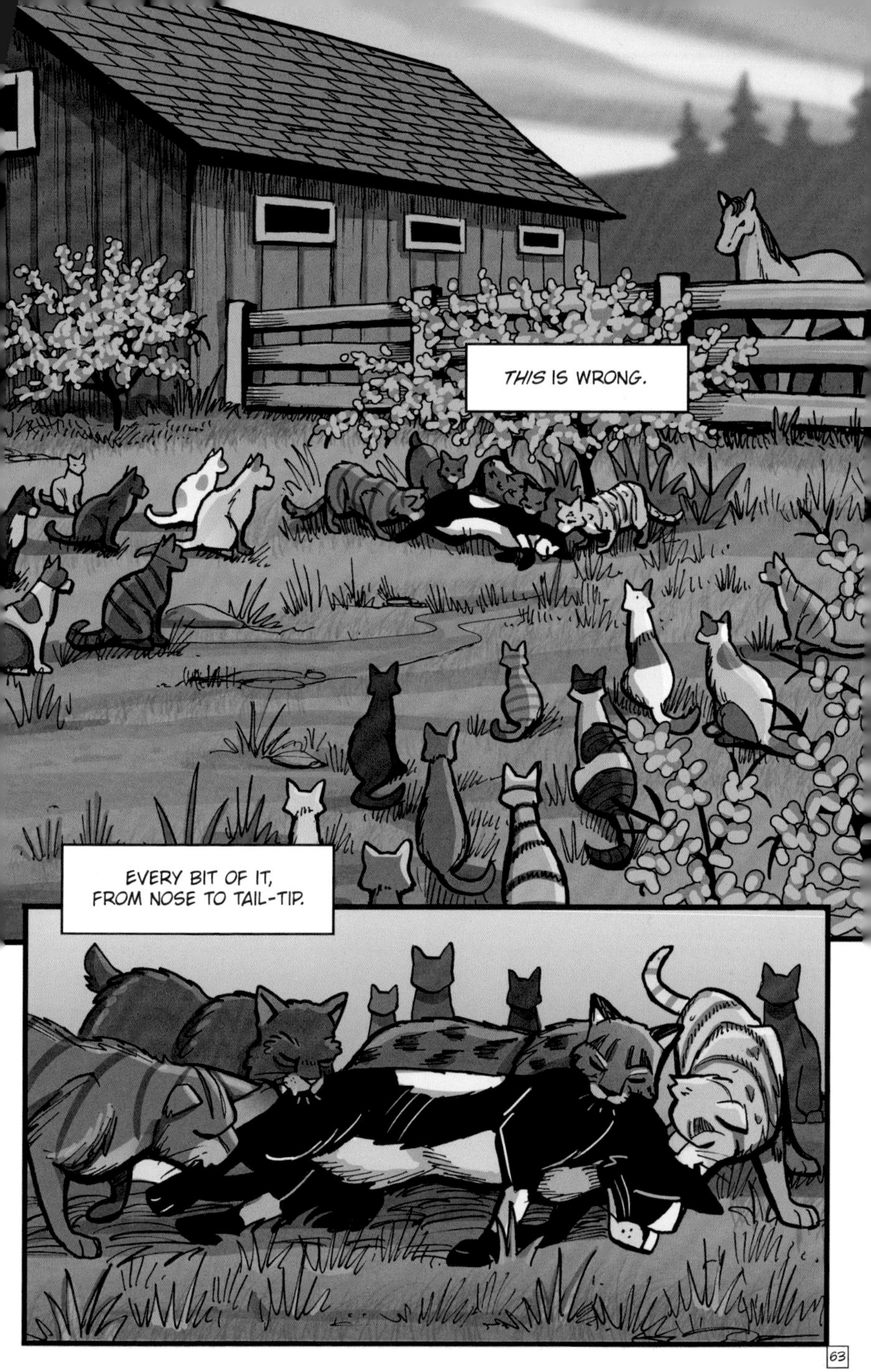
THIS IS WRONG.
EVERY BIT OF IT, FROM NOSE TO TAIL-TIP.

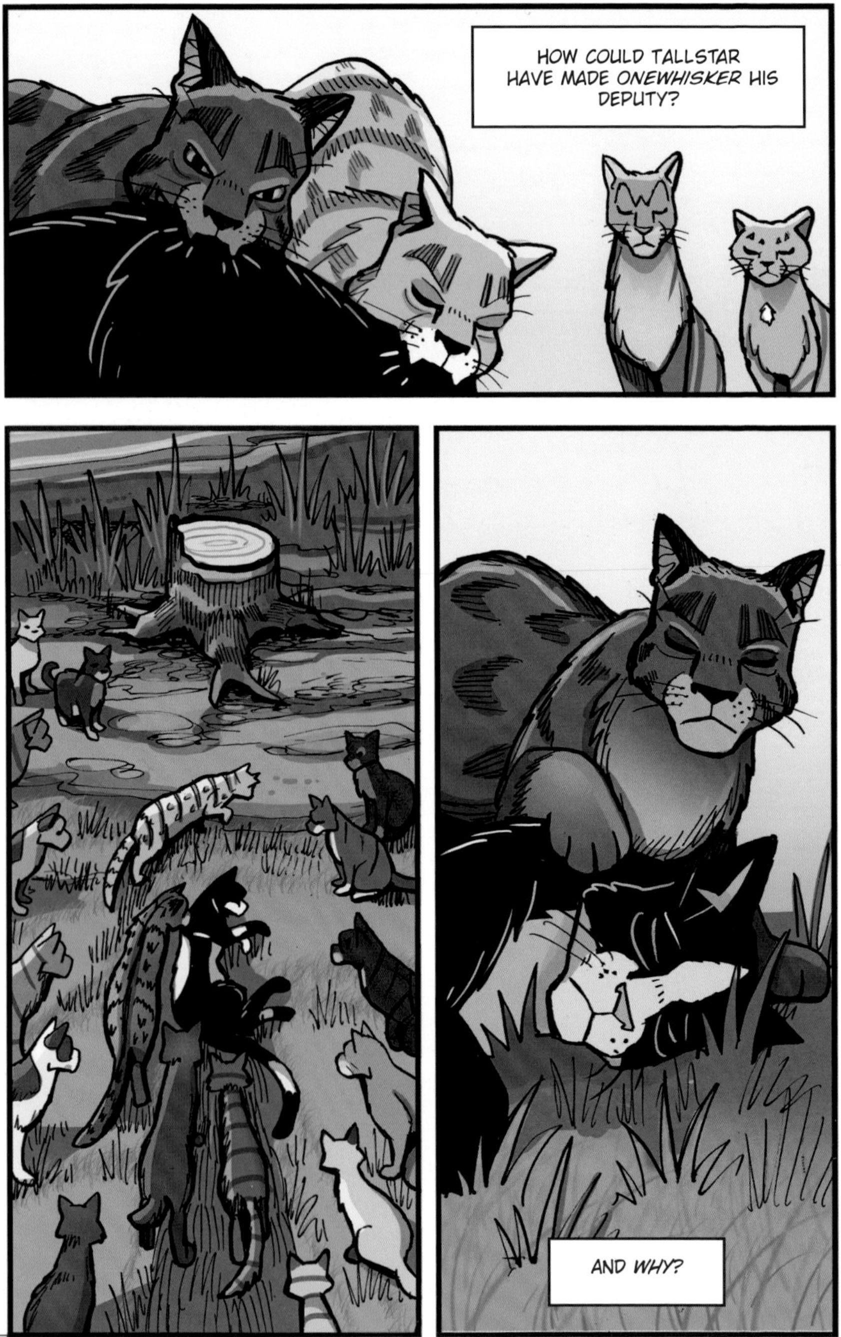
HOW COULD TALLSTAR HAVE MADE *ONEWHISKER* HIS DEPUTY?
AND *WHY*?

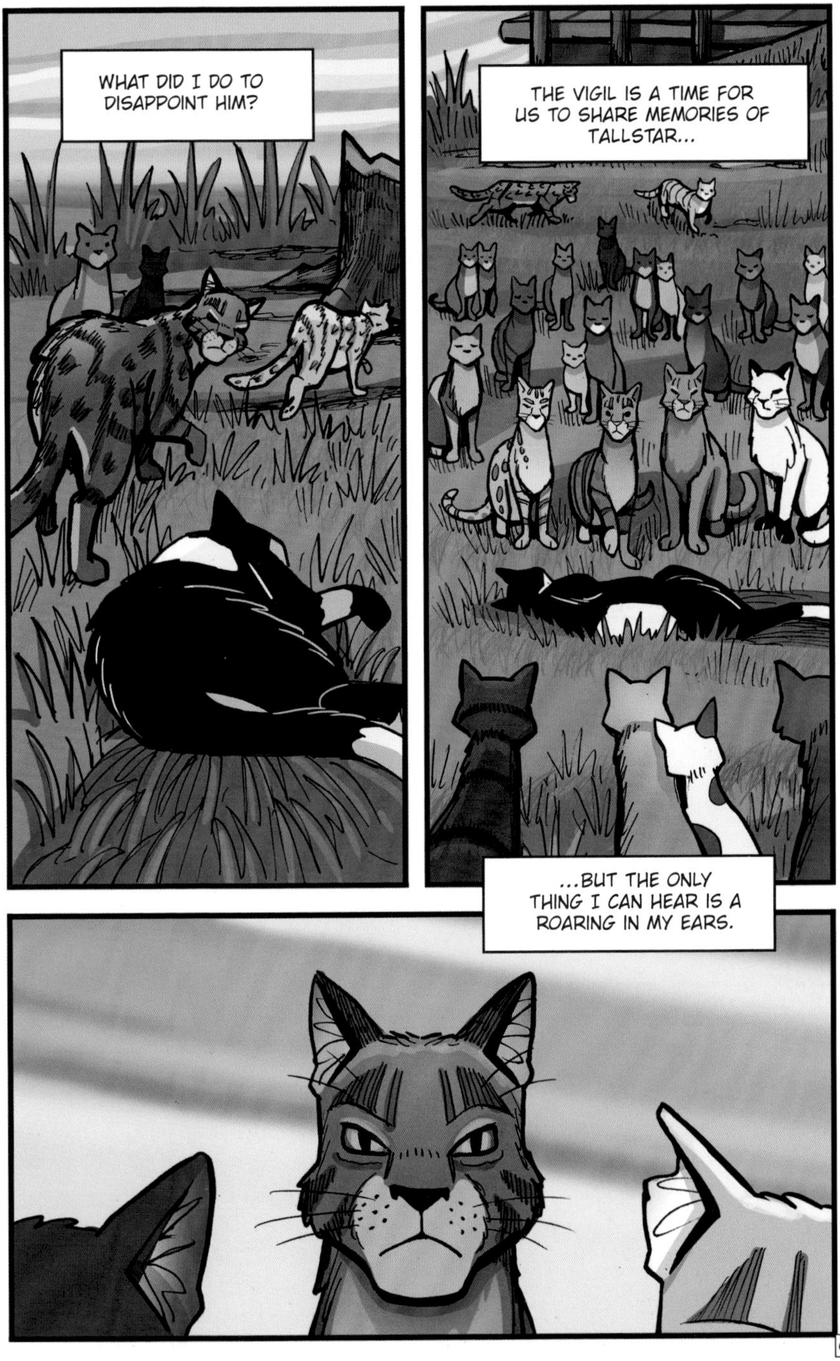
WHAT DID I DO TO DISAPPOINT HIM?
THE VIGIL IS A TIME FOR US TO SHARE MEMORIES OF TALLSTAR...
...BUT THE ONLY THING I CAN HEAR IS A ROARING IN MY EARS.

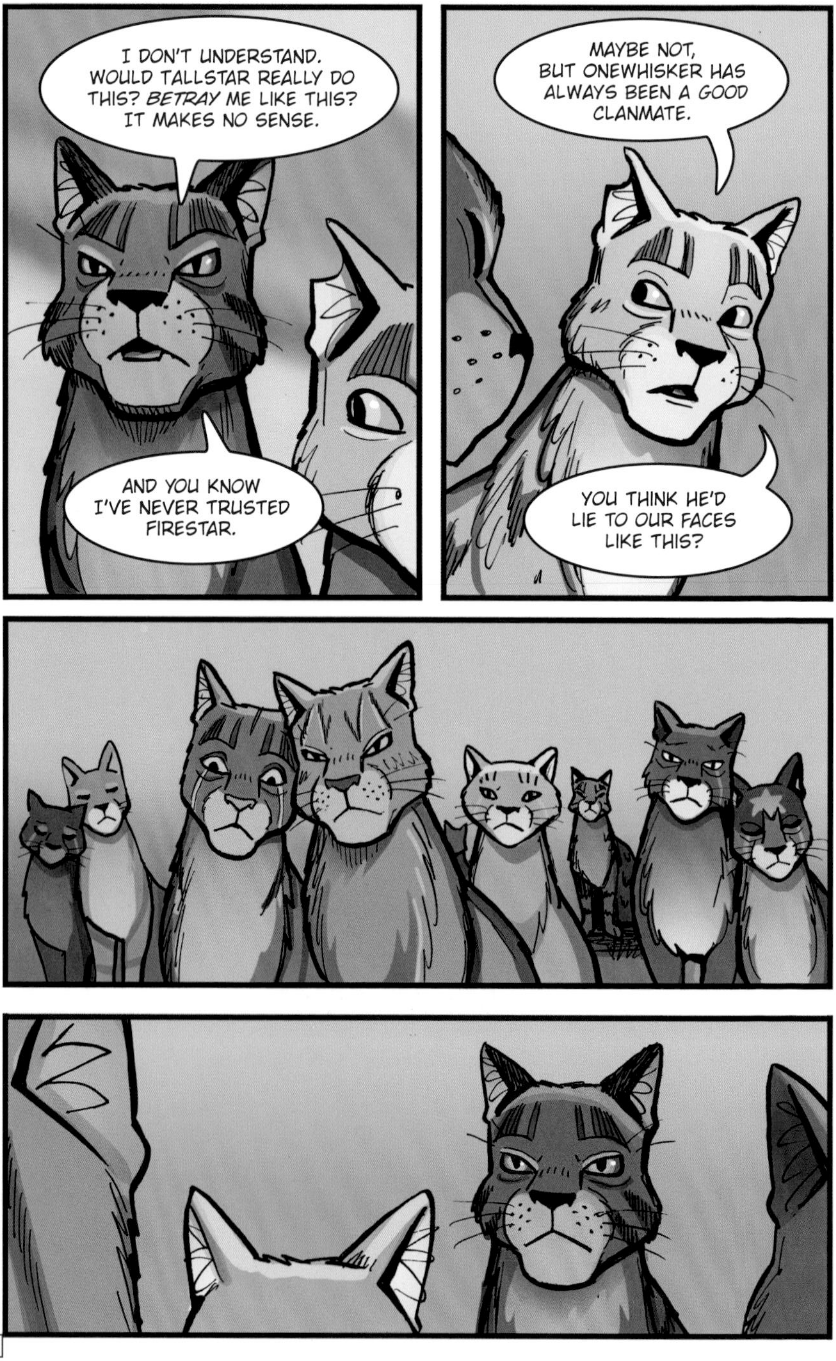
I DON'T UNDERSTAND. WOULD TALLSTAR REALLY DO THIS? *BETRAY* ME LIKE THIS? IT MAKES NO SENSE.
AND YOU KNOW I'VE NEVER TRUSTED FIRESTAR.
MAYBE NOT, BUT ONEWHISKER HAS ALWAYS BEEN A GOOD CLANMATE.
YOU THINK HE'D LIE TO OUR FACES LIKE THIS?

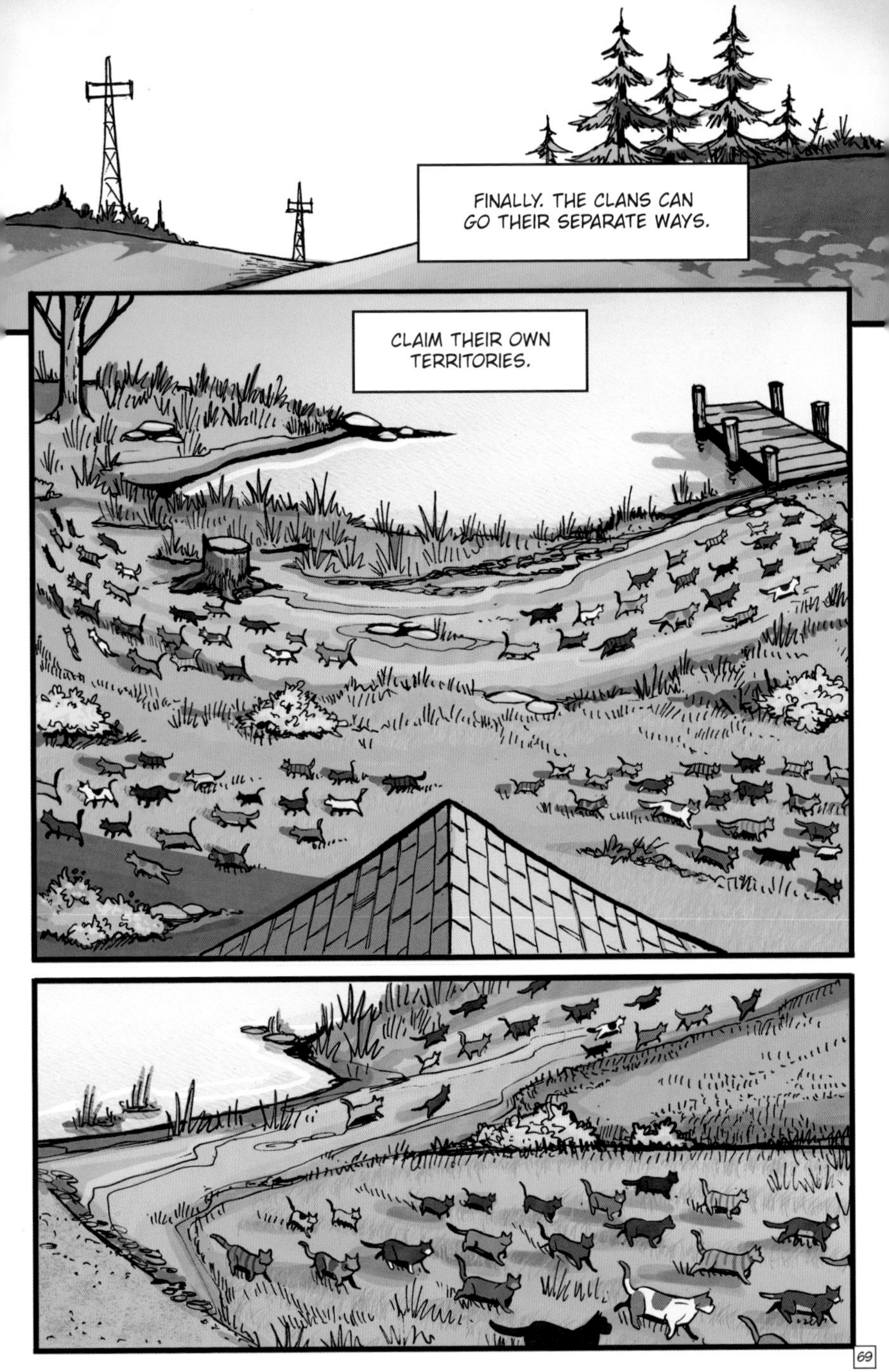
FINALLY. THE CLANS CAN GO THEIR SEPARATE WAYS.
CLAIM THEIR OWN TERRITORIES.

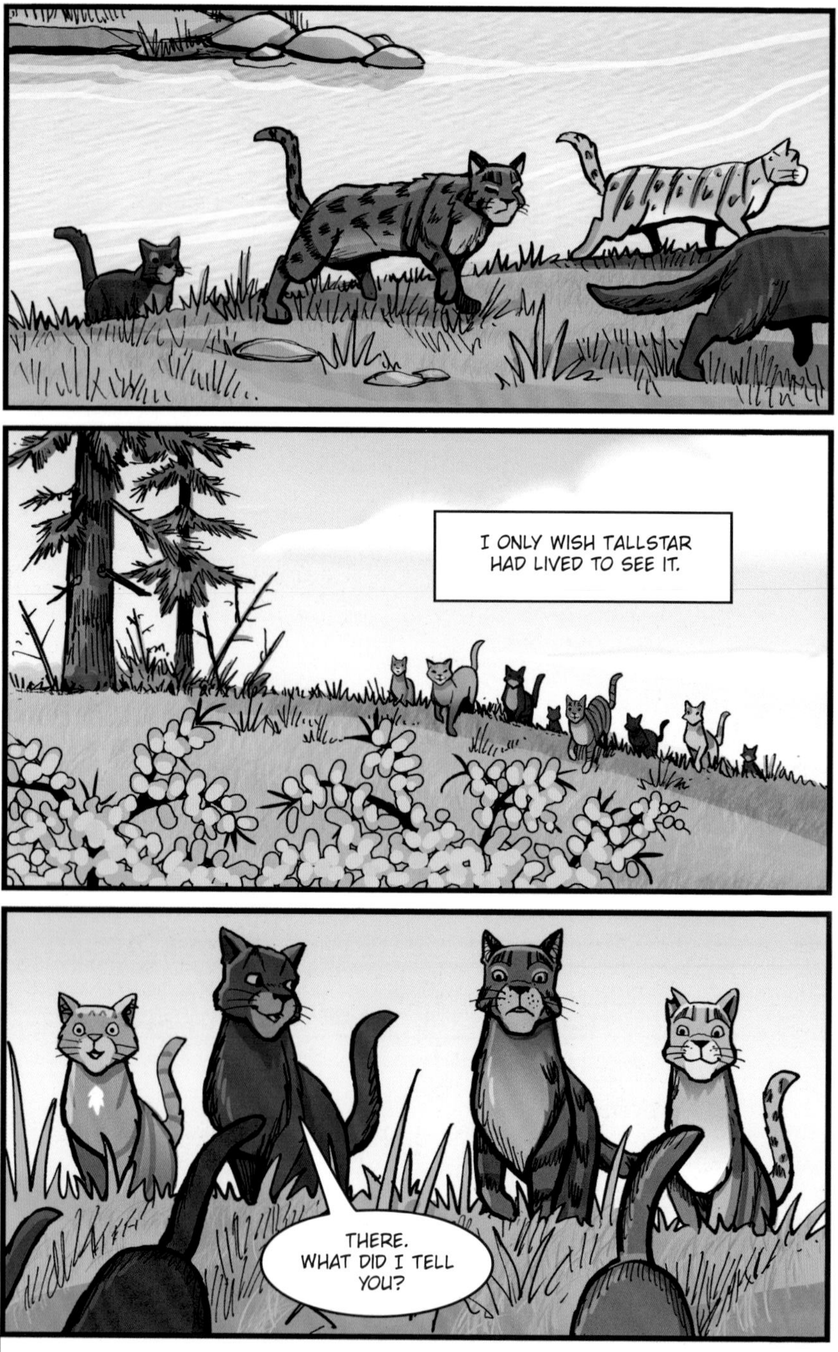
I ONLY WISH TALLSTAR HAD LIVED TO SEE IT.
THERE. WHAT DID I TELL YOU?

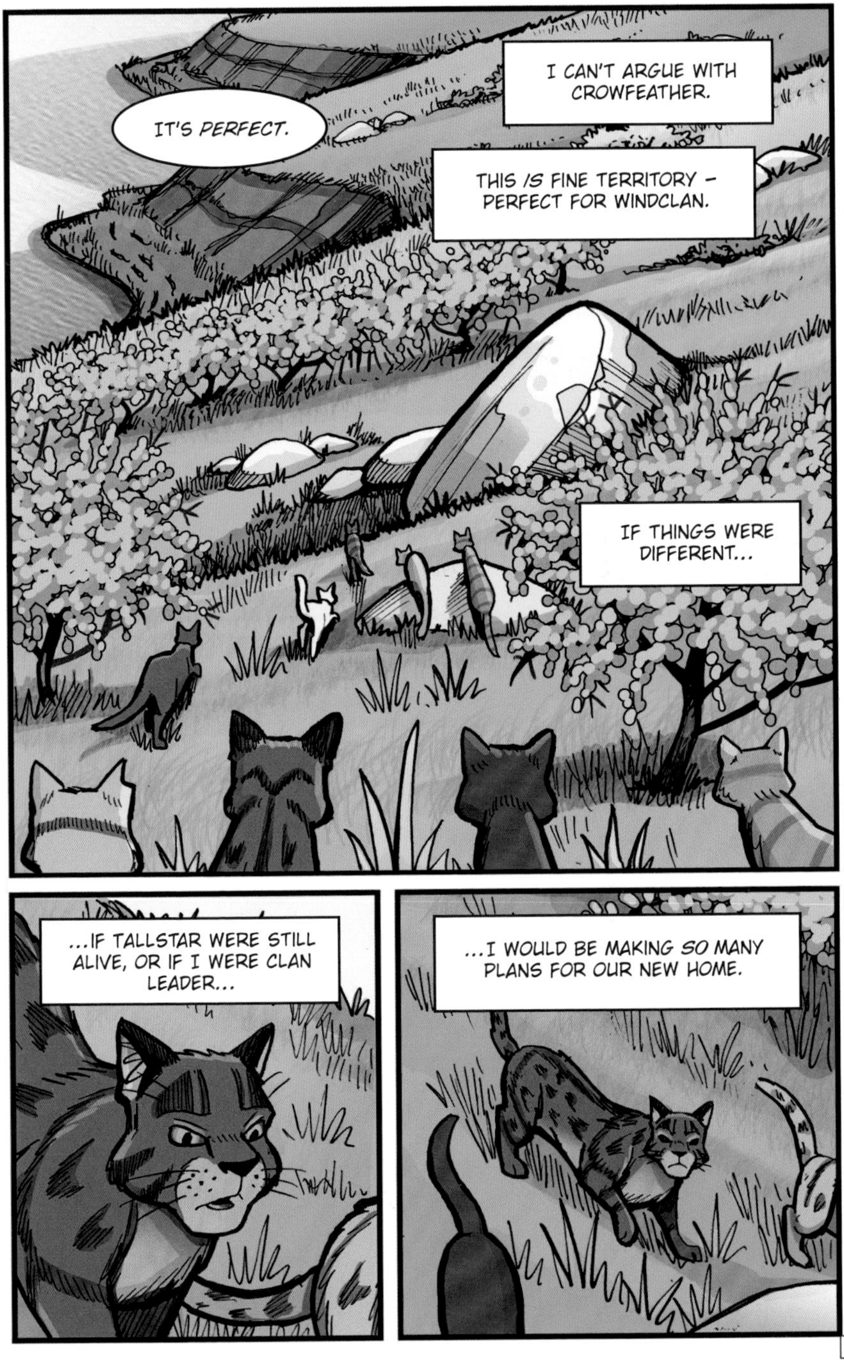
IT'S *PERFECT*.
I CAN'T ARGUE WITH CROWFEATHER.
THIS *IS* FINE TERRITORY – PERFECT FOR WINDCLAN.
IF THINGS WERE DIFFERENT...
...IF TALLSTAR WERE STILL ALIVE, OR IF I WERE CLAN LEADER...
...I WOULD BE MAKING *SO* MANY PLANS FOR OUR NEW HOME.

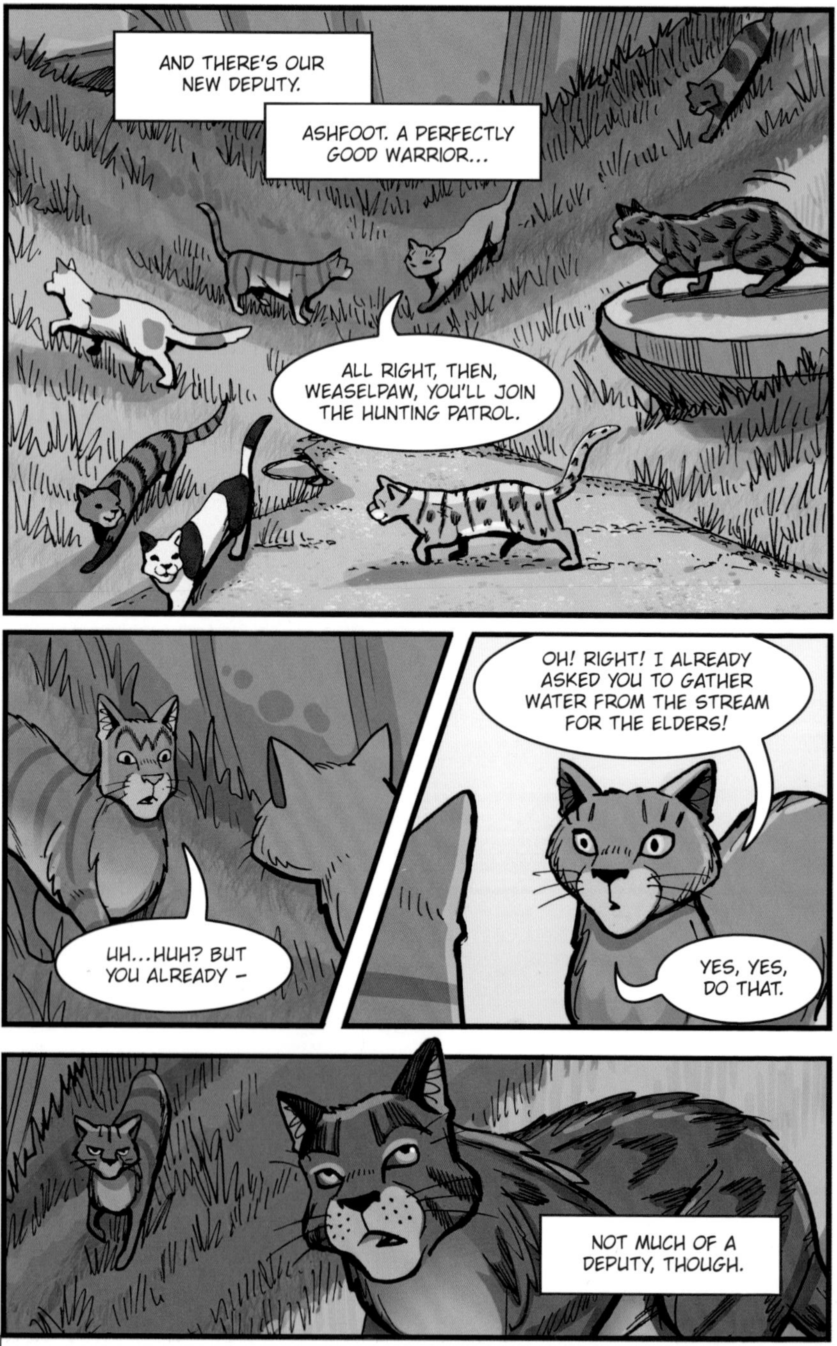
AND THERE'S OUR NEW DEPUTY.
ASHFOOT. A PERFECTLY GOOD WARRIOR...
ALL RIGHT, THEN, WEASELPAW, YOU'LL JOIN THE HUNTING PATROL.
UH...HUH? BUT YOU ALREADY –
OH! RIGHT! I ALREADY ASKED YOU TO GATHER WATER FROM THE STREAM FOR THE ELDERS!
YES, YES, DO THAT.
NOT MUCH OF A DEPUTY, THOUGH.

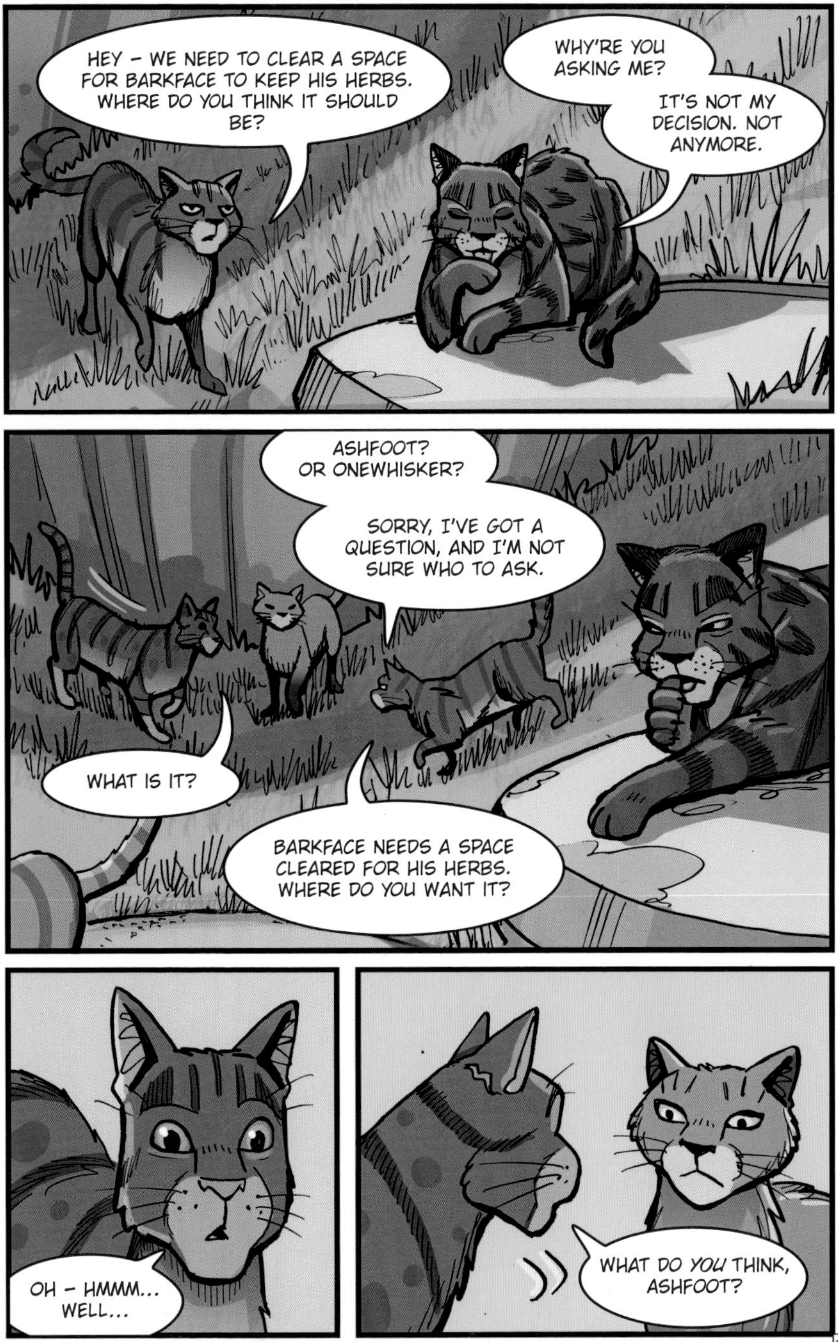
HEY – WE NEED TO CLEAR A SPACE FOR BARKFACE TO KEEP HIS HERBS. WHERE DO YOU THINK IT SHOULD BE?
WHY'RE YOU ASKING ME?
IT'S NOT MY DECISION. NOT ANYMORE.
ASHFOOT? OR ONEWHISKER?
SORRY, I'VE GOT A QUESTION, AND I'M NOT SURE WHO TO ASK.
WHAT IS IT?
BARKFACE NEEDS A SPACE CLEARED FOR HIS HERBS. WHERE DO YOU WANT IT?
OH – HMMM... WELL...
WHAT DO *YOU* THINK, ASHFOOT?

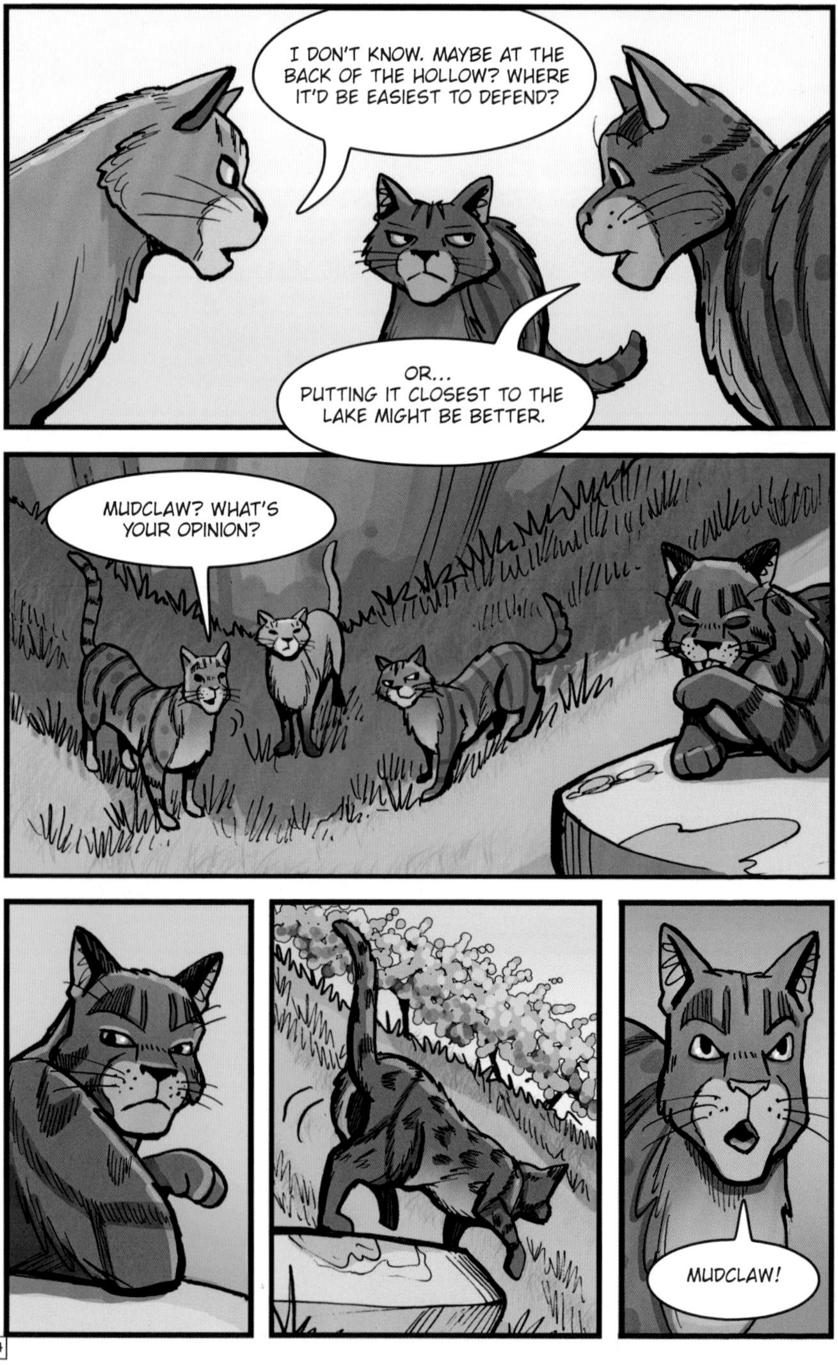
I DON'T KNOW. MAYBE AT THE BACK OF THE HOLLOW? WHERE IT'D BE EASIEST TO DEFEND?
OR... PUTTING IT CLOSEST TO THE LAKE MIGHT BE BETTER.
MUDCLAW? WHAT'S YOUR OPINION?
MUDCLAW!

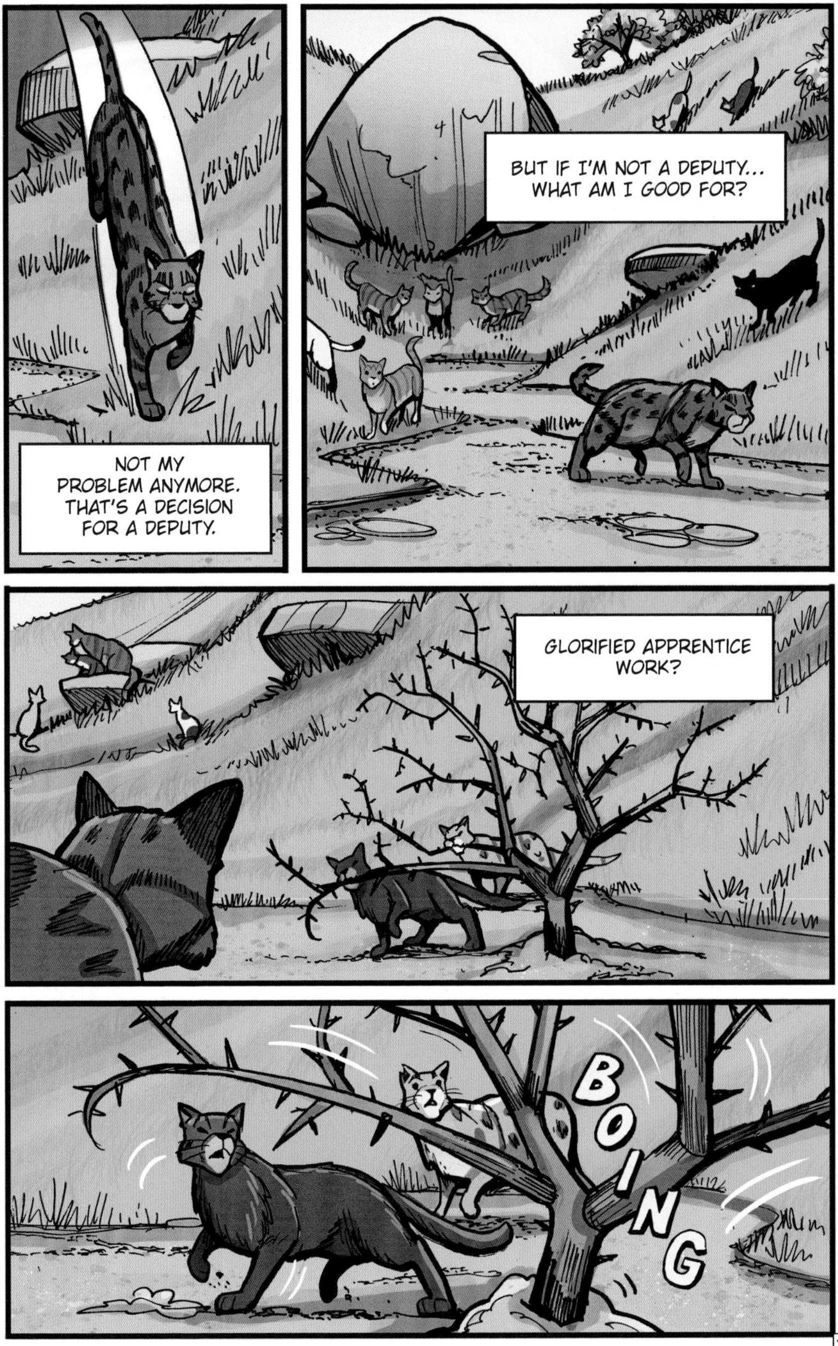
NOT MY PROBLEM ANYMORE. THAT'S A DECISION FOR A DEPUTY.
BUT IF I'M NOT A DEPUTY... WHAT AM I GOOD FOR?
GLORIFIED APPRENTICE WORK?
BOING

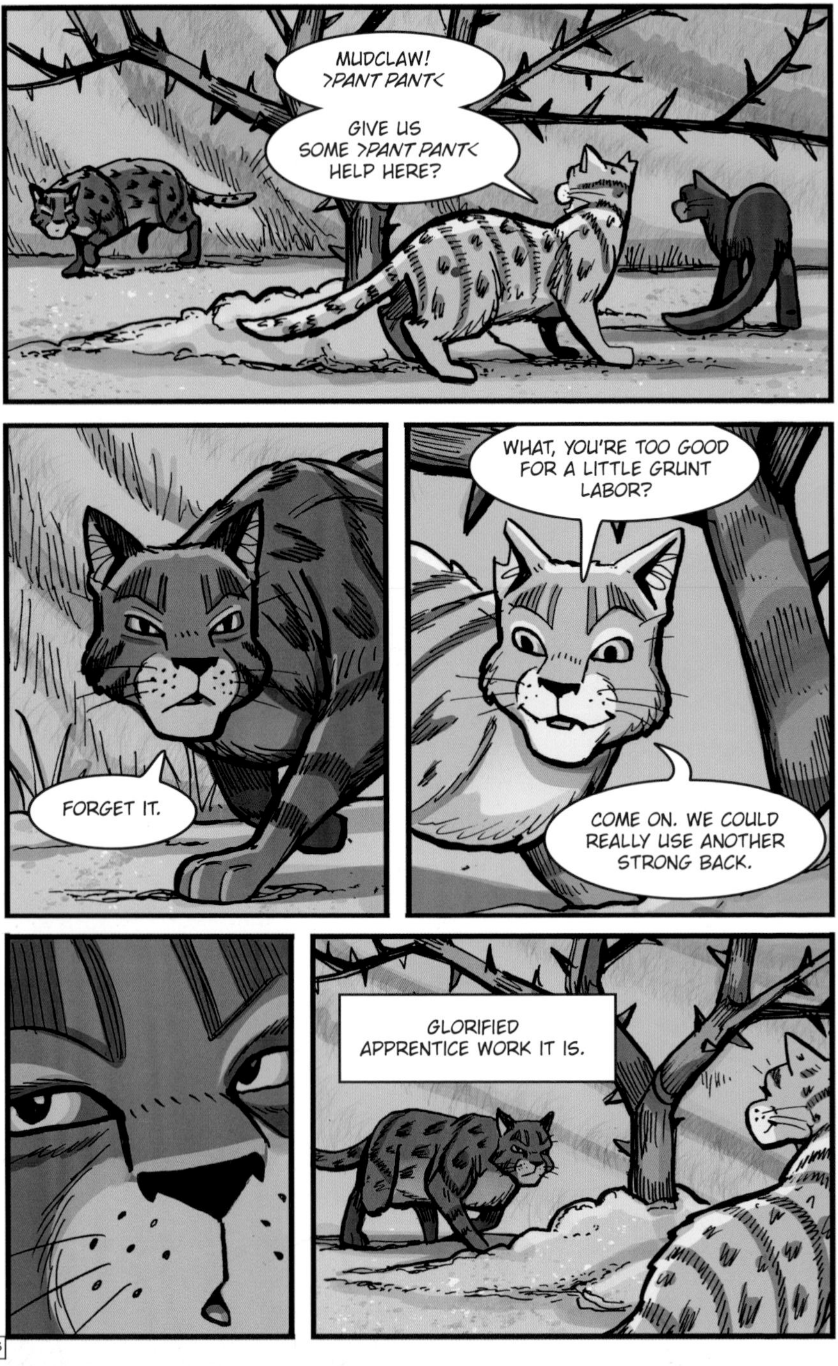
MUDCLAW! >PANT PANT<
GIVE US SOME >PANT PANT< HELP HERE?
FORGET IT.
WHAT, YOU'RE TOO GOOD FOR A LITTLE GRUNT LABOR?
COME ON. WE COULD REALLY USE ANOTHER STRONG BACK.
GLORIFIED APPRENTICE WORK IT IS.

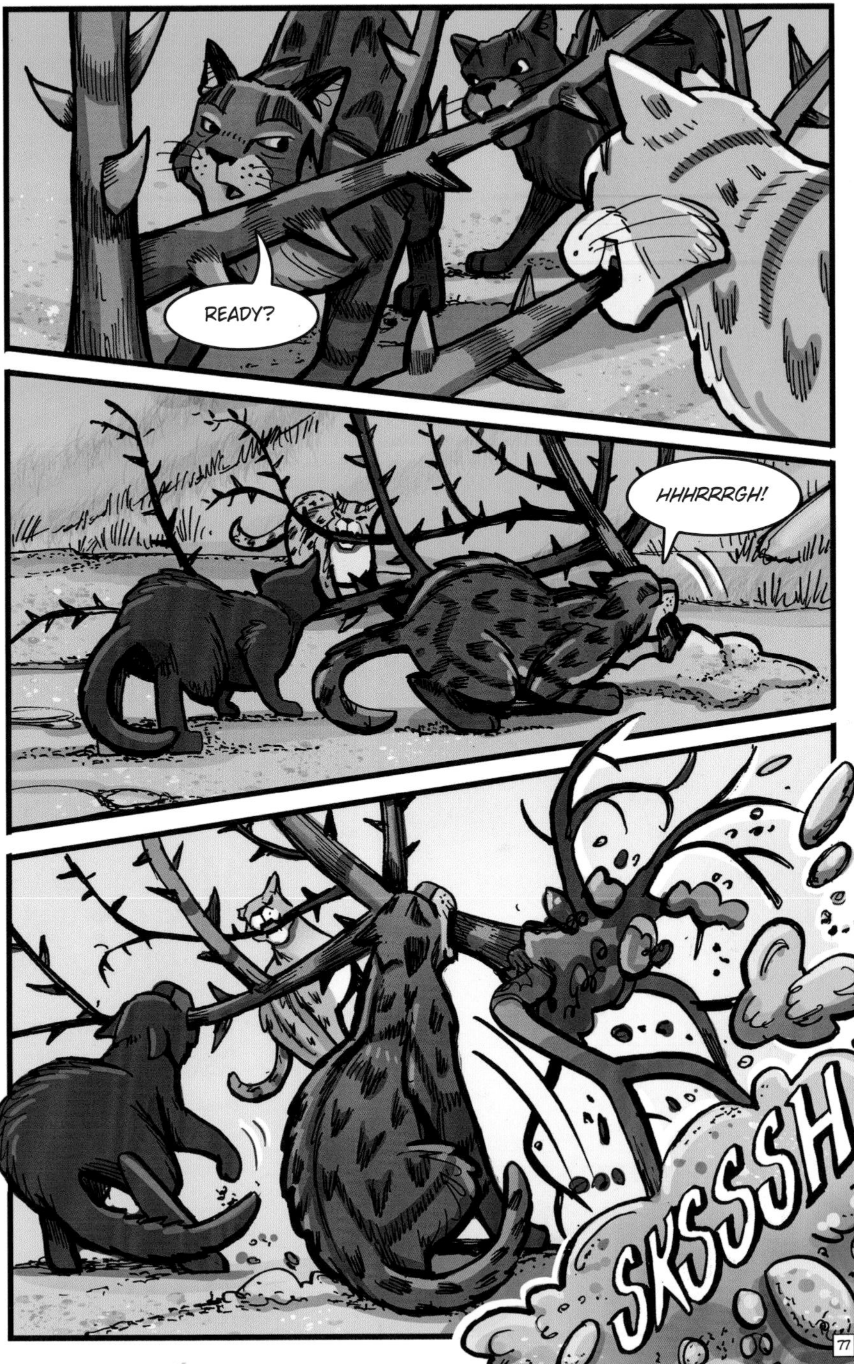
READY?
HHHRRRGH!
SKSSSH

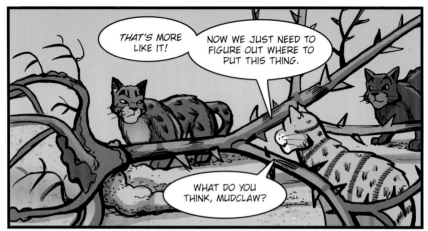

THAT'S MORE LIKE IT!

NOW WE JUST NEED TO FIGURE OUT WHERE TO PUT THIS THING.

WHAT DO YOU THINK, MUDCLAW?

YOU KNOW THAT'S NOT MY DECISION NOW.

LOOK, MUDCLAW, MAYBE YOU'RE NOT DEPUTY ANYMORE.

BUT YOU'RE STILL A *SENIOR WARRIOR*. IT'S NOT LIKE ALL THAT EXPERIENCE HAS JUST *DISAPPEARED.*

HE'S RIGHT. WE'RE BOTH SORRY ABOUT WHAT HAPPENED...

BUT YOU STILL MEAN A *LOT* TO WINDCLAN.

YOU *DO* KNOW THAT, RIGHT?

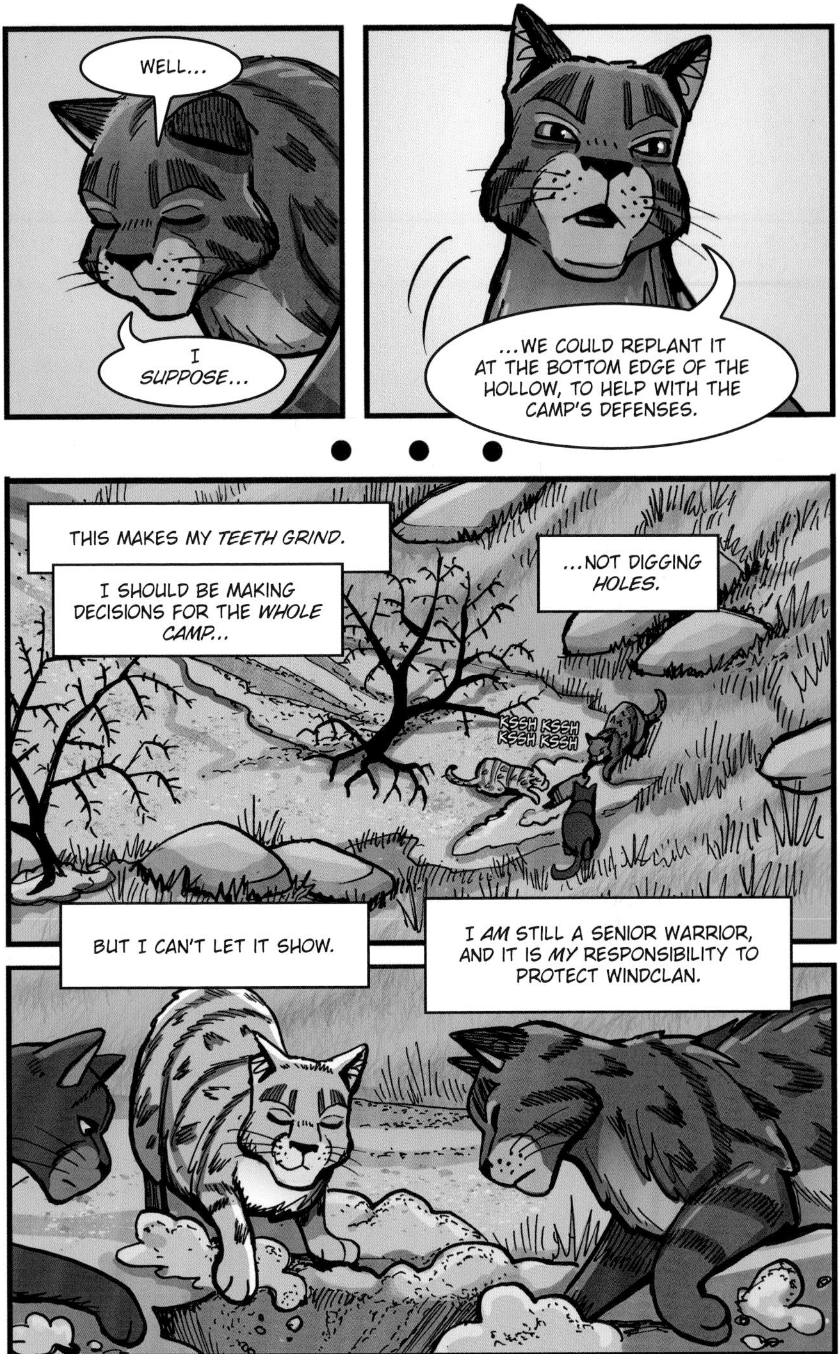
WELL...
I SUPPOSE...
...WE COULD REPLANT IT AT THE BOTTOM EDGE OF THE HOLLOW, TO HELP WITH THE CAMP'S DEFENSES.
THIS MAKES MY TEETH GRIND.
I SHOULD BE MAKING DECISIONS FOR THE WHOLE CAMP...
...NOT DIGGING HOLES.
KSSH KSSH KSSH KSSH
BUT I CAN'T LET IT SHOW.
I AM STILL A SENIOR WARRIOR, AND IT IS MY RESPONSIBILITY TO PROTECT WINDCLAN.

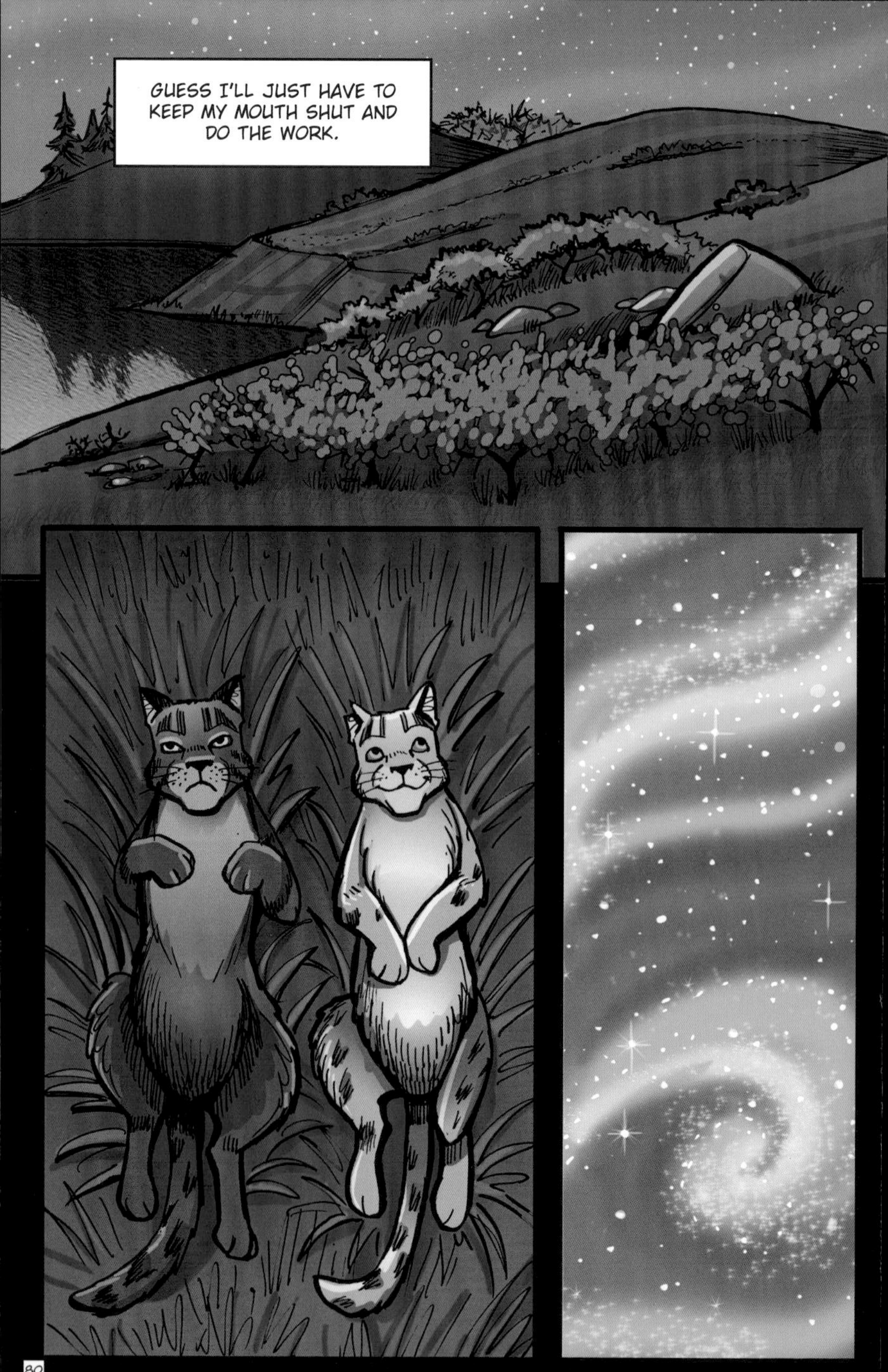
GUESS I'LL JUST HAVE TO KEEP MY MOUTH SHUT AND DO THE WORK.

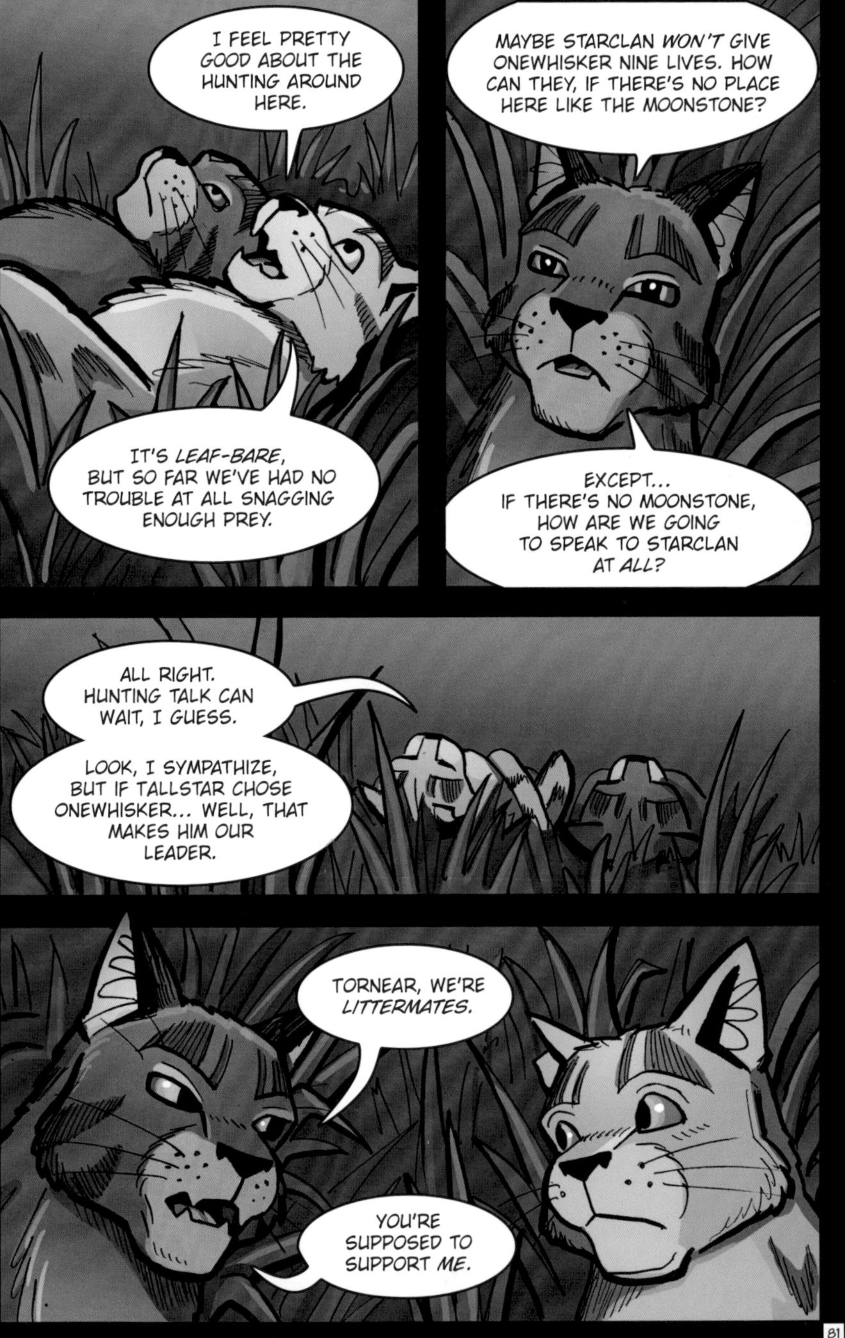
I FEEL PRETTY GOOD ABOUT THE HUNTING AROUND HERE.
IT'S *LEAF-BARE*, BUT SO FAR WE'VE HAD NO TROUBLE AT ALL SNAGGING ENOUGH PREY.
MAYBE STARCLAN *WON'T* GIVE ONEWHISKER NINE LIVES. HOW CAN THEY, IF THERE'S NO PLACE HERE LIKE THE MOONSTONE?
EXCEPT... IF THERE'S NO MOONSTONE, HOW ARE WE GOING TO SPEAK TO STARCLAN AT *ALL*?
ALL RIGHT. HUNTING TALK CAN WAIT, I GUESS.
LOOK, I SYMPATHIZE, BUT IF TALLSTAR CHOSE ONEWHISKER... WELL, THAT MAKES HIM OUR LEADER.
TORNEAR, WE'RE *LITTERMATES*.
YOU'RE SUPPOSED TO SUPPORT *ME*.

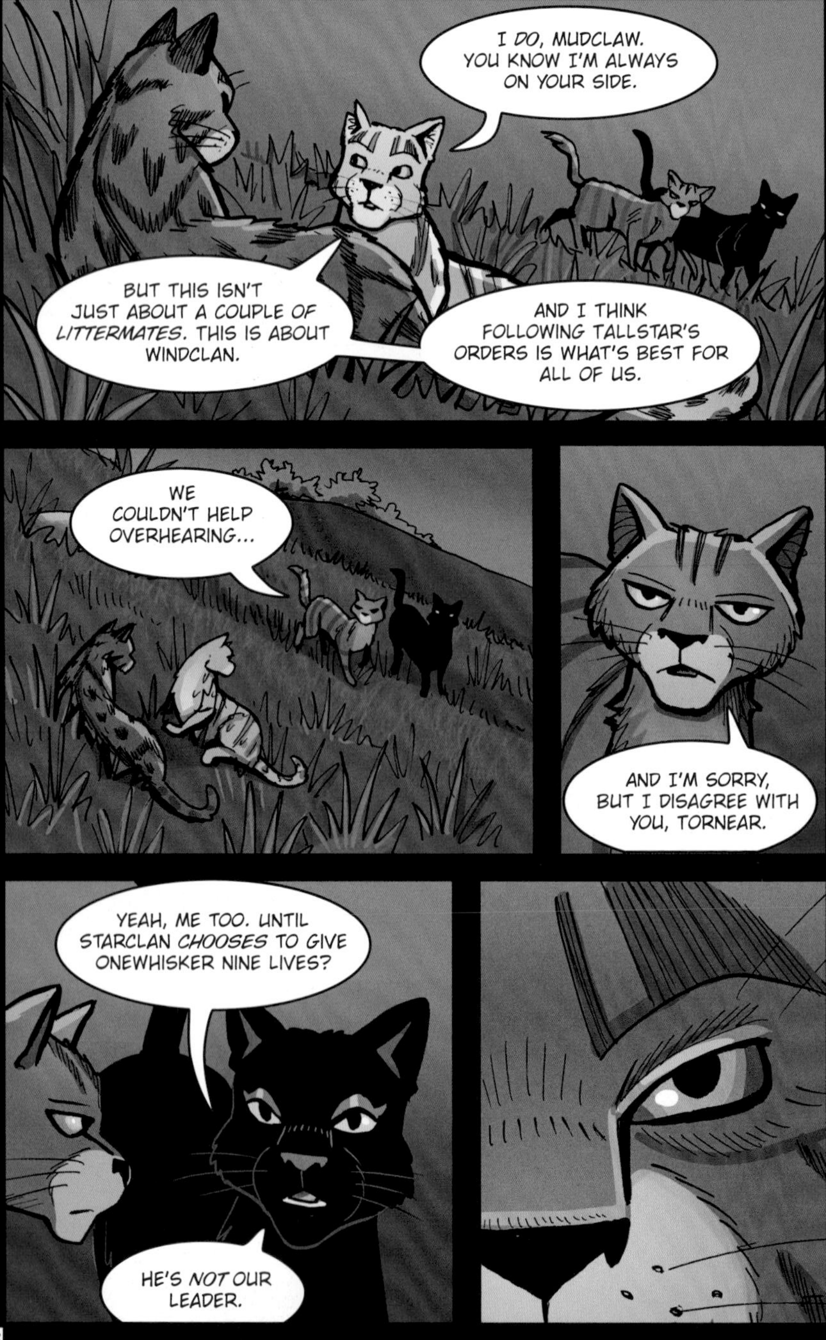
I *DO*, MUDCLAW. YOU KNOW I'M ALWAYS ON YOUR SIDE.
BUT THIS ISN'T JUST ABOUT A COUPLE OF *LITTERMATES*. THIS IS ABOUT WINDCLAN.
AND I THINK FOLLOWING TALLSTAR'S ORDERS IS WHAT'S BEST FOR ALL OF US.
WE COULDN'T HELP OVERHEARING...
AND I'M SORRY, BUT I DISAGREE WITH YOU, TORNEAR.
YEAH, ME TOO. UNTIL STARCLAN *CHOOSES* TO GIVE ONEWHISKER NINE LIVES?
HE'S *NOT* OUR LEADER.

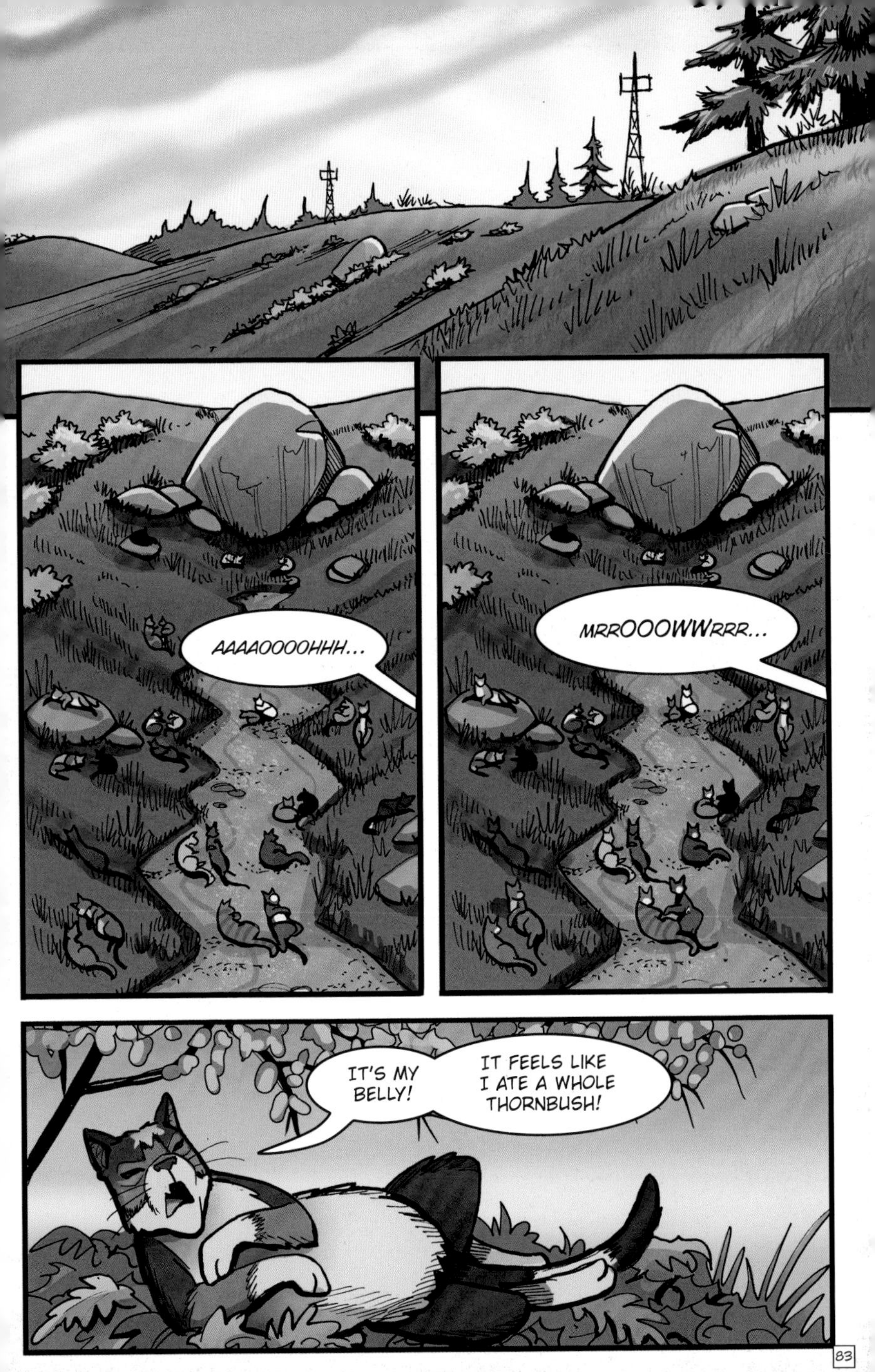
AAAAOOOOHHH...
MRROOOWWRRR...
IT'S MY BELLY!
IT FEELS LIKE I ATE A WHOLE THORNBUSH!

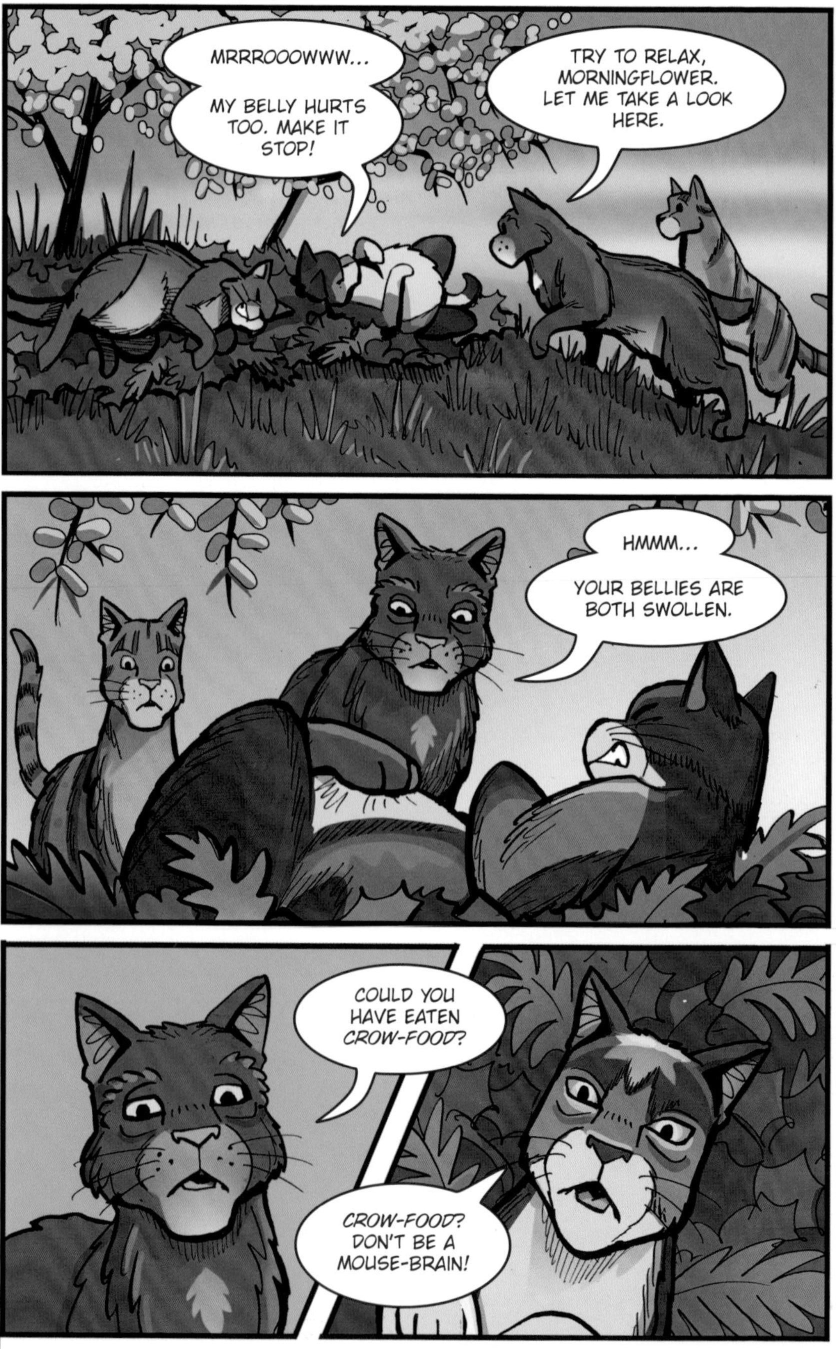
MRRROOOWWW...
MY BELLY HURTS TOO. MAKE IT STOP!
TRY TO RELAX, MORNINGFLOWER. LET ME TAKE A LOOK HERE.
HMMM...
YOUR BELLIES ARE BOTH SWOLLEN.
COULD YOU HAVE EATEN *CROW-FOOD*?
CROW-FOOD? DON'T BE A MOUSE-BRAIN!

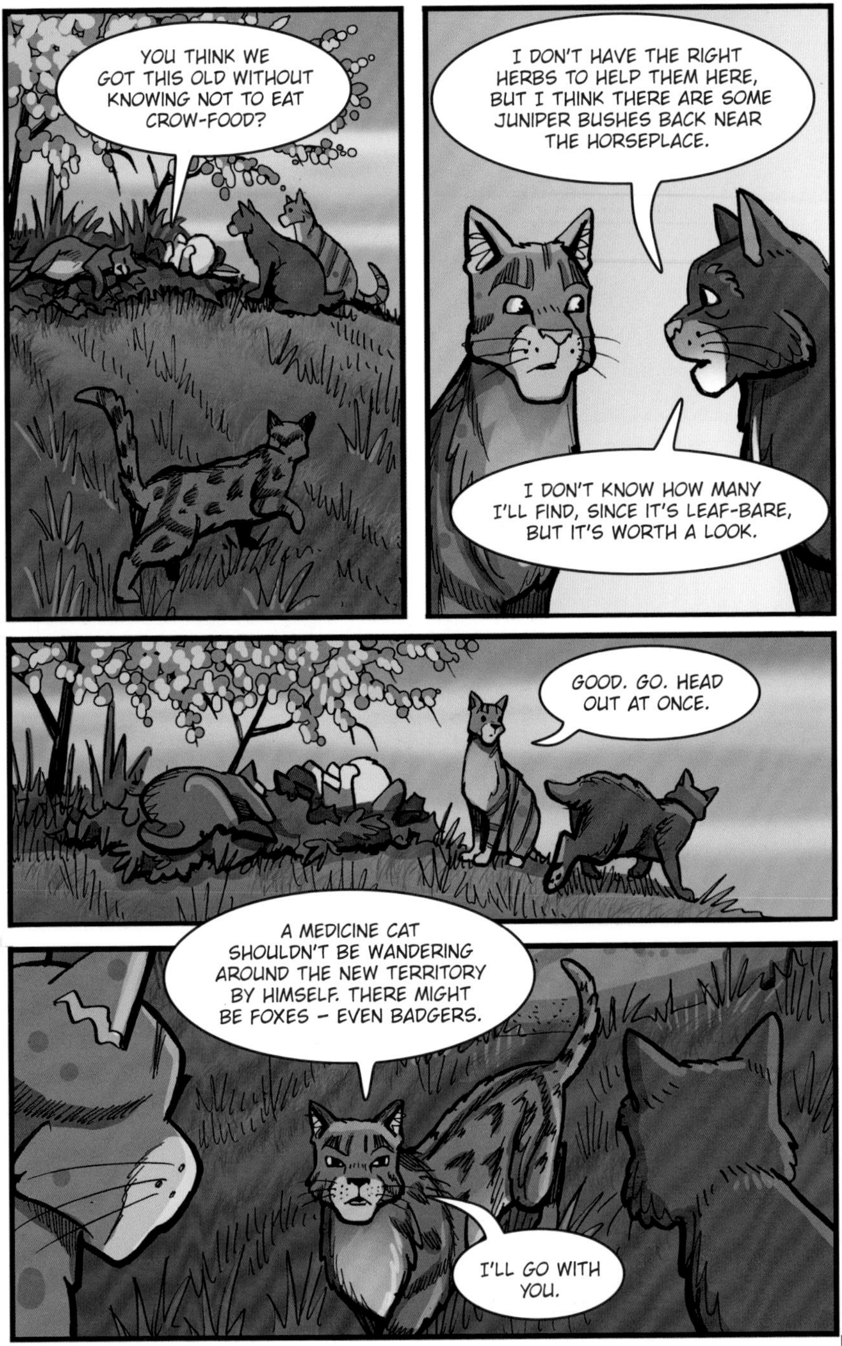
YOU THINK WE GOT THIS OLD WITHOUT KNOWING NOT TO EAT CROW-FOOD?
I DON'T HAVE THE RIGHT HERBS TO HELP THEM HERE, BUT I THINK THERE ARE SOME JUNIPER BUSHES BACK NEAR THE HORSEPLACE.
I DON'T KNOW HOW MANY I'LL FIND, SINCE IT'S LEAF-BARE, BUT IT'S WORTH A LOOK.
GOOD. GO. HEAD OUT AT ONCE.
A MEDICINE CAT SHOULDN'T BE WANDERING AROUND THE NEW TERRITORY BY HIMSELF. THERE MIGHT BE FOXES – EVEN BADGERS.
I'LL GO WITH YOU.

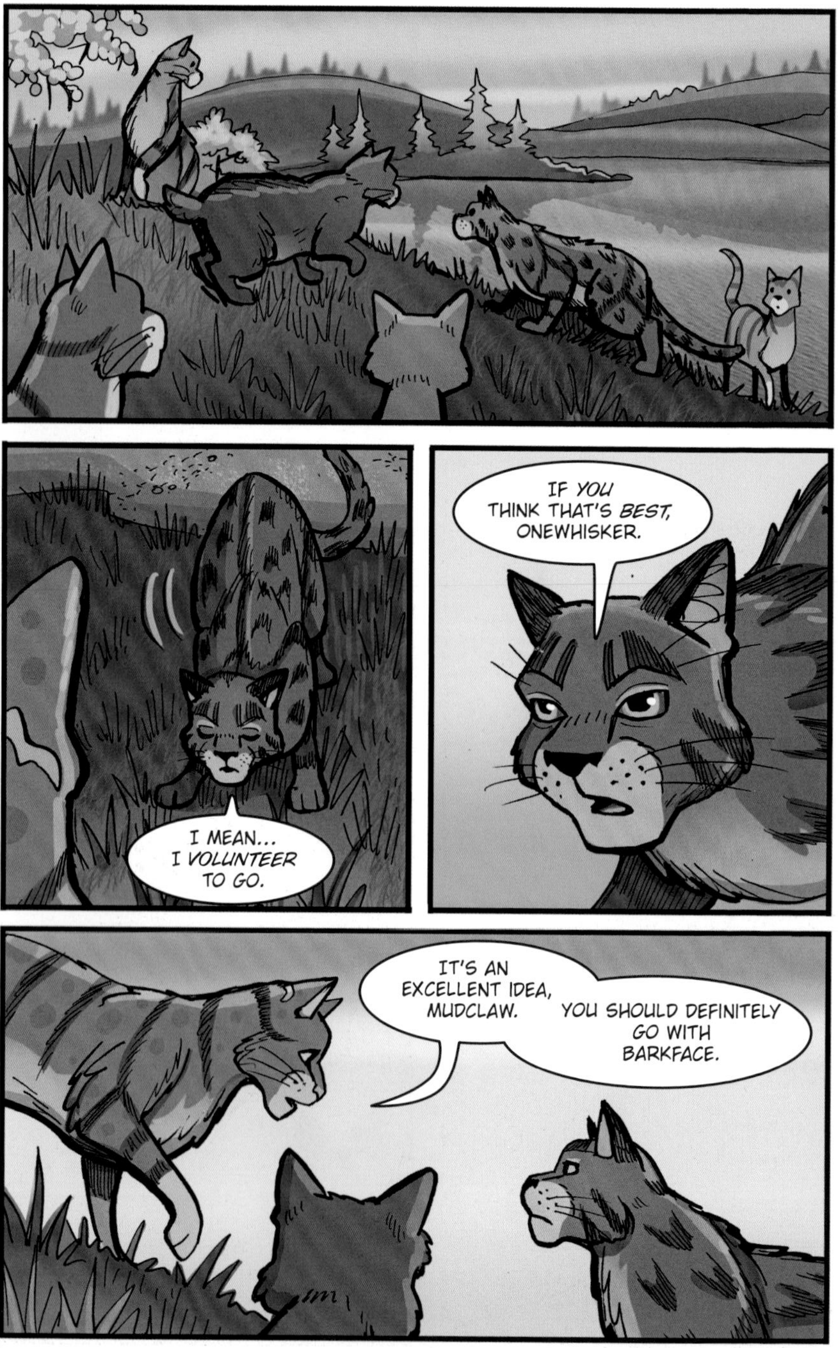
I MEAN...
I *VOLUNTEER*
TO GO.
IF *YOU*
THINK THAT'S *BEST*,
ONEWHISKER.
IT'S AN
EXCELLENT IDEA,
MUDCLAW.
YOU SHOULD DEFINITELY
GO WITH
BARKFACE.

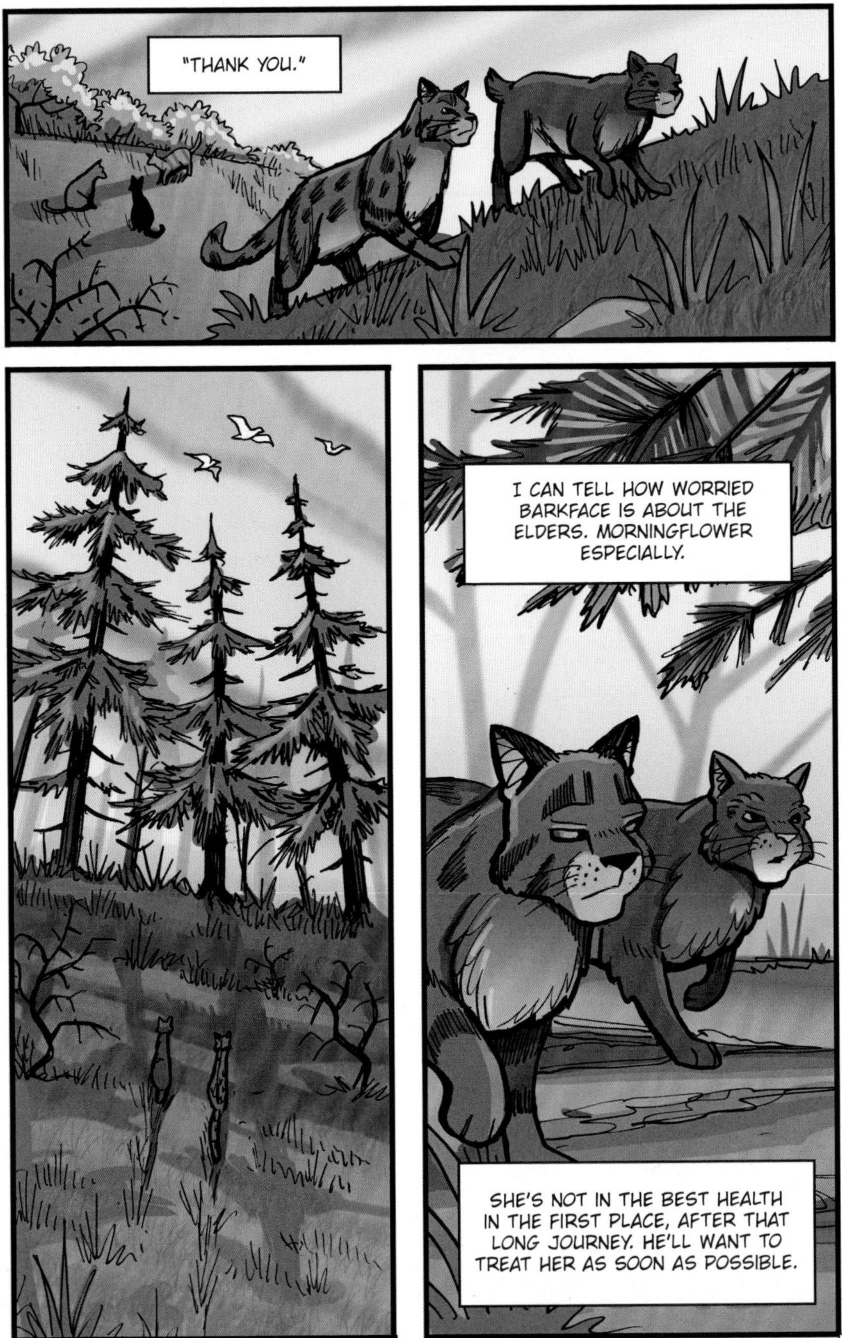
"THANK YOU."
I CAN TELL HOW WORRIED BARKFACE IS ABOUT THE ELDERS. MORNINGFLOWER ESPECIALLY.
SHE'S NOT IN THE BEST HEALTH IN THE FIRST PLACE, AFTER THAT LONG JOURNEY. HE'LL WANT TO TREAT HER AS SOON AS POSSIBLE.

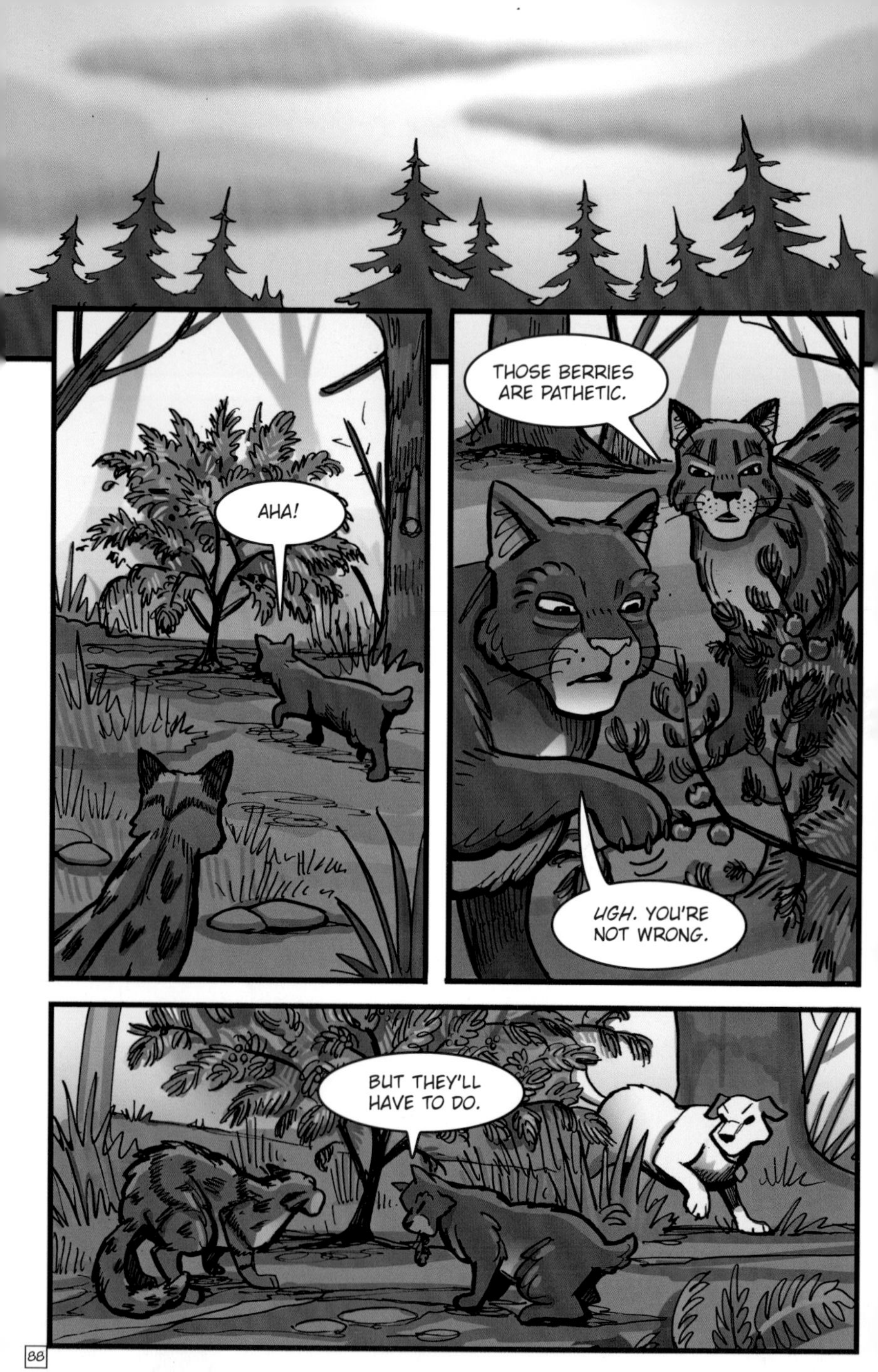
AHA!
THOSE BERRIES ARE PATHETIC.
UGH. YOU'RE NOT WRONG.
BUT THEY'LL HAVE TO DO.

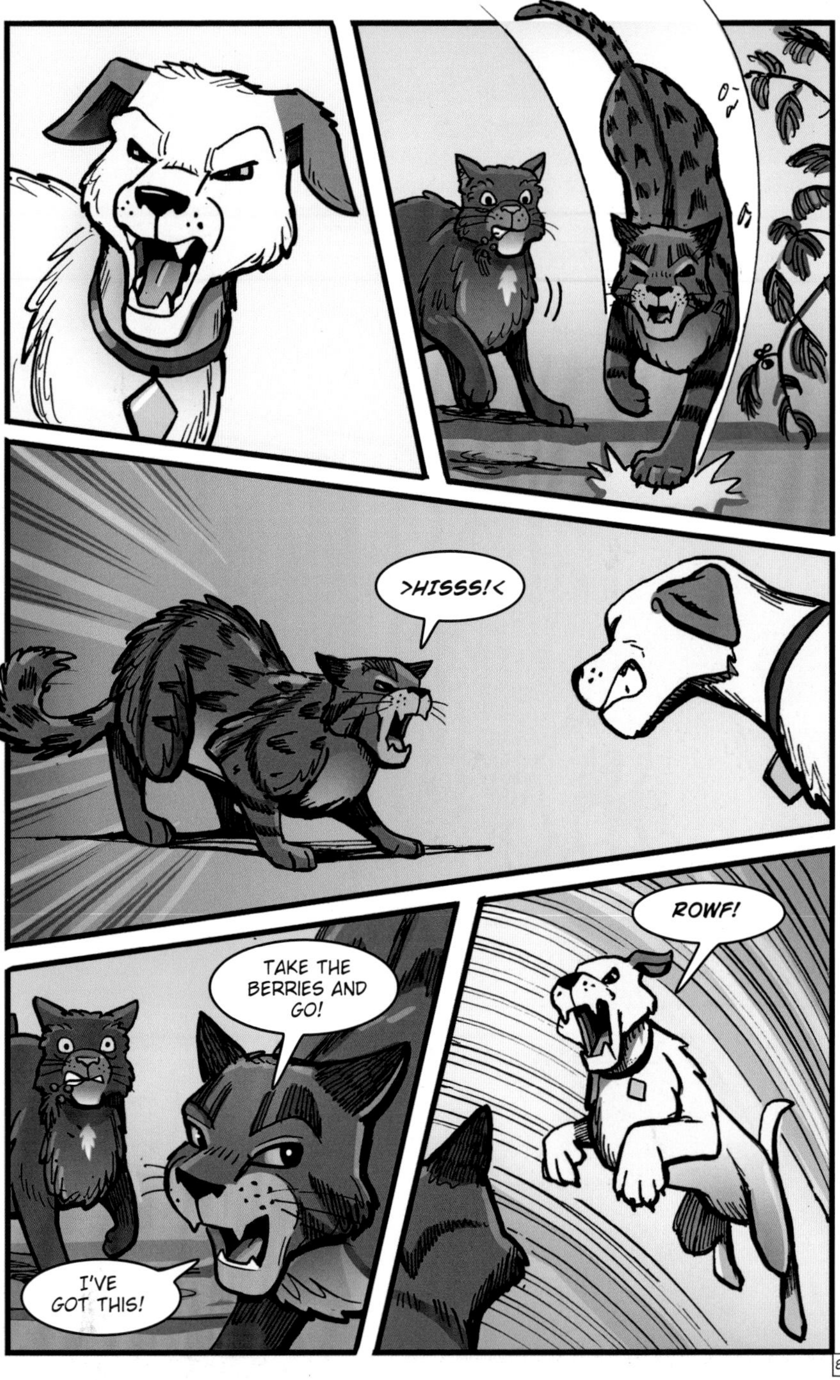
>HISSS!<
TAKE THE BERRIES AND GO!
I'VE GOT THIS!
ROWF!

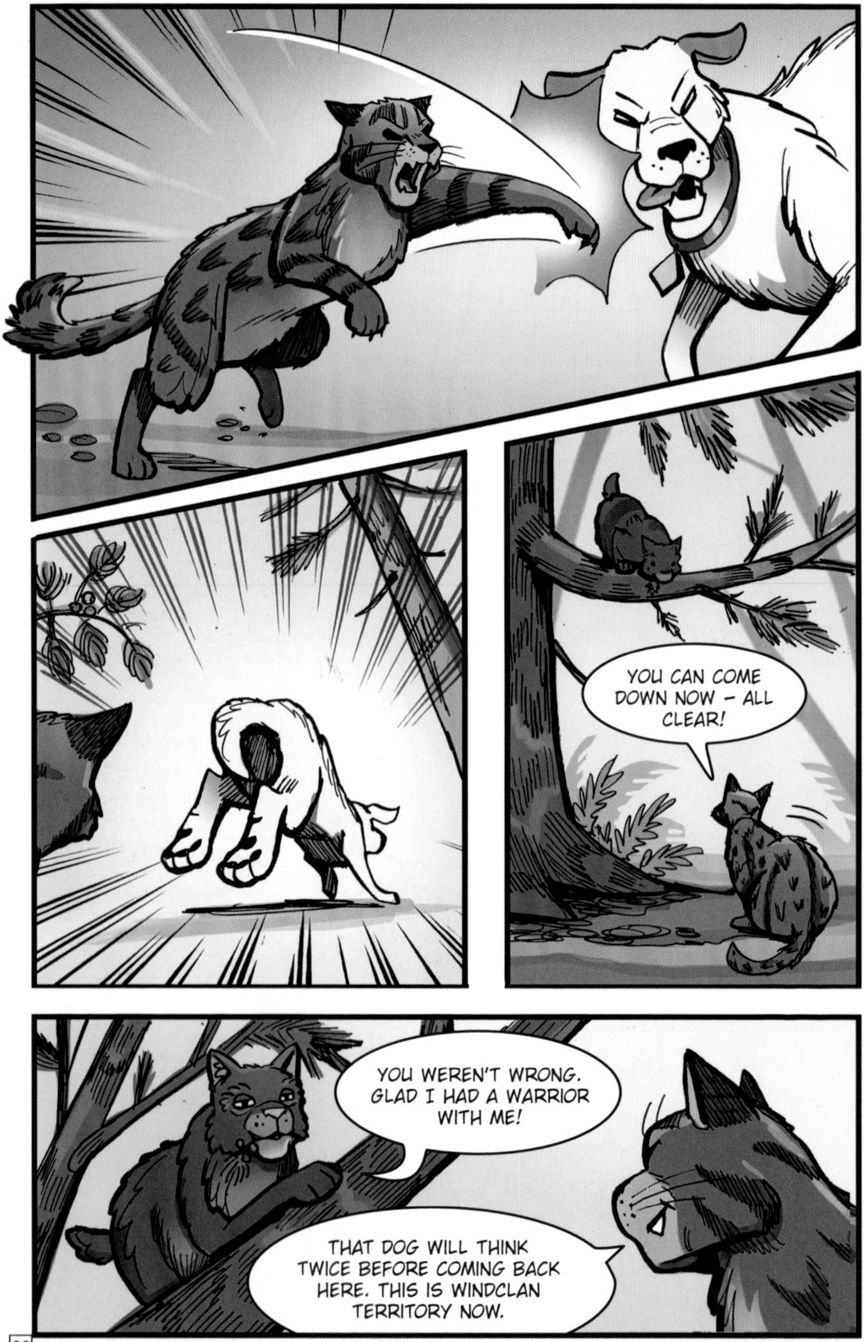
YOU CAN COME DOWN NOW – ALL CLEAR!
YOU WEREN'T WRONG. GLAD I HAD A WARRIOR WITH ME!
THAT DOG WILL THINK TWICE BEFORE COMING BACK HERE. THIS IS WINDCLAN TERRITORY NOW.

BARKFACE...DO YOU KNOW IF STARCLAN HAS COME HERE WITH US? DO YOU KNOW FOR *CERTAIN*?

I ASK BECAUSE...WELL... WHAT IF IT TURNS OUT THAT WE CAN ONLY REACH THEM IN OUR OLD TERRITORY?

WHAT IF STARCLAN CAN NEVER GIVE ANY OF OUR LEADERS NINE LIVES AGAIN?

ALL WILL BE WELL, MUDCLAW. I KNOW IT. I CAN FEEL IT.

YOU JUST HAVE TO HAVE *FAITH* IN STARCLAN.

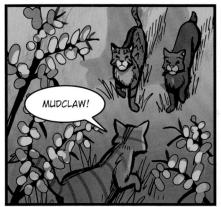

MUDCLAW!

WHAT IS IT? IS SOMETHING WRONG?

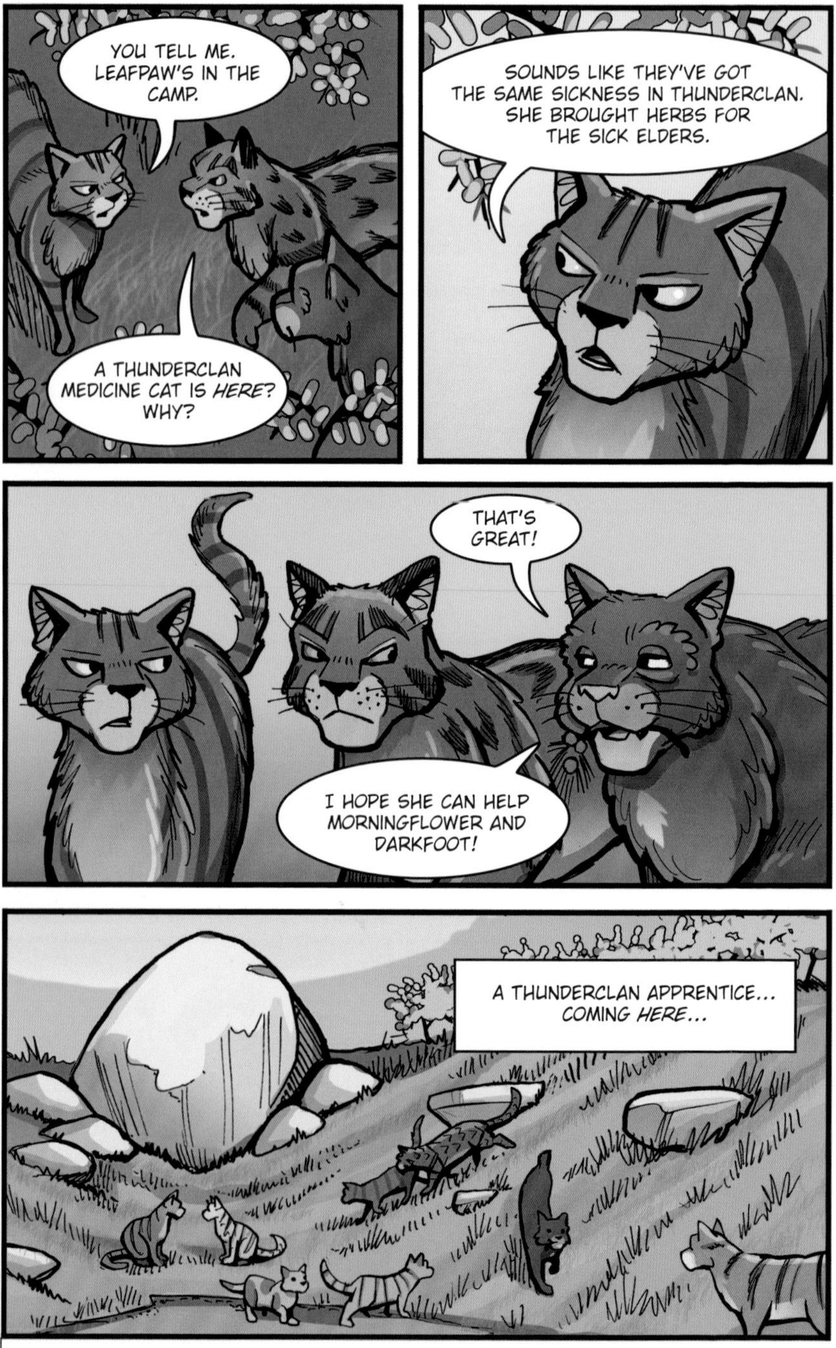
YOU TELL ME. LEAFPAW'S IN THE CAMP.
A THUNDERCLAN MEDICINE CAT IS *HERE*? WHY?
SOUNDS LIKE THEY'VE GOT THE SAME SICKNESS IN THUNDERCLAN. SHE BROUGHT HERBS FOR THE SICK ELDERS.
THAT'S GREAT!
I HOPE SHE CAN HELP MORNINGFLOWER AND DARKFOOT!
A THUNDERCLAN APPRENTICE... COMING *HERE*...

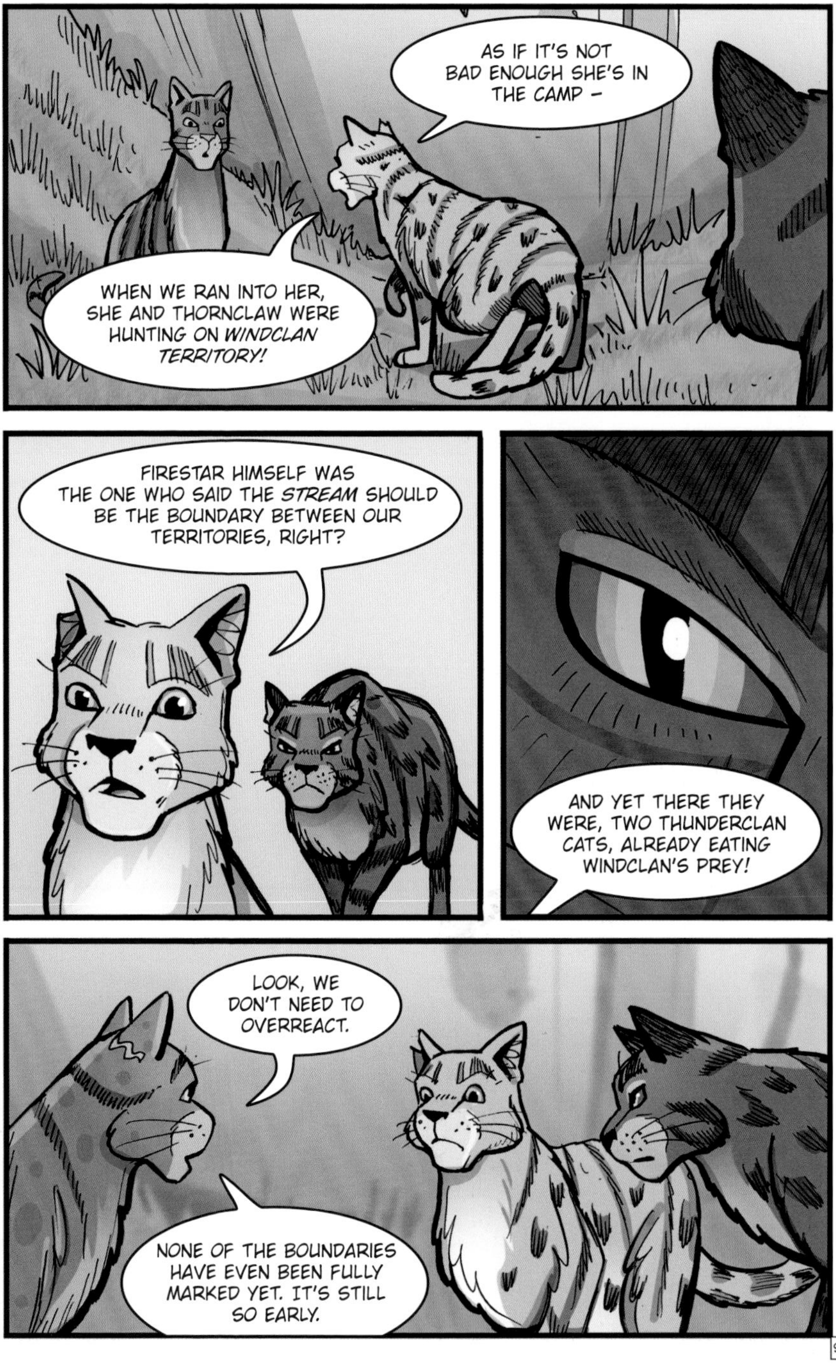
AS IF IT'S NOT BAD ENOUGH SHE'S IN THE CAMP –
WHEN WE RAN INTO HER, SHE AND THORNCLAW WERE HUNTING ON *WINDCLAN TERRITORY!*
FIRESTAR HIMSELF WAS THE ONE WHO SAID THE *STREAM* SHOULD BE THE BOUNDARY BETWEEN OUR TERRITORIES, RIGHT?
AND YET THERE THEY WERE, TWO THUNDERCLAN CATS, ALREADY EATING WINDCLAN'S PREY!
LOOK, WE DON'T NEED TO OVERREACT.
NONE OF THE BOUNDARIES HAVE EVEN BEEN FULLY MARKED YET. IT'S STILL SO EARLY.

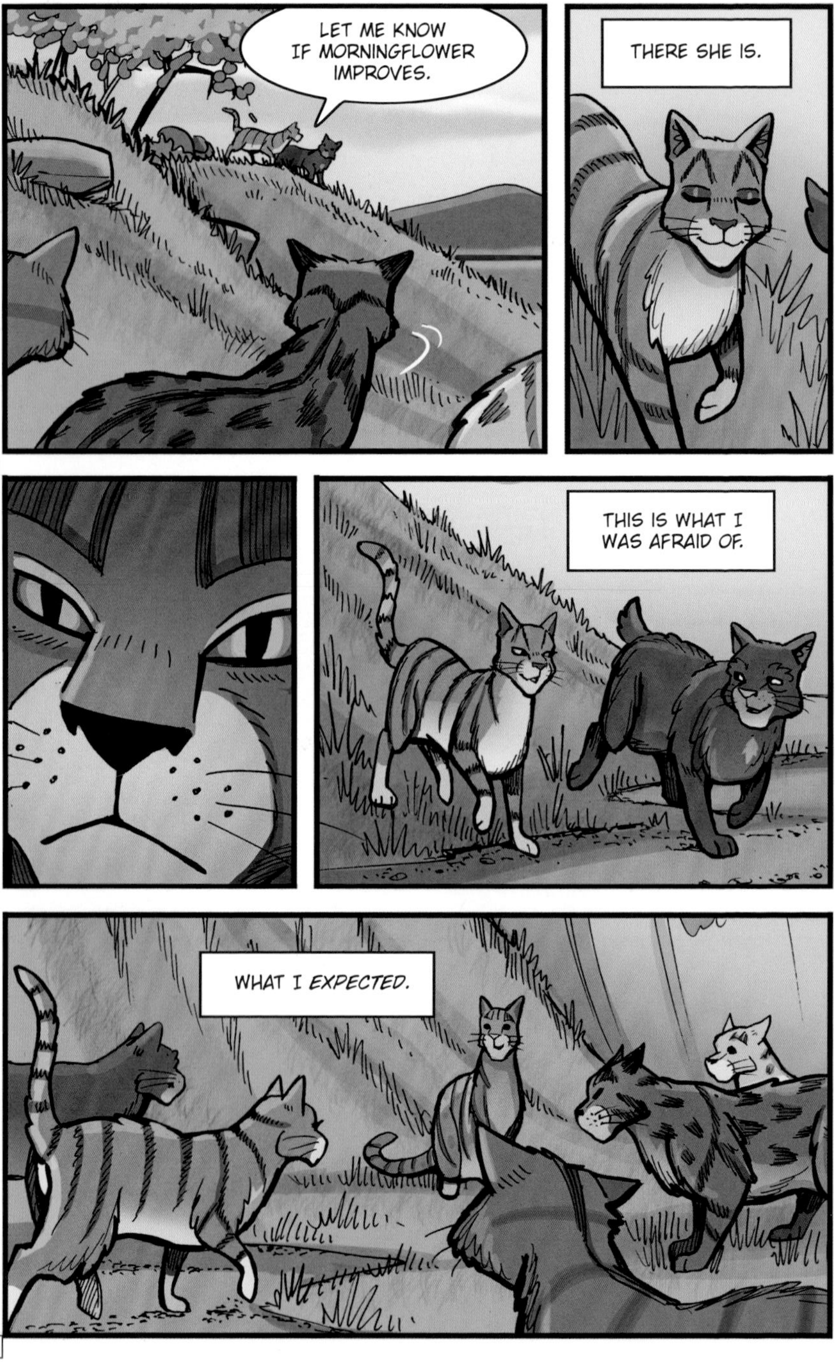
LET ME KNOW IF MORNINGFLOWER IMPROVES.
THERE SHE IS.
THIS IS WHAT I WAS AFRAID OF.
WHAT I *EXPECTED.*

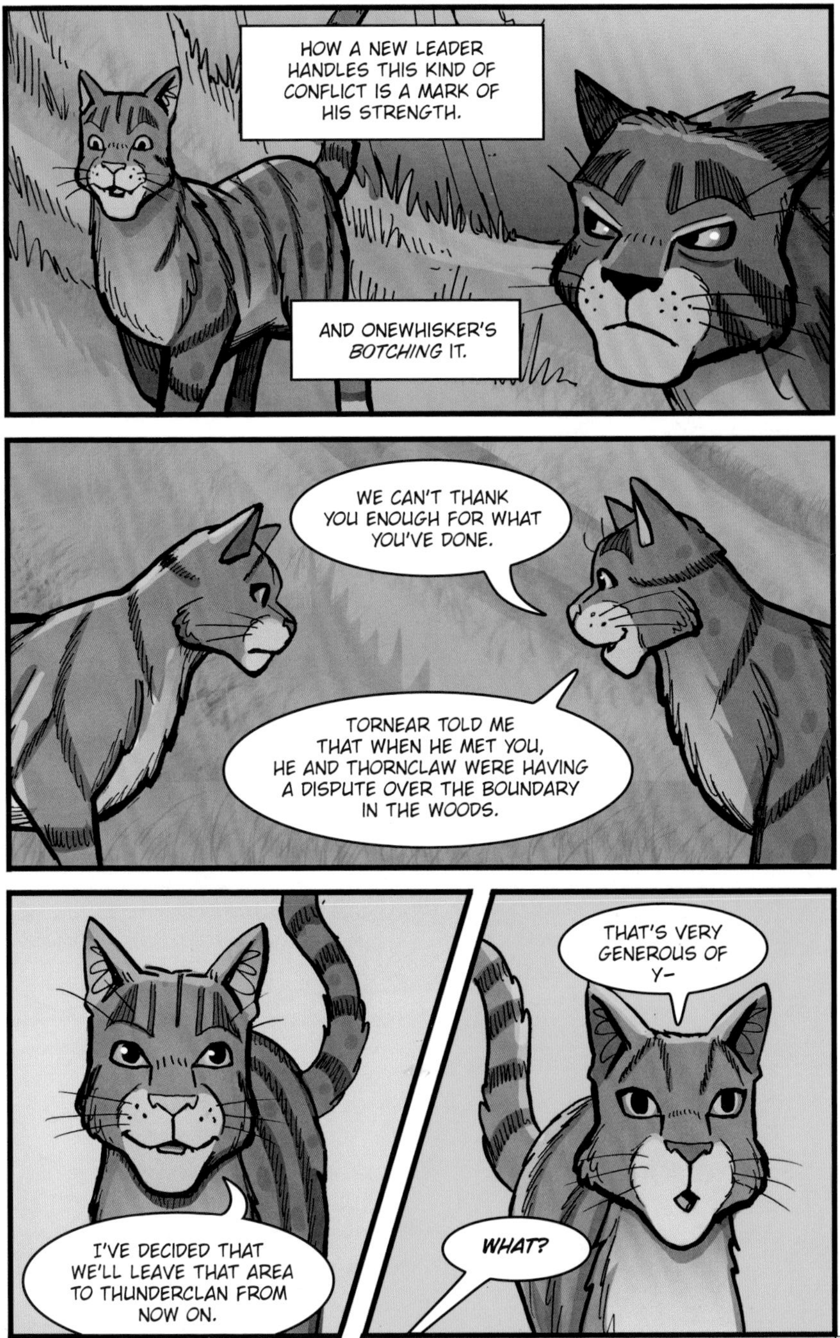
HOW A NEW LEADER HANDLES THIS KIND OF CONFLICT IS A MARK OF HIS STRENGTH.
AND ONEWHISKER'S *BOTCHING* IT.
WE CAN'T THANK YOU ENOUGH FOR WHAT YOU'VE DONE.
TORNEAR TOLD ME THAT WHEN HE MET YOU, HE AND THORNCLAW WERE HAVING A DISPUTE OVER THE BOUNDARY IN THE WOODS.
I'VE DECIDED THAT WE'LL LEAVE THAT AREA TO THUNDERCLAN FROM NOW ON.
THAT'S VERY GENEROUS OF Y–
WHAT?

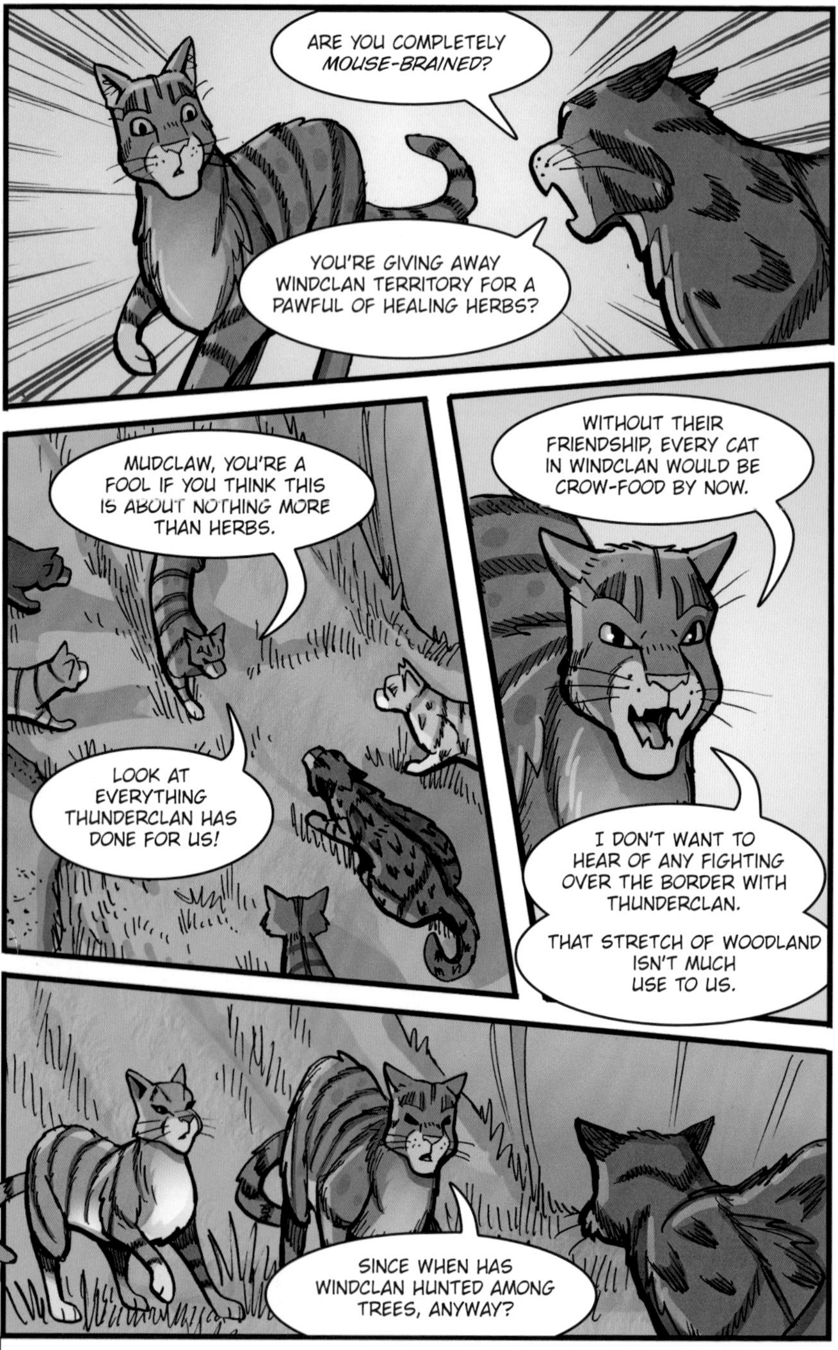
ARE YOU COMPLETELY *MOUSE-BRAINED?*
YOU'RE GIVING AWAY WINDCLAN TERRITORY FOR A PAWFUL OF HEALING HERBS?
MUDCLAW, YOU'RE A FOOL IF YOU THINK THIS IS ABOUT NOTHING MORE THAN HERBS.
LOOK AT EVERYTHING THUNDERCLAN HAS DONE FOR US!
WITHOUT THEIR FRIENDSHIP, EVERY CAT IN WINDCLAN WOULD BE CROW-FOOD BY NOW.
I DON'T WANT TO HEAR OF ANY FIGHTING OVER THE BORDER WITH THUNDERCLAN.
THAT STRETCH OF WOODLAND ISN'T MUCH USE TO US.
SINCE WHEN HAS WINDCLAN HUNTED AMONG TREES, ANYWAY?

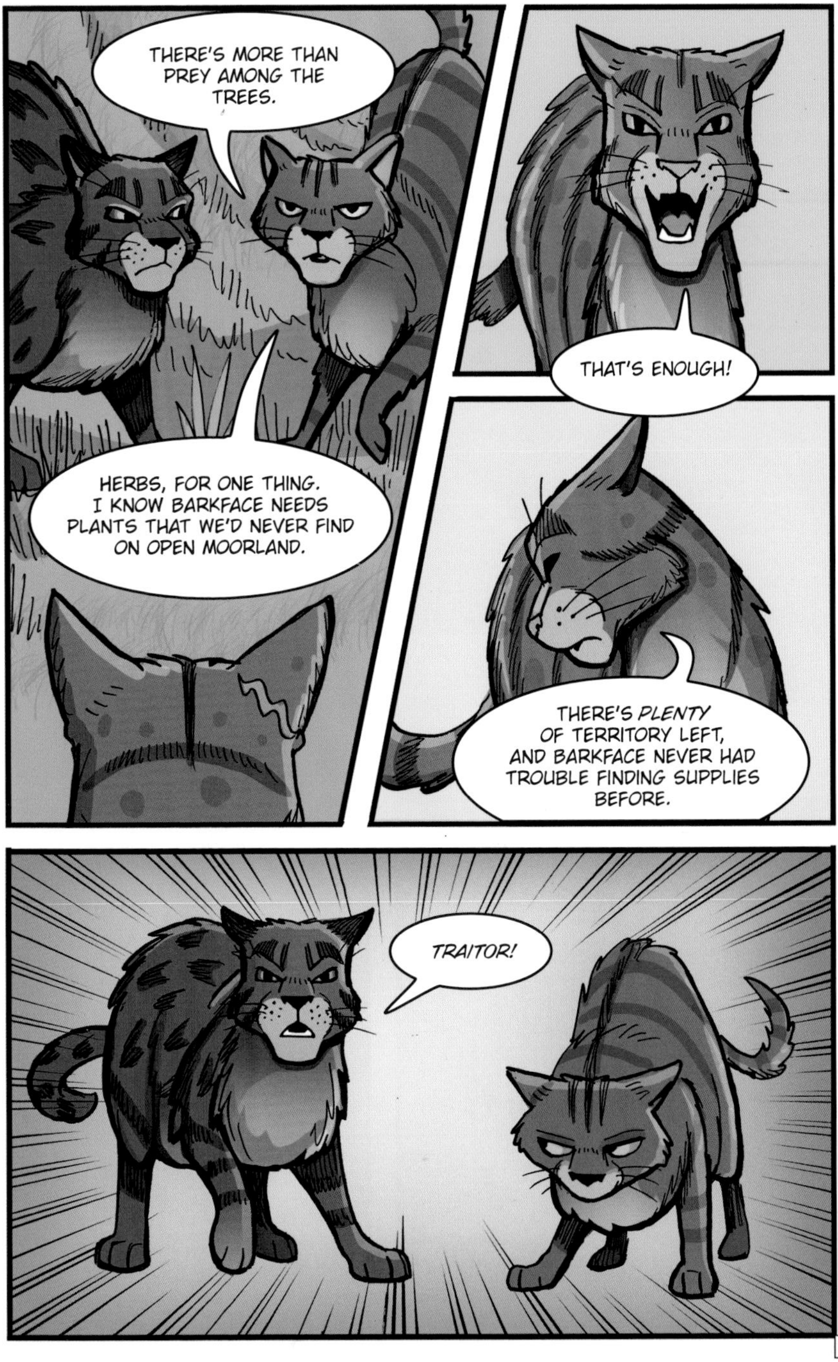
THERE'S MORE THAN PREY AMONG THE TREES.
HERBS, FOR ONE THING. I KNOW BARKFACE NEEDS PLANTS THAT WE'D NEVER FIND ON OPEN MOORLAND.
THAT'S ENOUGH!
THERE'S *PLENTY* OF TERRITORY LEFT, AND BARKFACE NEVER HAD TROUBLE FINDING SUPPLIES BEFORE.
TRAITOR!

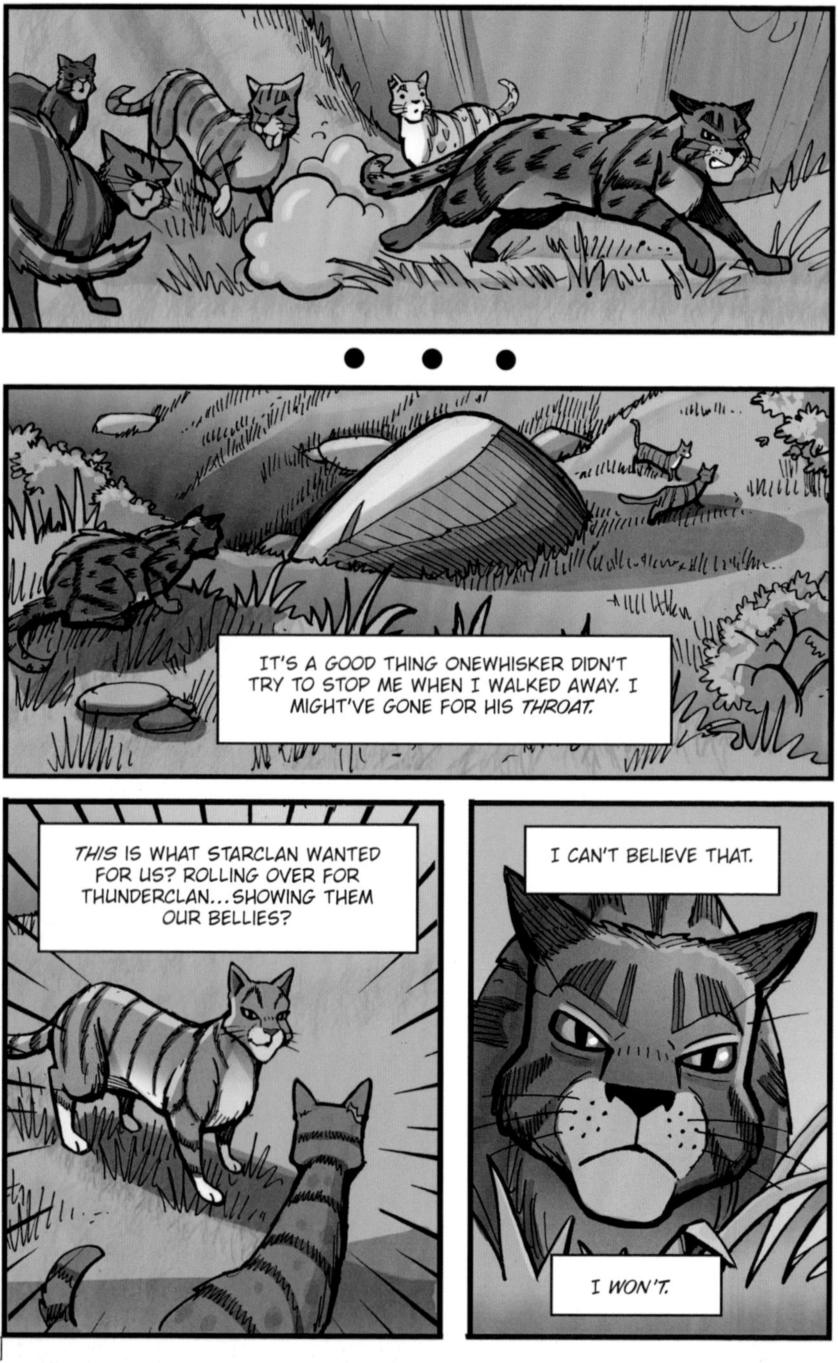

IT'S A GOOD THING ONEWHISKER DIDN'T TRY TO STOP ME WHEN I WALKED AWAY. I MIGHT'VE GONE FOR HIS *THROAT.*
THIS IS WHAT STARCLAN WANTED FOR US? ROLLING OVER FOR THUNDERCLAN...SHOWING THEM OUR BELLIES?
I CAN'T BELIEVE THAT.
I *WON'T.*

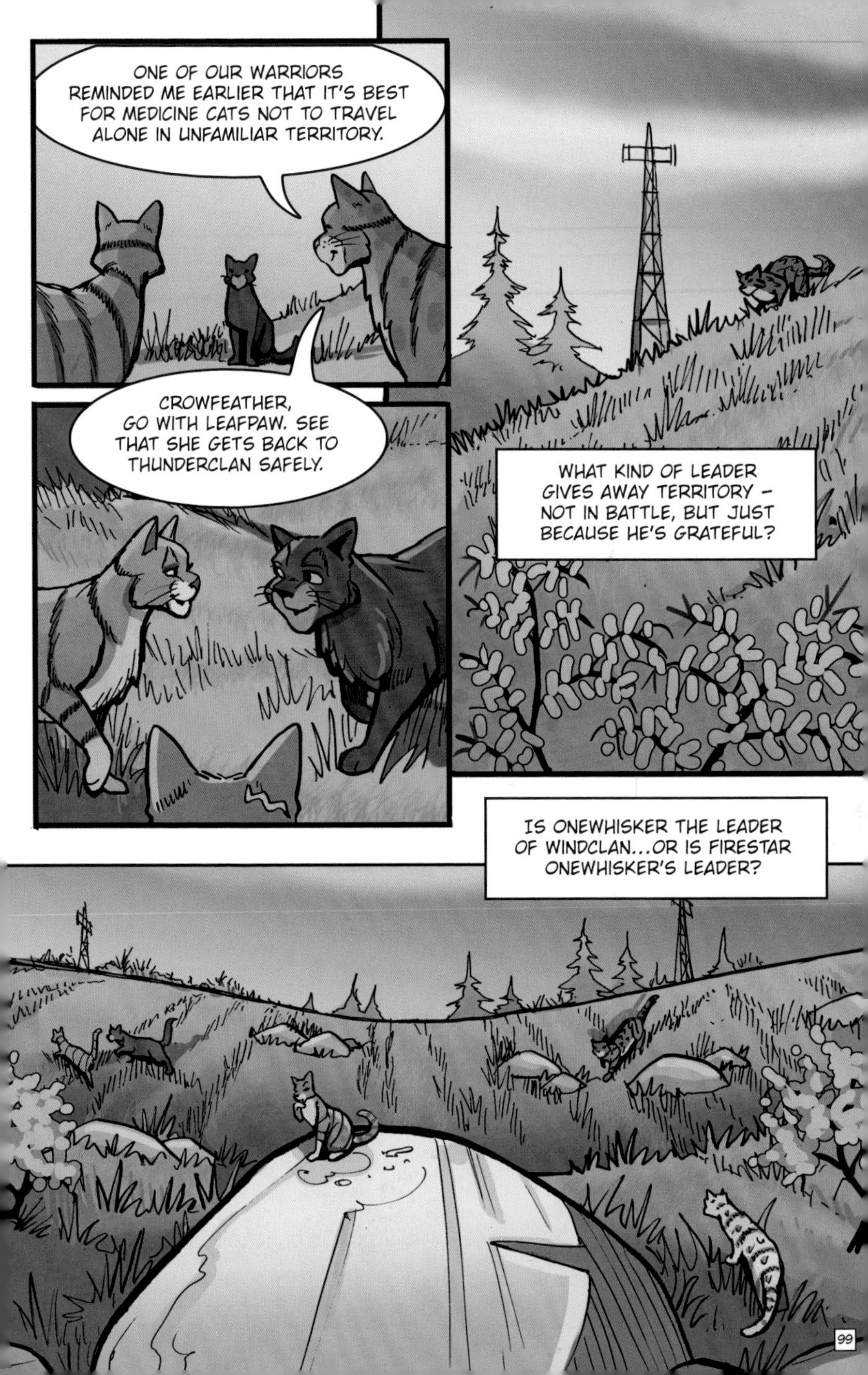
ONE OF OUR WARRIORS REMINDED ME EARLIER THAT IT'S BEST FOR MEDICINE CATS NOT TO TRAVEL ALONE IN UNFAMILIAR TERRITORY.
CROWFEATHER, GO WITH LEAFPAW. SEE THAT SHE GETS BACK TO THUNDERCLAN SAFELY.
WHAT KIND OF LEADER GIVES AWAY TERRITORY – NOT IN BATTLE, BUT JUST BECAUSE HE'S GRATEFUL?
IS ONEWHISKER THE LEADER OF WINDCLAN...OR IS FIRESTAR ONEWHISKER'S LEADER?

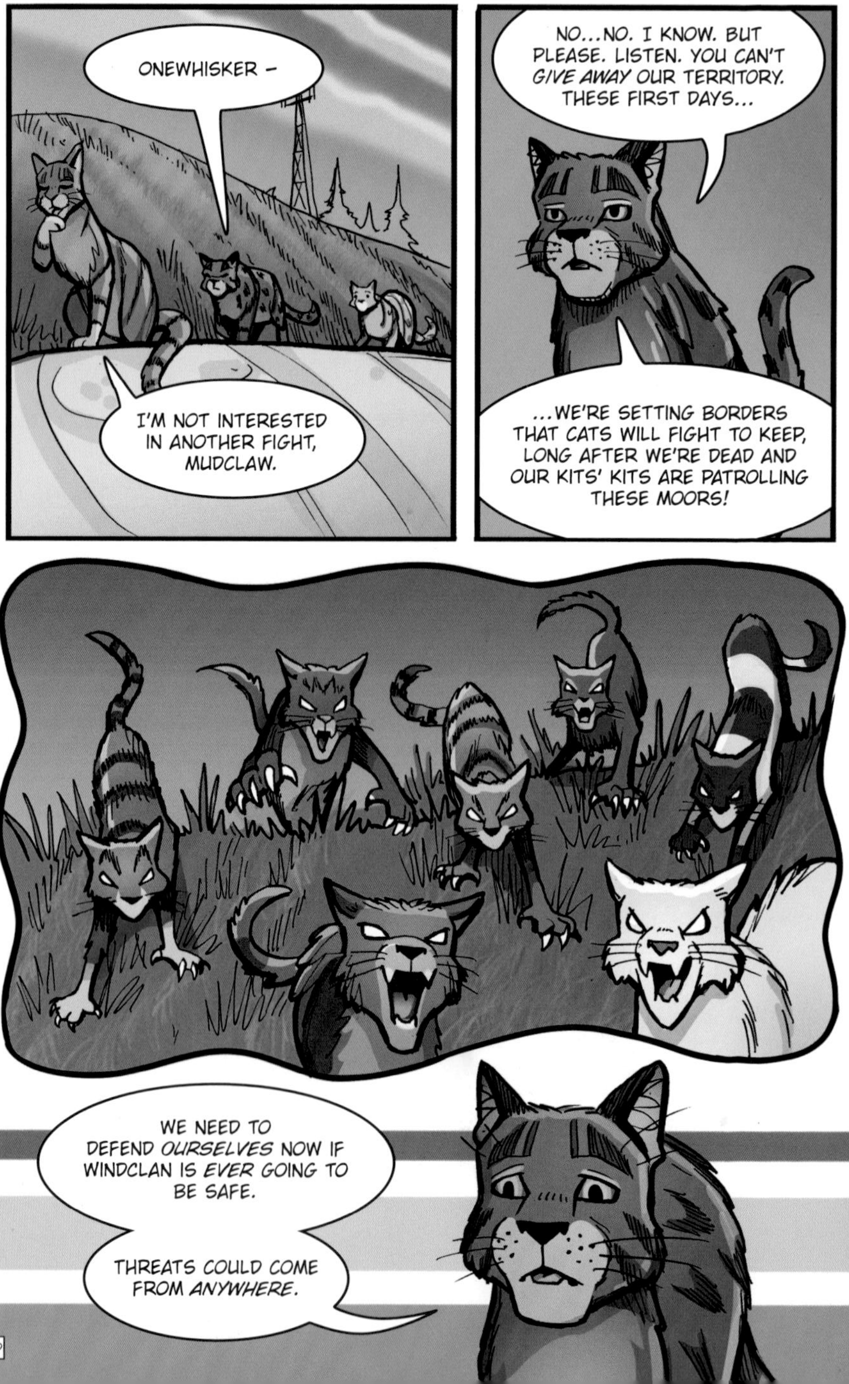
ONEWHISKER –
I'M NOT INTERESTED IN ANOTHER FIGHT, MUDCLAW.
NO...NO. I KNOW. BUT PLEASE. LISTEN. YOU CAN'T *GIVE AWAY* OUR TERRITORY. THESE FIRST DAYS...
...WE'RE SETTING BORDERS THAT CATS WILL FIGHT TO KEEP, LONG AFTER WE'RE DEAD AND OUR KITS' KITS ARE PATROLLING THESE MOORS!
WE NEED TO DEFEND *OURSELVES* NOW IF WINDCLAN IS *EVER* GOING TO BE SAFE.
THREATS COULD COME FROM *ANYWHERE*.

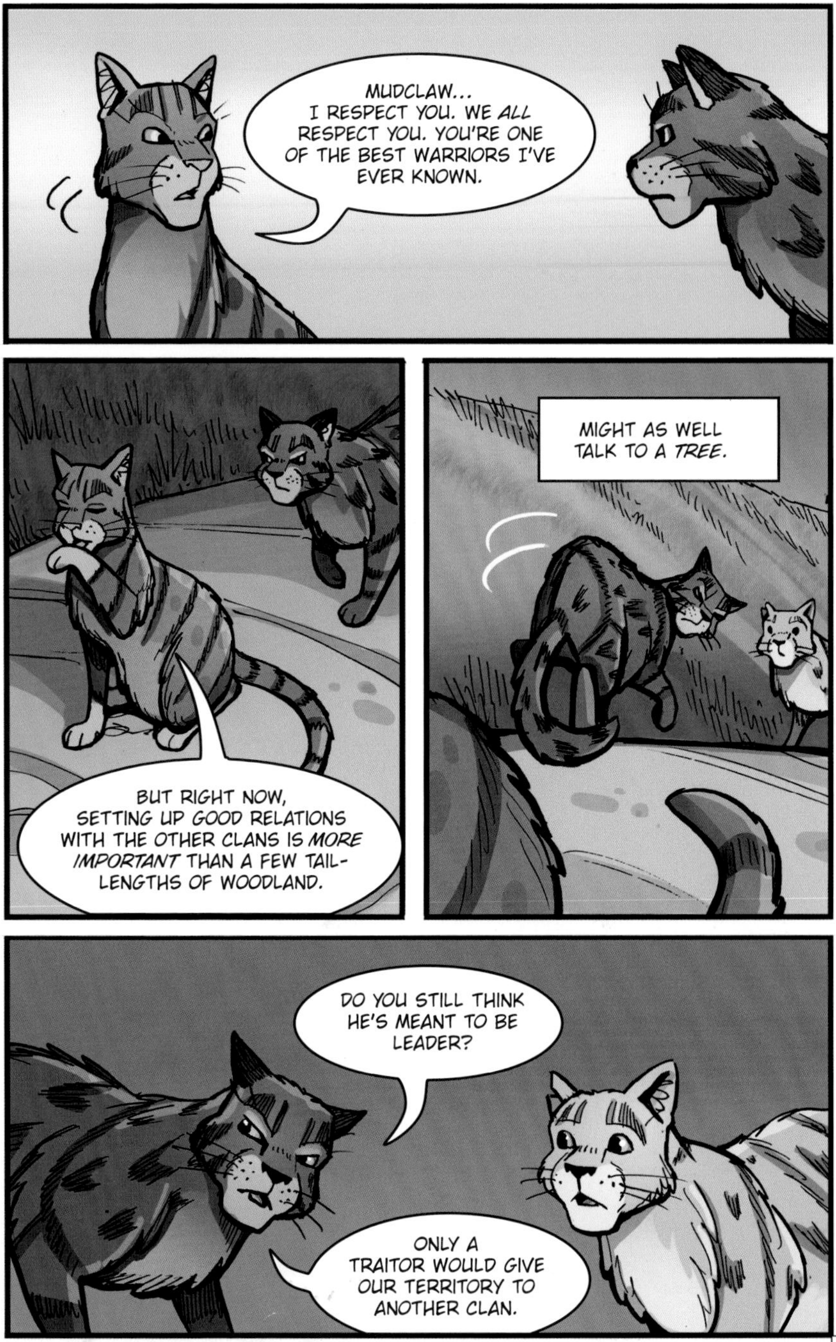
MUDCLAW... I RESPECT YOU. WE *ALL* RESPECT YOU. YOU'RE ONE OF THE BEST WARRIORS I'VE EVER KNOWN.
BUT RIGHT NOW, SETTING UP *GOOD* RELATIONS WITH THE OTHER CLANS IS *MORE IMPORTANT* THAN A FEW TAIL-LENGTHS OF WOODLAND.
MIGHT AS WELL TALK TO A *TREE.*
DO YOU STILL THINK HE'S MEANT TO BE LEADER?
ONLY A TRAITOR WOULD GIVE OUR TERRITORY TO ANOTHER CLAN.

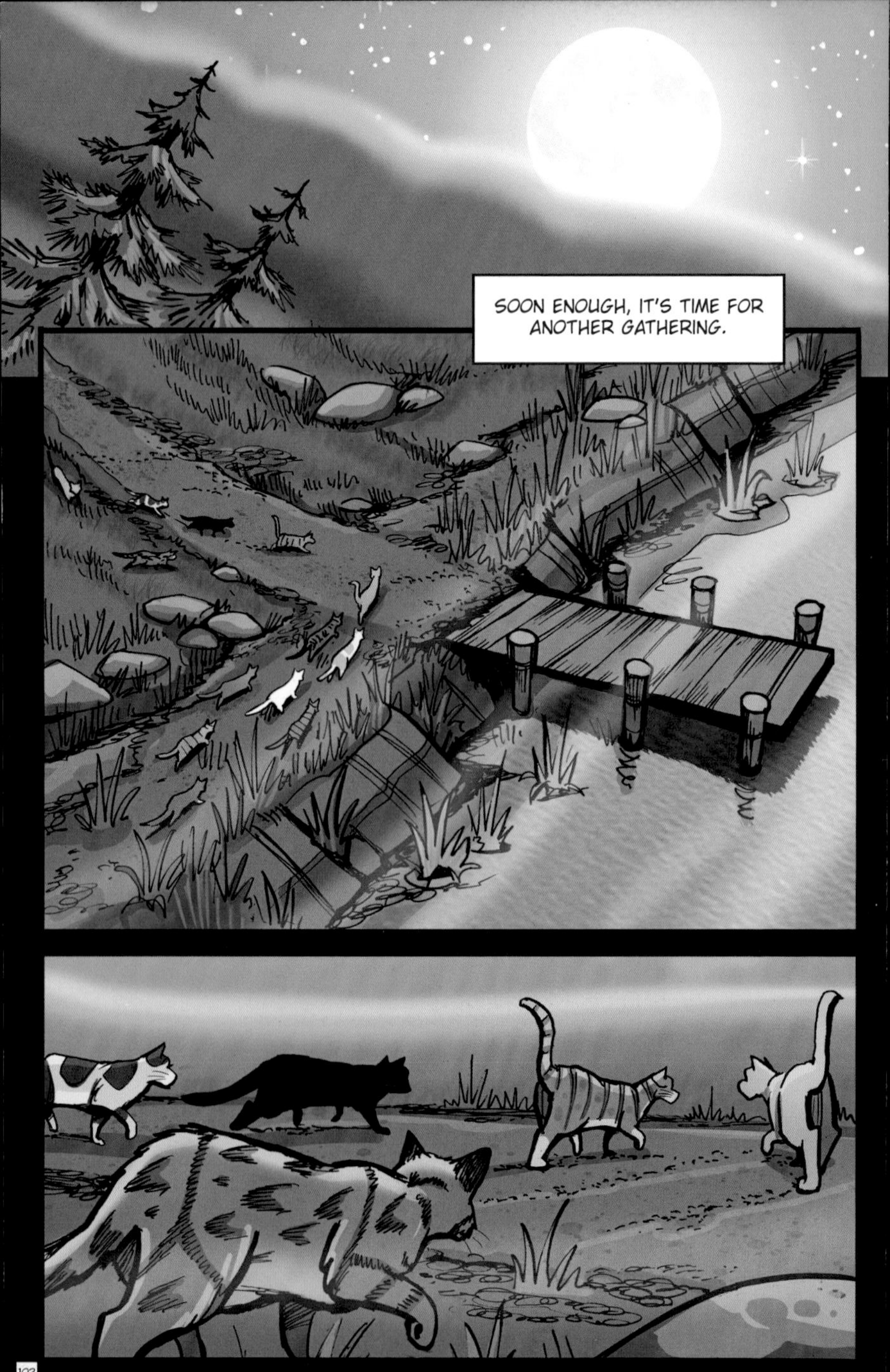
SOON ENOUGH, IT'S TIME FOR ANOTHER GATHERING.

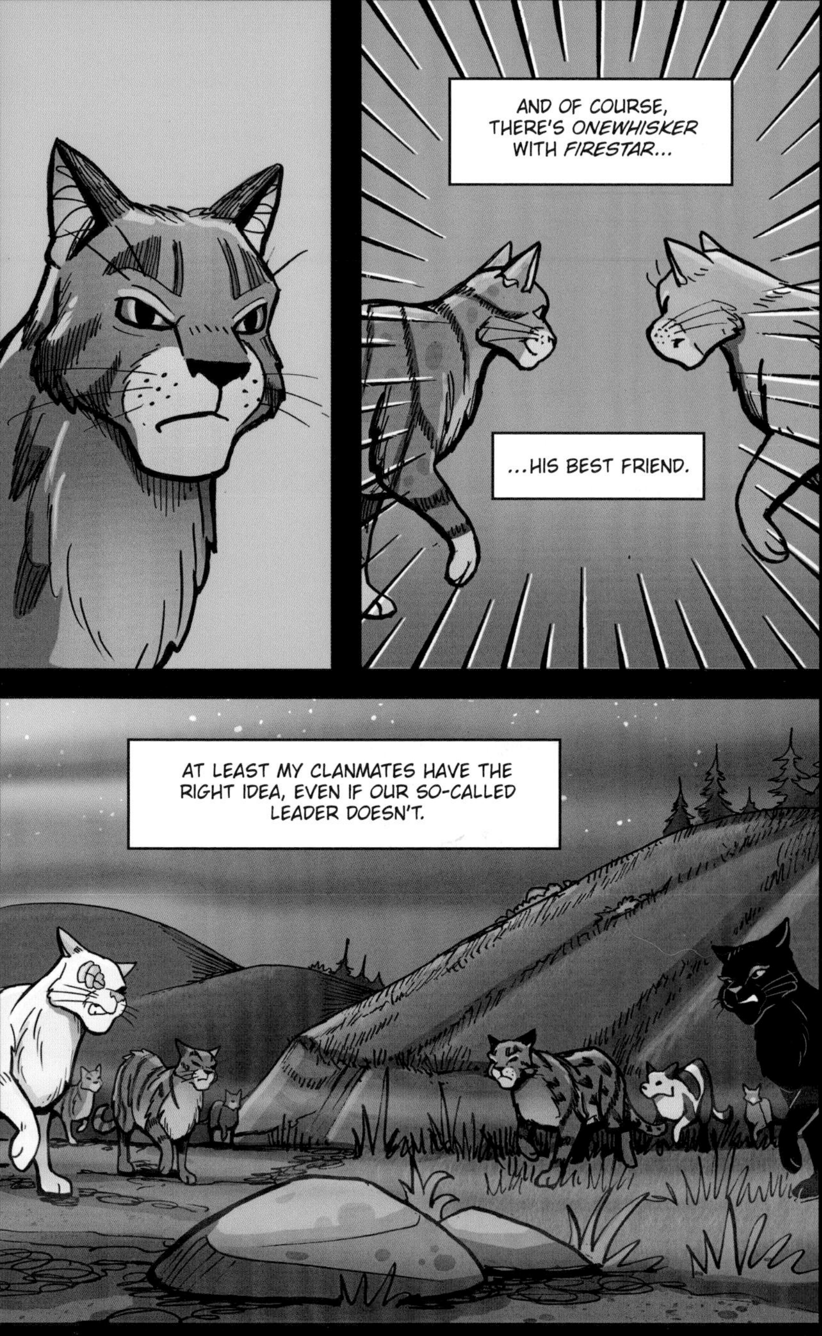
AND OF COURSE, THERE'S *ONEWHISKER* WITH *FIRESTAR*...
...HIS BEST FRIEND.
AT LEAST MY CLANMATES HAVE THE RIGHT IDEA, EVEN IF OUR SO-CALLED LEADER DOESN'T.

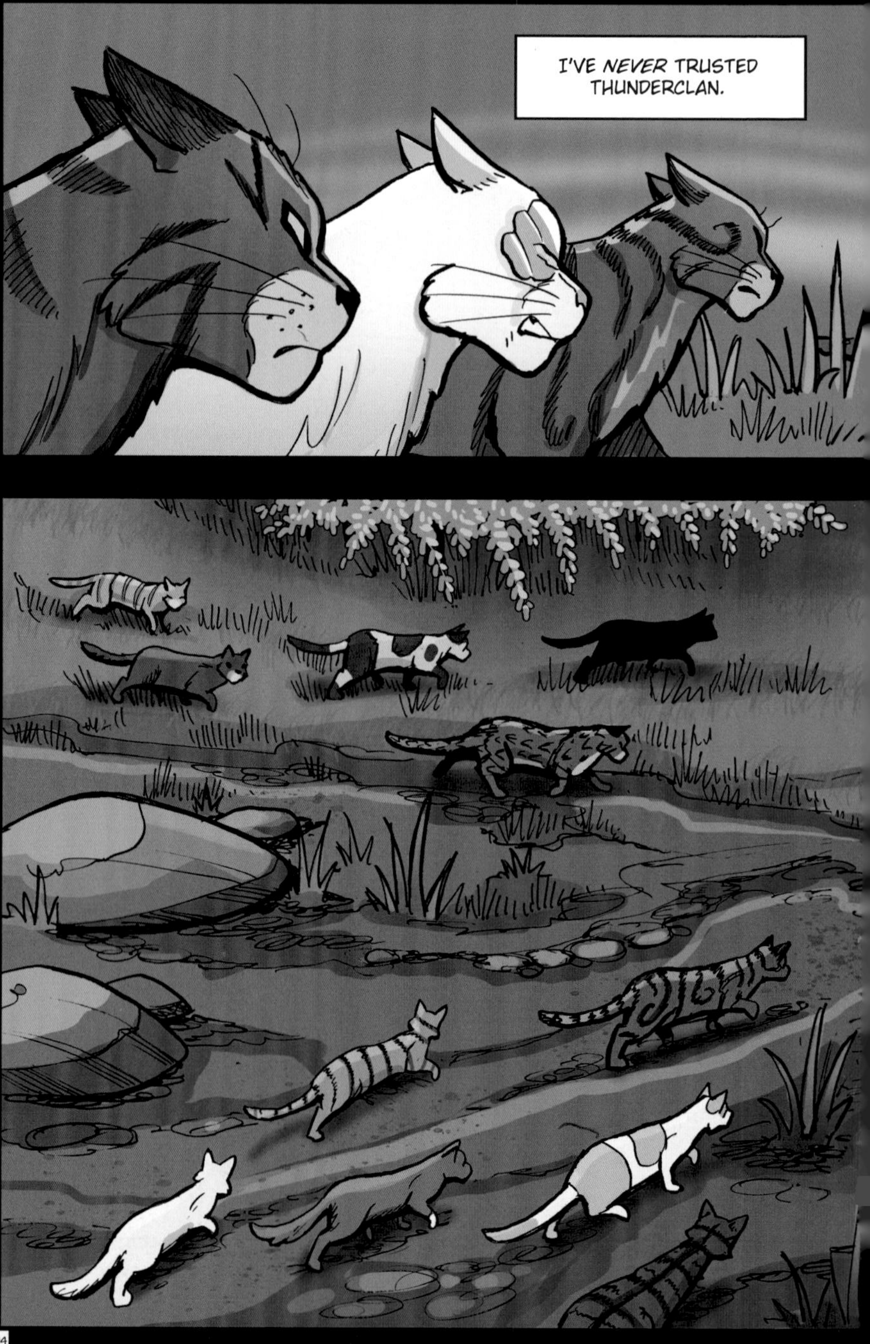
I'VE *NEVER* TRUSTED THUNDERCLAN.

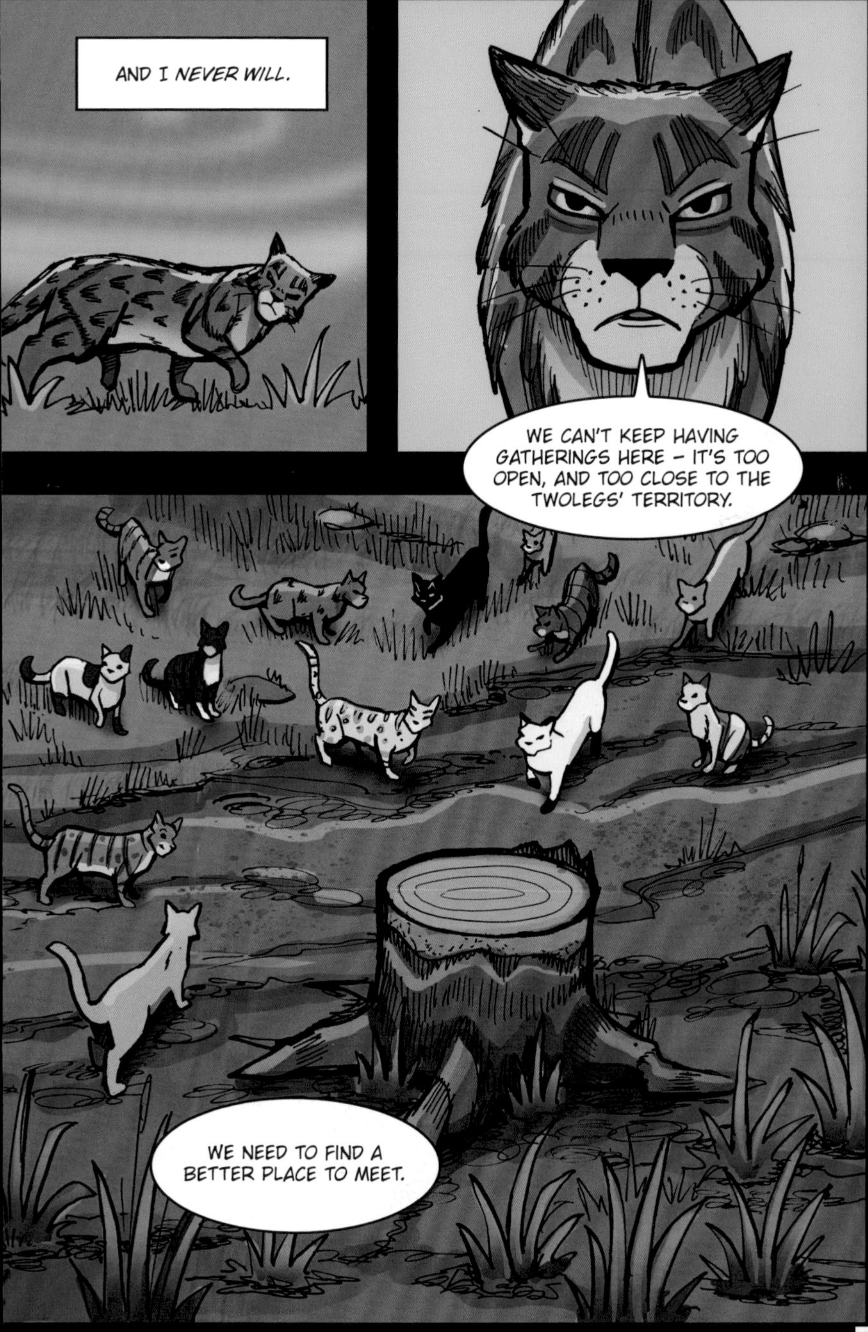
AND I *NEVER WILL.*
WE CAN'T KEEP HAVING GATHERINGS HERE – IT'S TOO OPEN, AND TOO CLOSE TO THE TWOLEGS' TERRITORY.
WE NEED TO FIND A BETTER PLACE TO MEET.

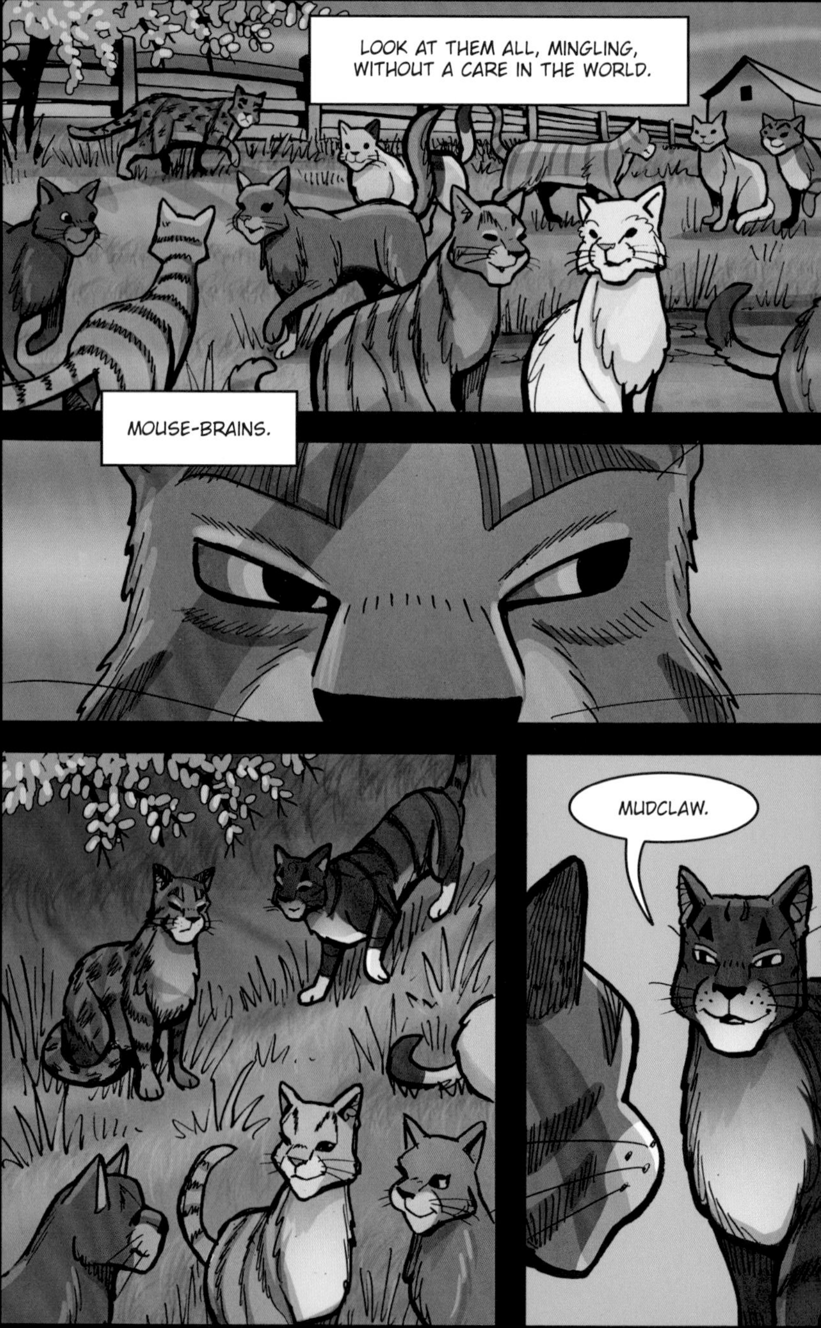
LOOK AT THEM ALL, MINGLING, WITHOUT A CARE IN THE WORLD.
MOUSE-BRAINS.
MUDCLAW.

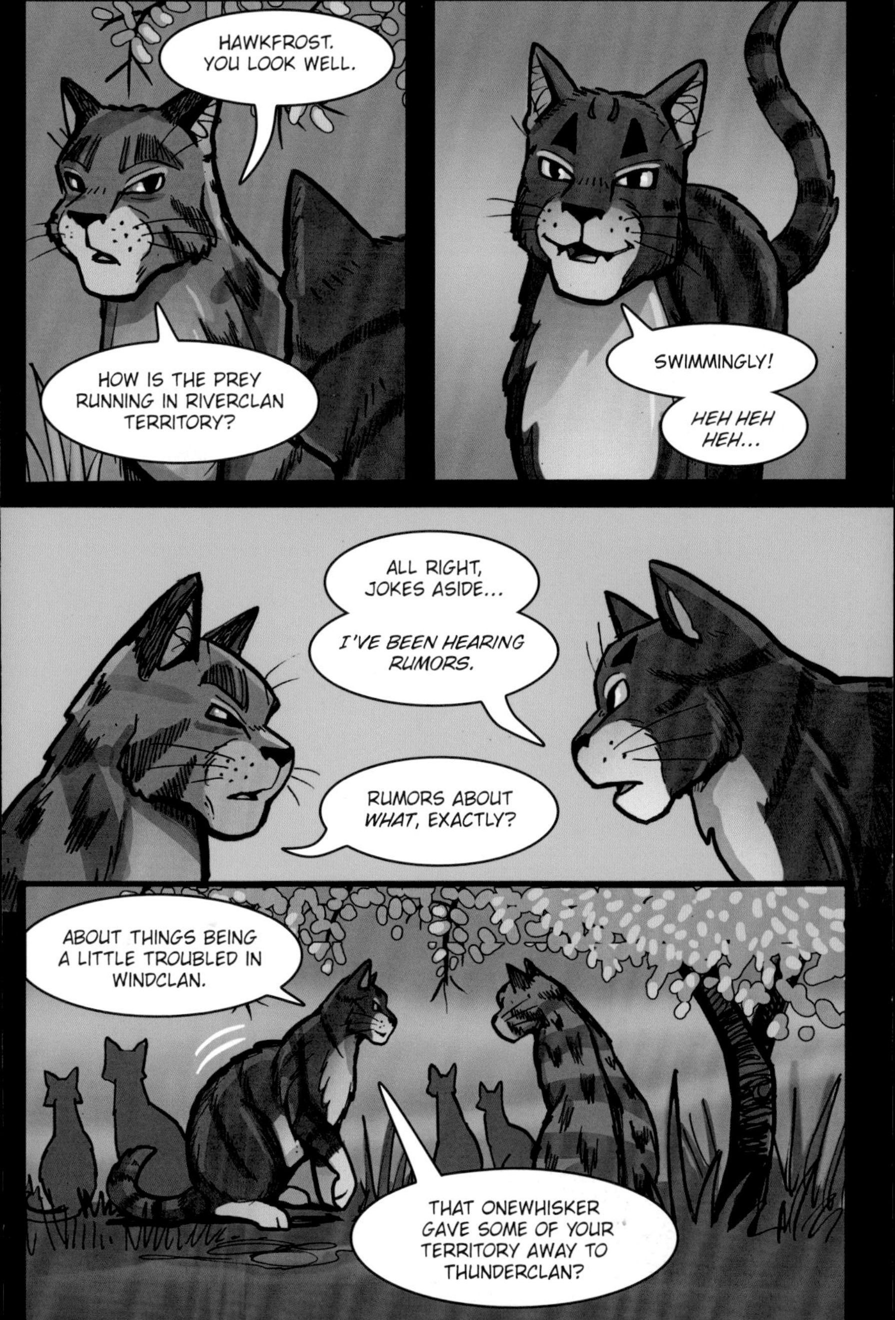
HAWKFROST. YOU LOOK WELL.
HOW IS THE PREY RUNNING IN RIVERCLAN TERRITORY?
SWIMMINGLY!
HEH HEH HEH...
ALL RIGHT, JOKES ASIDE...
I'VE BEEN HEARING RUMORS.
RUMORS ABOUT *WHAT*, EXACTLY?
ABOUT THINGS BEING A LITTLE TROUBLED IN WINDCLAN.
THAT ONEWHISKER GAVE SOME OF YOUR TERRITORY AWAY TO THUNDERCLAN?

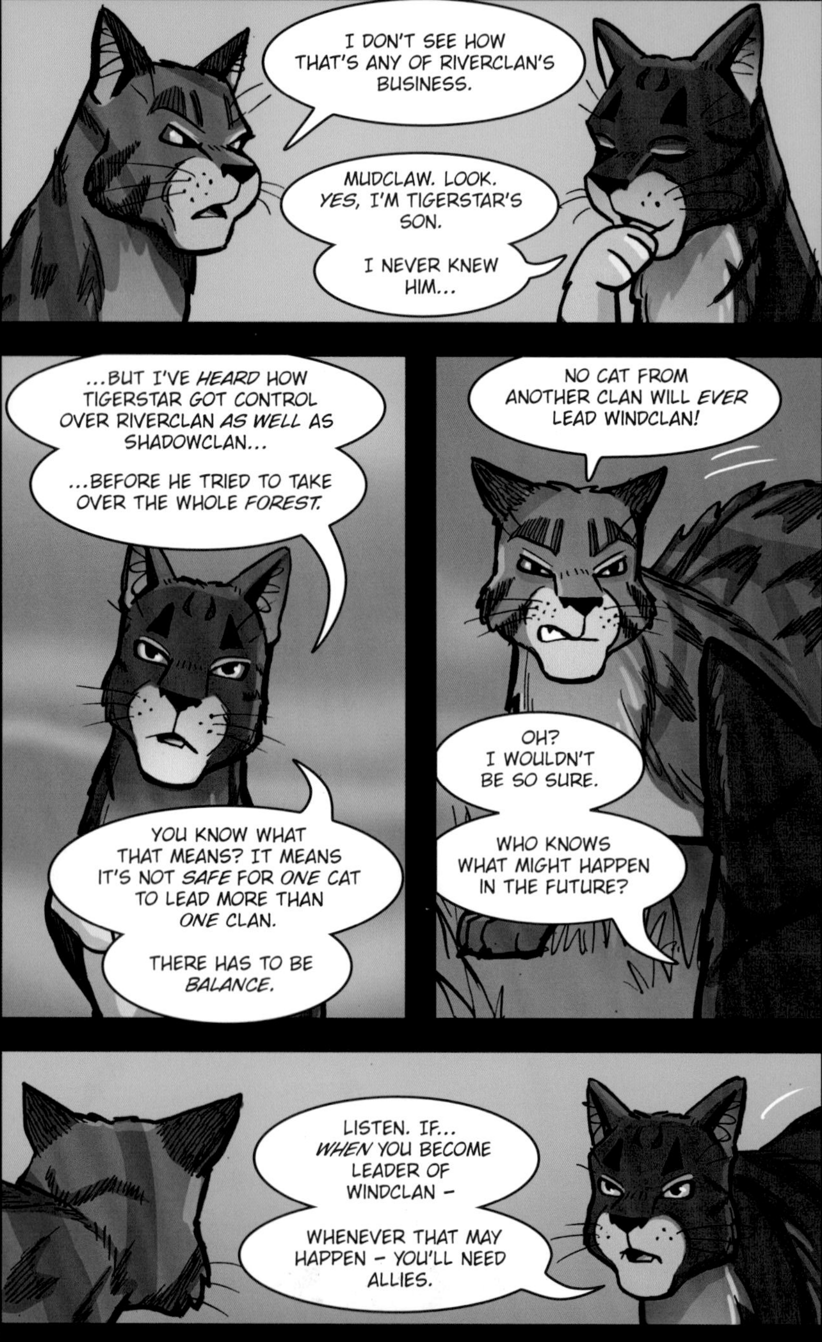

I DON'T SEE HOW THAT'S ANY OF RIVERCLAN'S BUSINESS.
MUDCLAW. LOOK. *YES*, I'M TIGERSTAR'S SON.
I NEVER KNEW HIM...
...BUT I'VE *HEARD* HOW TIGERSTAR GOT CONTROL OVER RIVERCLAN *AS WELL* AS SHADOWCLAN...
...BEFORE HE TRIED TO TAKE OVER THE WHOLE *FOREST*.
YOU KNOW WHAT THAT MEANS? IT MEANS IT'S NOT *SAFE* FOR *ONE* CAT TO LEAD MORE THAN *ONE* CLAN.
THERE HAS TO BE *BALANCE*.
NO CAT FROM ANOTHER CLAN WILL *EVER* LEAD WINDCLAN!
OH? I WOULDN'T BE SO SURE.
WHO KNOWS WHAT MIGHT HAPPEN IN THE FUTURE?
LISTEN. IF... *WHEN* YOU BECOME LEADER OF WINDCLAN –
WHENEVER THAT MAY HAPPEN – YOU'LL NEED ALLIES.

JUST THINK ABOUT IT.

"THINK ABOUT IT," HE SAYS.

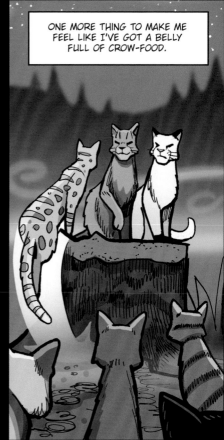

ONE MORE THING TO MAKE ME FEEL LIKE I'VE GOT A BELLY FULL OF CROW-FOOD.

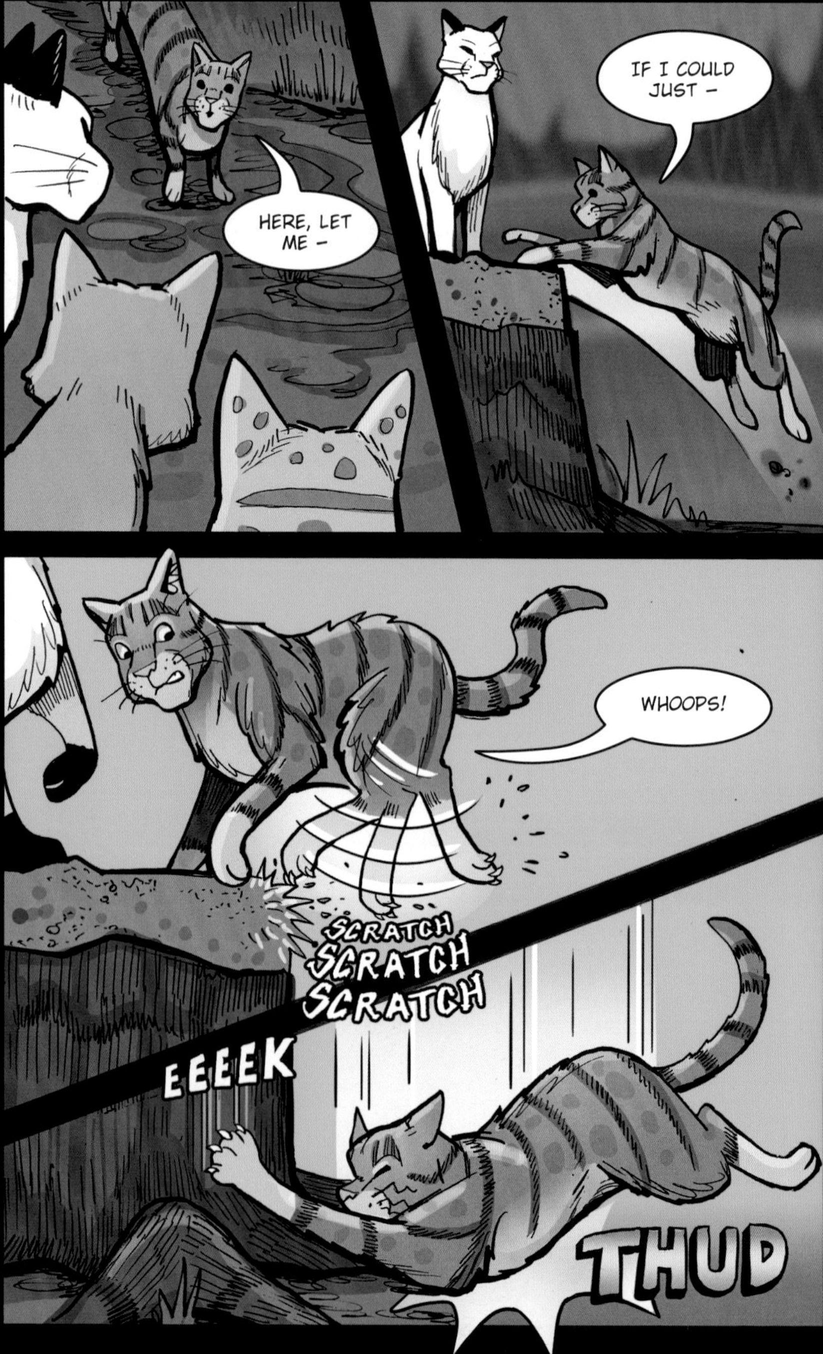
HERE, LET ME –
IF I COULD JUST –
WHOOPS!
SCRATCH SCRATCH SCRATCH
EEEEK
THUD

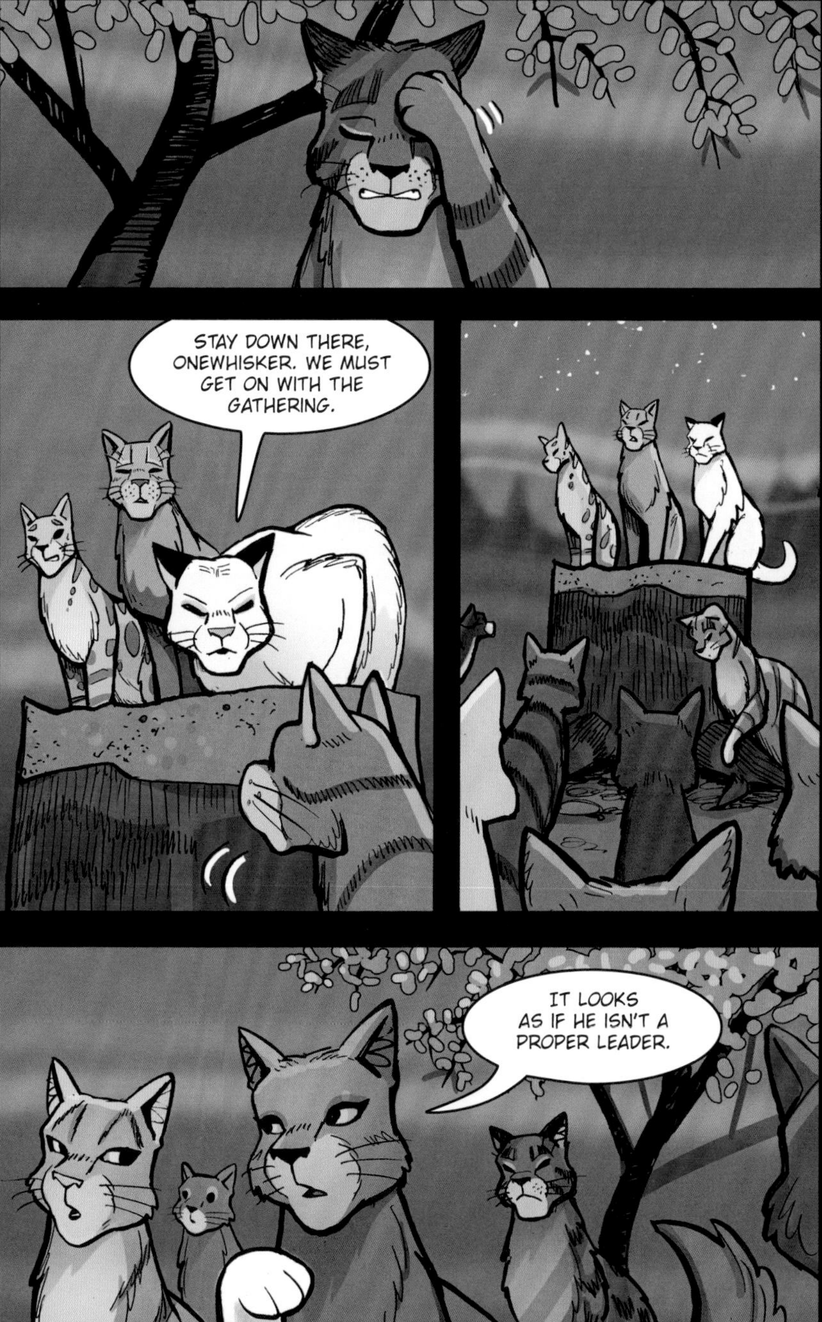
STAY DOWN THERE, ONEWHISKER. WE MUST GET ON WITH THE GATHERING.
IT LOOKS AS IF HE ISN'T A PROPER LEADER.

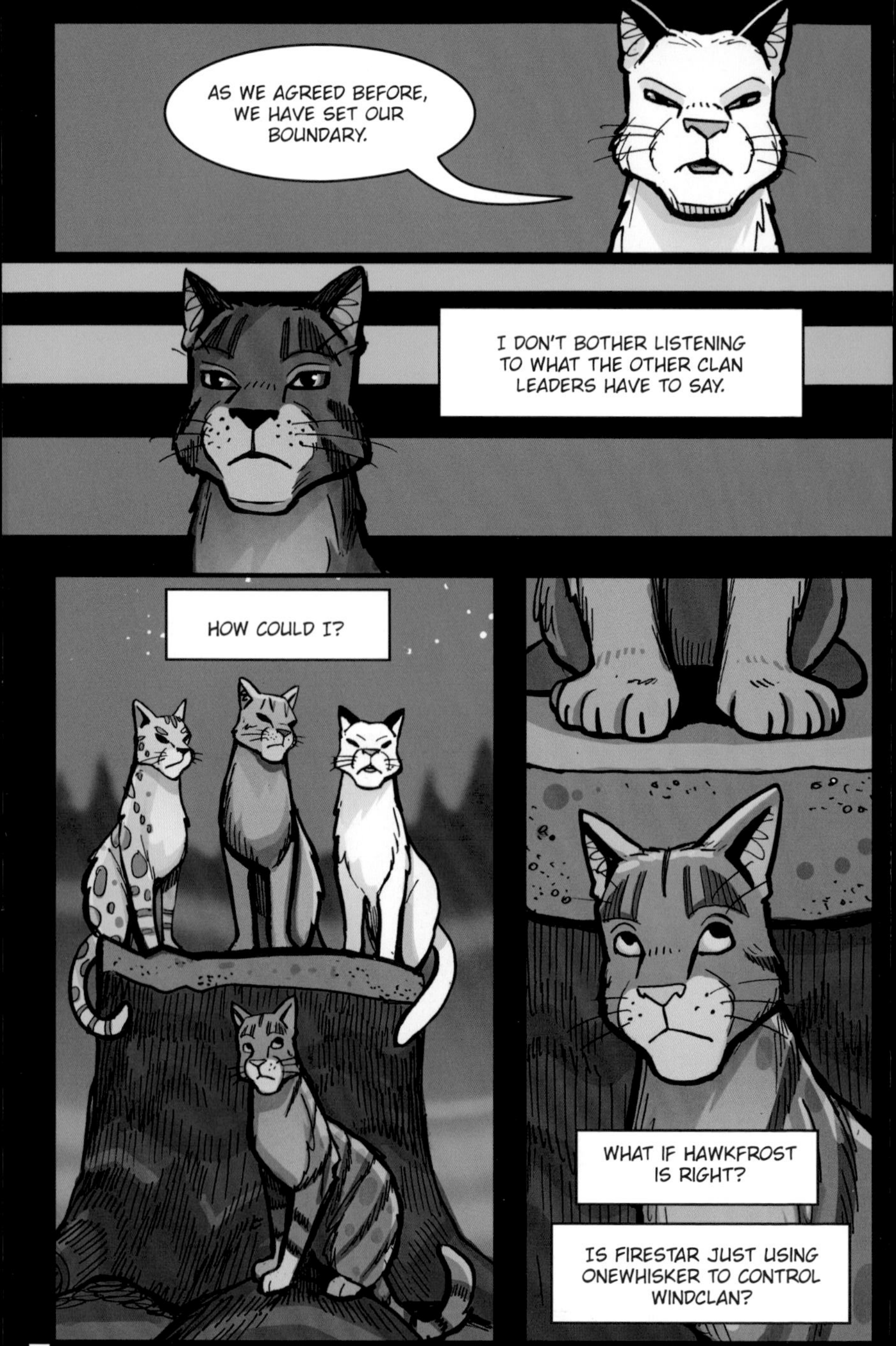
AS WE AGREED BEFORE, WE HAVE SET OUR BOUNDARY.
I DON'T BOTHER LISTENING TO WHAT THE OTHER CLAN LEADERS HAVE TO SAY.
HOW COULD I?
WHAT IF HAWKFROST IS RIGHT?
IS FIRESTAR JUST USING ONEWHISKER TO CONTROL WINDCLAN?

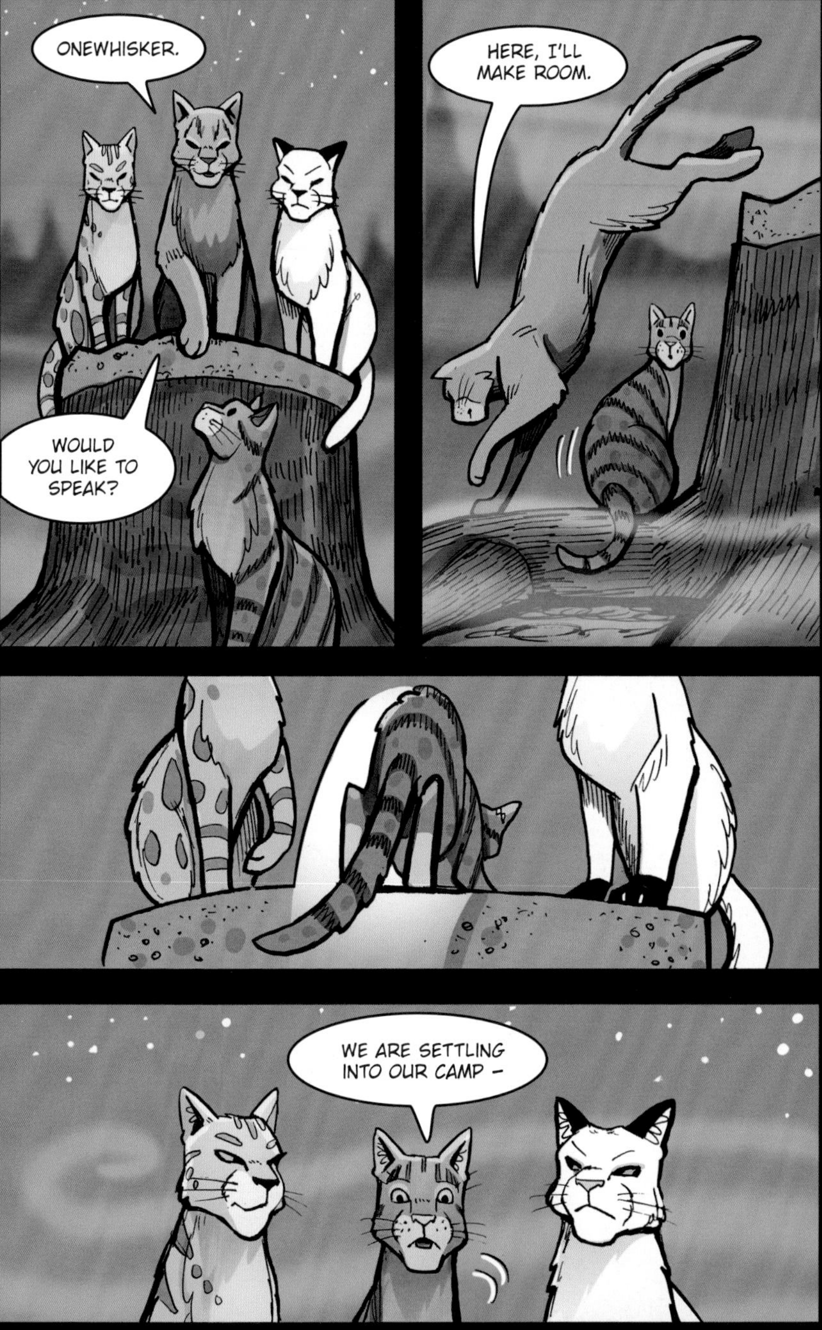
ONEWHISKER.
HERE, I'LL MAKE ROOM.
WOULD YOU LIKE TO SPEAK?
WE ARE SETTLING INTO OUR CAMP –

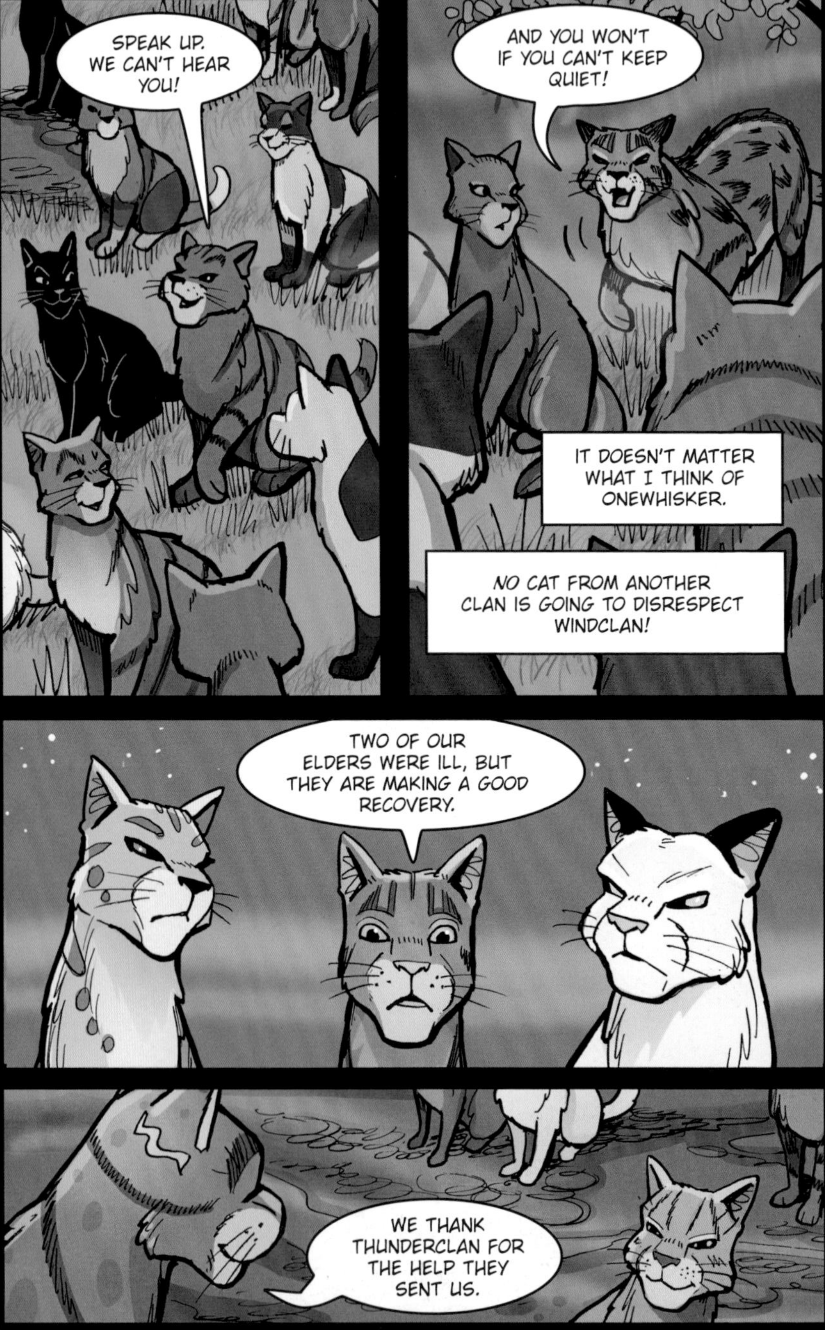
SPEAK UP. WE CAN'T HEAR YOU!
AND YOU WON'T IF YOU CAN'T KEEP QUIET!
IT DOESN'T MATTER WHAT I THINK OF ONEWHISKER.
NO CAT FROM ANOTHER CLAN IS GOING TO DISRESPECT WINDCLAN!
TWO OF OUR ELDERS WERE ILL, BUT THEY ARE MAKING A GOOD RECOVERY.
WE THANK THUNDERCLAN FOR THE HELP THEY SENT US.

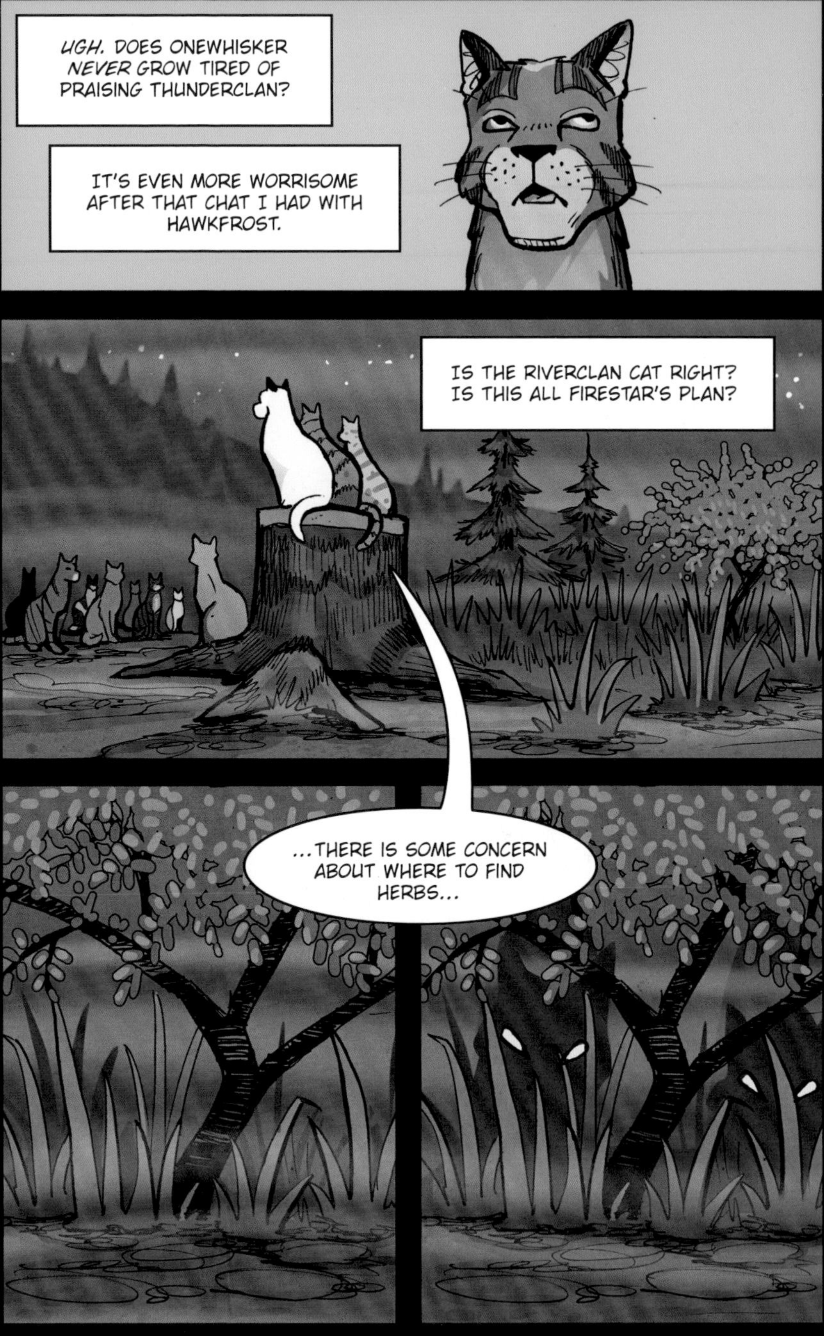
UGH. DOES ONEWHISKER NEVER GROW TIRED OF PRAISING THUNDERCLAN?
IT'S EVEN MORE WORRISOME AFTER THAT CHAT I HAD WITH HAWKFROST.
IS THE RIVERCLAN CAT RIGHT? IS THIS ALL FIRESTAR'S PLAN?
...THERE IS SOME CONCERN ABOUT WHERE TO FIND HERBS...

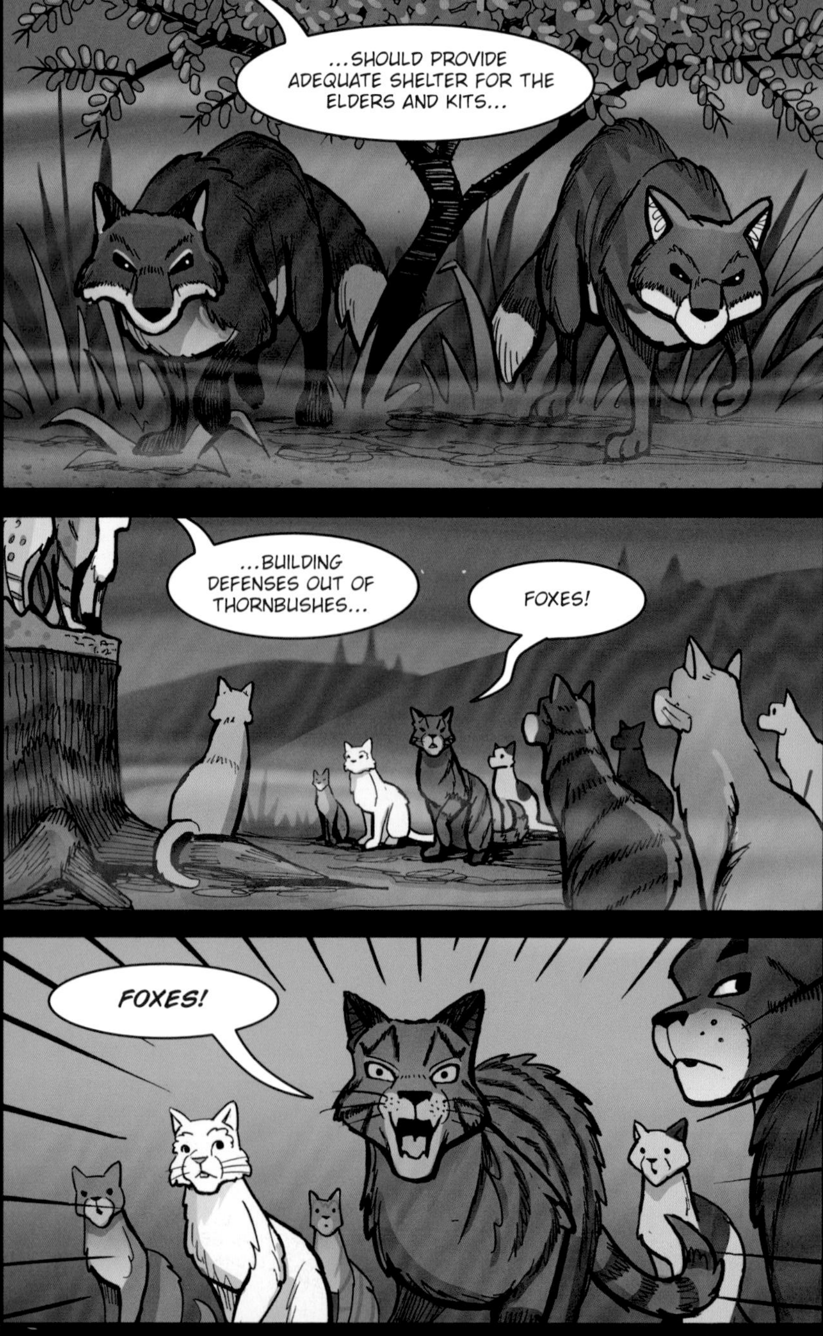
...SHOULD PROVIDE ADEQUATE SHELTER FOR THE ELDERS AND KITS...
...BUILDING DEFENSES OUT OF THORNBUSHES...
FOXES!
FOXES!

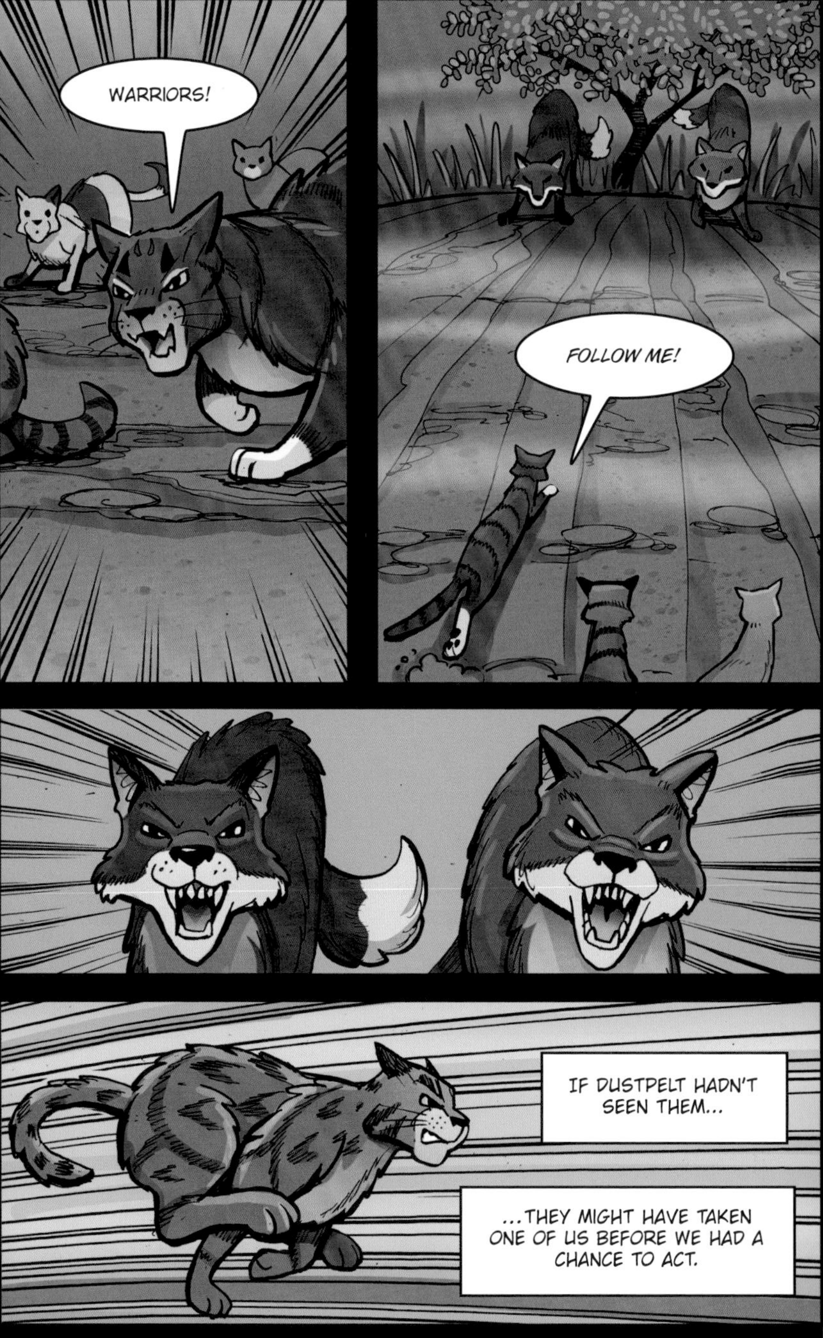
WARRIORS!
FOLLOW ME!
IF DUSTPELT HADN'T SEEN THEM...
...THEY MIGHT HAVE TAKEN ONE OF US BEFORE WE HAD A CHANCE TO ACT.

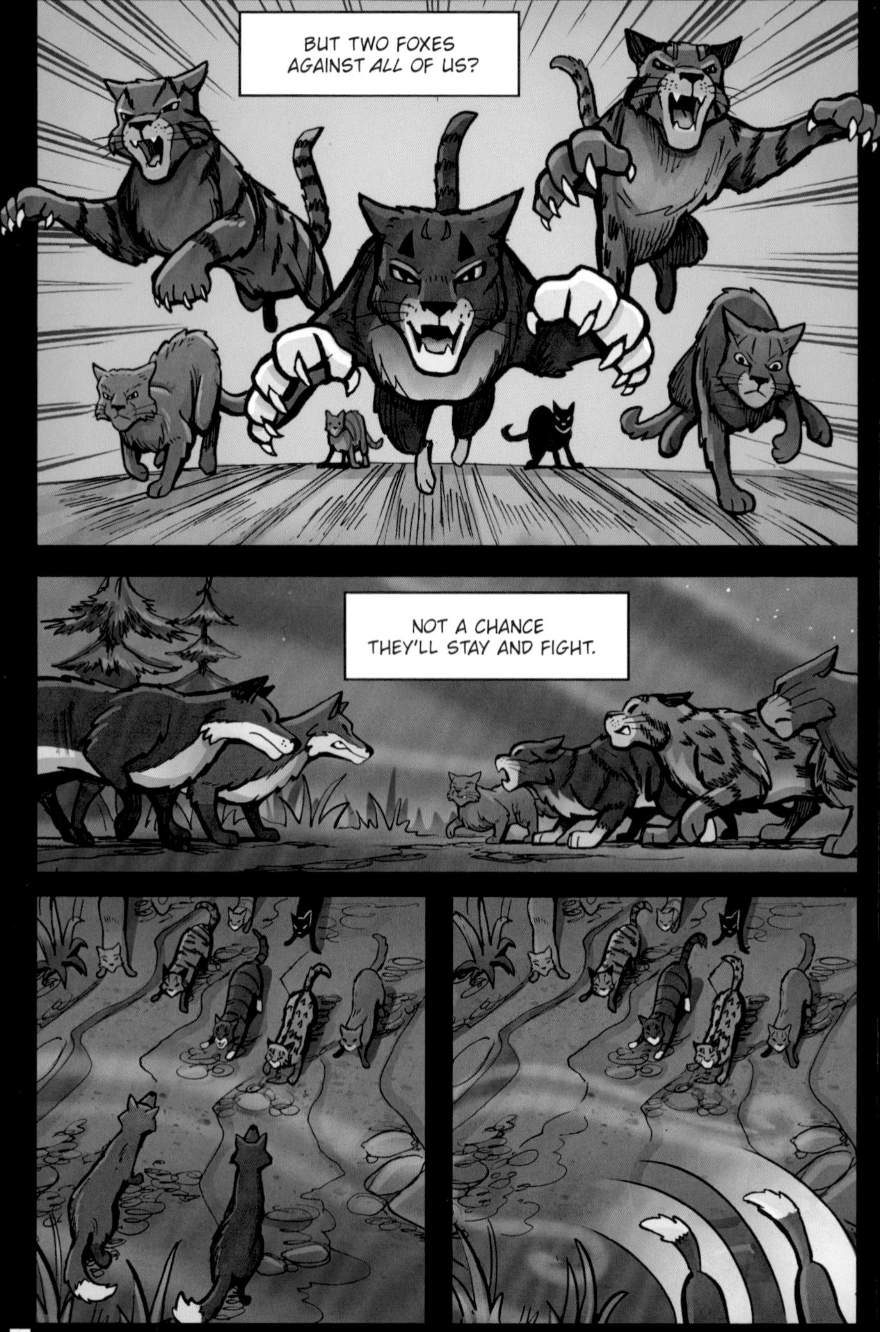
BUT TWO FOXES
AGAINST ALL OF US?
NOT A CHANCE
THEY'LL STAY AND FIGHT.

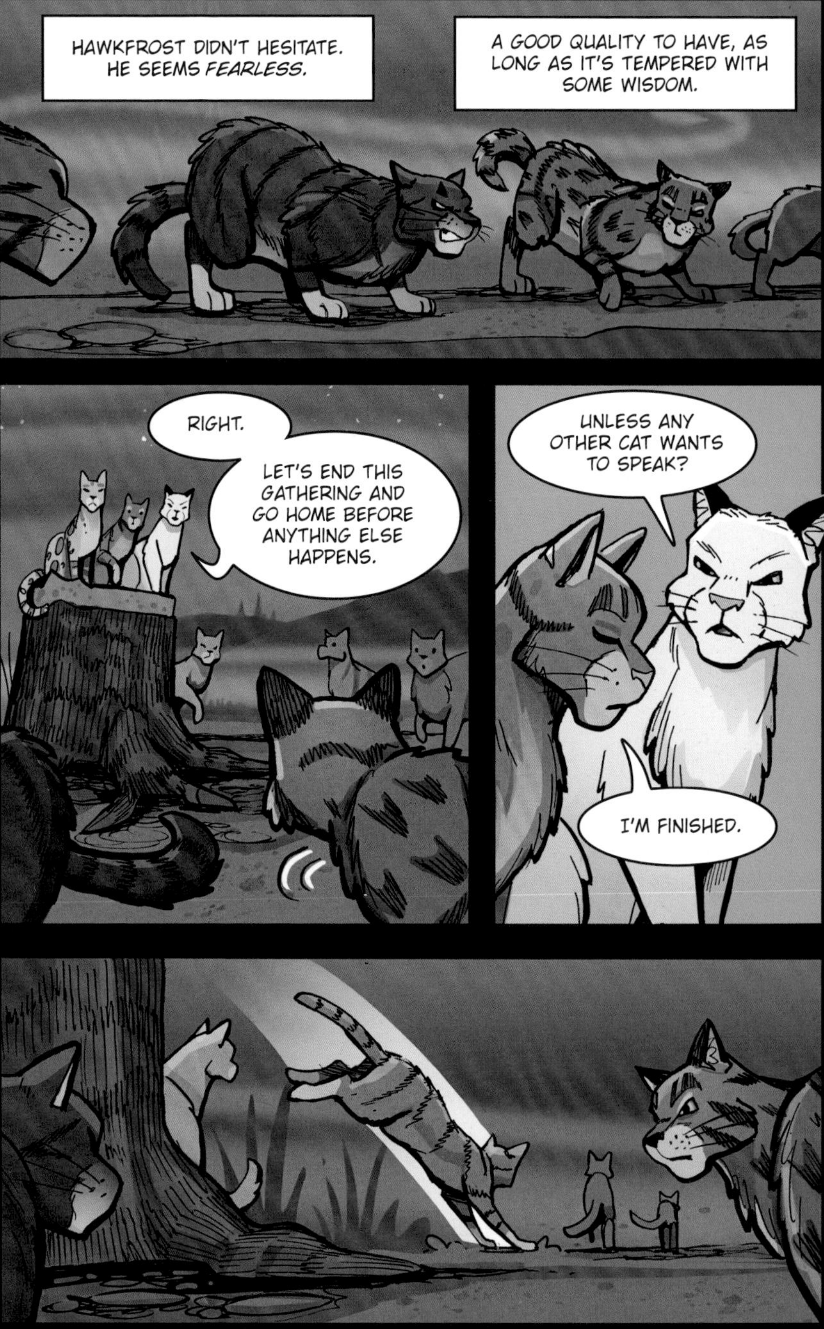
HAWKFROST DIDN'T HESITATE. HE SEEMS *FEARLESS.*
A GOOD QUALITY TO HAVE, AS LONG AS IT'S TEMPERED WITH SOME WISDOM.
RIGHT.
LET'S END THIS GATHERING AND GO HOME BEFORE ANYTHING ELSE HAPPENS.
UNLESS ANY OTHER CAT WANTS TO SPEAK?
I'M FINISHED.

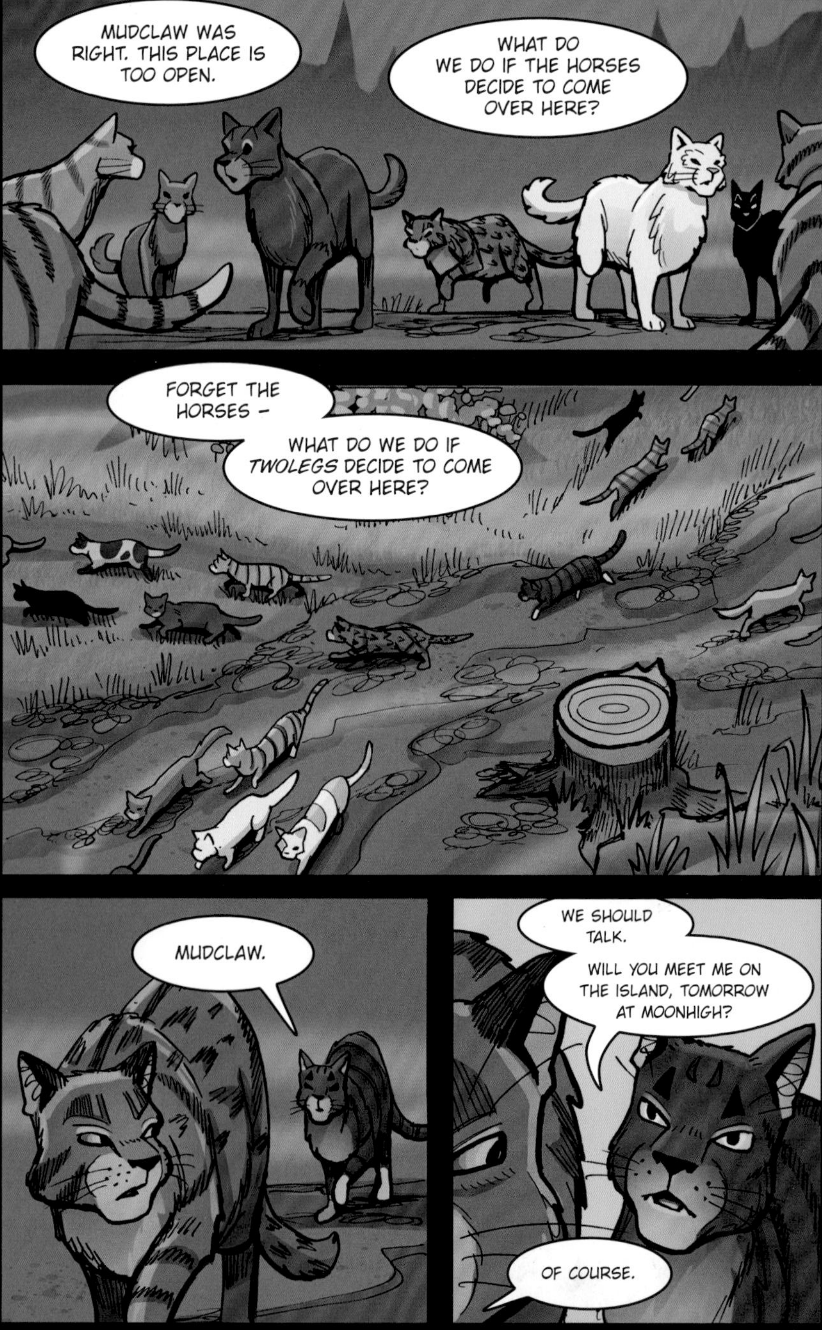
MUDCLAW WAS RIGHT. THIS PLACE IS TOO OPEN.
WHAT DO WE DO IF THE HORSES DECIDE TO COME OVER HERE?
FORGET THE HORSES –
WHAT DO WE DO IF *TWOLEGS* DECIDE TO COME OVER HERE?
MUDCLAW.
WE SHOULD TALK.
WILL YOU MEET ME ON THE ISLAND, TOMORROW AT MOONHIGH?
OF COURSE.

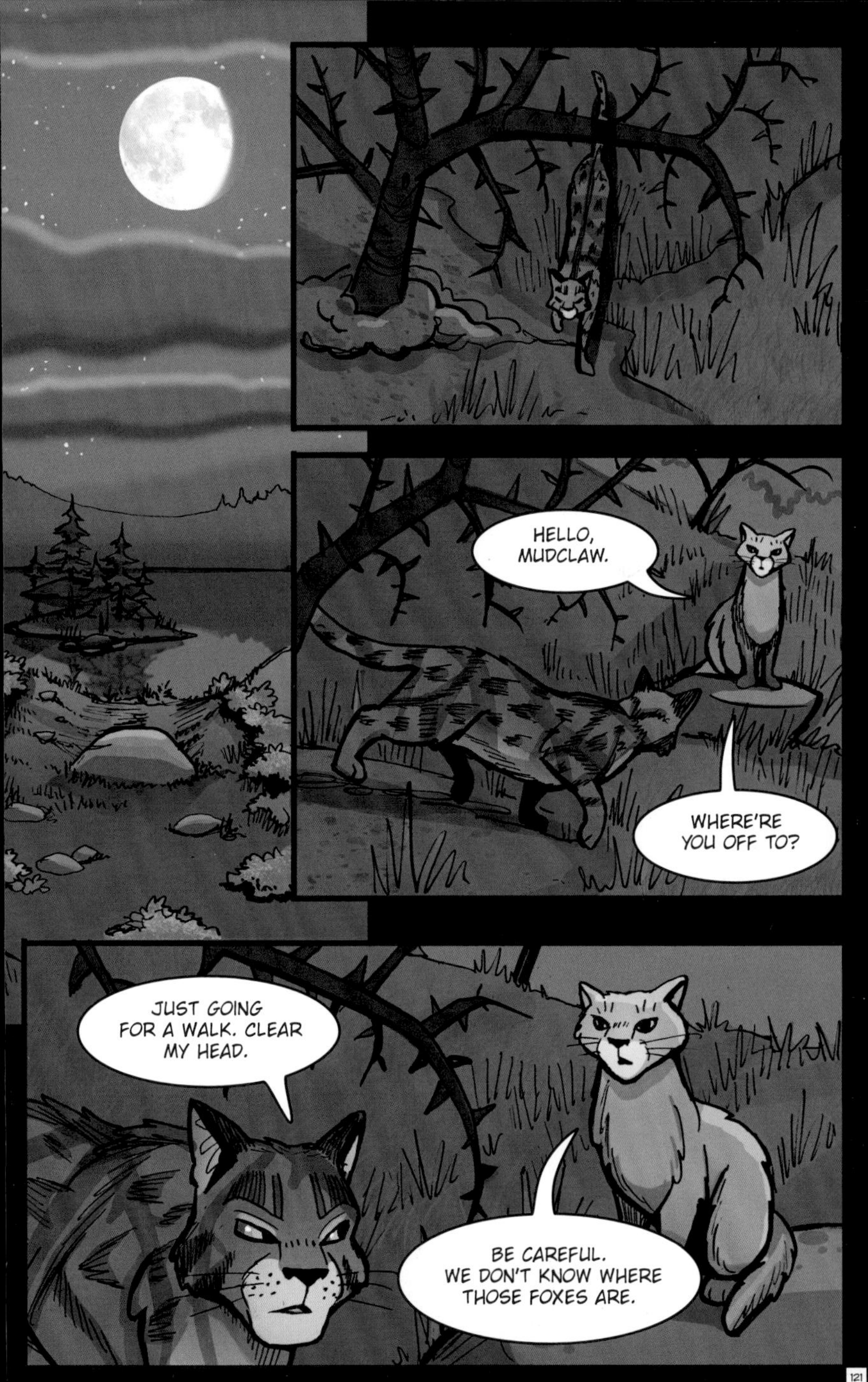
HELLO, MUDCLAW.
WHERE'RE YOU OFF TO?
JUST GOING FOR A WALK. CLEAR MY HEAD.
BE CAREFUL. WE DON'T KNOW WHERE THOSE FOXES ARE.

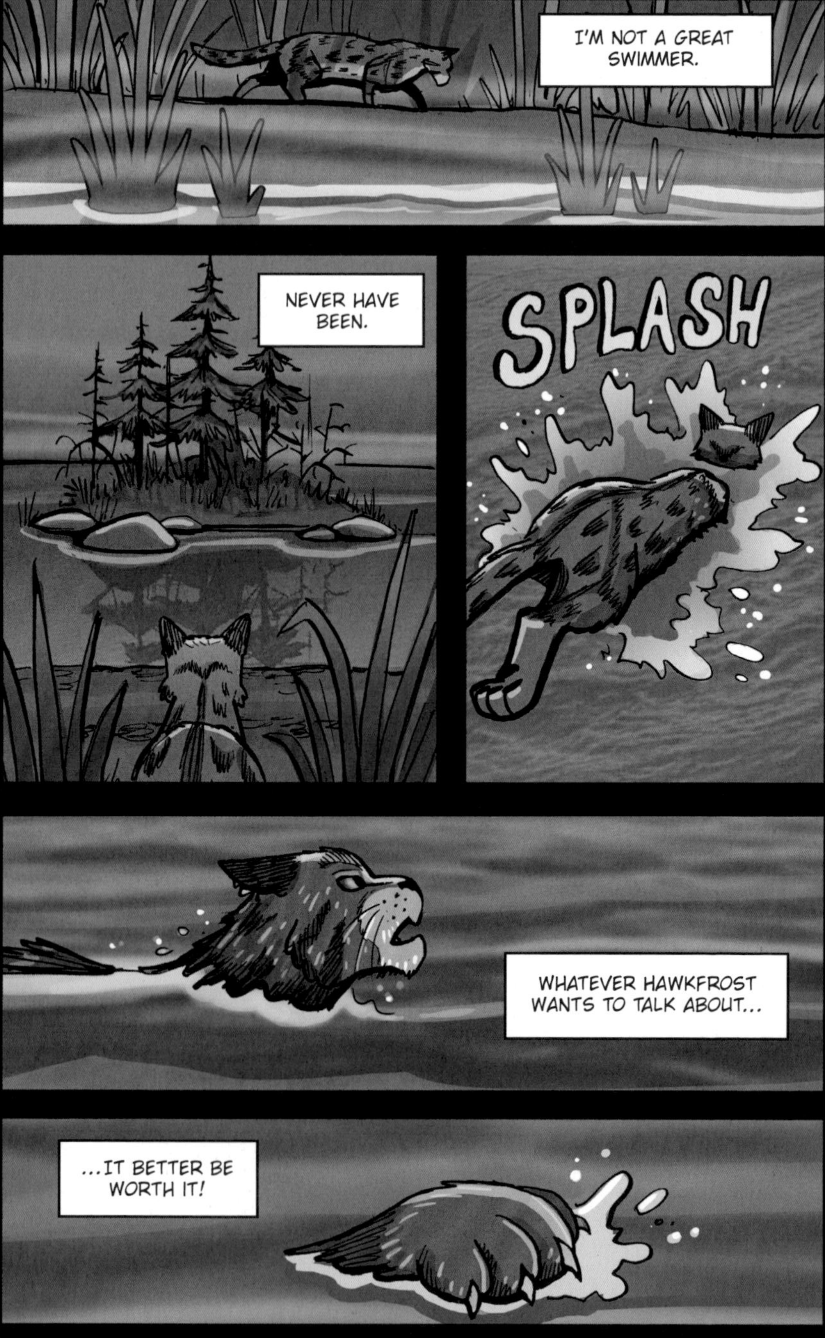
I'M NOT A GREAT SWIMMER.
NEVER HAVE BEEN.
SPLASH
WHATEVER HAWKFROST WANTS TO TALK ABOUT...
...IT BETTER BE WORTH IT!

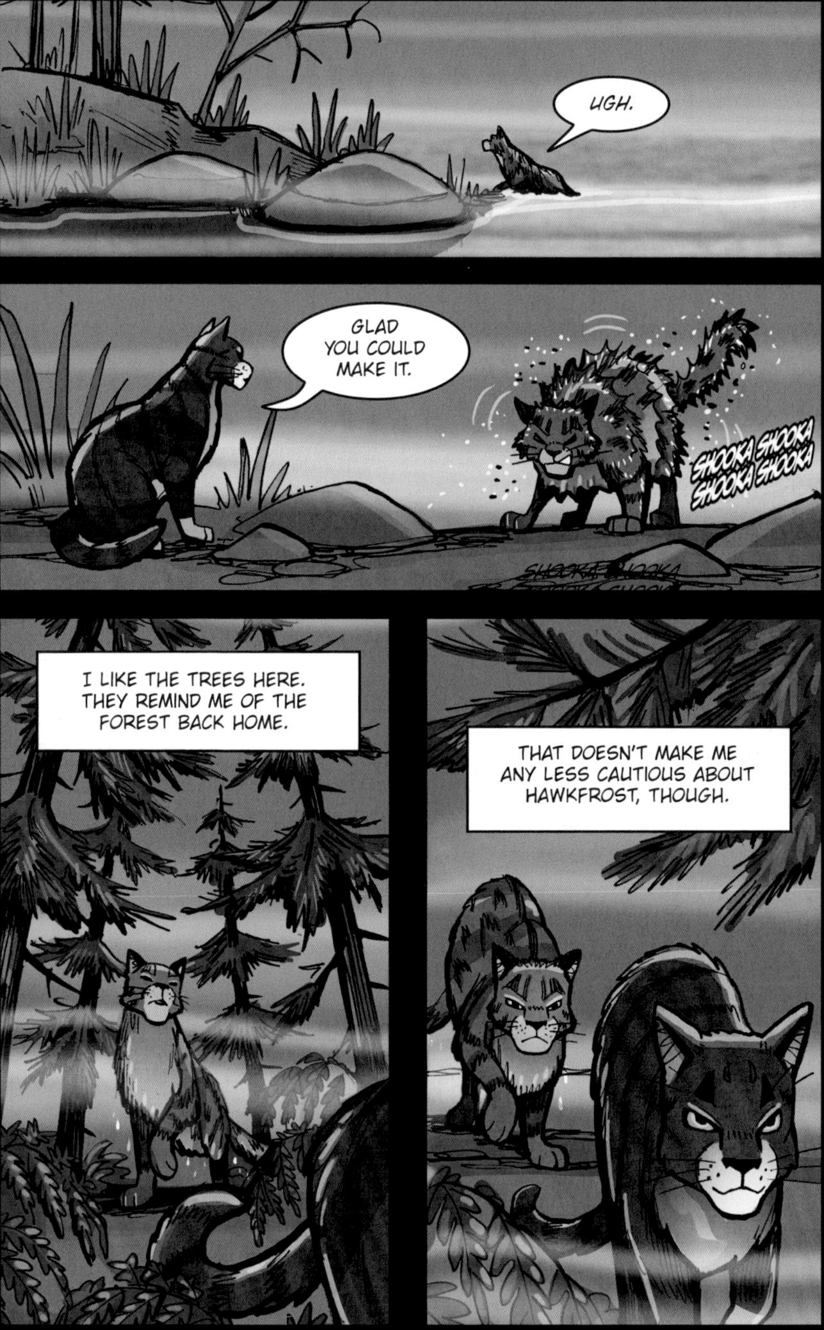
UGH.
GLAD YOU COULD MAKE IT.
SHOOKA SHOOKA SHOOKA SHOOKA
I LIKE THE TREES HERE. THEY REMIND ME OF THE FOREST BACK HOME.
THAT DOESN'T MAKE ME ANY LESS CAUTIOUS ABOUT HAWKFROST, THOUGH.

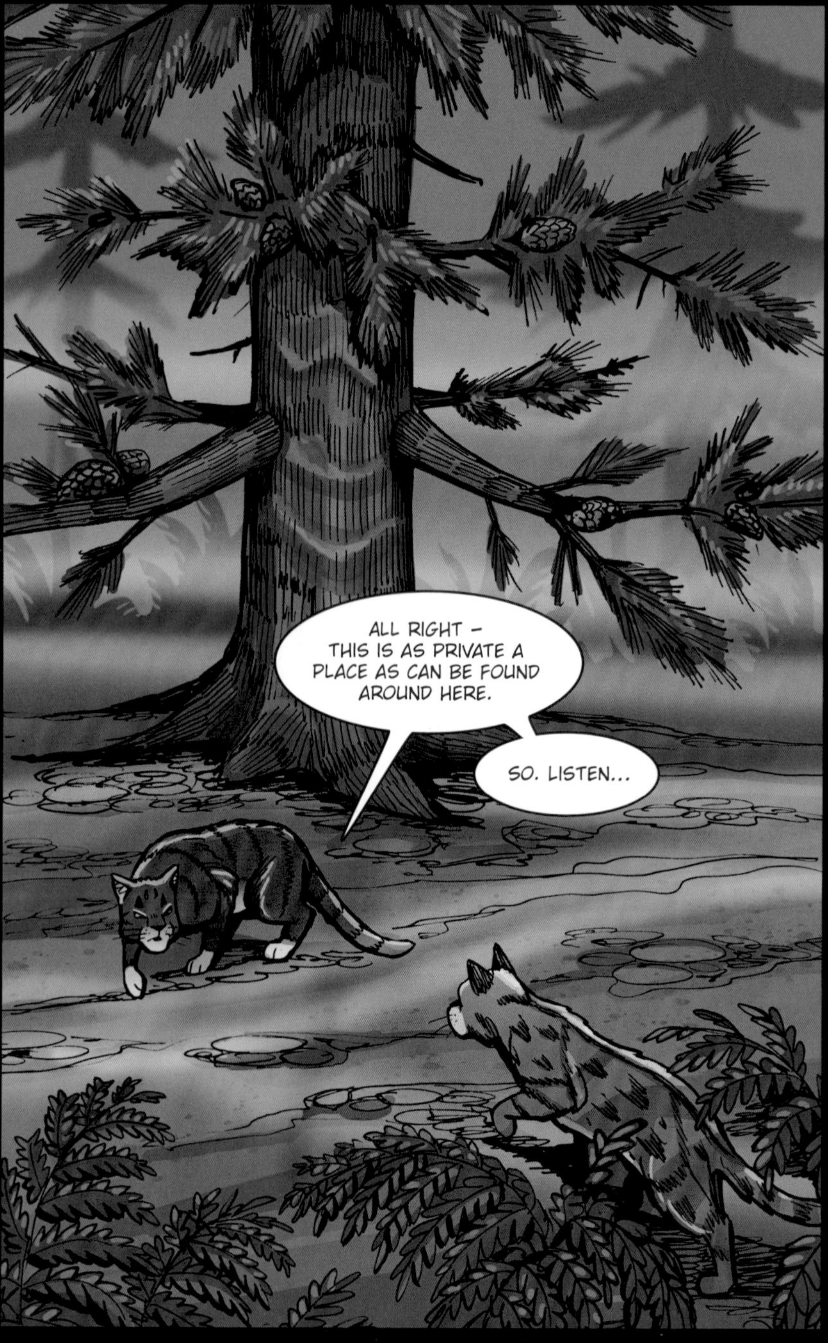
ALL RIGHT – THIS IS AS PRIVATE A PLACE AS CAN BE FOUND AROUND HERE.
SO. LISTEN...

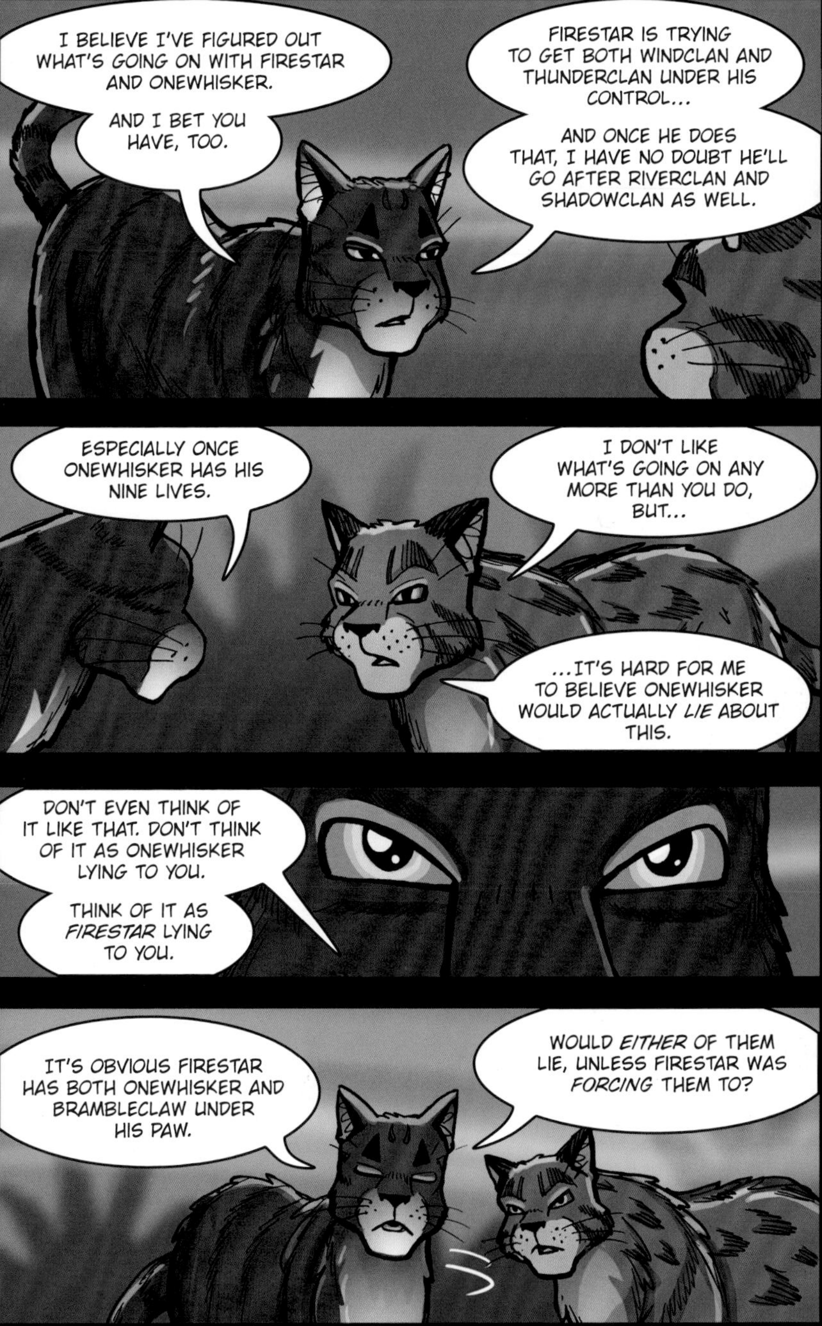
I BELIEVE I'VE FIGURED OUT WHAT'S GOING ON WITH FIRESTAR AND ONEWHISKER.
AND I BET YOU HAVE, TOO.
FIRESTAR IS TRYING TO GET BOTH WINDCLAN AND THUNDERCLAN UNDER HIS CONTROL...
AND ONCE HE DOES THAT, I HAVE NO DOUBT HE'LL GO AFTER RIVERCLAN AND SHADOWCLAN AS WELL.
ESPECIALLY ONCE ONEWHISKER HAS HIS NINE LIVES.
I DON'T LIKE WHAT'S GOING ON ANY MORE THAN YOU DO, BUT...
...IT'S HARD FOR ME TO BELIEVE ONEWHISKER WOULD ACTUALLY *LIE* ABOUT THIS.
DON'T EVEN THINK OF IT LIKE THAT. DON'T THINK OF IT AS ONEWHISKER LYING TO YOU.
THINK OF IT AS *FIRESTAR* LYING TO YOU.
IT'S OBVIOUS FIRESTAR HAS BOTH ONEWHISKER AND BRAMBLECLAW UNDER HIS PAW.
WOULD *EITHER* OF THEM LIE, UNLESS FIRESTAR WAS *FORCING* THEM TO?

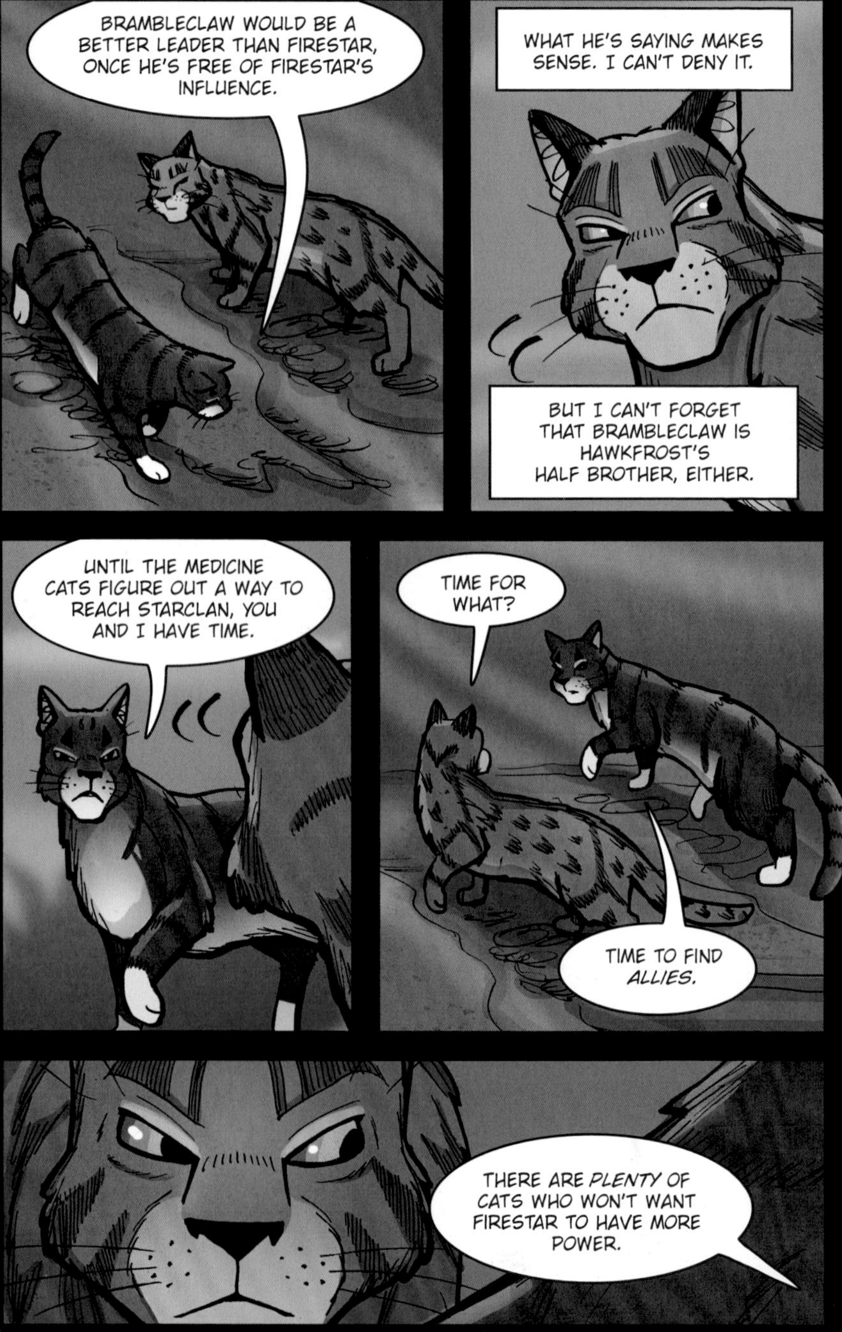
BRAMBLECLAW WOULD BE A BETTER LEADER THAN FIRESTAR, ONCE HE'S FREE OF FIRESTAR'S INFLUENCE.
WHAT HE'S SAYING MAKES SENSE. I CAN'T DENY IT.
BUT I CAN'T FORGET THAT BRAMBLECLAW IS HAWKFROST'S HALF BROTHER, EITHER.
UNTIL THE MEDICINE CATS FIGURE OUT A WAY TO REACH STARCLAN, YOU AND I HAVE TIME.
TIME FOR WHAT?
TIME TO FIND *ALLIES.*
THERE ARE *PLENTY* OF CATS WHO WON'T WANT FIRESTAR TO HAVE MORE POWER.

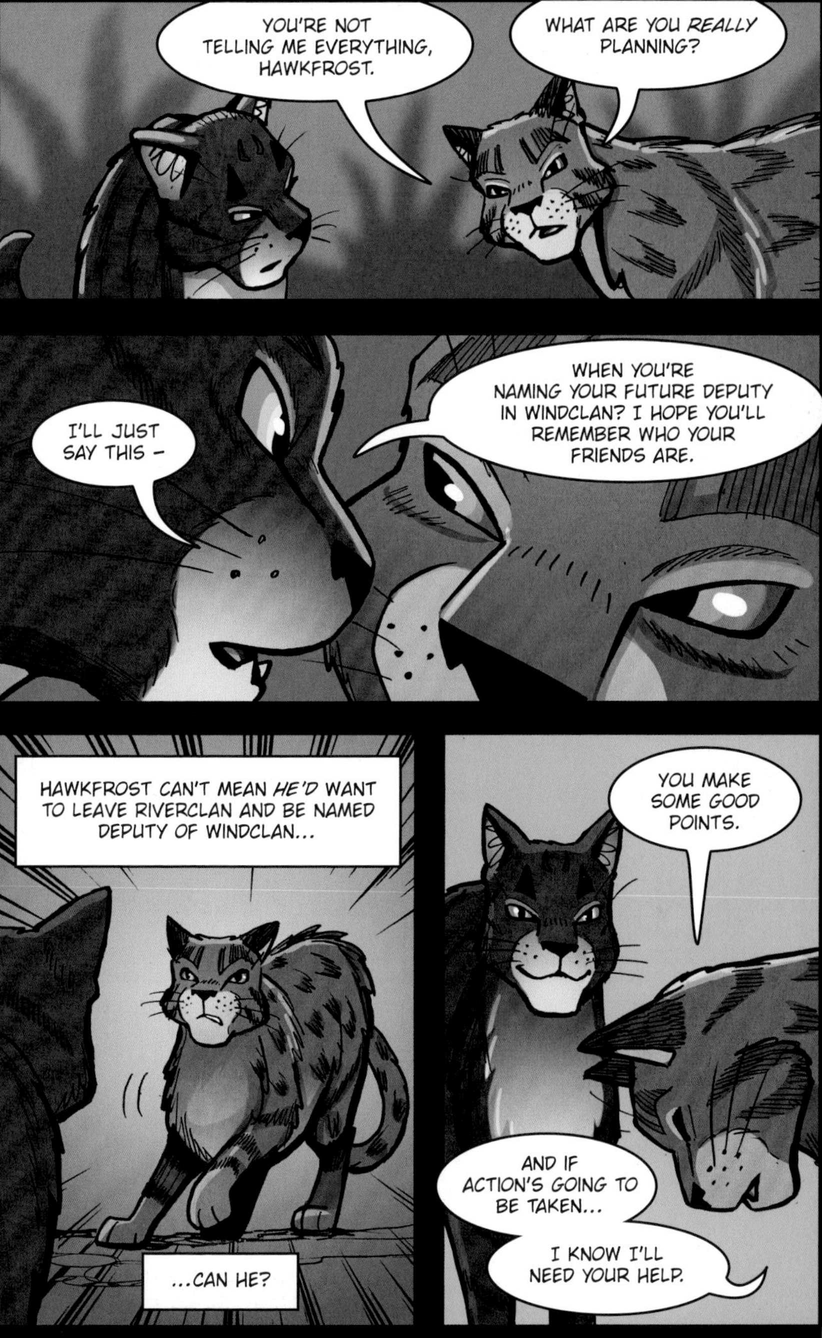
YOU'RE NOT TELLING ME EVERYTHING, HAWKFROST.
WHAT ARE YOU *REALLY* PLANNING?
I'LL JUST SAY THIS –
WHEN YOU'RE NAMING YOUR FUTURE DEPUTY IN WINDCLAN? I HOPE YOU'LL REMEMBER WHO YOUR FRIENDS ARE.
HAWKFROST CAN'T MEAN *HE'D* WANT TO LEAVE RIVERCLAN AND BE NAMED DEPUTY OF WINDCLAN...
...CAN HE?
YOU MAKE SOME GOOD POINTS.
AND IF ACTION'S GOING TO BE TAKEN...
I KNOW I'LL NEED YOUR HELP.

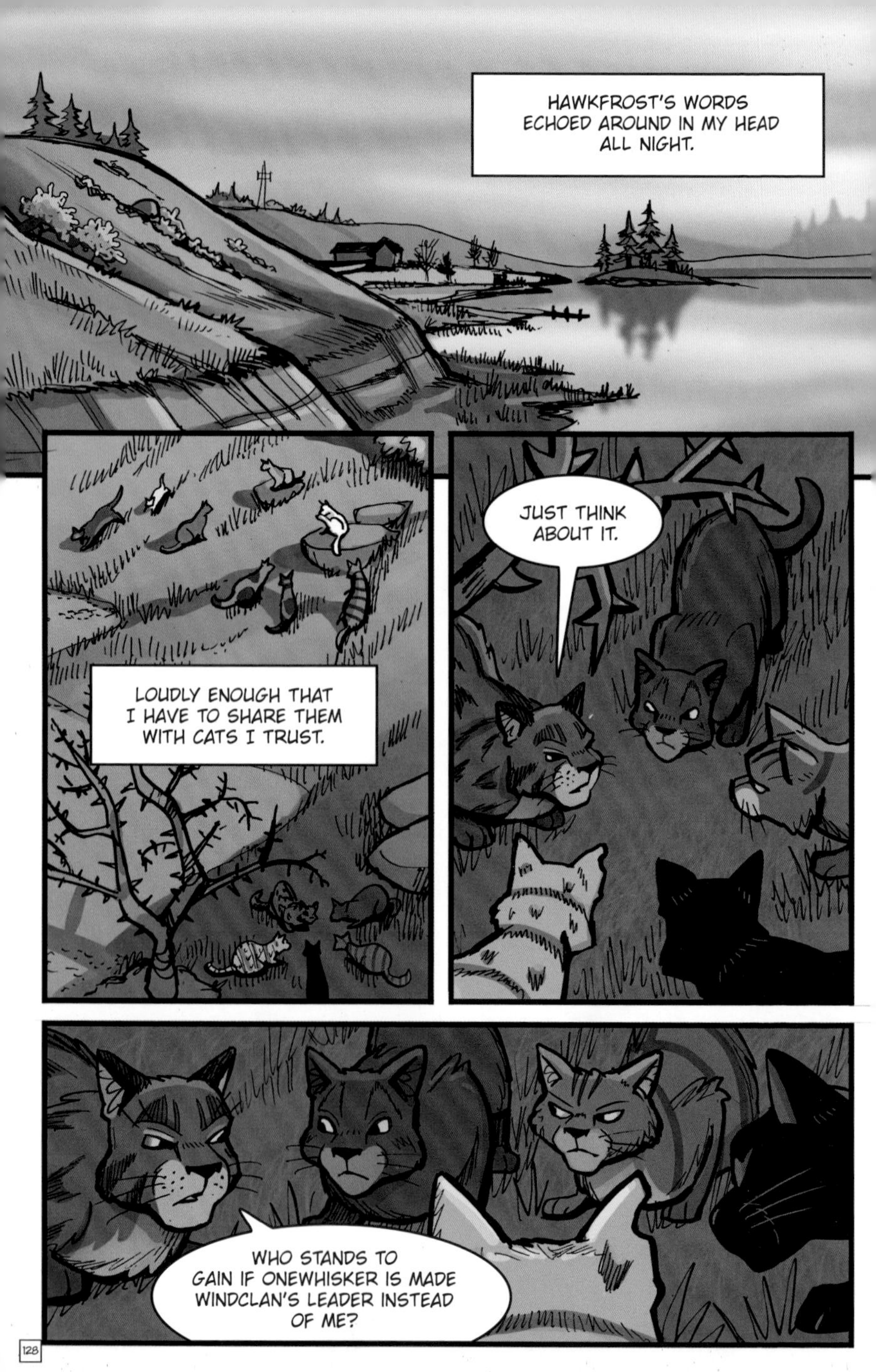
HAWKFROST'S WORDS ECHOED AROUND IN MY HEAD ALL NIGHT.
LOUDLY ENOUGH THAT I HAVE TO SHARE THEM WITH CATS I TRUST.
JUST THINK ABOUT IT.
WHO STANDS TO GAIN IF ONEWHISKER IS MADE WINDCLAN'S LEADER INSTEAD OF ME?

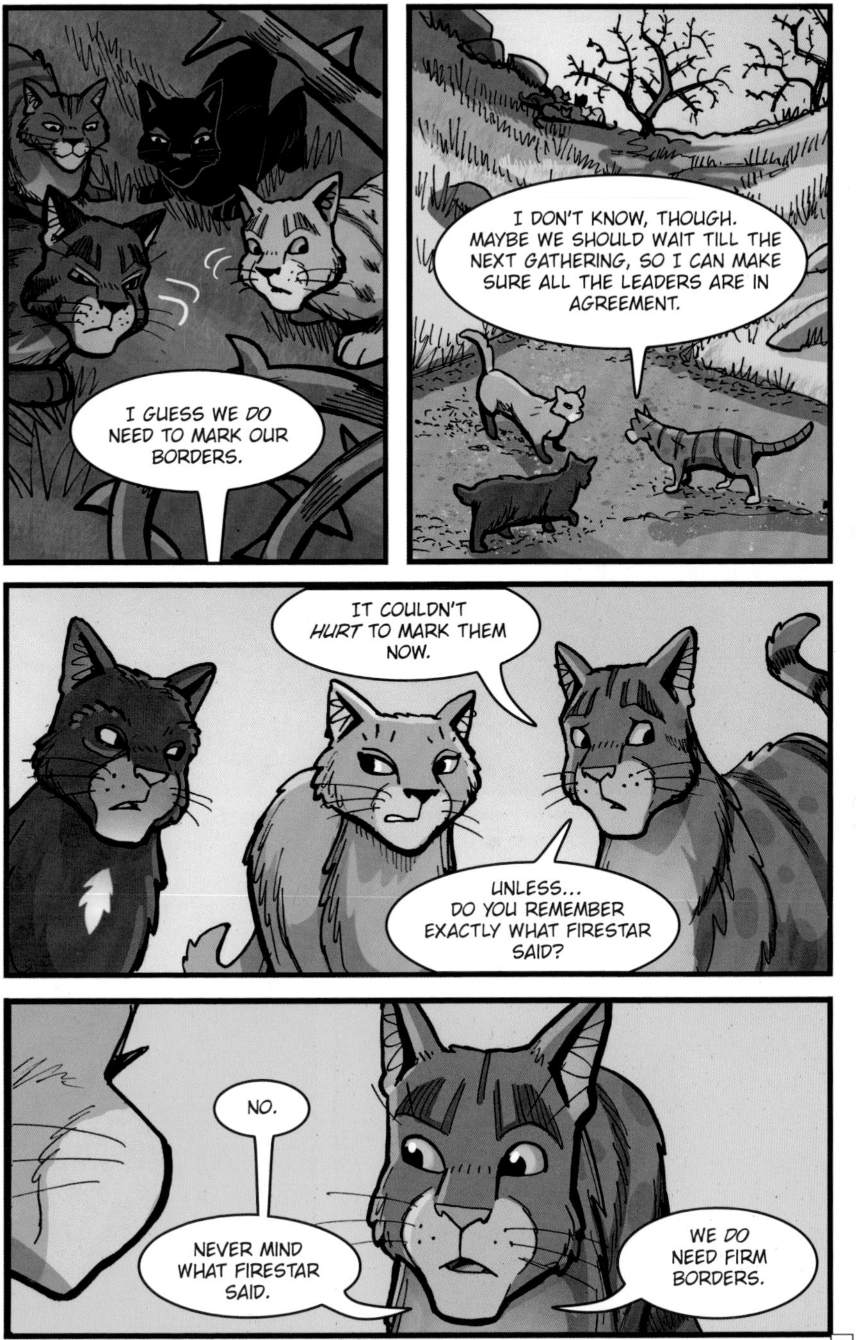
I GUESS WE *DO* NEED TO MARK OUR BORDERS.
I DON'T KNOW, THOUGH. MAYBE WE SHOULD WAIT TILL THE NEXT GATHERING, SO I CAN MAKE SURE ALL THE LEADERS ARE IN AGREEMENT.
IT COULDN'T *HURT* TO MARK THEM NOW.
UNLESS... DO YOU REMEMBER EXACTLY WHAT FIRESTAR SAID?
NO.
NEVER MIND WHAT FIRESTAR SAID.
WE *DO* NEED FIRM BORDERS.

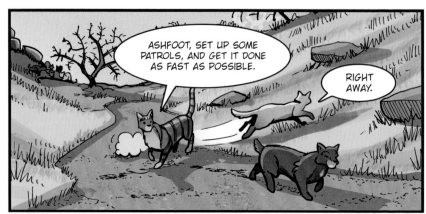

ASHFOOT, SET UP SOME PATROLS, AND GET IT DONE AS FAST AS POSSIBLE.

RIGHT AWAY.

EXACTLY HOW CERTAIN ARE WE THAT TALLSTAR CHOSE *HIM* TO LEAD US?

HOW CERTAIN ARE WE THAT THAT WASN'T JUST WHAT FIRESTAR *TOLD* US?

I DON'T LIKE YOUR WORDS, MUDCLAW, AND I DON'T LIKE THE THOUGHTS BEHIND THEM.

WHATEVER IT IS YOU'RE PLANNING, I WANT NO PART OF IT.

NEVER MIND HIM.

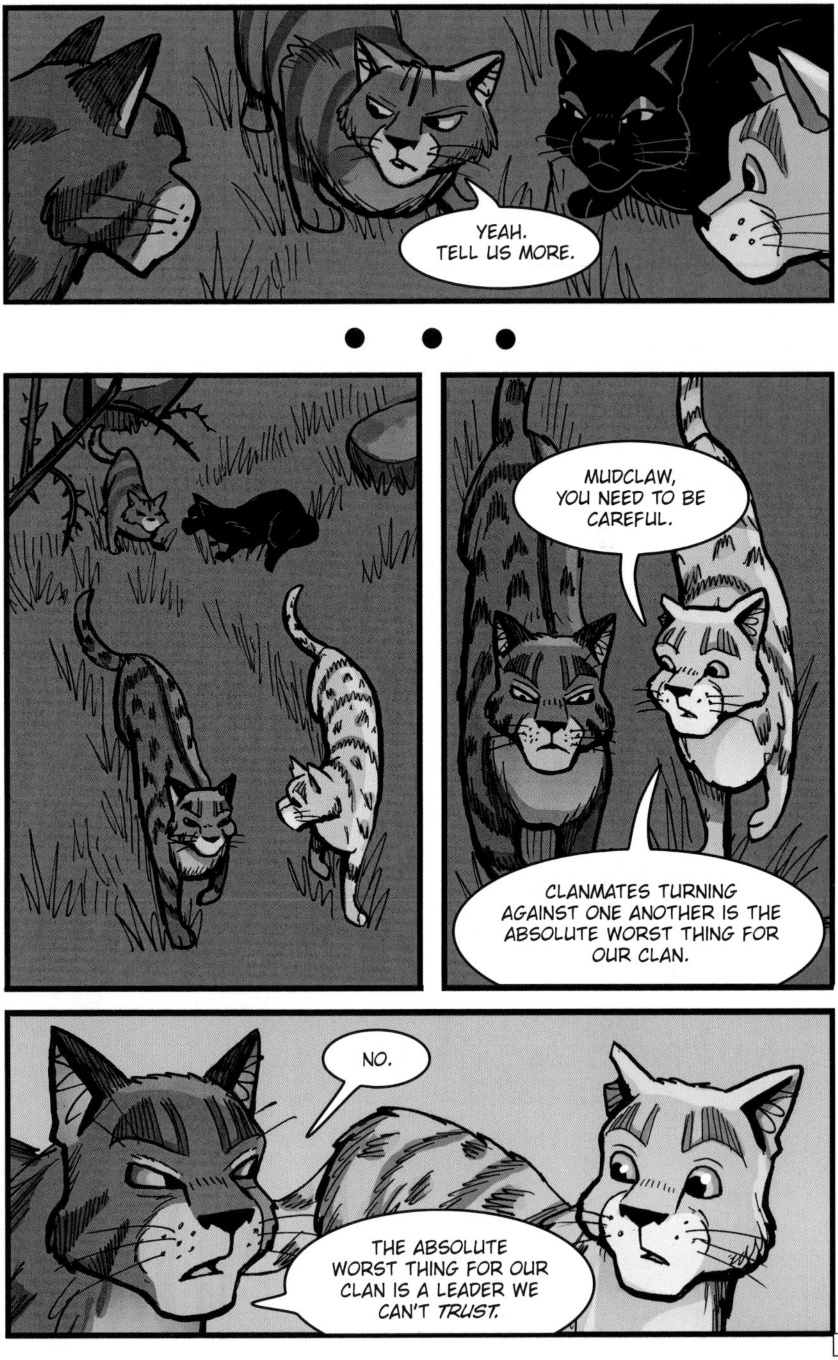
YEAH. TELL US MORE.
MUDCLAW, YOU NEED TO BE CAREFUL.
CLANMATES TURNING AGAINST ONE ANOTHER IS THE ABSOLUTE WORST THING FOR OUR CLAN.
NO.
THE ABSOLUTE WORST THING FOR OUR CLAN IS A LEADER WE CAN'T *TRUST.*

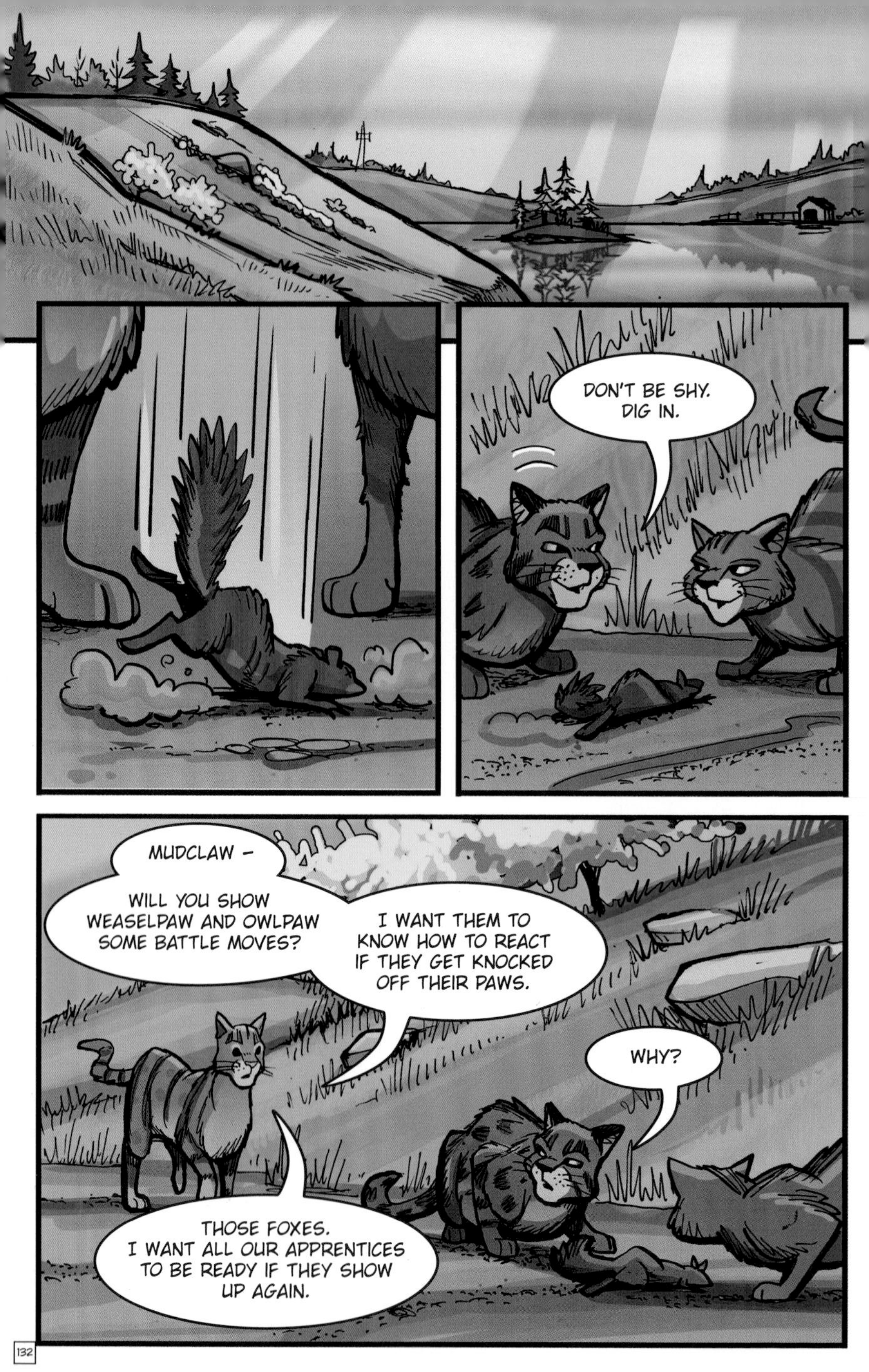
DON'T BE SHY. DIG IN.
MUDCLAW –
WILL YOU SHOW WEASELPAW AND OWLPAW SOME BATTLE MOVES?
I WANT THEM TO KNOW HOW TO REACT IF THEY GET KNOCKED OFF THEIR PAWS.
WHY?
THOSE FOXES. I WANT ALL OUR APPRENTICES TO BE READY IF THEY SHOW UP AGAIN.

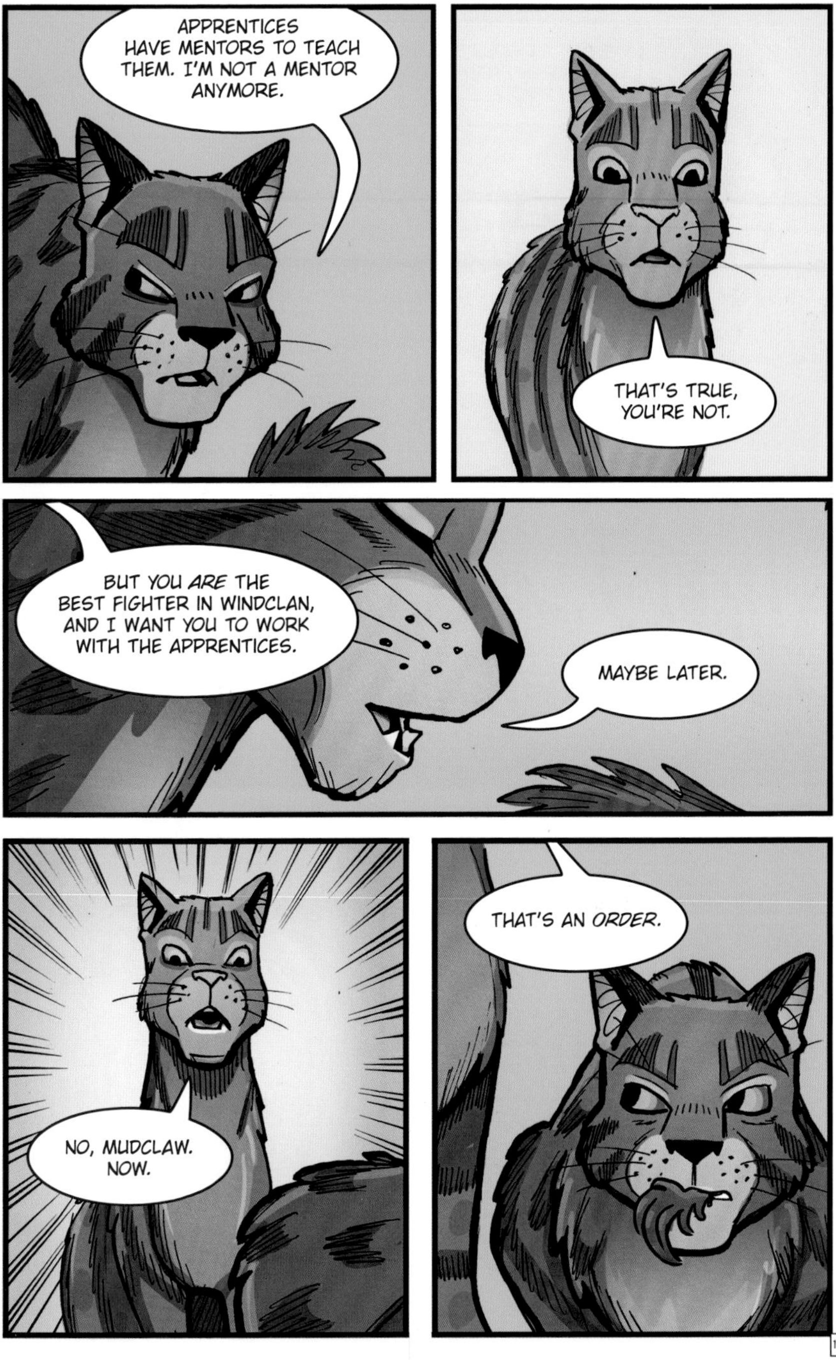
APPRENTICES HAVE MENTORS TO TEACH THEM. I'M NOT A MENTOR ANYMORE.
THAT'S TRUE, YOU'RE NOT.
BUT YOU *ARE* THE BEST FIGHTER IN WINDCLAN, AND I WANT YOU TO WORK WITH THE APPRENTICES.
MAYBE LATER.
NO, MUDCLAW. NOW.
THAT'S AN *ORDER*.

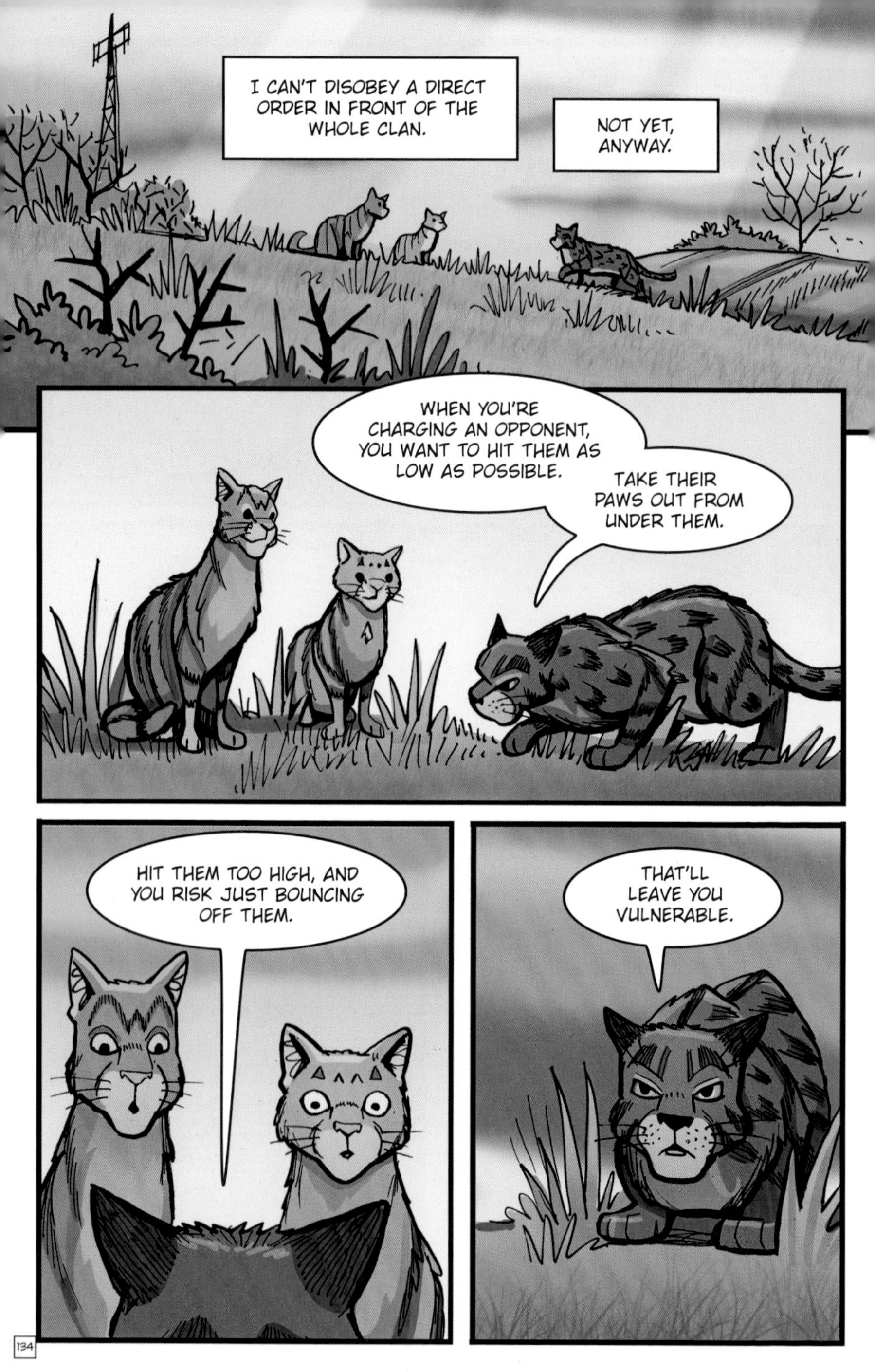
I CAN'T DISOBEY A DIRECT ORDER IN FRONT OF THE WHOLE CLAN.
NOT YET, ANYWAY.
WHEN YOU'RE CHARGING AN OPPONENT, YOU WANT TO HIT THEM AS LOW AS POSSIBLE.
TAKE THEIR PAWS OUT FROM UNDER THEM.
HIT THEM TOO HIGH, AND YOU RISK JUST BOUNCING OFF THEM.
THAT'LL LEAVE YOU VULNERABLE.

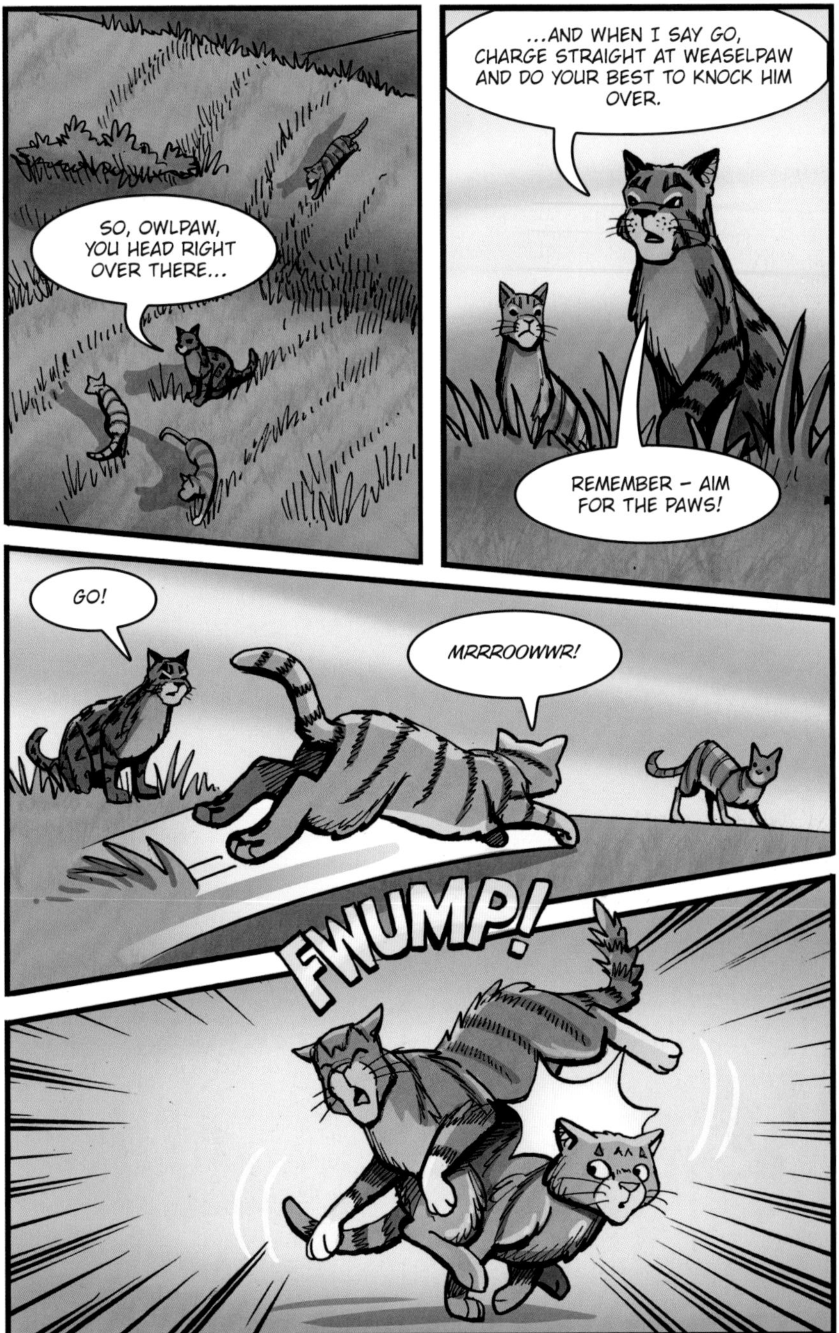
SO, OWLPAW, YOU HEAD RIGHT OVER THERE...
...AND WHEN I SAY GO, CHARGE STRAIGHT AT WEASELPAW AND DO YOUR BEST TO KNOCK HIM OVER.
REMEMBER – AIM FOR THE PAWS!
GO!
MRRROOWWR!
FWUMP!

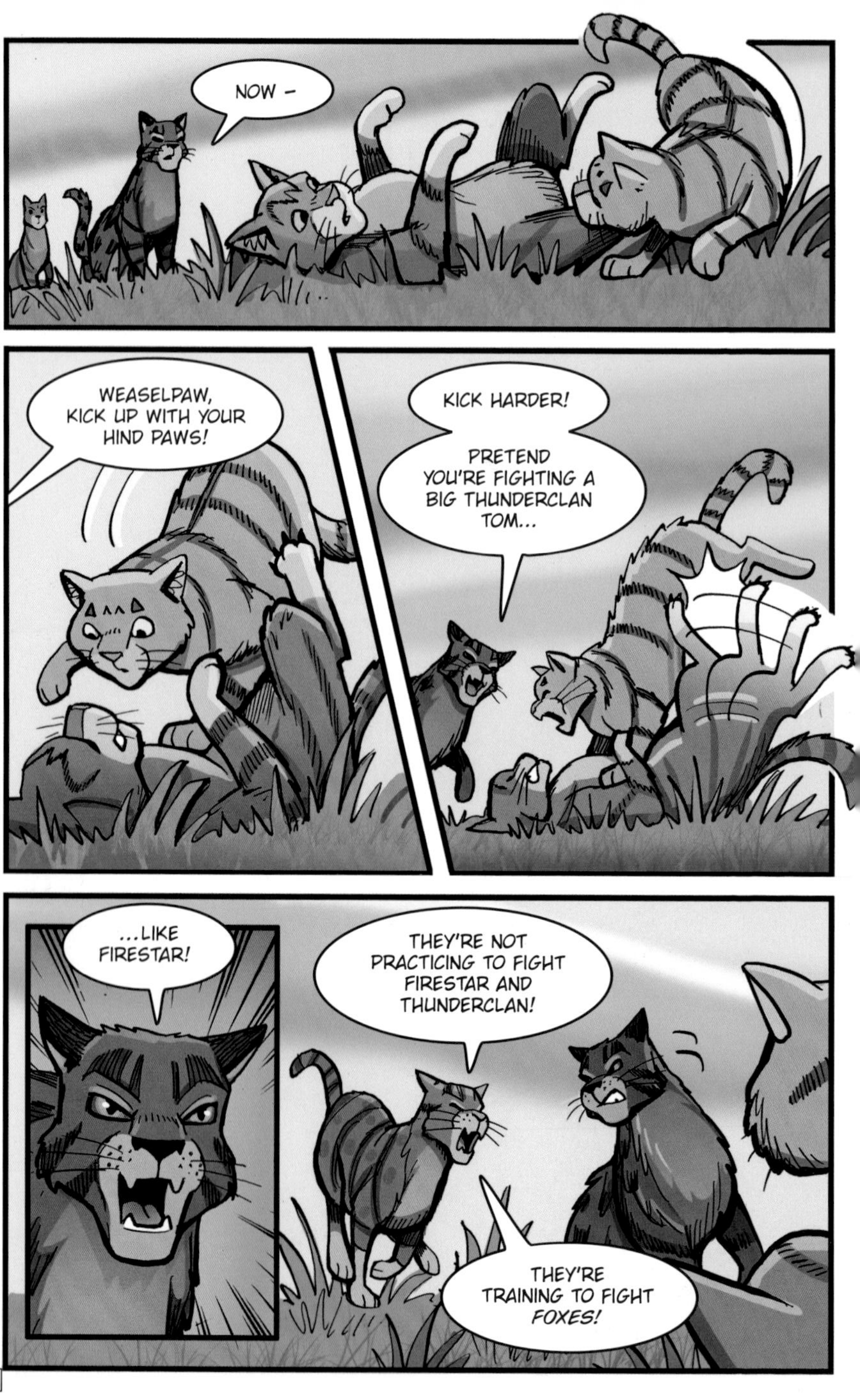
NOW –
WEASELPAW, KICK UP WITH YOUR HIND PAWS!
KICK HARDER!
PRETEND YOU'RE FIGHTING A BIG THUNDERCLAN TOM...
...LIKE FIRESTAR!
THEY'RE NOT PRACTICING TO FIGHT FIRESTAR AND THUNDERCLAN!
THEY'RE TRAINING TO FIGHT *FOXES!*

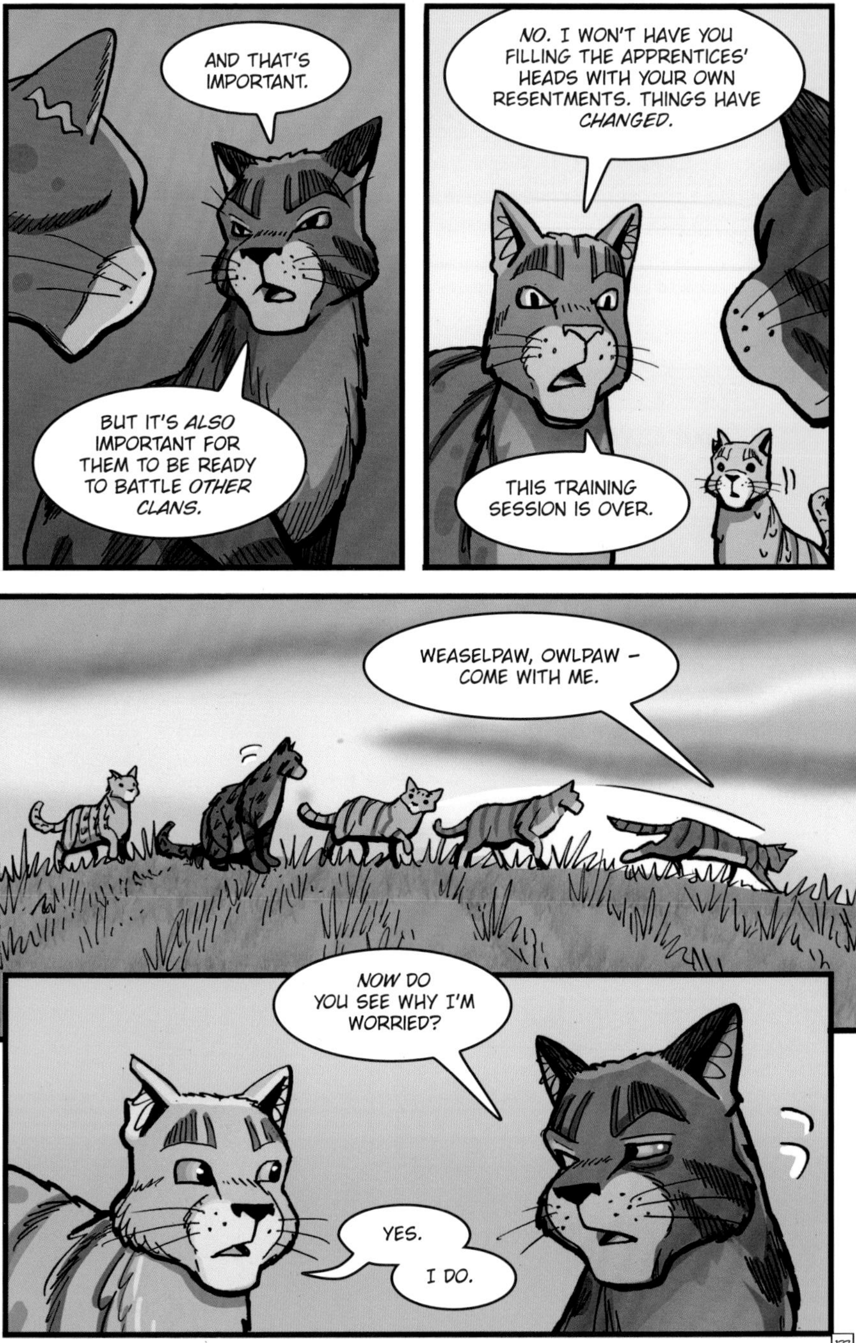
AND THAT'S IMPORTANT.
BUT IT'S *ALSO* IMPORTANT FOR THEM TO BE READY TO BATTLE *OTHER* CLANS.
NO. I WON'T HAVE YOU FILLING THE APPRENTICES' HEADS WITH YOUR OWN RESENTMENTS. THINGS HAVE *CHANGED*.
THIS TRAINING SESSION IS OVER.
WEASELPAW, OWLPAW – COME WITH ME.
NOW DO YOU SEE WHY I'M WORRIED?
YES.
I DO.

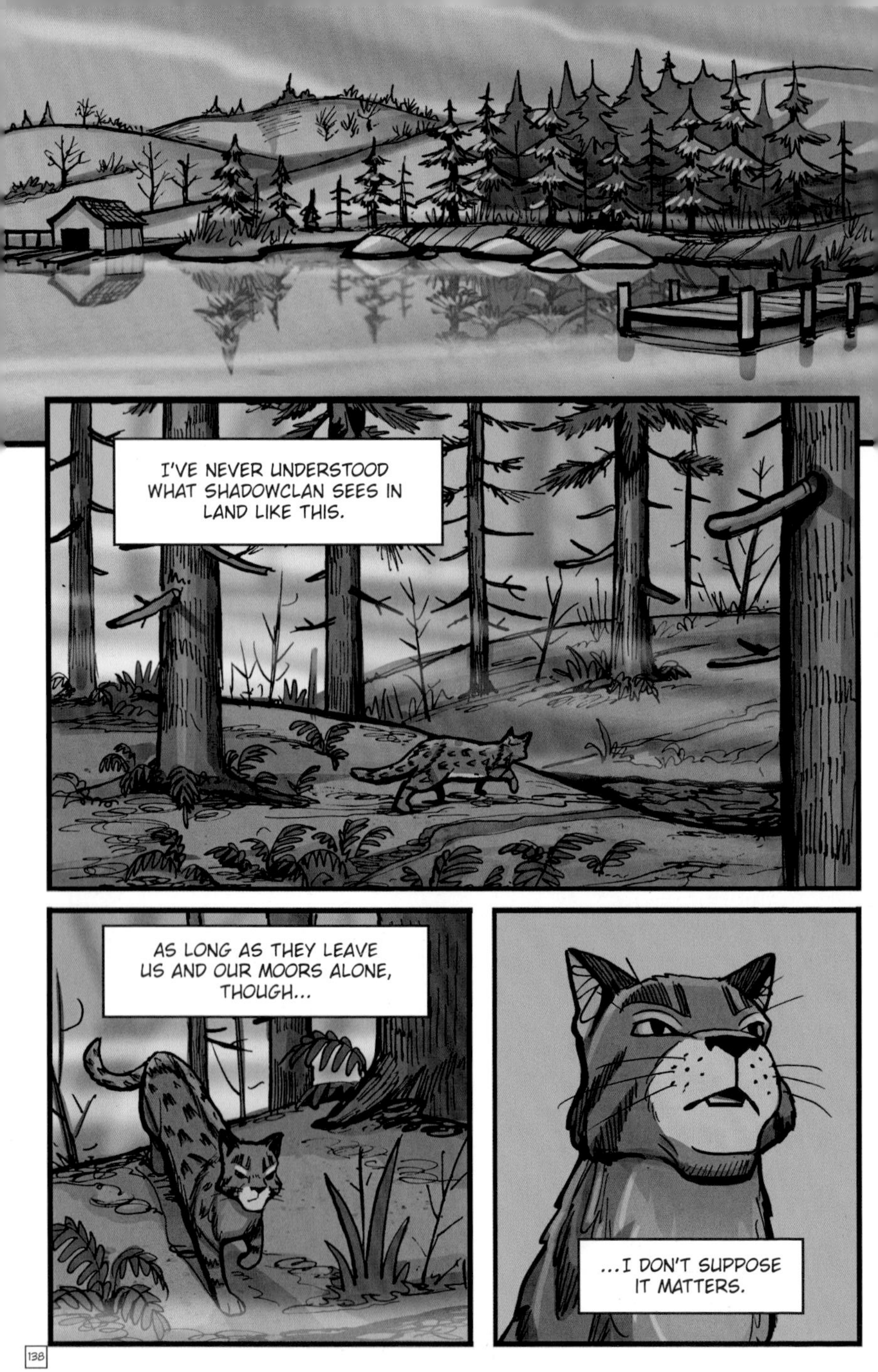
I'VE NEVER UNDERSTOOD WHAT SHADOWCLAN SEES IN LAND LIKE THIS.
AS LONG AS THEY LEAVE US AND OUR MOORS ALONE, THOUGH...
...I DON'T SUPPOSE IT MATTERS.

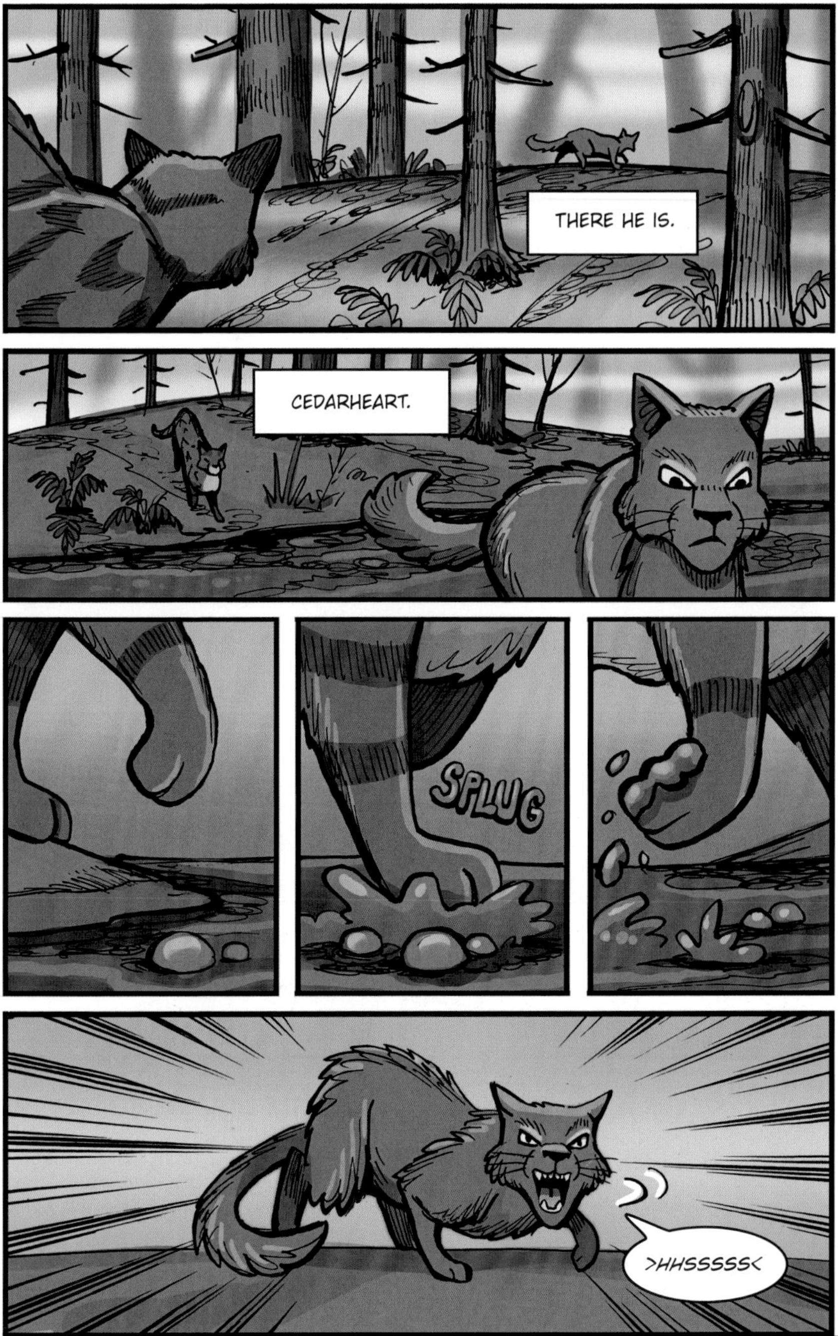
THERE HE IS.
CEDARHEART.
SPLUG
>HHSSSSS<

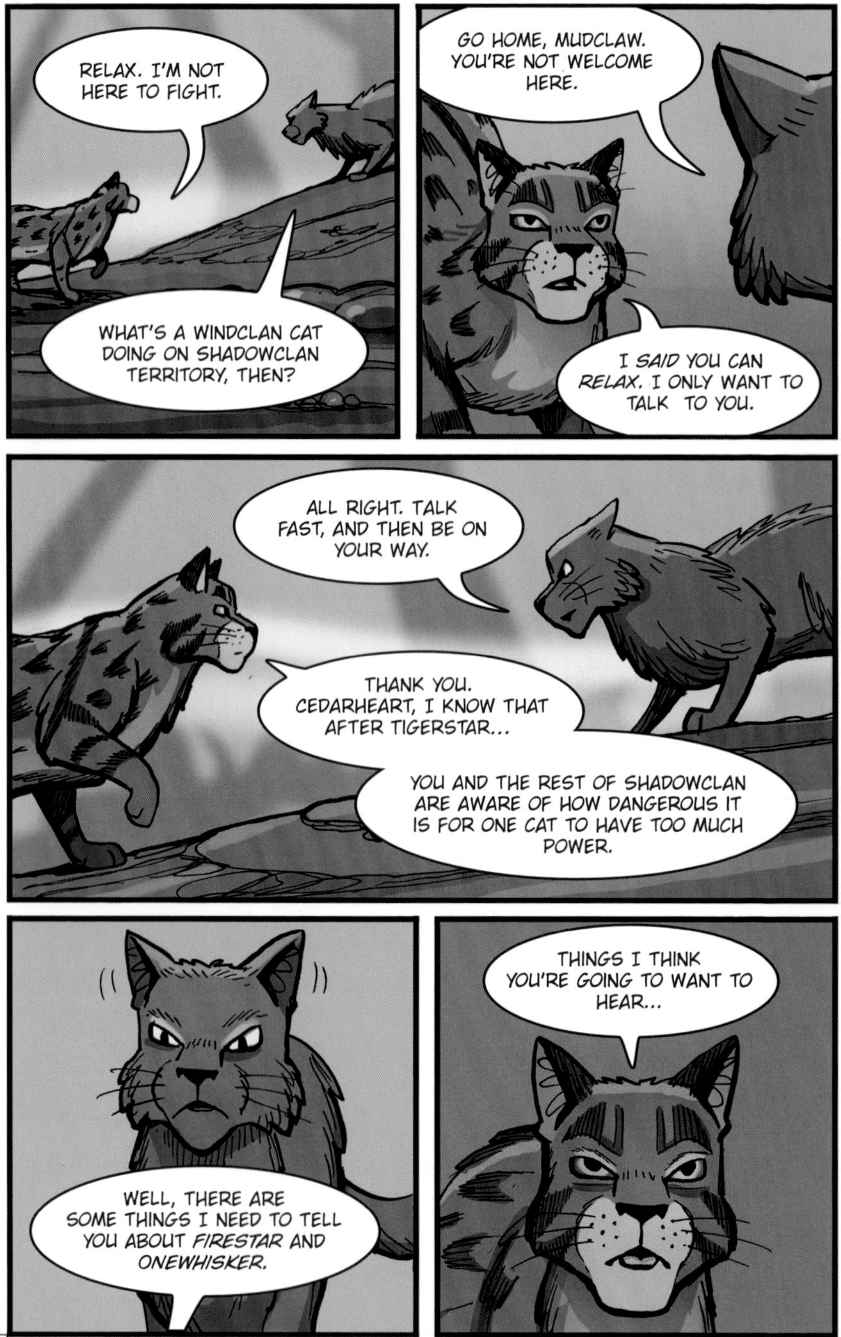
RELAX. I'M NOT HERE TO FIGHT.
WHAT'S A WINDCLAN CAT DOING ON SHADOWCLAN TERRITORY, THEN?
GO HOME, MUDCLAW. YOU'RE NOT WELCOME HERE.
I *SAID* YOU CAN *RELAX.* I ONLY WANT TO TALK TO YOU.
ALL RIGHT. TALK FAST, AND THEN BE ON YOUR WAY.
THANK YOU. CEDARHEART, I KNOW THAT AFTER TIGERSTAR...
YOU AND THE REST OF SHADOWCLAN ARE AWARE OF HOW DANGEROUS IT IS FOR ONE CAT TO HAVE TOO MUCH POWER.
WELL, THERE ARE SOME THINGS I NEED TO TELL YOU ABOUT *FIRESTAR* AND *ONEWHISKER.*
THINGS I THINK YOU'RE GOING TO WANT TO HEAR...

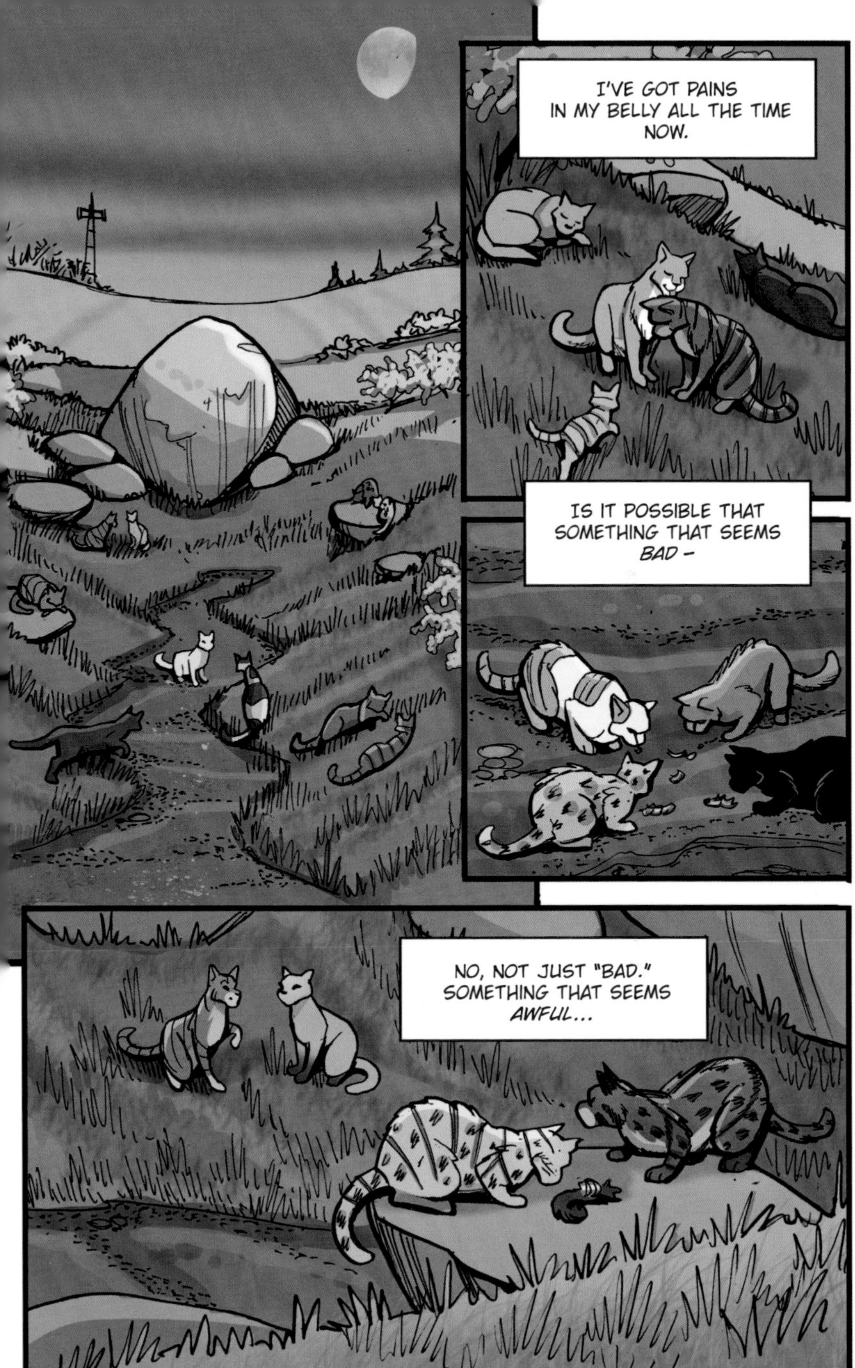
I'VE GOT PAINS IN MY BELLY ALL THE TIME NOW.
IS IT POSSIBLE THAT SOMETHING THAT SEEMS *BAD* –
NO, NOT JUST "BAD." SOMETHING THAT SEEMS *AWFUL*...

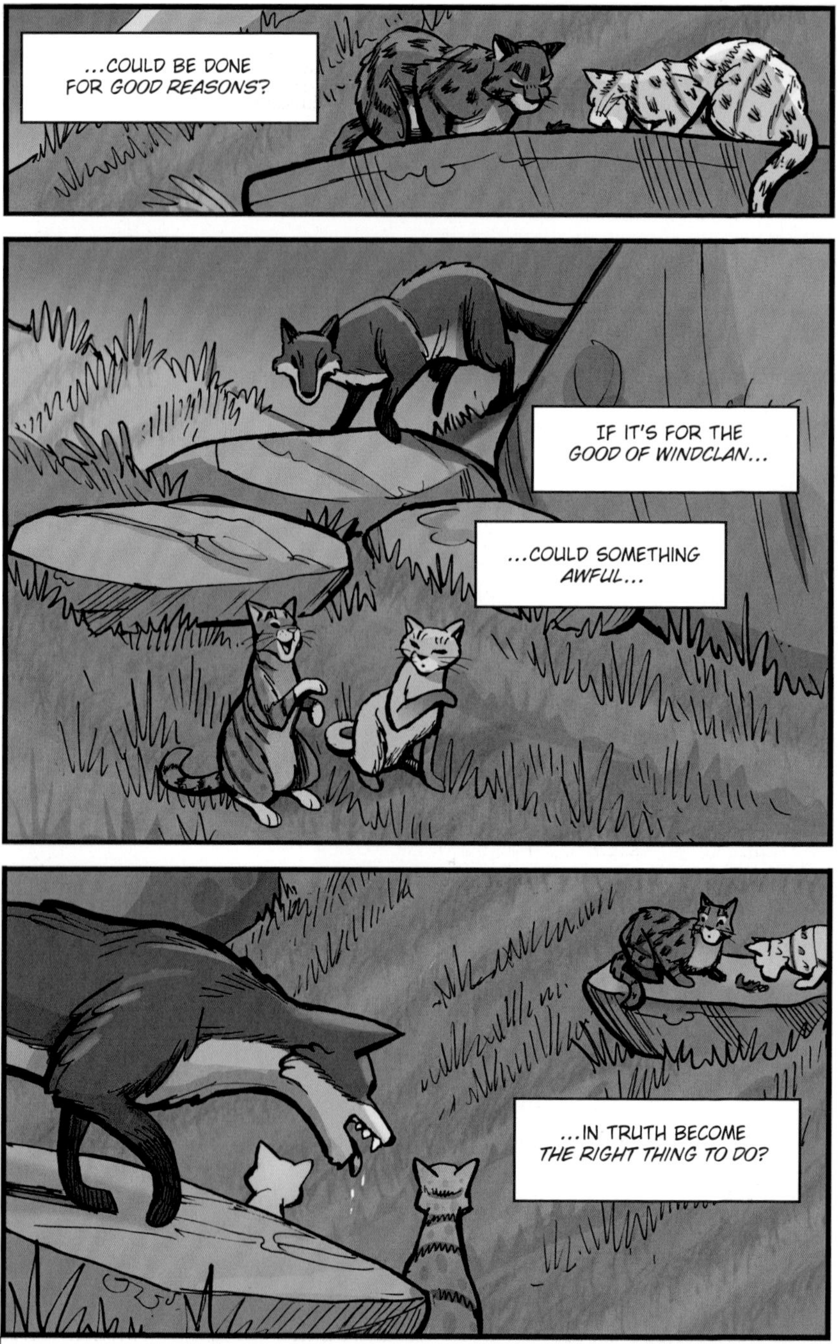
...COULD BE DONE FOR GOOD REASONS?
IF IT'S FOR THE GOOD OF WINDCLAN...
...COULD SOMETHING AWFUL...
...IN TRUTH BECOME THE RIGHT THING TO DO?

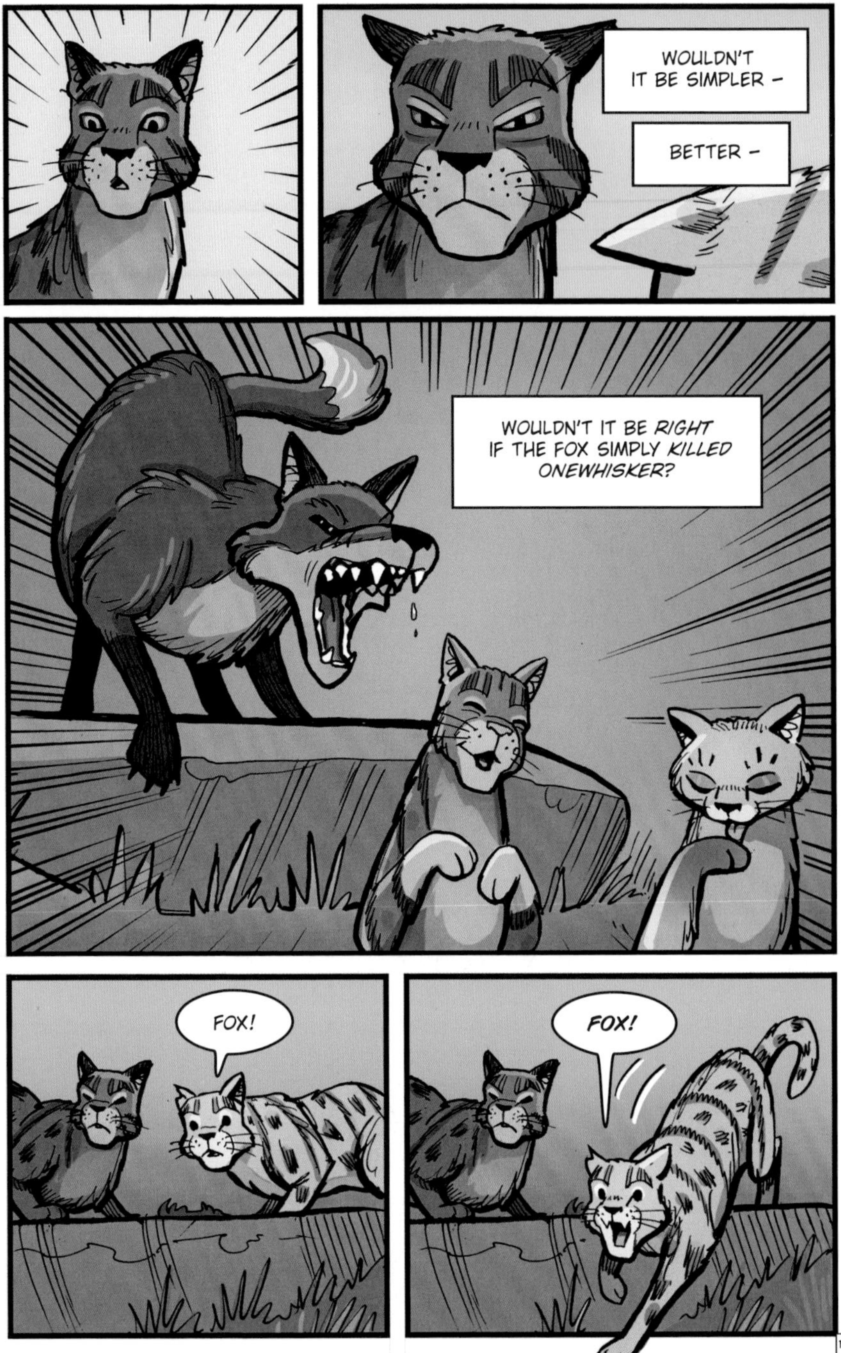
WOULDN'T IT BE SIMPLER –
BETTER –
WOULDN'T IT BE *RIGHT* IF THE FOX SIMPLY *KILLED* ONEWHISKER?
FOX!
FOX!

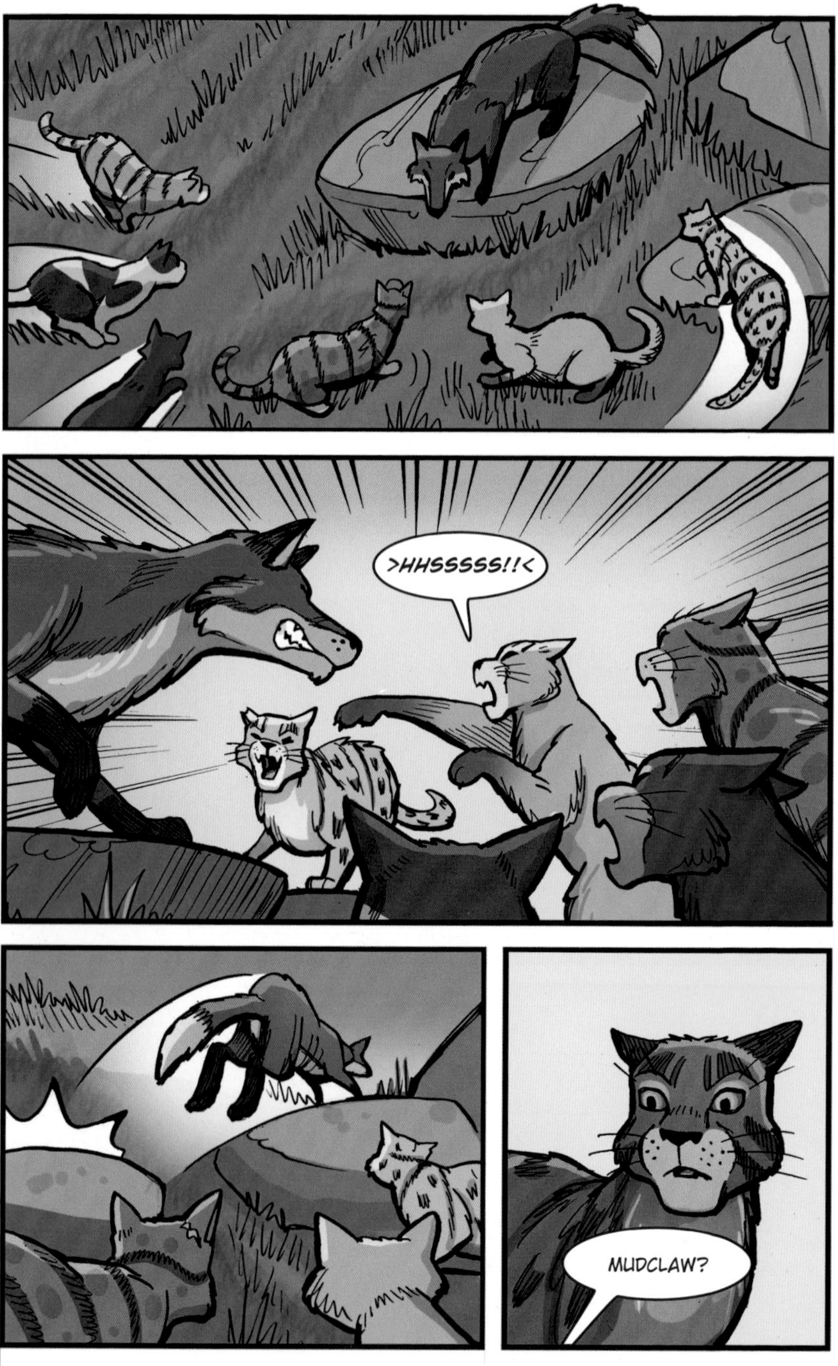
>HHSSSSSS!!<
MUDCLAW?

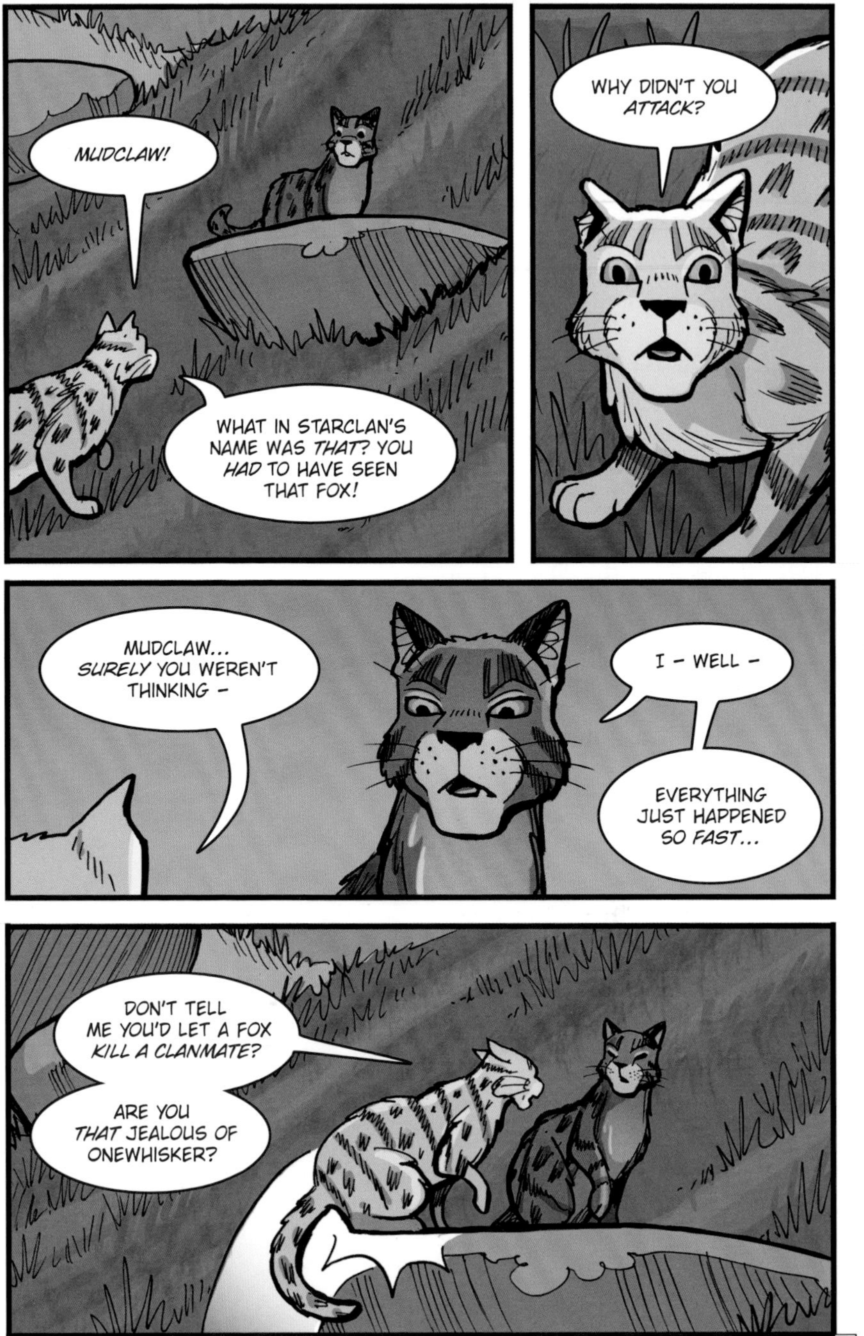
MUDCLAW!
WHAT IN STARCLAN'S NAME WAS *THAT*? YOU *HAD* TO HAVE SEEN THAT FOX!
WHY DIDN'T YOU *ATTACK*?
MUDCLAW... *SURELY* YOU WEREN'T THINKING –
I – WELL –
EVERYTHING JUST HAPPENED SO *FAST*...
DON'T TELL ME YOU'D LET A FOX *KILL A CLANMATE*?
ARE YOU *THAT* JEALOUS OF ONEWHISKER?

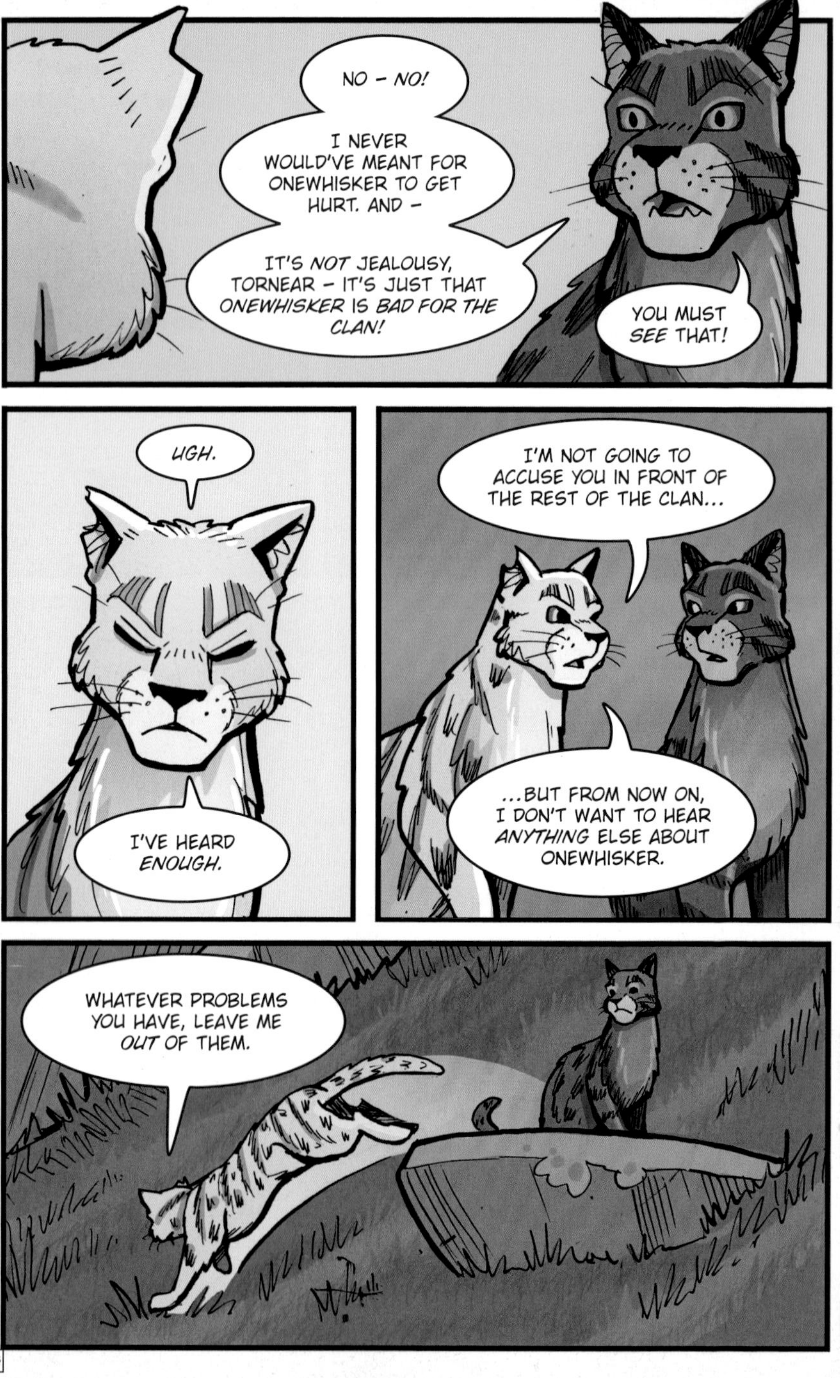
NO - NO!
I NEVER WOULD'VE MEANT FOR ONEWHISKER TO GET HURT. AND -
IT'S NOT JEALOUSY, TORNEAR - IT'S JUST THAT ONEWHISKER IS BAD FOR THE CLAN!
YOU MUST SEE THAT!
UGH.
I'VE HEARD ENOUGH.
I'M NOT GOING TO ACCUSE YOU IN FRONT OF THE REST OF THE CLAN...
...BUT FROM NOW ON, I DON'T WANT TO HEAR ANYTHING ELSE ABOUT ONEWHISKER.
WHATEVER PROBLEMS YOU HAVE, LEAVE ME OUT OF THEM.

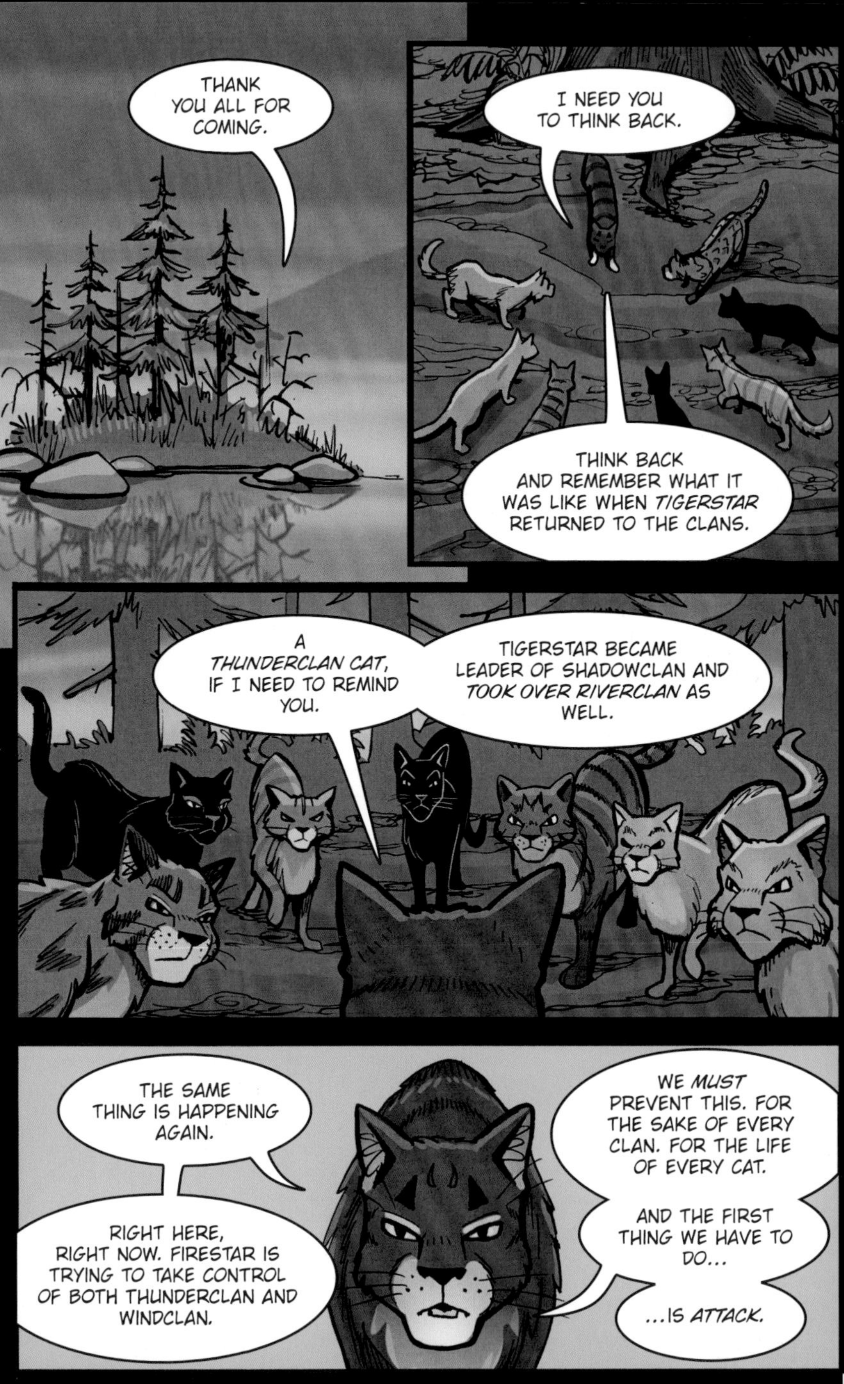
THANK YOU ALL FOR COMING.
I NEED YOU TO THINK BACK.
THINK BACK AND REMEMBER WHAT IT WAS LIKE WHEN *TIGERSTAR* RETURNED TO THE CLANS.
A *THUNDERCLAN CAT*, IF I NEED TO REMIND YOU.
TIGERSTAR BECAME LEADER OF SHADOWCLAN AND *TOOK OVER RIVERCLAN* AS WELL.
THE SAME THING IS HAPPENING AGAIN.
RIGHT HERE, RIGHT NOW. FIRESTAR IS TRYING TO TAKE CONTROL OF BOTH THUNDERCLAN AND WINDCLAN.
WE *MUST* PREVENT THIS. FOR THE SAKE OF EVERY CLAN. FOR THE LIFE OF EVERY CAT.
AND THE FIRST THING WE HAVE TO DO...
...IS *ATTACK*.

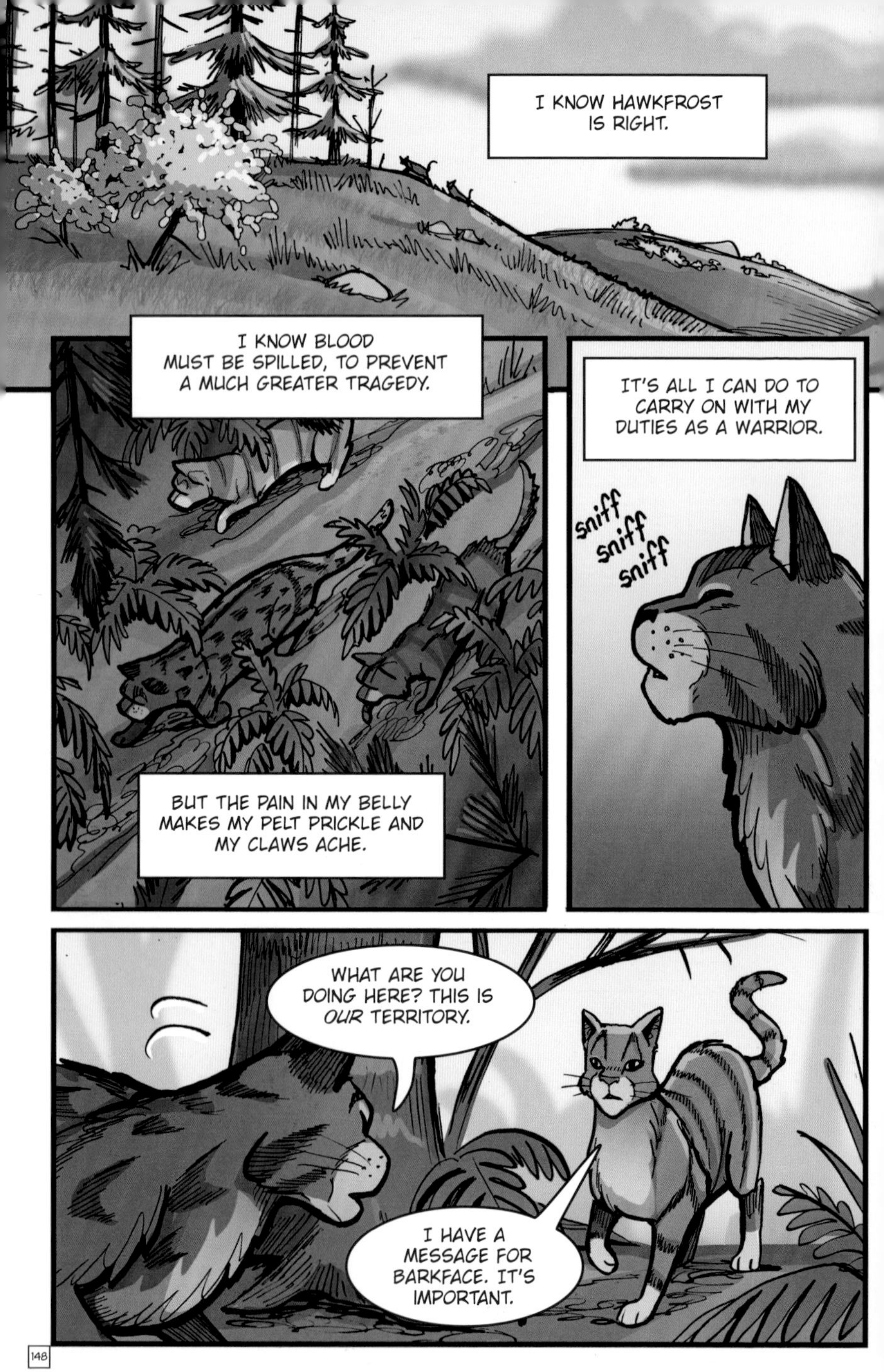
I KNOW HAWKFROST IS RIGHT.
I KNOW BLOOD MUST BE SPILLED, TO PREVENT A MUCH GREATER TRAGEDY.
BUT THE PAIN IN MY BELLY MAKES MY PELT PRICKLE AND MY CLAWS ACHE.
IT'S ALL I CAN DO TO CARRY ON WITH MY DUTIES AS A WARRIOR.
sniff sniff sniff
WHAT ARE YOU DOING HERE? THIS IS *OUR* TERRITORY.
I HAVE A MESSAGE FOR BARKFACE. IT'S IMPORTANT.

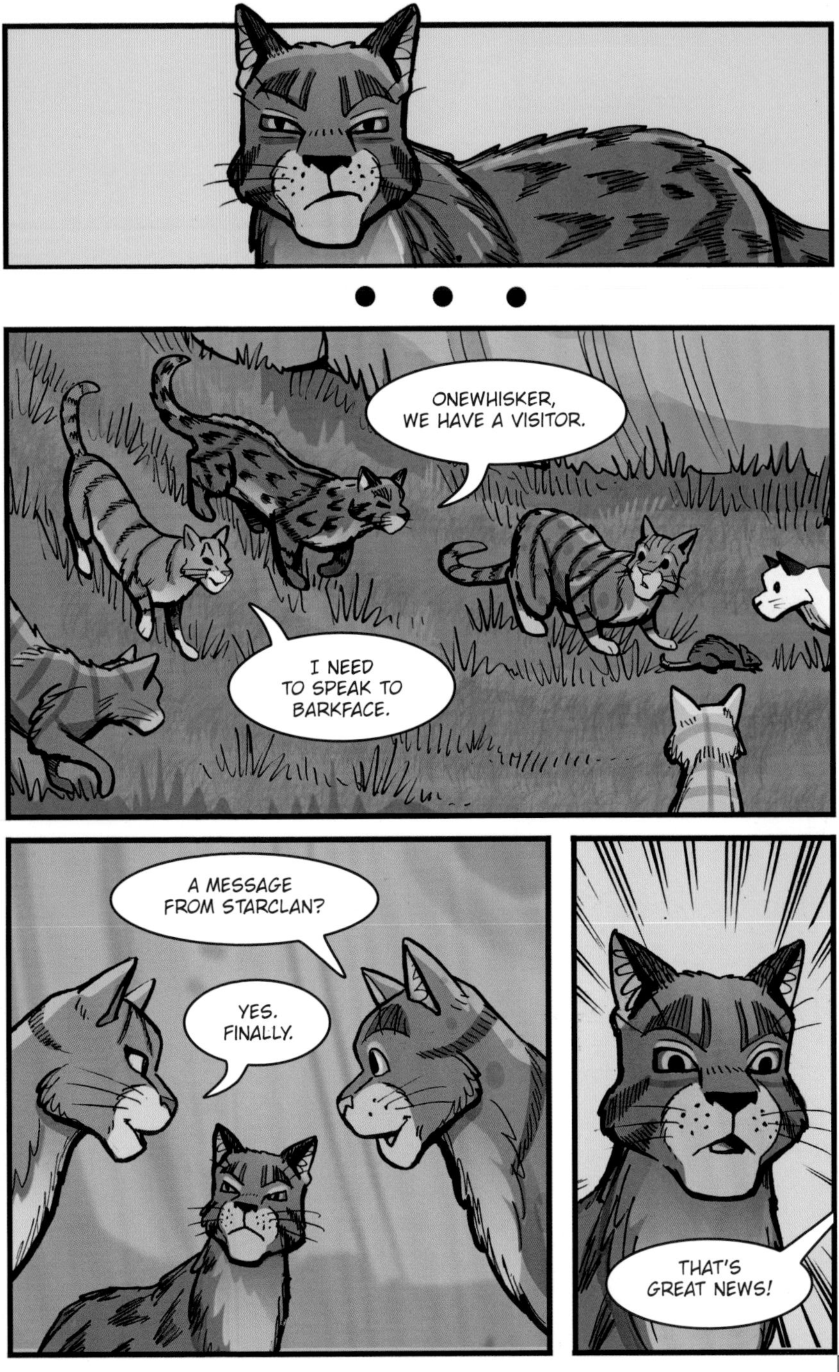
ONEWHISKER, WE HAVE A VISITOR.
I NEED TO SPEAK TO BARKFACE.
A MESSAGE FROM STARCLAN?
YES. FINALLY.
THAT'S GREAT NEWS!

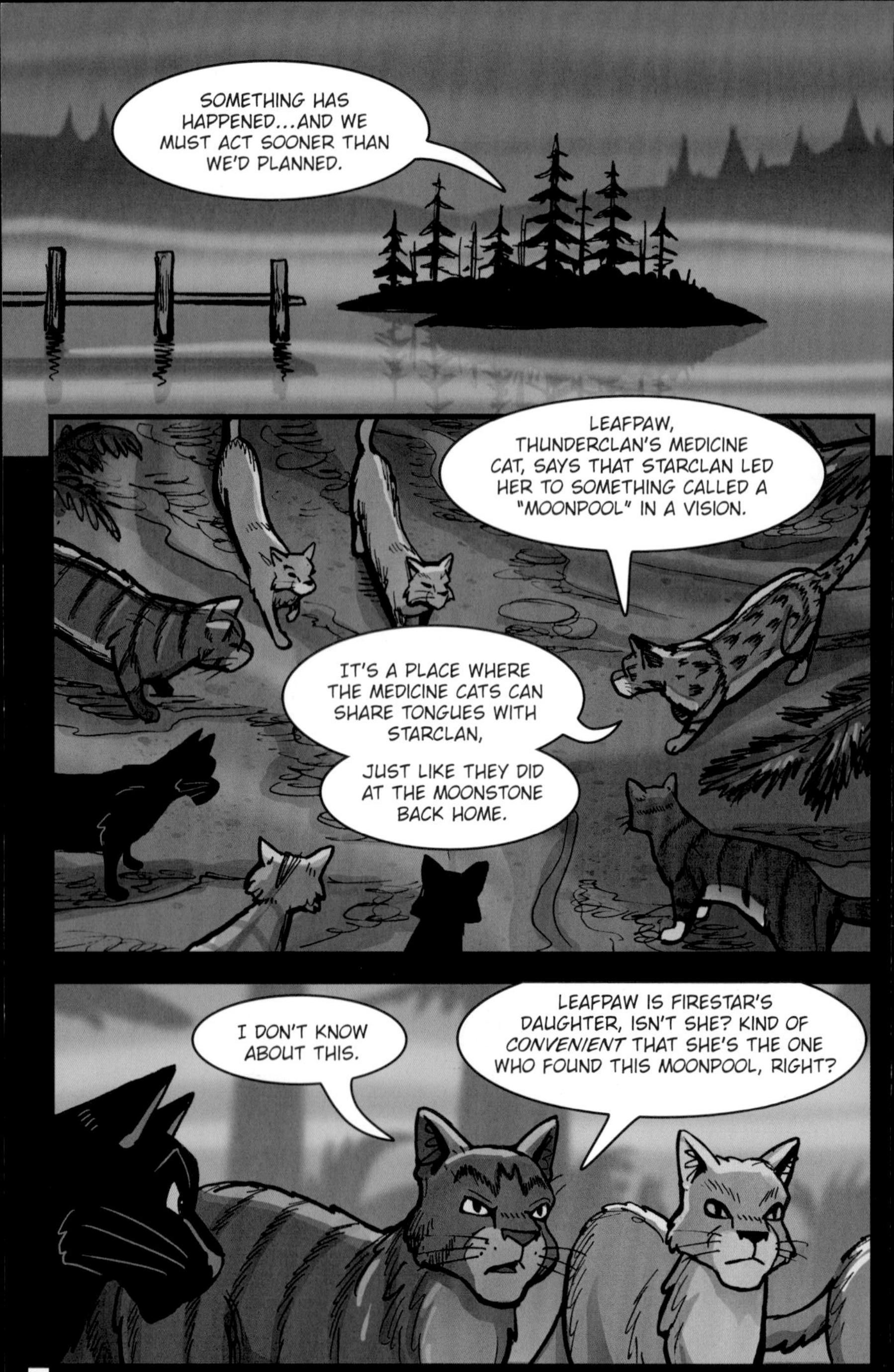
SOMETHING HAS HAPPENED...AND WE MUST ACT SOONER THAN WE'D PLANNED.
LEAFPAW, THUNDERCLAN'S MEDICINE CAT, SAYS THAT STARCLAN LED HER TO SOMETHING CALLED A "MOONPOOL" IN A VISION.
IT'S A PLACE WHERE THE MEDICINE CATS CAN SHARE TONGUES WITH STARCLAN,
JUST LIKE THEY DID AT THE MOONSTONE BACK HOME.
I DON'T KNOW ABOUT THIS.
LEAFPAW IS FIRESTAR'S DAUGHTER, ISN'T SHE? KIND OF *CONVENIENT* THAT SHE'S THE ONE WHO FOUND THIS MOONPOOL, RIGHT?

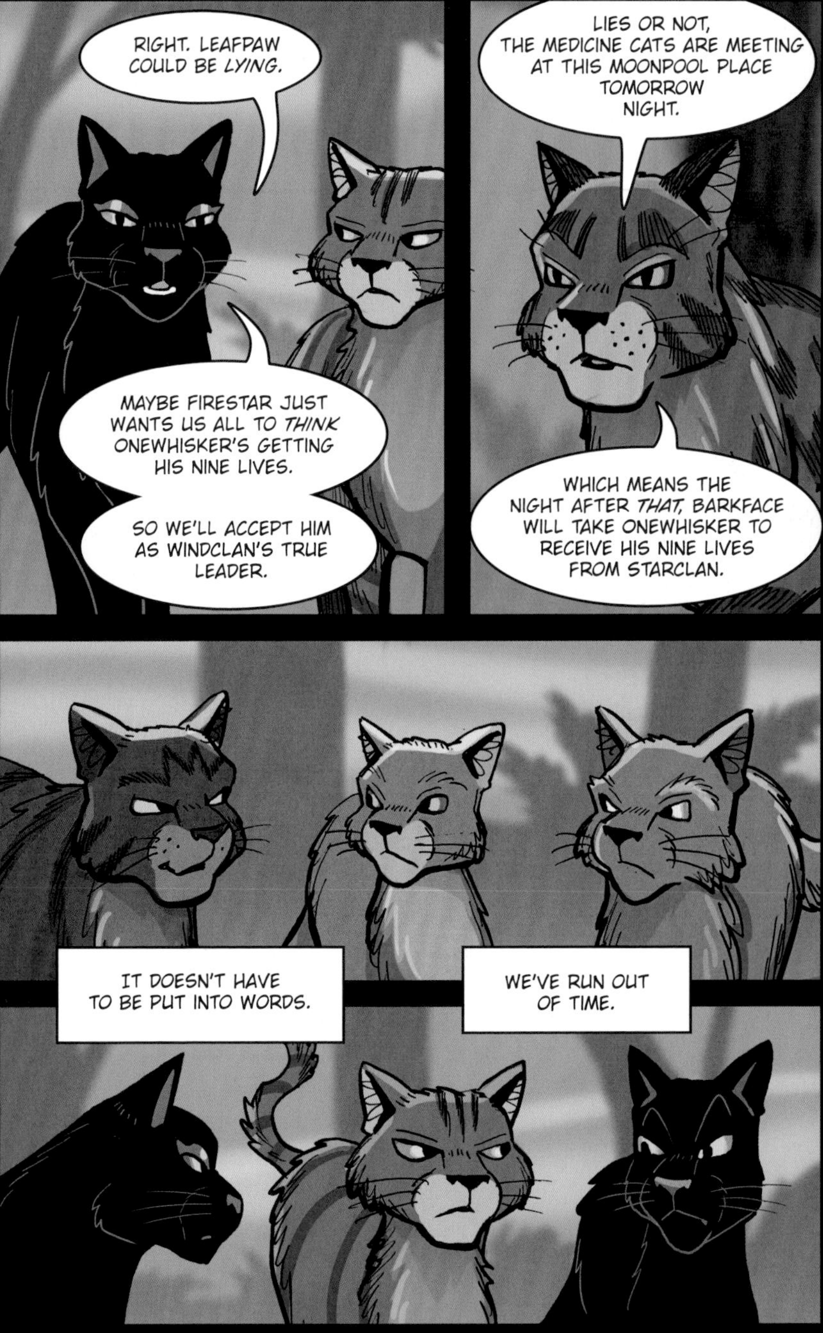

RIGHT. LEAFPAW COULD BE *LYING.*
MAYBE FIRESTAR JUST WANTS US ALL TO *THINK* ONEWHISKER'S GETTING HIS NINE LIVES.
SO WE'LL ACCEPT HIM AS WINDCLAN'S TRUE LEADER.
LIES OR NOT, THE MEDICINE CATS ARE MEETING AT THIS MOONPOOL PLACE TOMORROW NIGHT.
WHICH MEANS THE NIGHT AFTER *THAT,* BARKFACE WILL TAKE ONEWHISKER TO RECEIVE HIS NINE LIVES FROM STARCLAN.
IT DOESN'T HAVE TO BE PUT INTO WORDS.
WE'VE RUN OUT OF TIME.

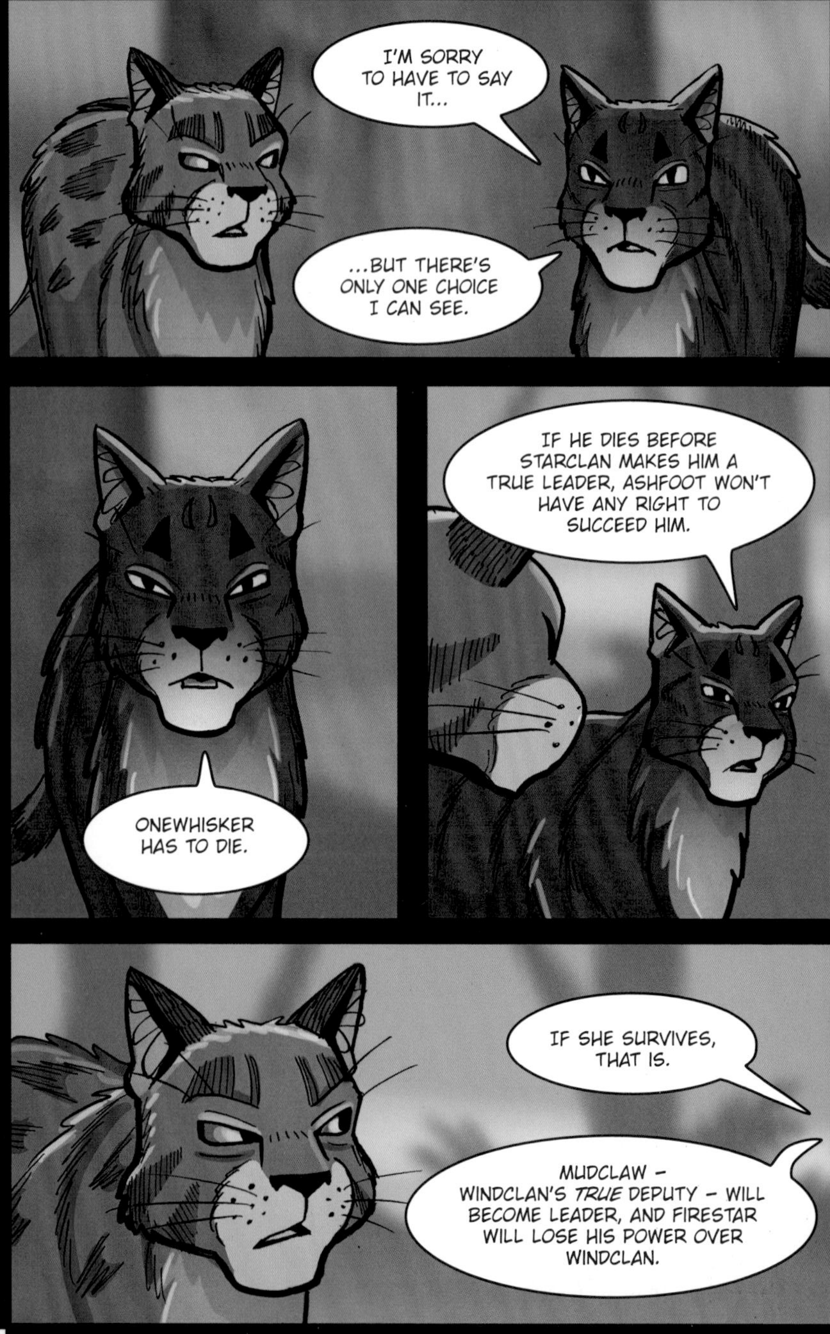
I'M SORRY TO HAVE TO SAY IT...
...BUT THERE'S ONLY ONE CHOICE I CAN SEE.
ONEWHISKER HAS TO DIE.
IF HE DIES BEFORE STARCLAN MAKES HIM A TRUE LEADER, ASHFOOT WON'T HAVE ANY RIGHT TO SUCCEED HIM.
IF SHE SURVIVES, THAT IS.
MUDCLAW – WINDCLAN'S *TRUE* DEPUTY – WILL BECOME LEADER, AND FIRESTAR WILL LOSE HIS POWER OVER WINDCLAN.

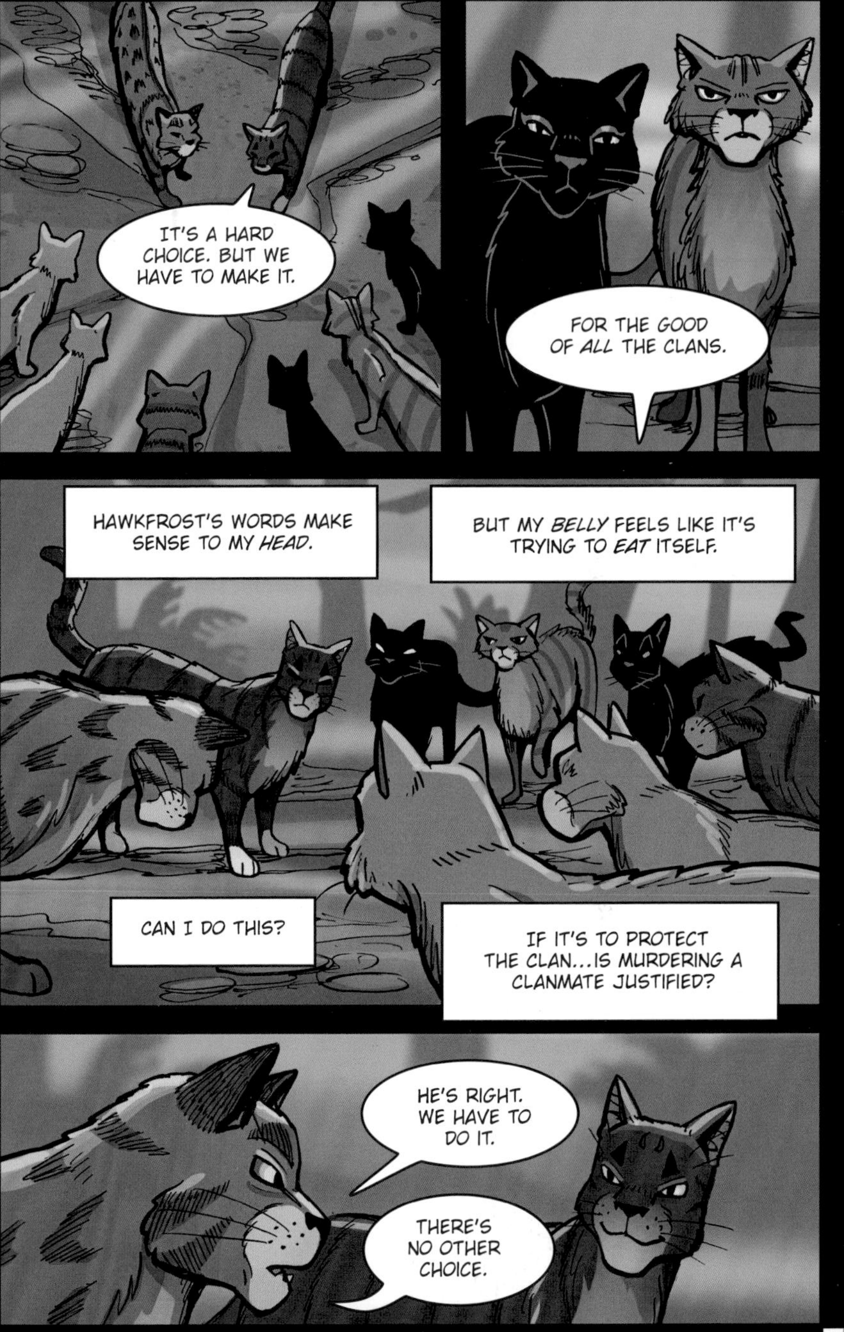
IT'S A HARD CHOICE. BUT WE HAVE TO MAKE IT.
FOR THE GOOD OF *ALL* THE CLANS.
HAWKFROST'S WORDS MAKE SENSE TO MY *HEAD*.
BUT MY *BELLY* FEELS LIKE IT'S TRYING TO *EAT* ITSELF.
CAN I DO THIS?
IF IT'S TO PROTECT THE CLAN...IS MURDERING A CLANMATE JUSTIFIED?
HE'S RIGHT. WE HAVE TO DO IT.
THERE'S NO OTHER CHOICE.

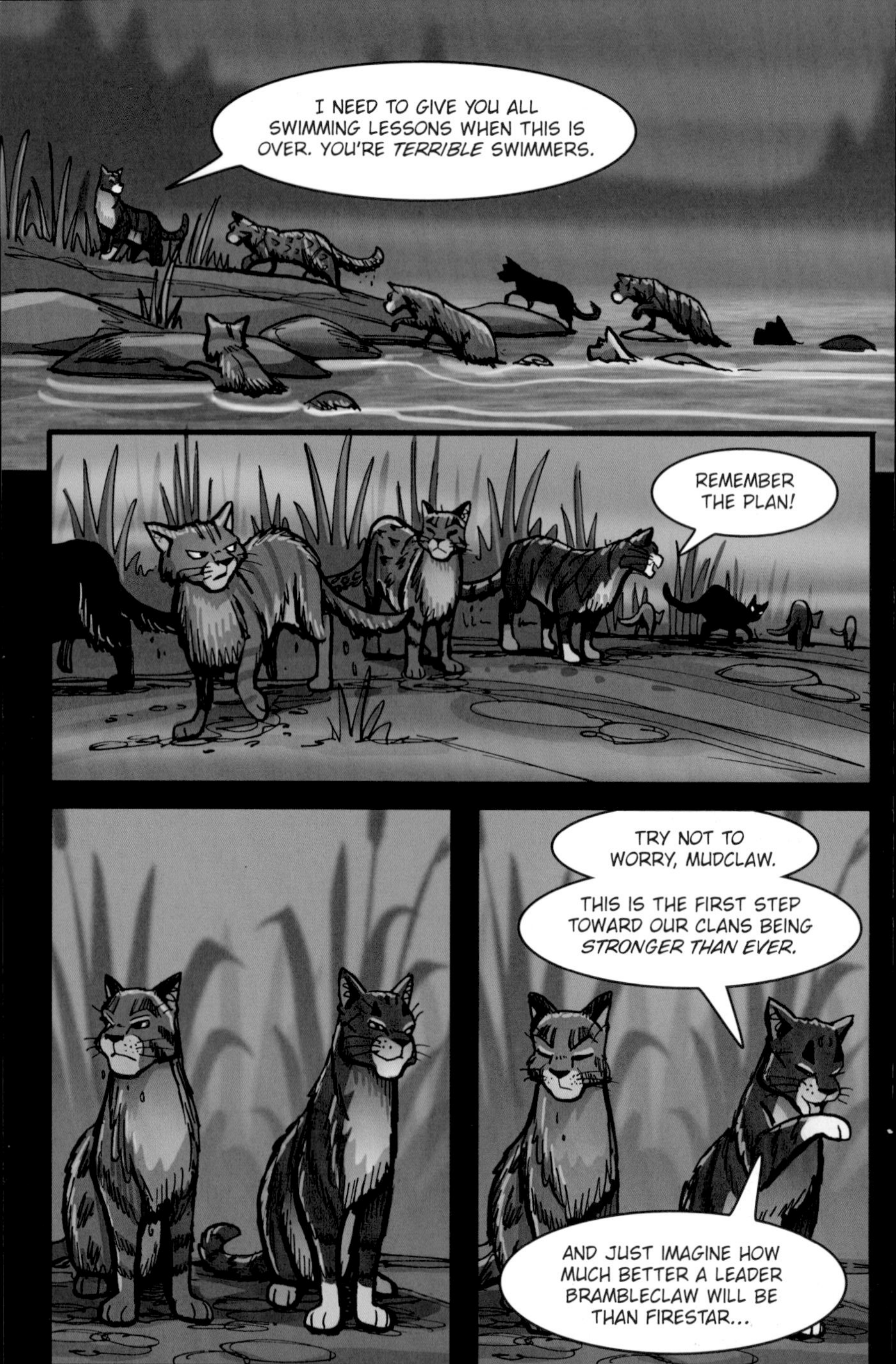
I NEED TO GIVE YOU ALL SWIMMING LESSONS WHEN THIS IS OVER. YOU'RE *TERRIBLE* SWIMMERS.
REMEMBER THE PLAN!
TRY NOT TO WORRY, MUDCLAW.
THIS IS THE FIRST STEP TOWARD OUR CLANS BEING *STRONGER THAN EVER.*
AND JUST IMAGINE HOW MUCH BETTER A LEADER BRAMBLECLAW WILL BE THAN FIRESTAR...

WAIT, *WHAT?* YOU REALLY WANT BRAMBLECLAW LEADING THUNDERCLAN?

HE'S BACKED FIRESTAR ALL THE WAY!

HE WAS FIRESTAR'S *APPRENTICE*, FOR STARCLAN'S SAKE!

DON'T WORRY. ONCE HE'S OUT FROM UNDER FIRESTAR'S PAW...

...BRAMBLECLAW WILL COME AROUND TO OUR WAY OF THINKING.

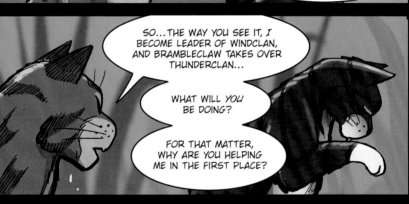

SO...THE WAY YOU SEE IT, *I* BECOME LEADER OF WINDCLAN, AND BRAMBLECLAW TAKES OVER THUNDERCLAN...

WHAT WILL *YOU* BE DOING?

FOR THAT MATTER, WHY ARE YOU HELPING ME IN THE FIRST PLACE?

YOU *HAVEN'T FORGOTTEN* WHAT I SAID ABOUT MAKING ME YOUR SECOND IN COMMAND, HAVE YOU?

OF *COURSE* I WAS SERIOUS. JUST IMAGINE IT. THE TWO OF US TAKE OVER FROM ONEWHISKER AND ASHFOOT...

WH –

YOU WERE *SERIOUS?* YOU'D LEAVE RIVERCLAN TO BE WINDCLAN'S DEPUTY?

AND *THEN*...

WE'D BE FREE TO FOCUS *ALL* ON RIVERCLAN, WOULDN'T WE?

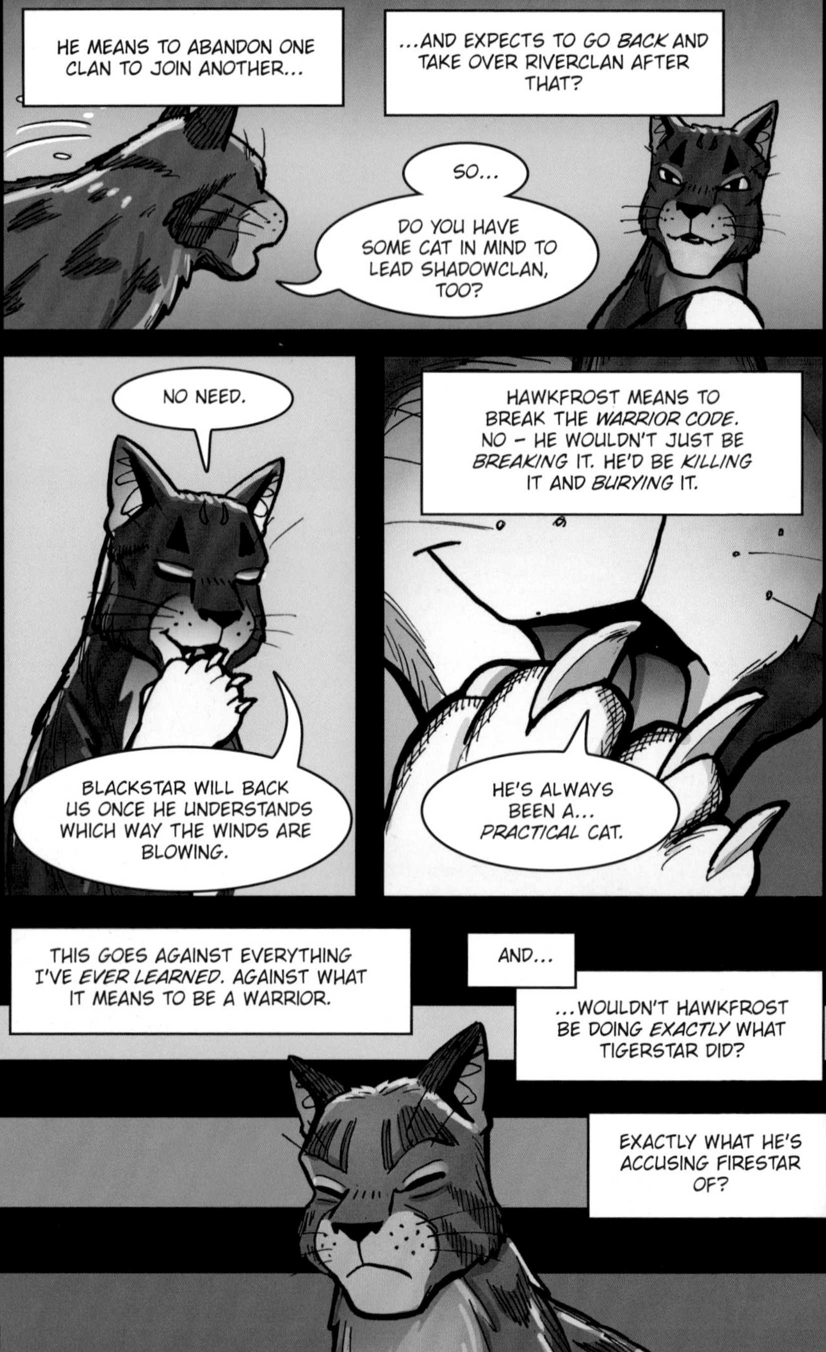
HE MEANS TO ABANDON ONE CLAN TO JOIN ANOTHER...
...AND EXPECTS TO GO *BACK* AND TAKE OVER RIVERCLAN AFTER THAT?
SO...
DO YOU HAVE SOME CAT IN MIND TO LEAD SHADOWCLAN, TOO?
NO NEED.
HAWKFROST MEANS TO BREAK THE *WARRIOR CODE*. NO – HE WOULDN'T JUST BE *BREAKING* IT. HE'D BE *KILLING* IT AND *BURYING* IT.
BLACKSTAR WILL BACK US ONCE HE UNDERSTANDS WHICH WAY THE WINDS ARE BLOWING.
HE'S ALWAYS BEEN A... *PRACTICAL* CAT.
THIS GOES AGAINST EVERYTHING I'VE *EVER LEARNED*. AGAINST WHAT IT MEANS TO BE A WARRIOR.
AND...
...WOULDN'T HAWKFROST BE DOING *EXACTLY* WHAT TIGERSTAR DID?
EXACTLY WHAT HE'S ACCUSING FIRESTAR OF?

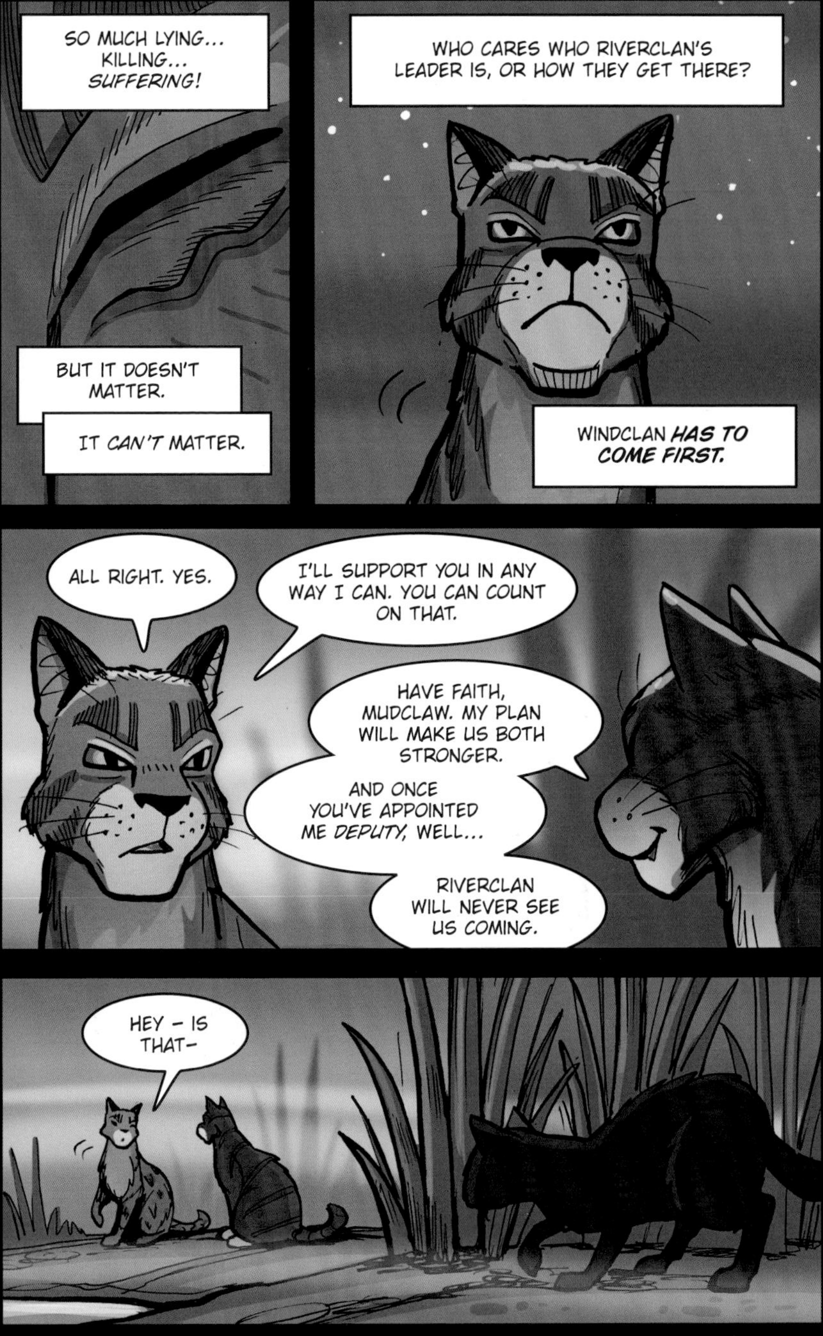
SO MUCH LYING... KILLING... *SUFFERING!*
WHO CARES WHO RIVERCLAN'S LEADER IS, OR HOW THEY GET THERE?
BUT IT DOESN'T MATTER.
IT *CAN'T* MATTER.
WINDCLAN ***HAS TO COME FIRST.***
ALL RIGHT. YES.
I'LL SUPPORT YOU IN ANY WAY I CAN. YOU CAN COUNT ON THAT.
HAVE FAITH, MUDCLAW. MY PLAN WILL MAKE US BOTH STRONGER.
AND ONCE YOU'VE APPOINTED ME *DEPUTY,* WELL...
RIVERCLAN WILL NEVER SEE US COMING.
HEY – IS THAT–

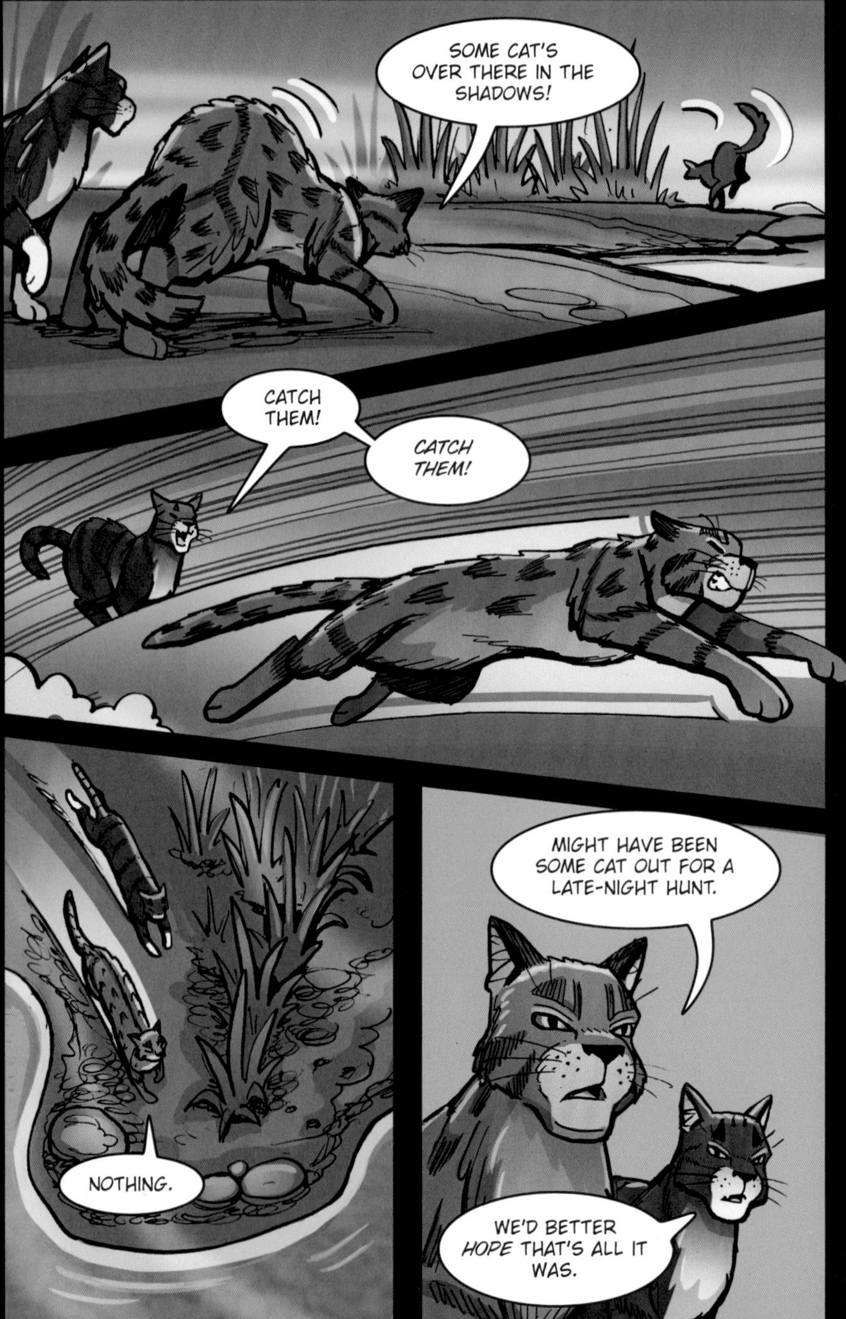
SOME CAT'S OVER THERE IN THE SHADOWS!
CATCH THEM!
CATCH THEM!
NOTHING.
MIGHT HAVE BEEN SOME CAT OUT FOR A LATE-NIGHT HUNT.
WE'D BETTER HOPE THAT'S ALL IT WAS.

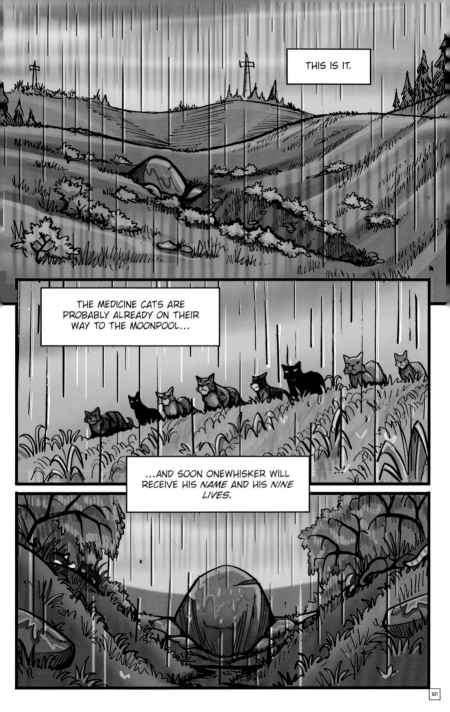

THIS IS IT.

THE MEDICINE CATS ARE PROBABLY ALREADY ON THEIR WAY TO THE MOONPOOL...

...AND SOON ONEWHISKER WILL RECEIVE HIS *NAME* AND HIS *NINE LIVES.*

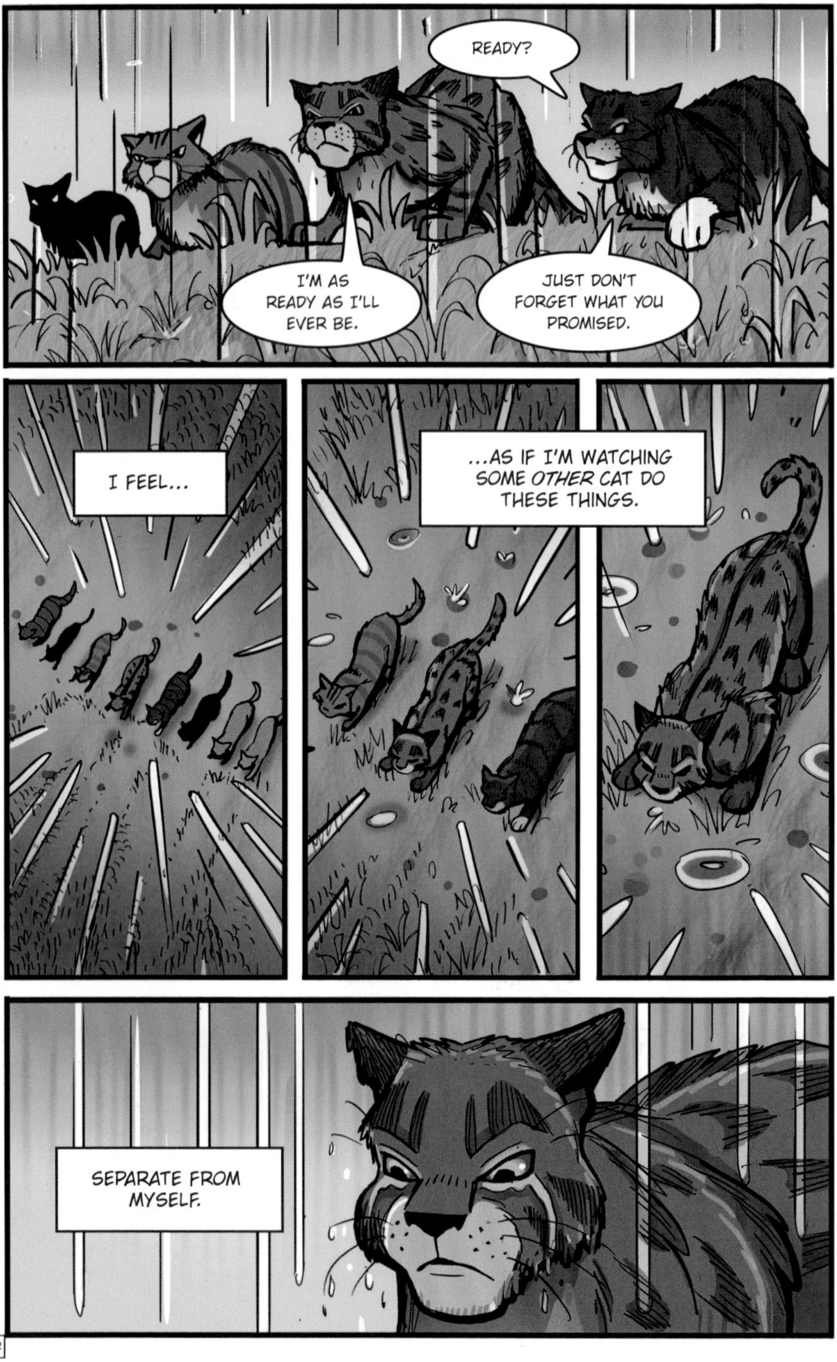
READY?
I'M AS READY AS I'LL EVER BE.
JUST DON'T FORGET WHAT YOU PROMISED.
I FEEL...
...AS IF I'M WATCHING SOME *OTHER* CAT DO THESE THINGS.
SEPARATE FROM MYSELF.

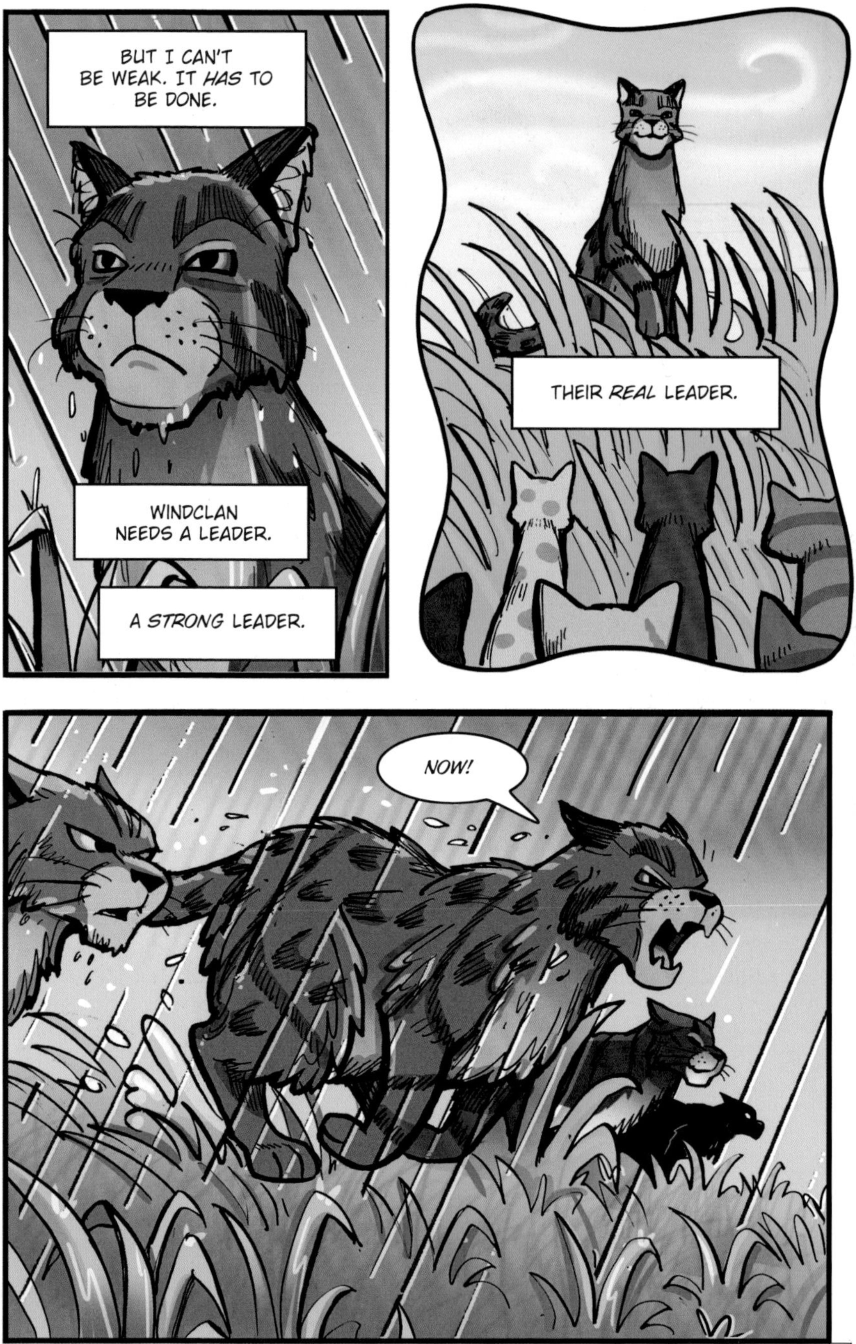
BUT I CAN'T BE WEAK. IT HAS TO BE DONE.
WINDCLAN NEEDS A LEADER.
A STRONG LEADER.
THEIR REAL LEADER.
NOW!

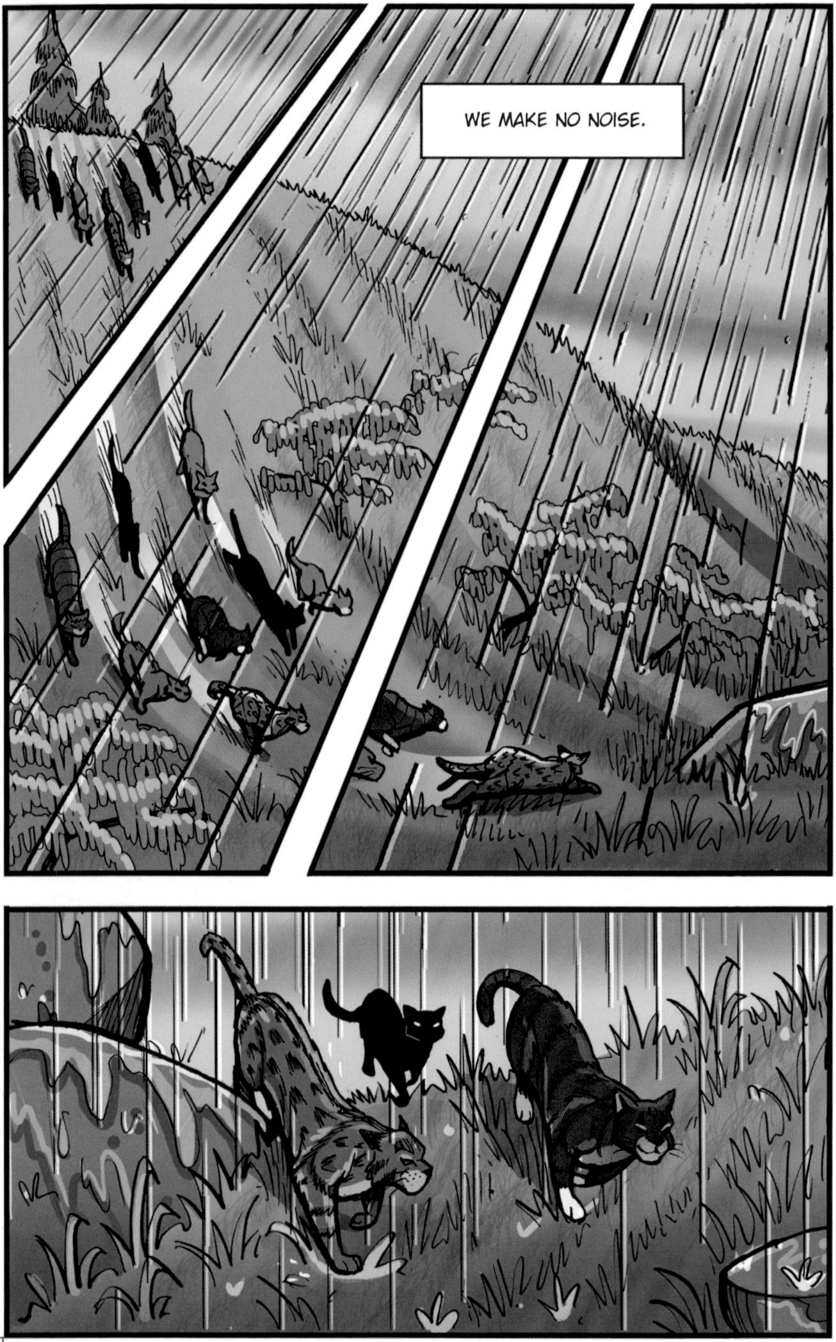
WE MAKE NO NOISE.

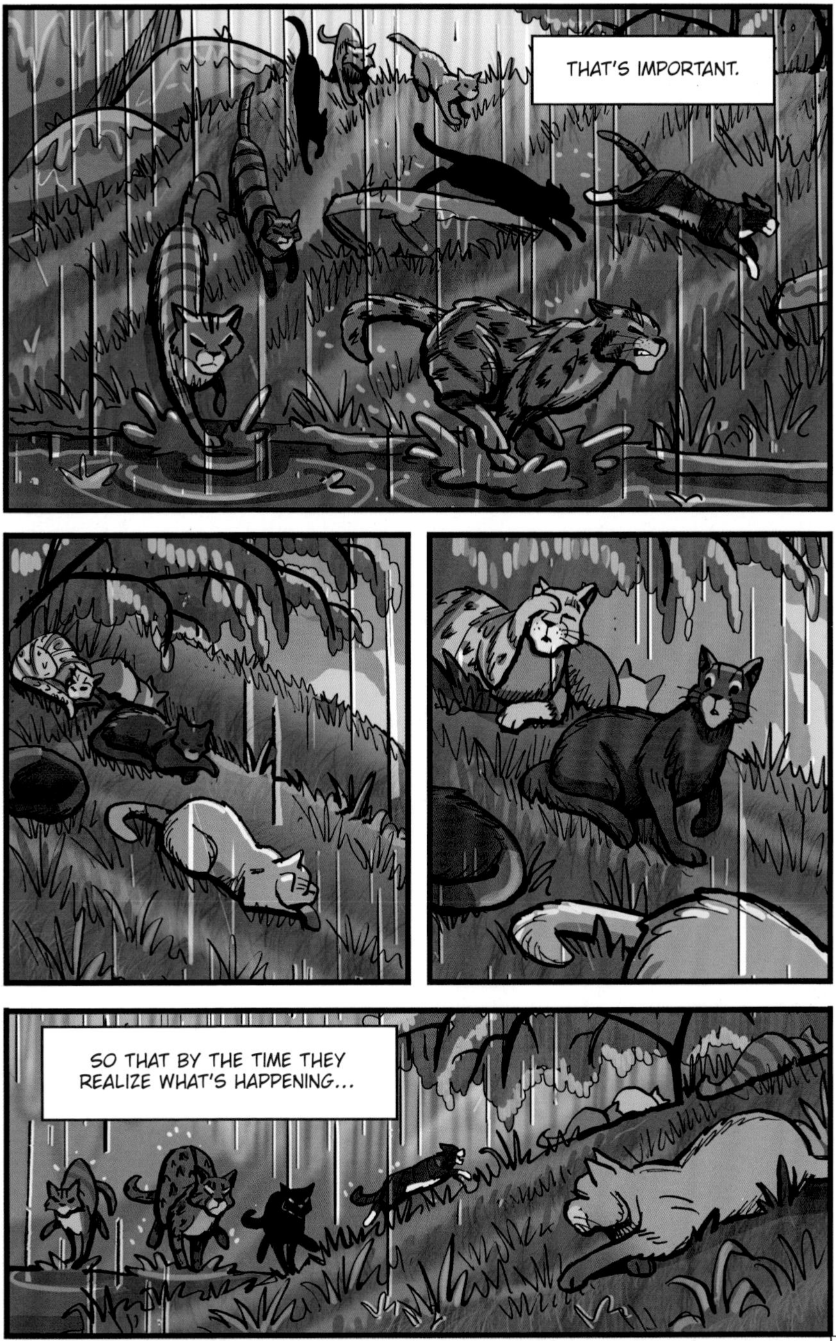
THAT'S IMPORTANT.
SO THAT BY THE TIME THEY REALIZE WHAT'S HAPPENING...

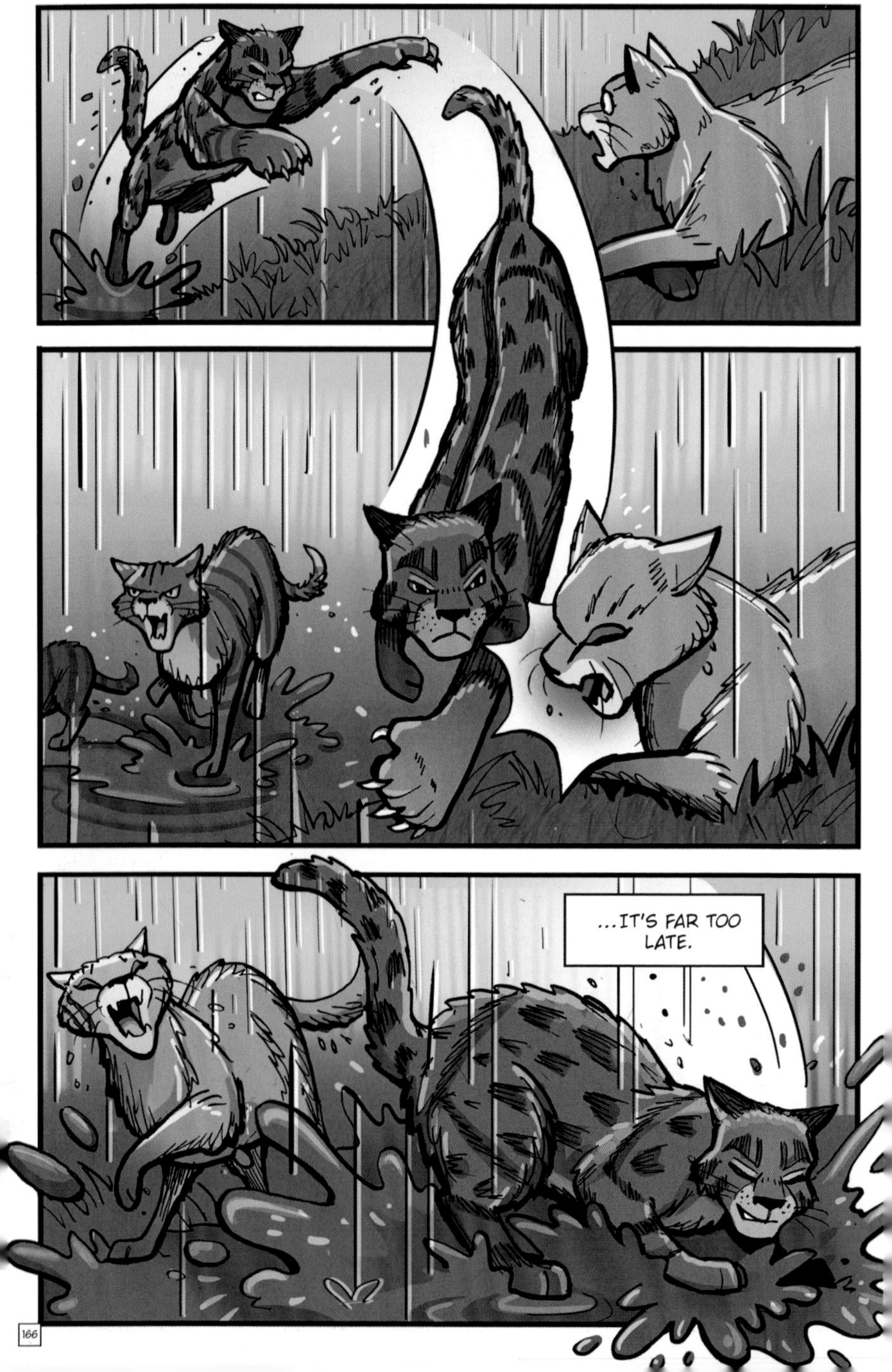
...IT'S FAR TOO LATE.

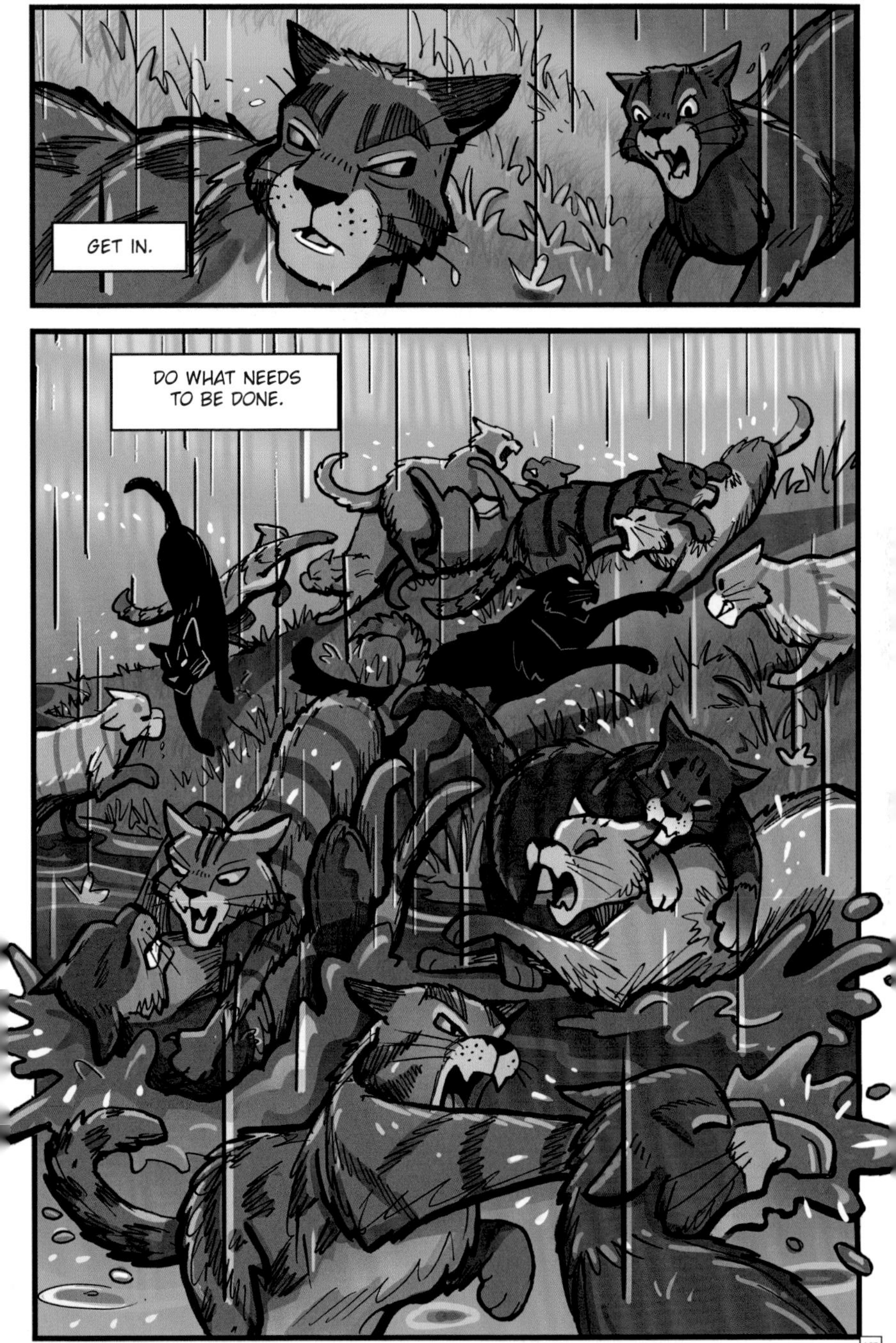
GET IN.
DO WHAT NEEDS TO BE DONE.

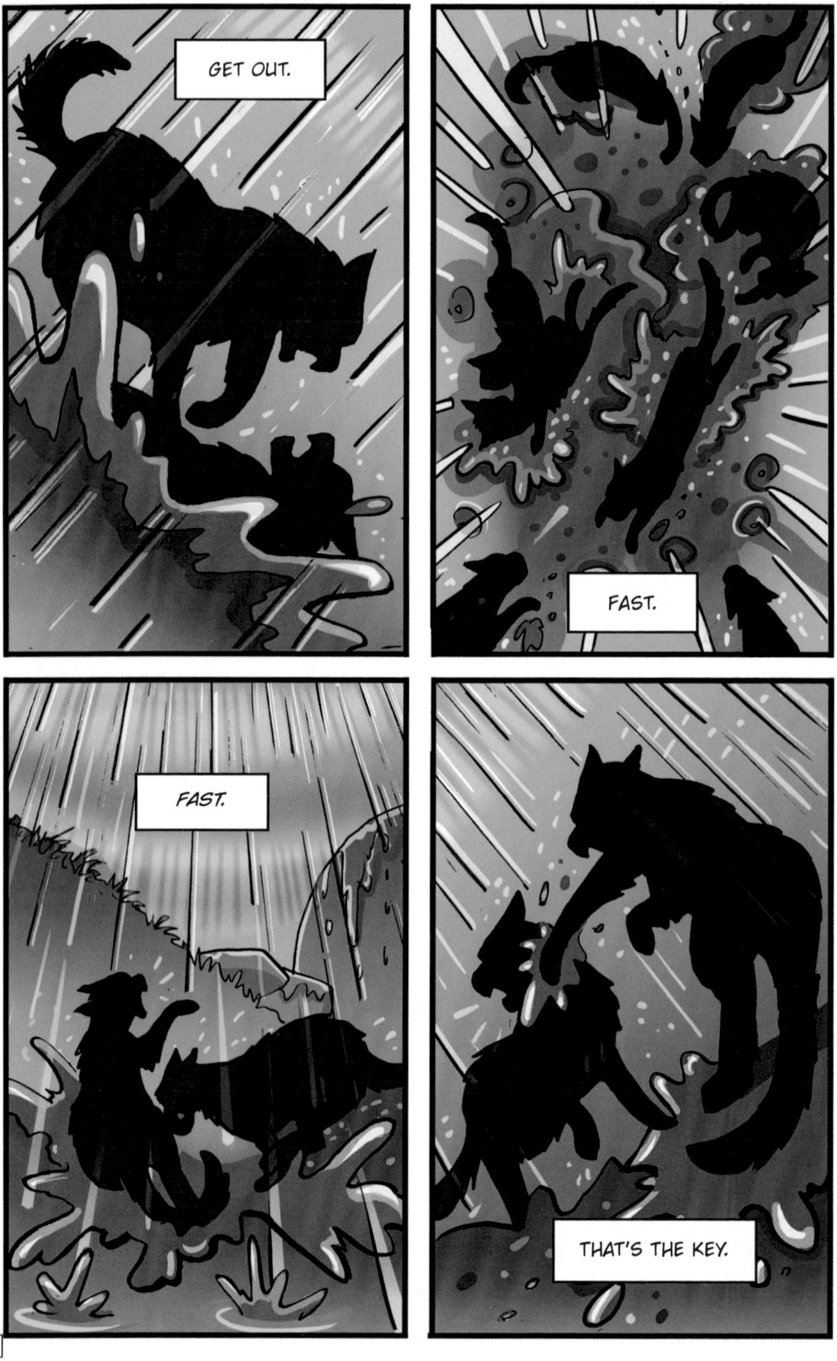
GET OUT.
FAST.
FAST.
THAT'S THE KEY.

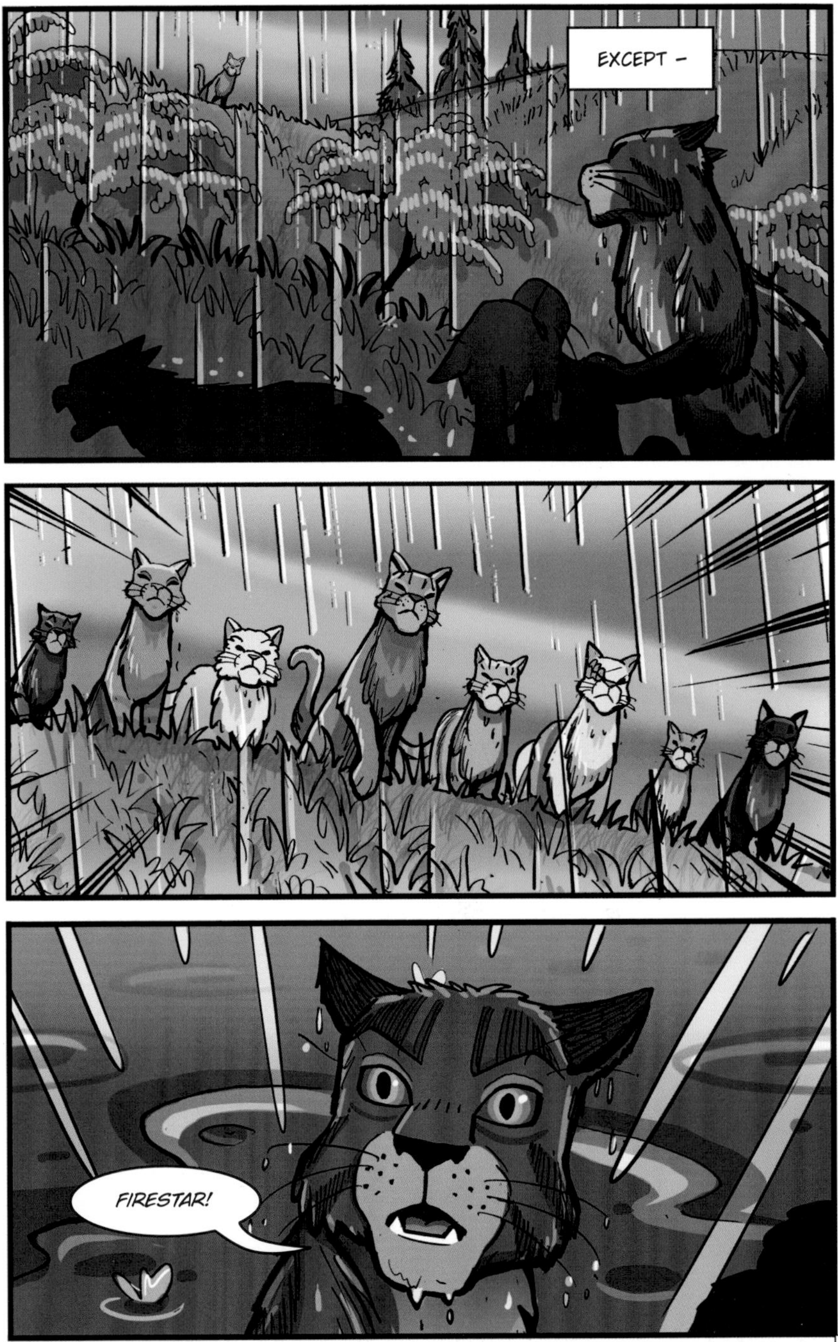
EXCEPT –
FIRESTAR!

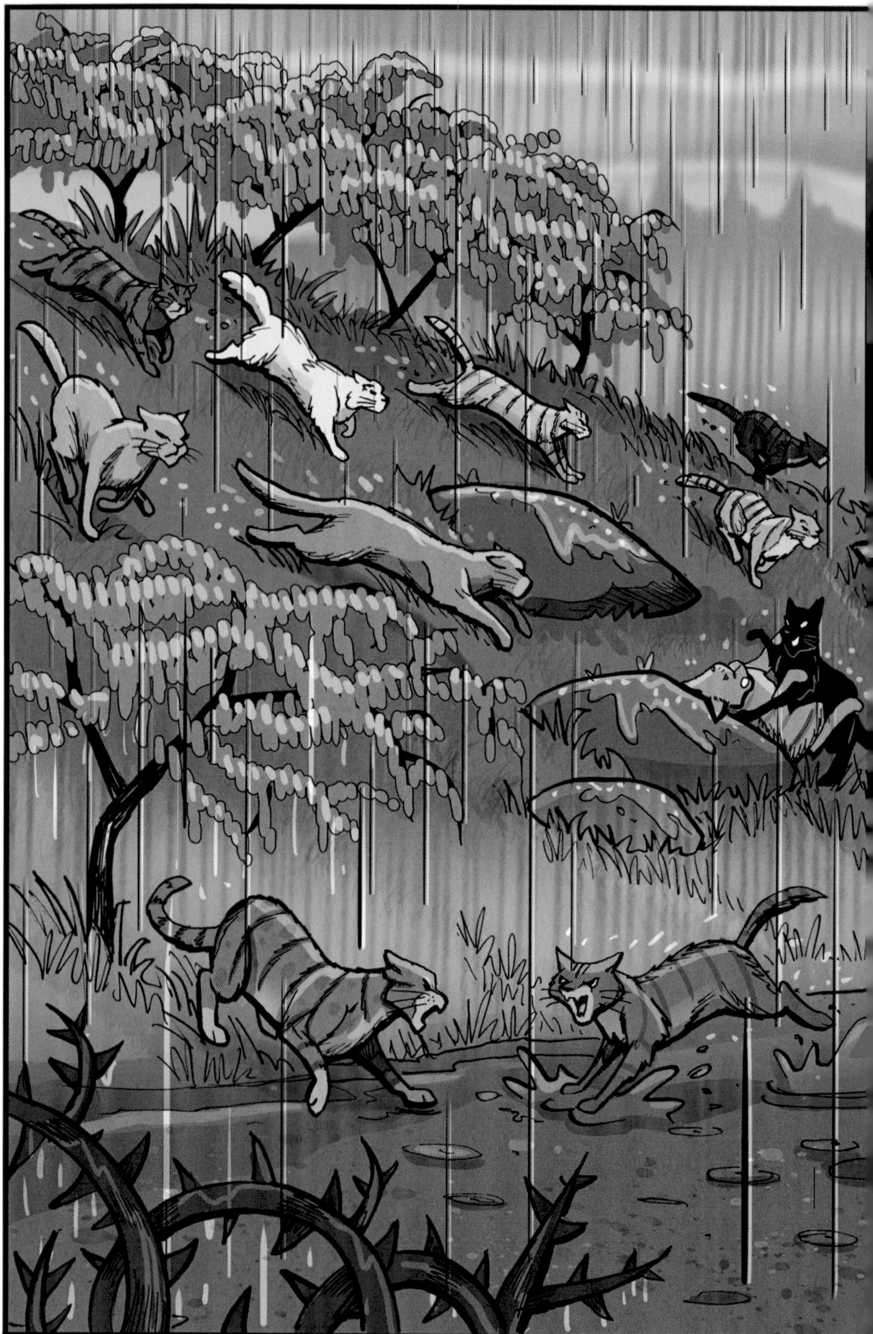

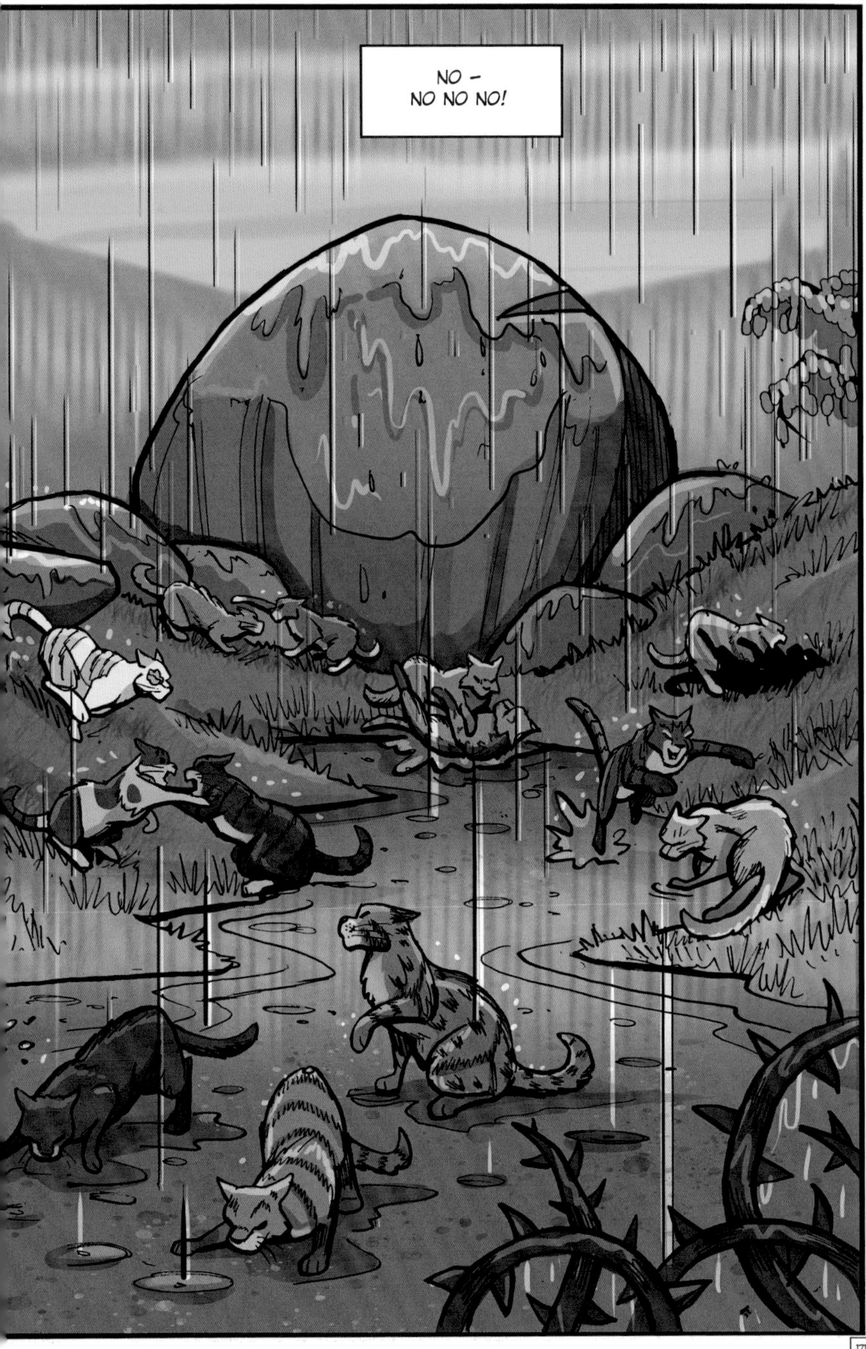
NO –
NO NO NO!

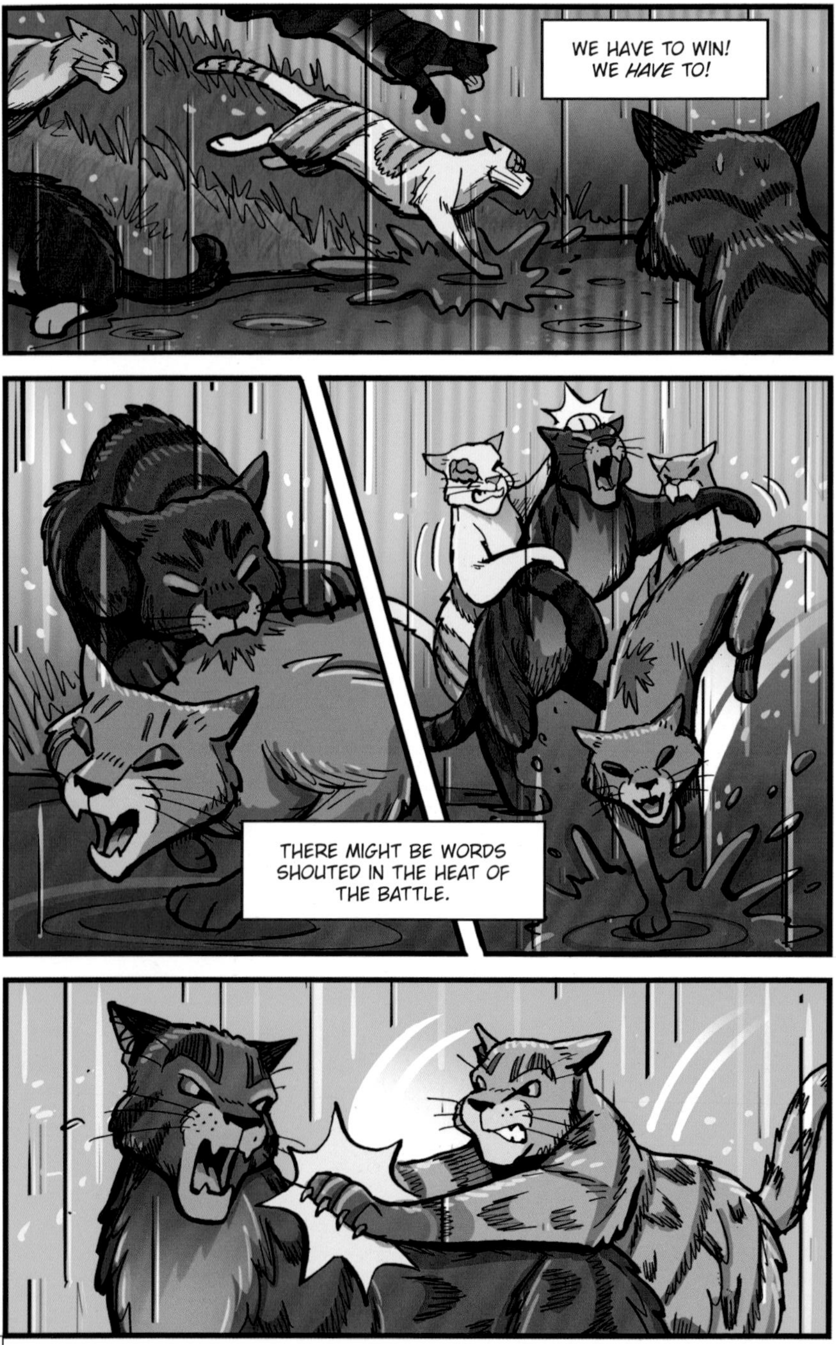
WE HAVE TO WIN!
WE *HAVE* TO!
THERE MIGHT BE WORDS SHOUTED IN THE HEAT OF THE BATTLE.

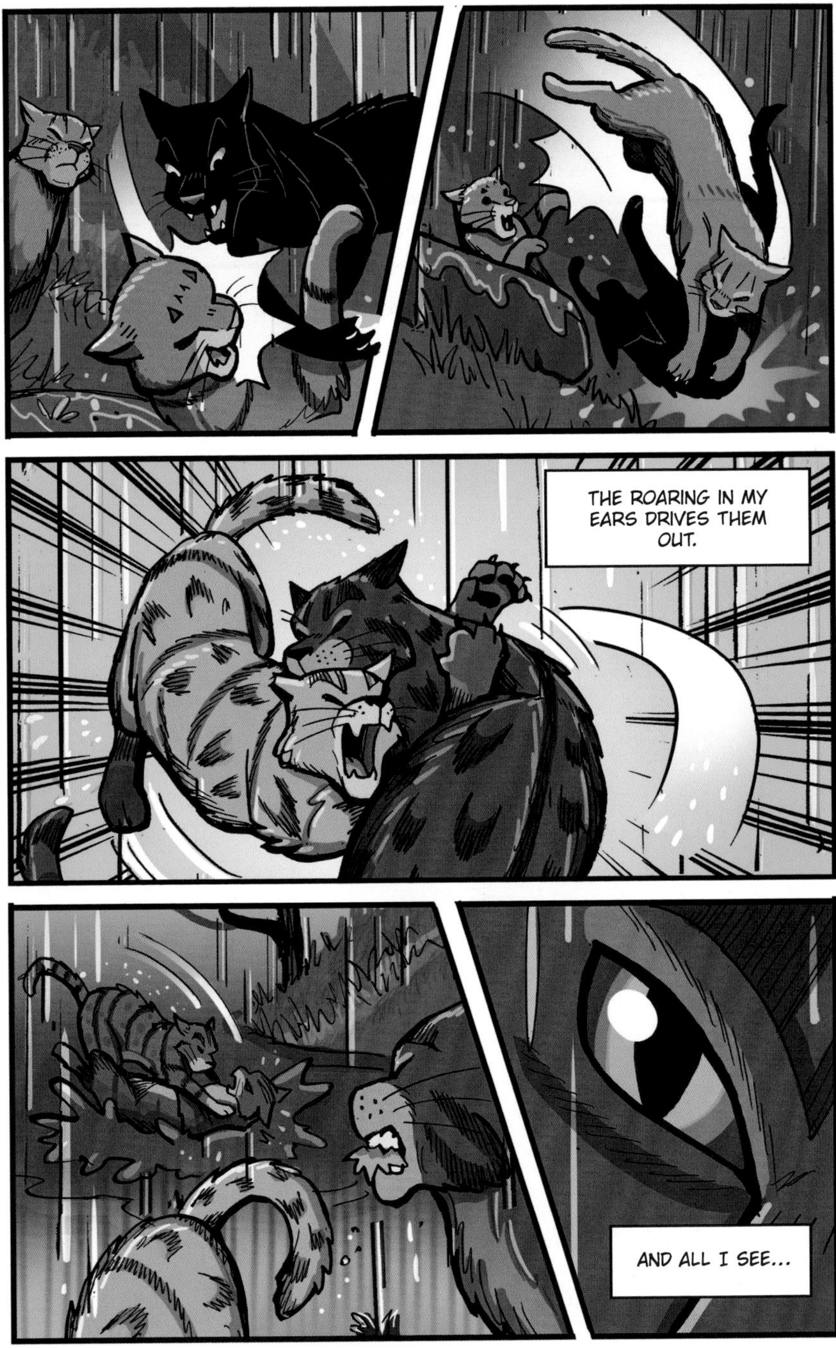
THE ROARING IN MY EARS DRIVES THEM OUT.
AND ALL I SEE...

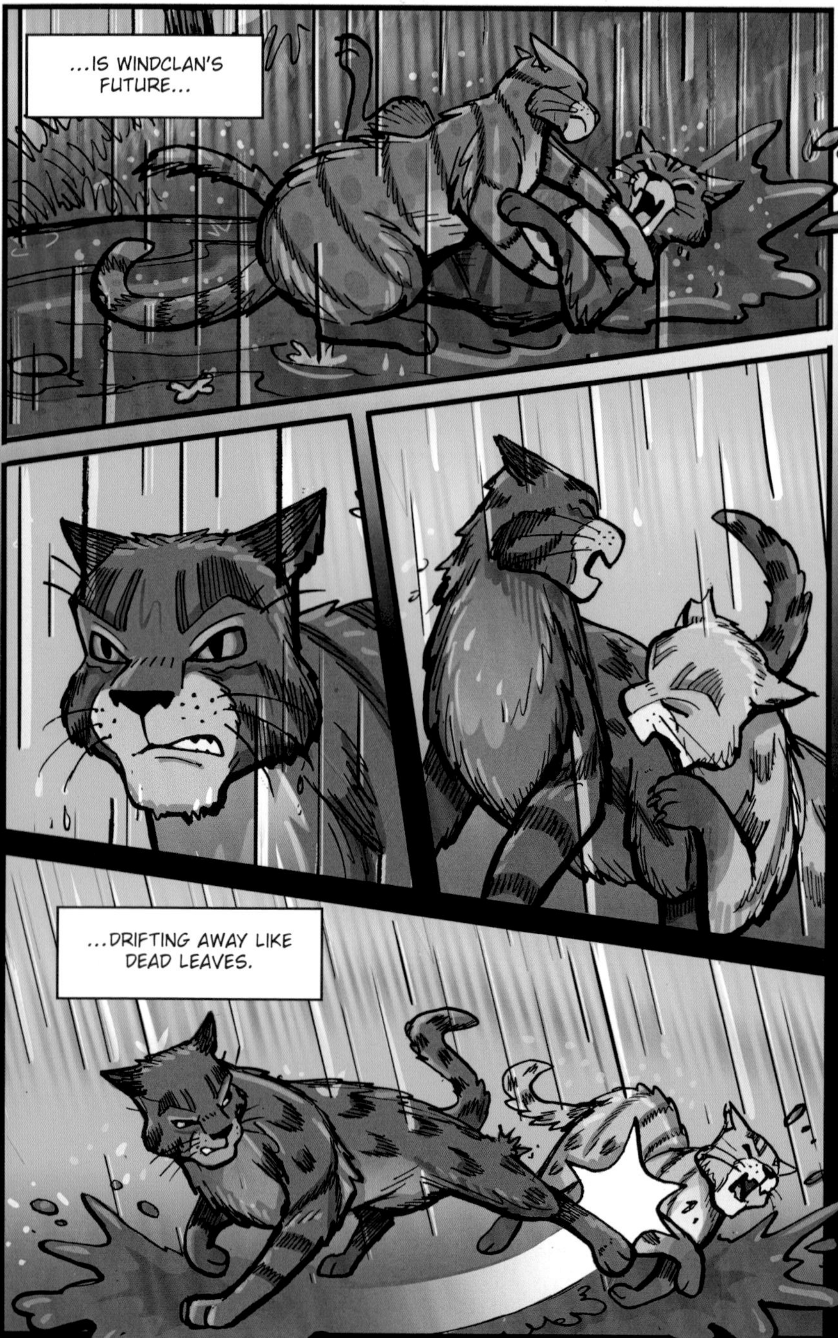
...IS WINDCLAN'S FUTURE...
...DRIFTING AWAY LIKE DEAD LEAVES.

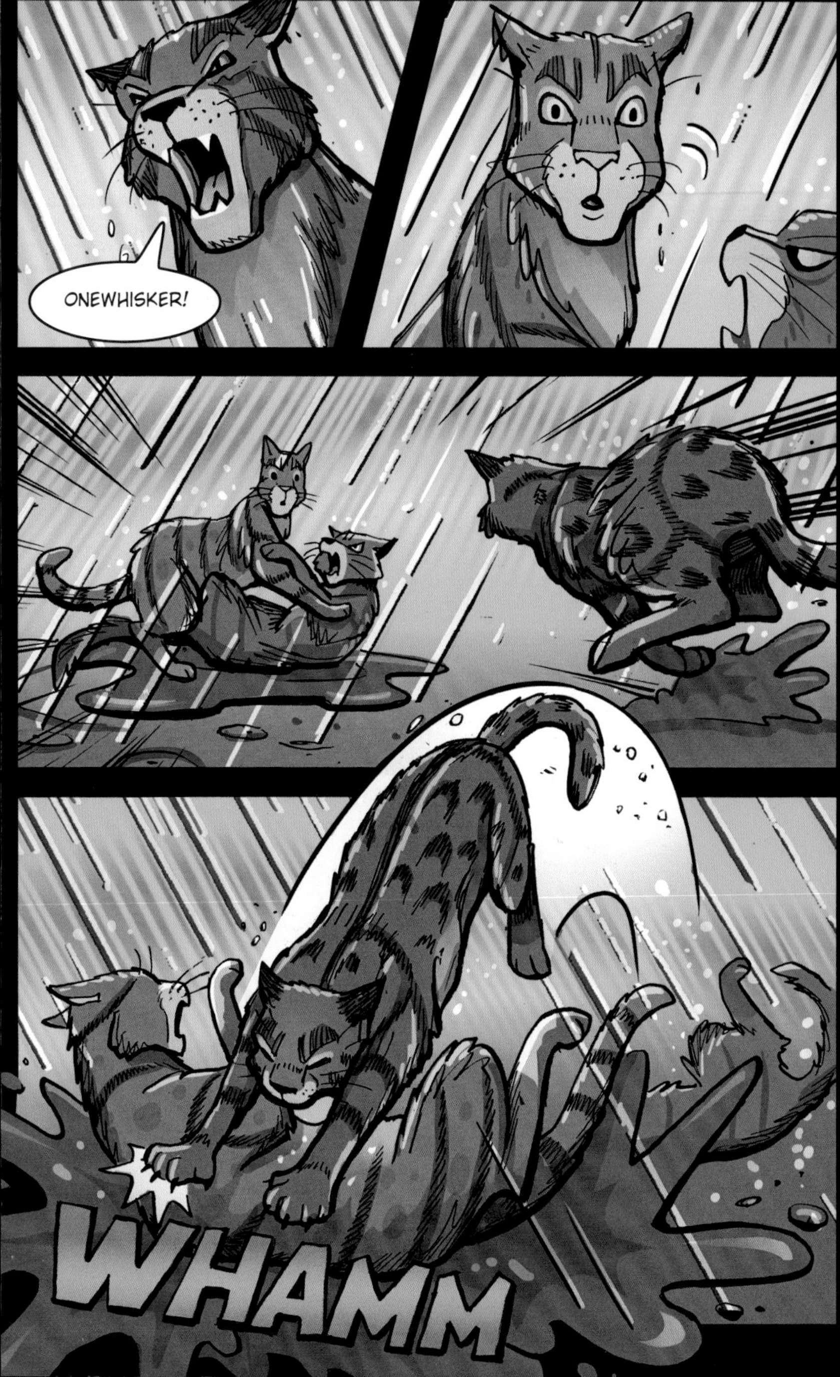
ONEWHISKER!
WHAMM

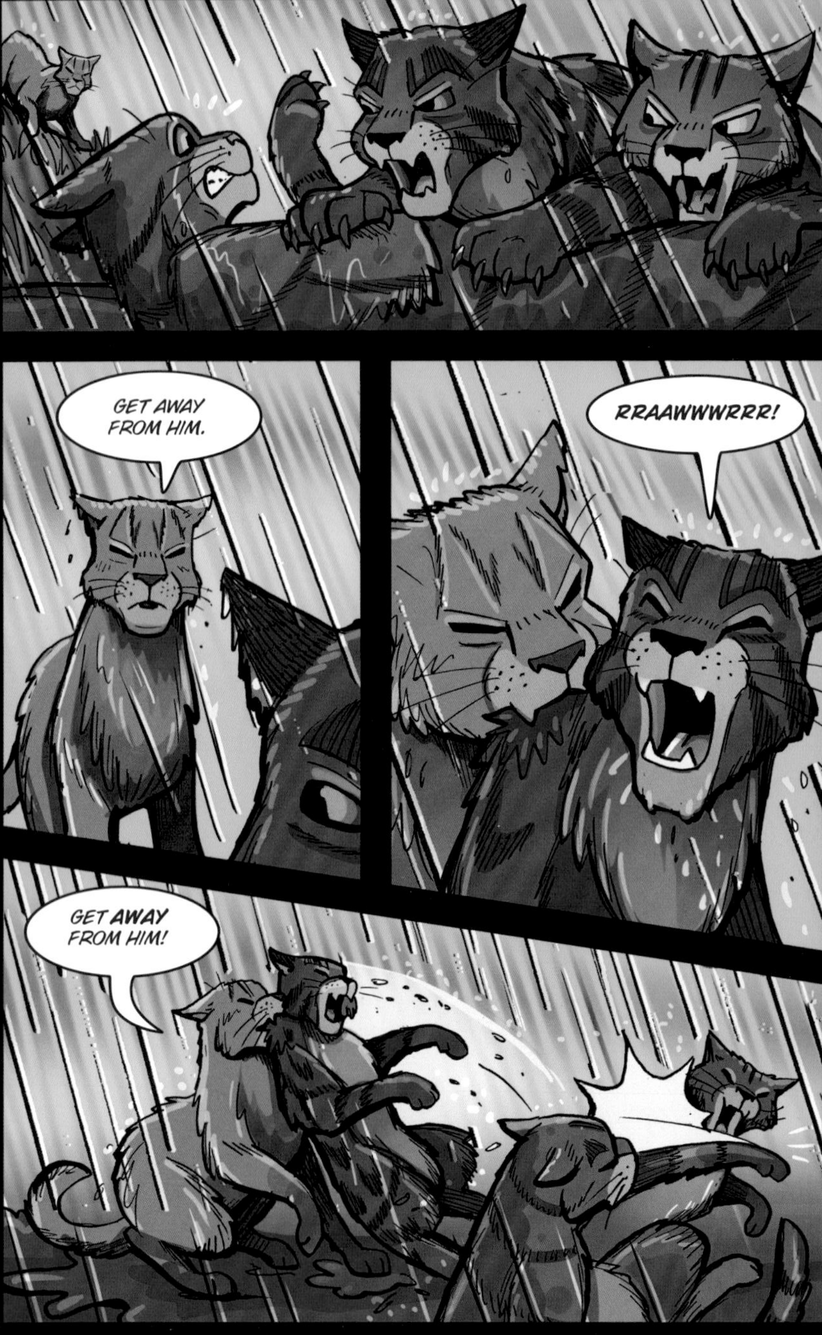
GET AWAY FROM HIM.
RRAAWWWRRR!
GET AWAY FROM HIM!

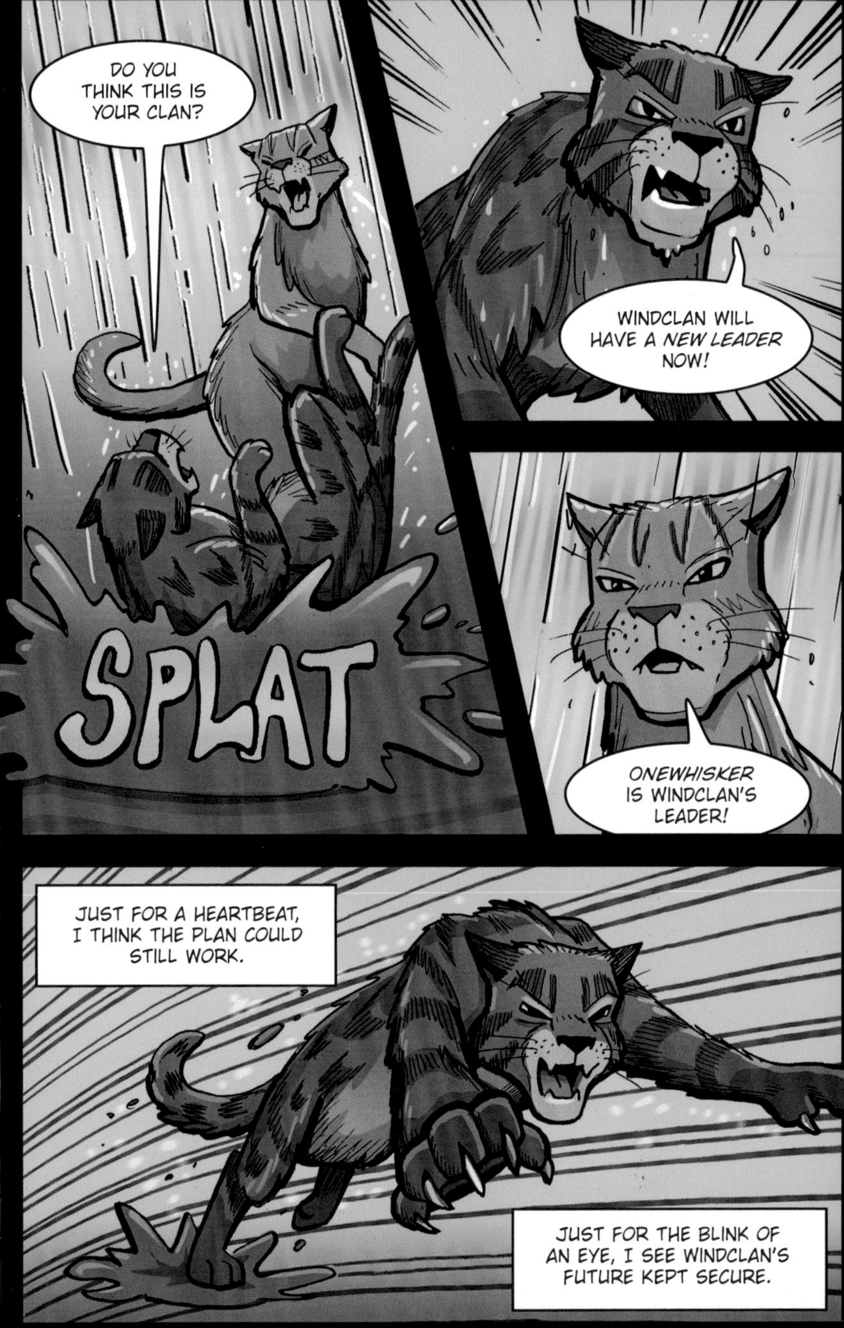
DO YOU THINK THIS IS YOUR CLAN?
SPLAT
WINDCLAN WILL HAVE A *NEW LEADER* NOW!
ONEWHISKER IS WINDCLAN'S LEADER!
JUST FOR A HEARTBEAT, I THINK THE PLAN COULD STILL WORK.
JUST FOR THE BLINK OF AN EYE, I SEE WINDCLAN'S FUTURE KEPT SECURE.

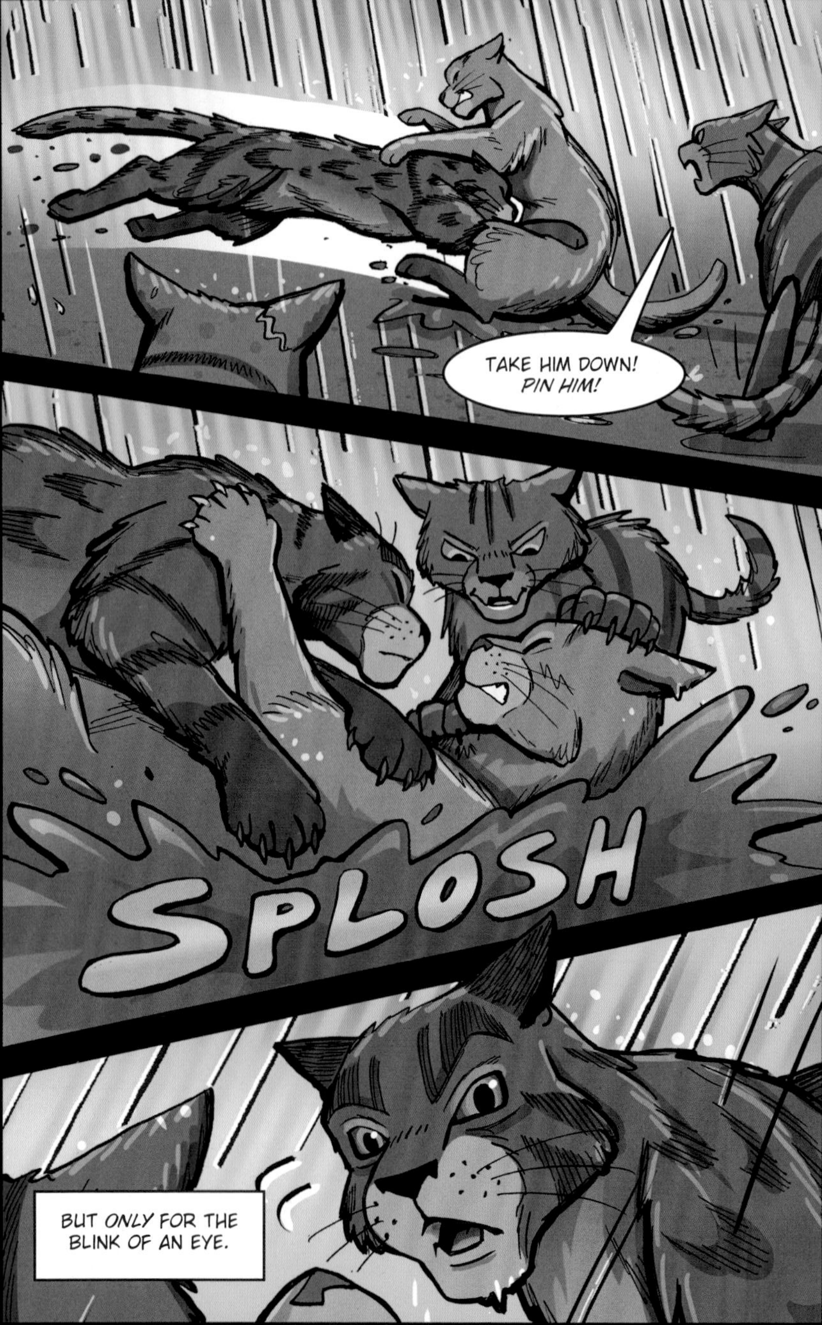
TAKE HIM DOWN! *PIN HIM!*
SPLOSH
BUT *ONLY* FOR THE BLINK OF AN EYE.

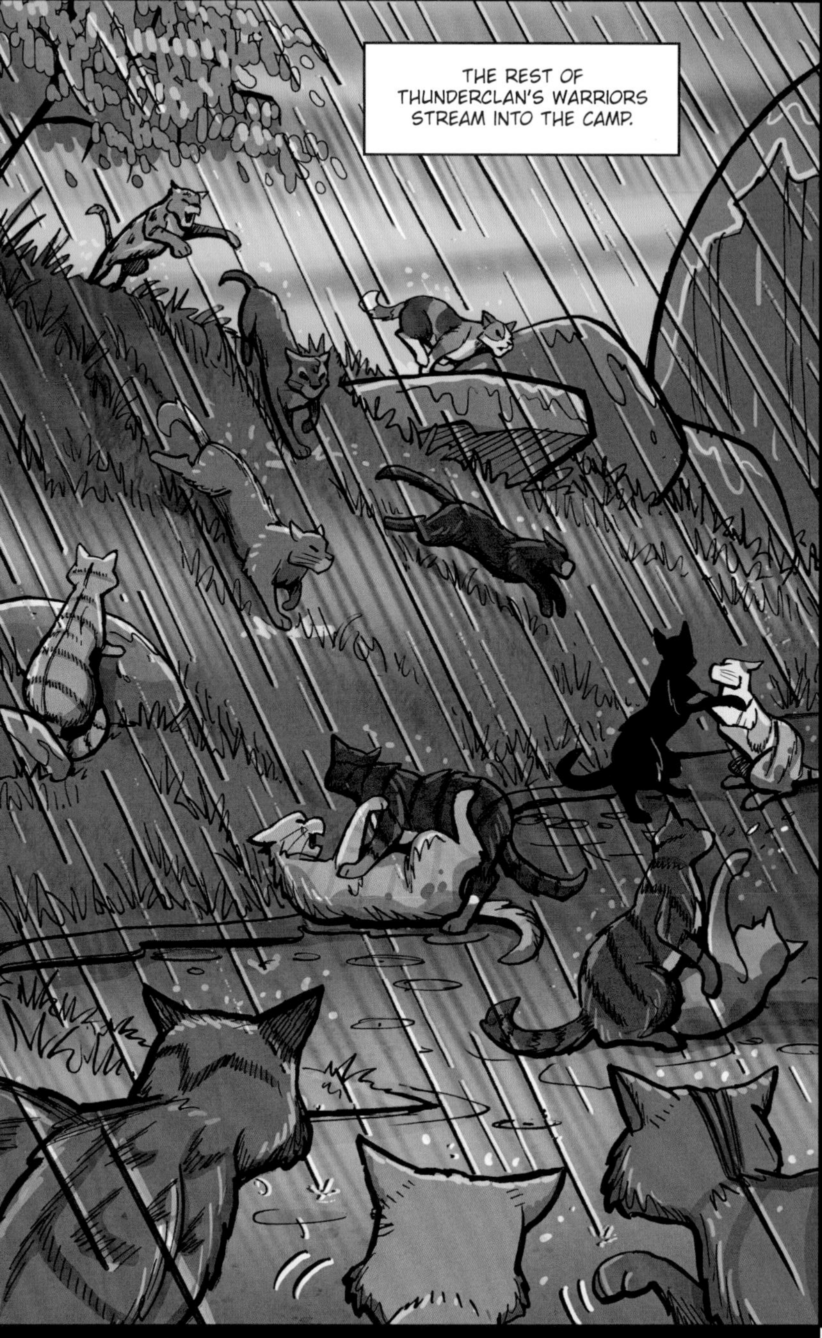
THE REST OF THUNDERCLAN'S WARRIORS STREAM INTO THE CAMP.

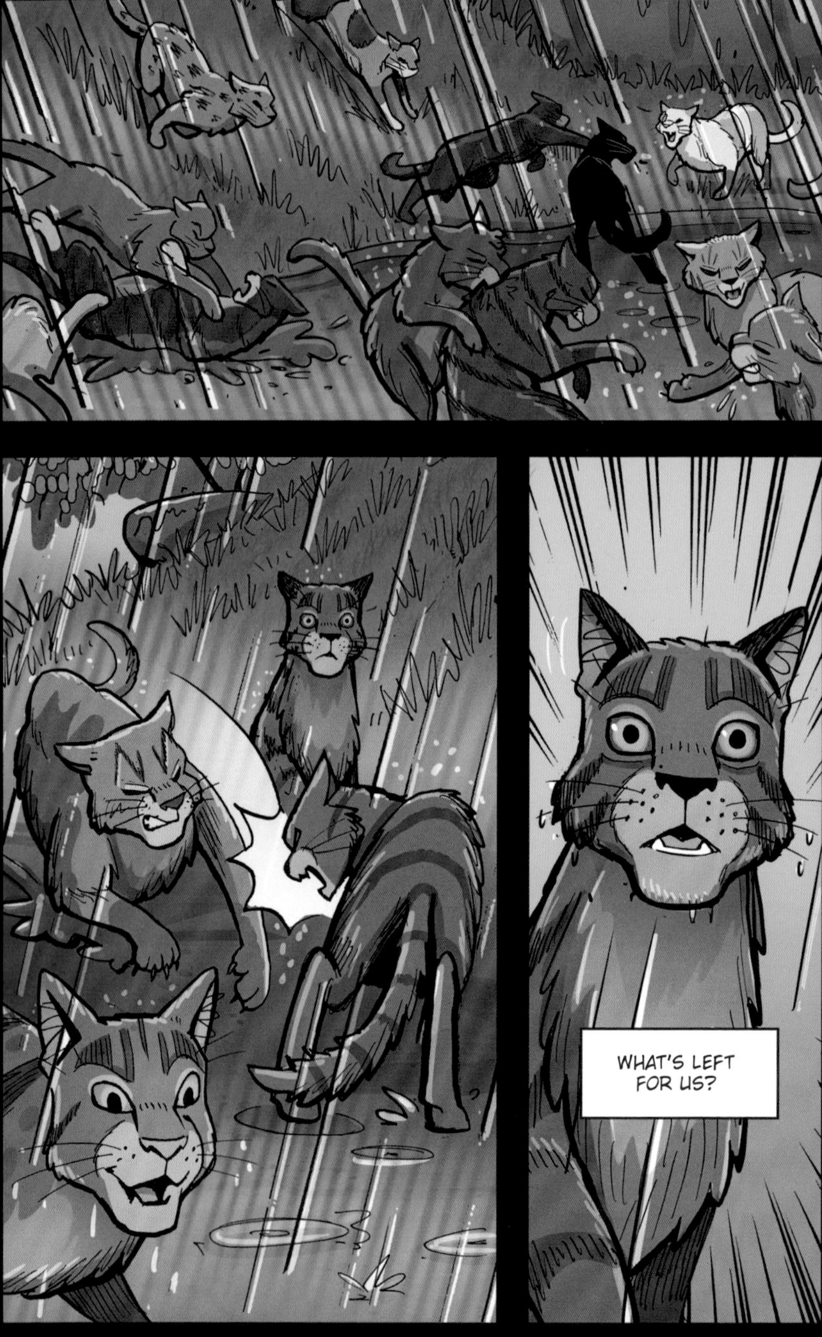
WHAT'S LEFT
FOR US?

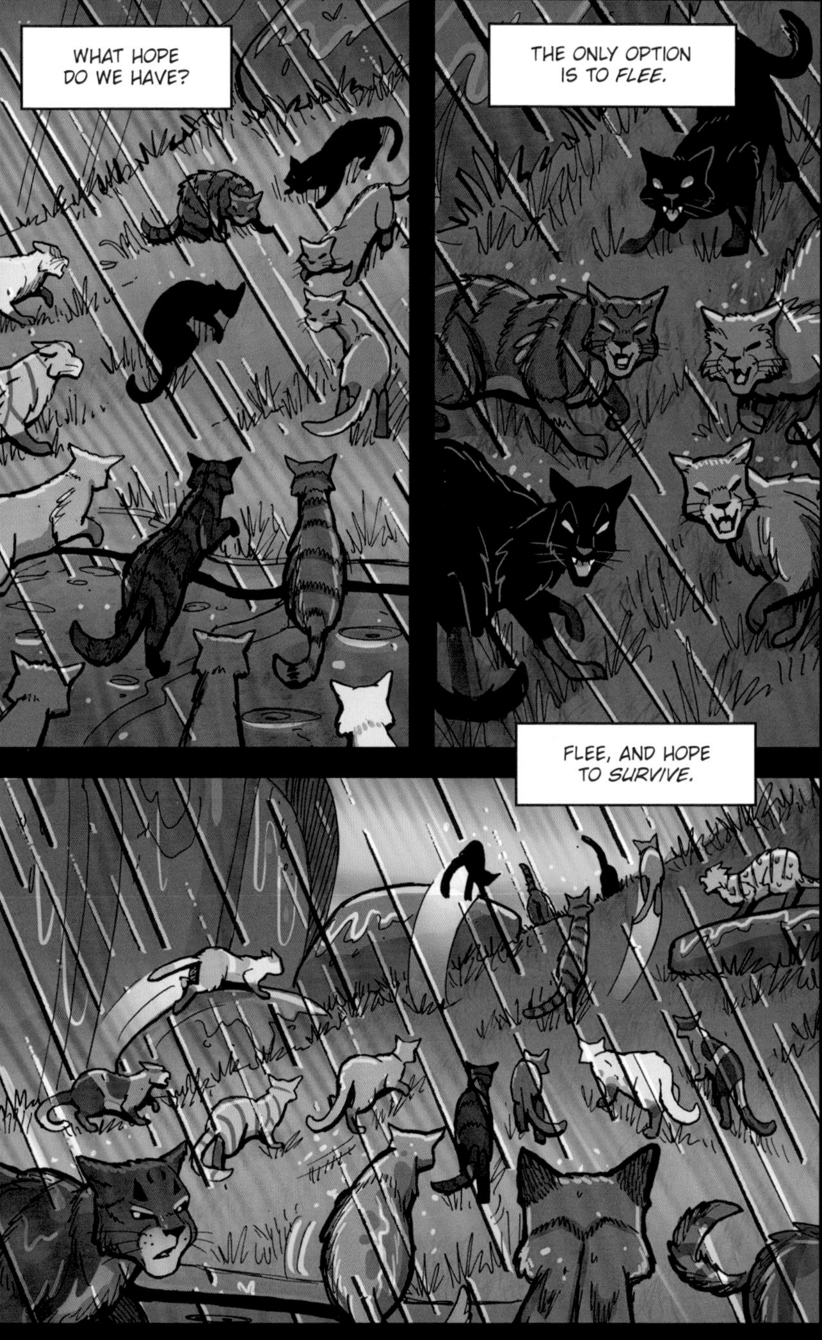
WHAT HOPE DO WE HAVE?
THE ONLY OPTION IS TO *FLEE.*
FLEE, AND HOPE TO *SURVIVE.*

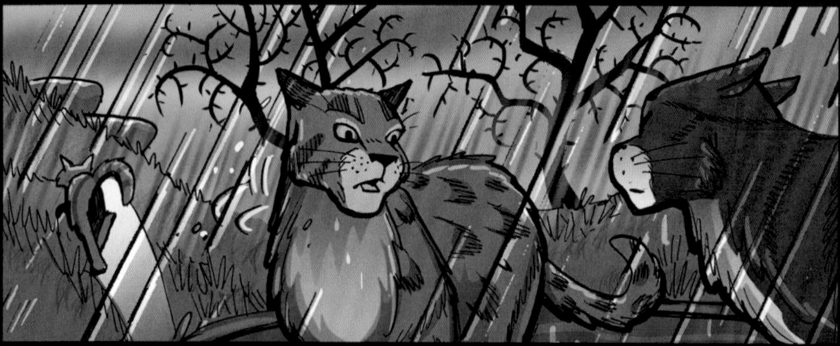

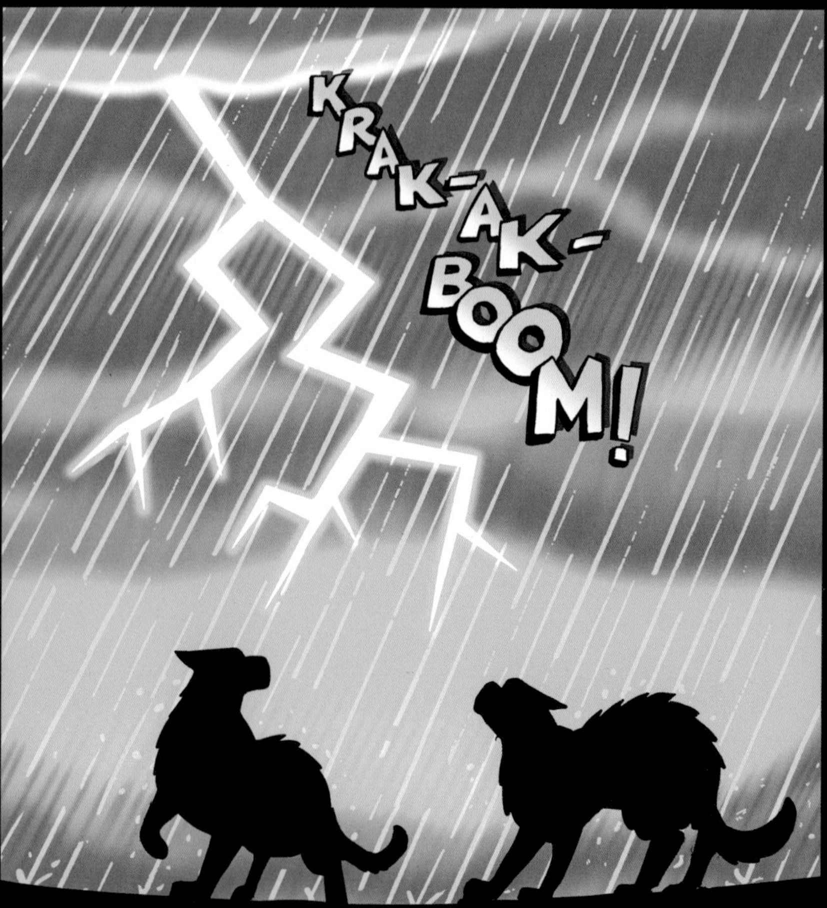
KRAK-AK-BOOM!

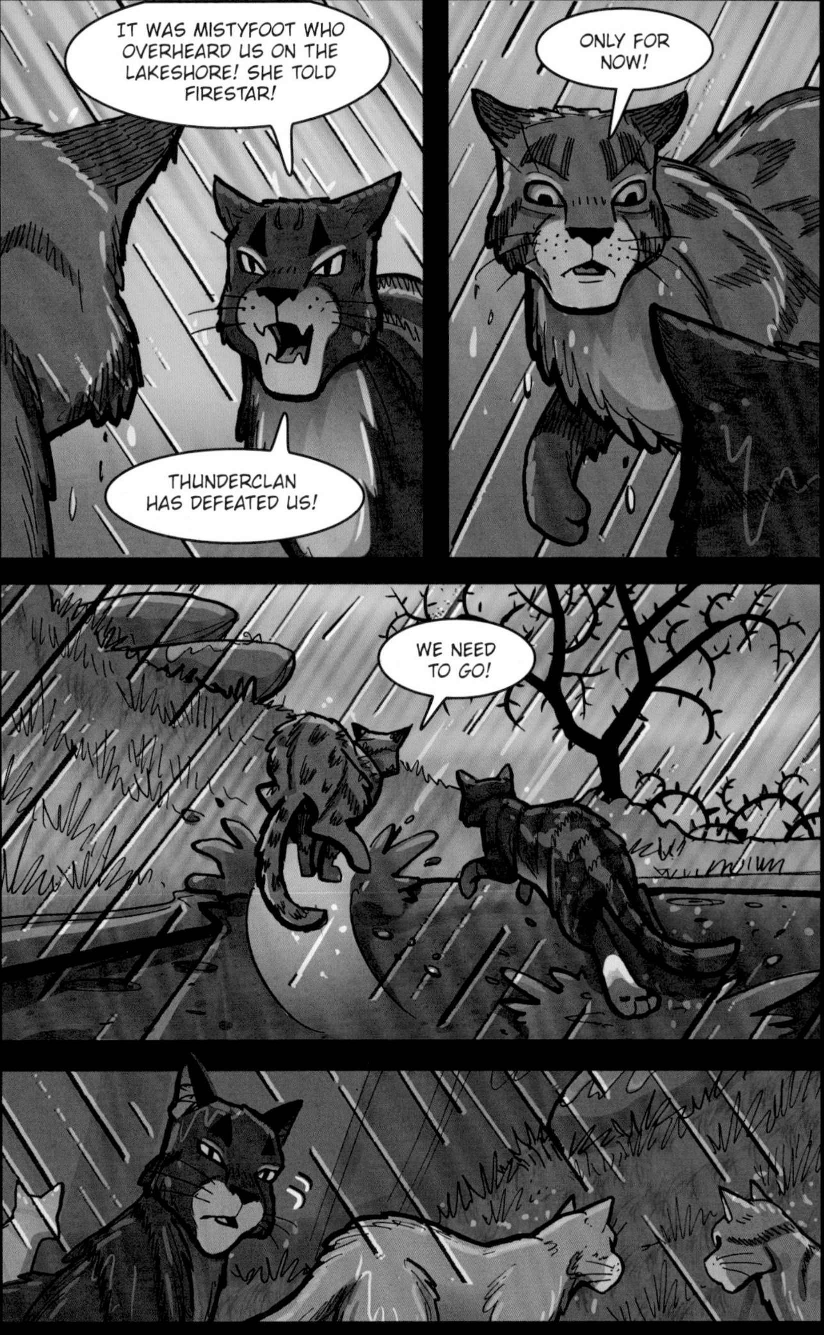
IT WAS MISTYFOOT WHO OVERHEARD US ON THE LAKESHORE! SHE TOLD FIRESTAR!
THUNDERCLAN HAS DEFEATED US!
ONLY FOR NOW!
WE NEED TO GO!

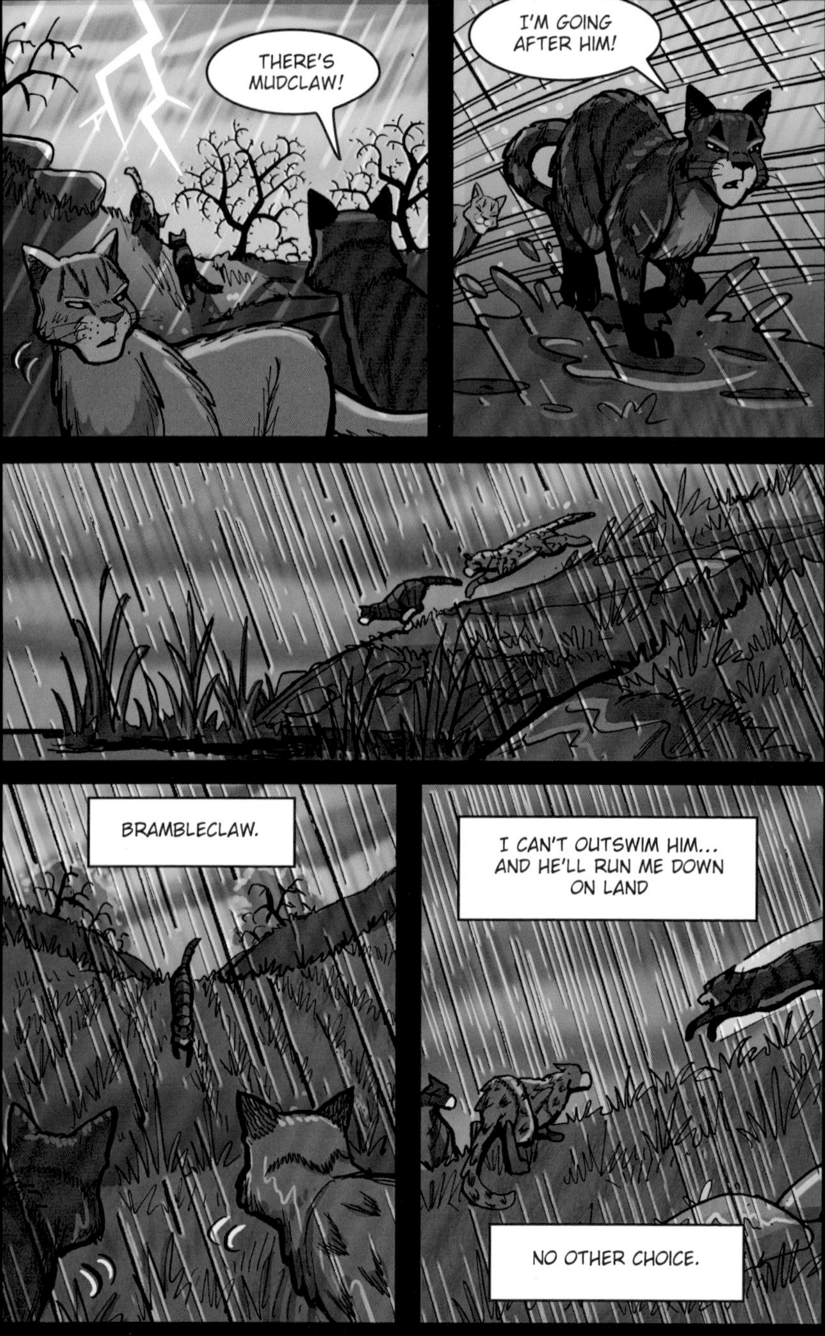
THERE'S MUDCLAW!
I'M GOING AFTER HIM!
BRAMBLECLAW.
I CAN'T OUTSWIM HIM... AND HE'LL RUN ME DOWN ON LAND
NO OTHER CHOICE.

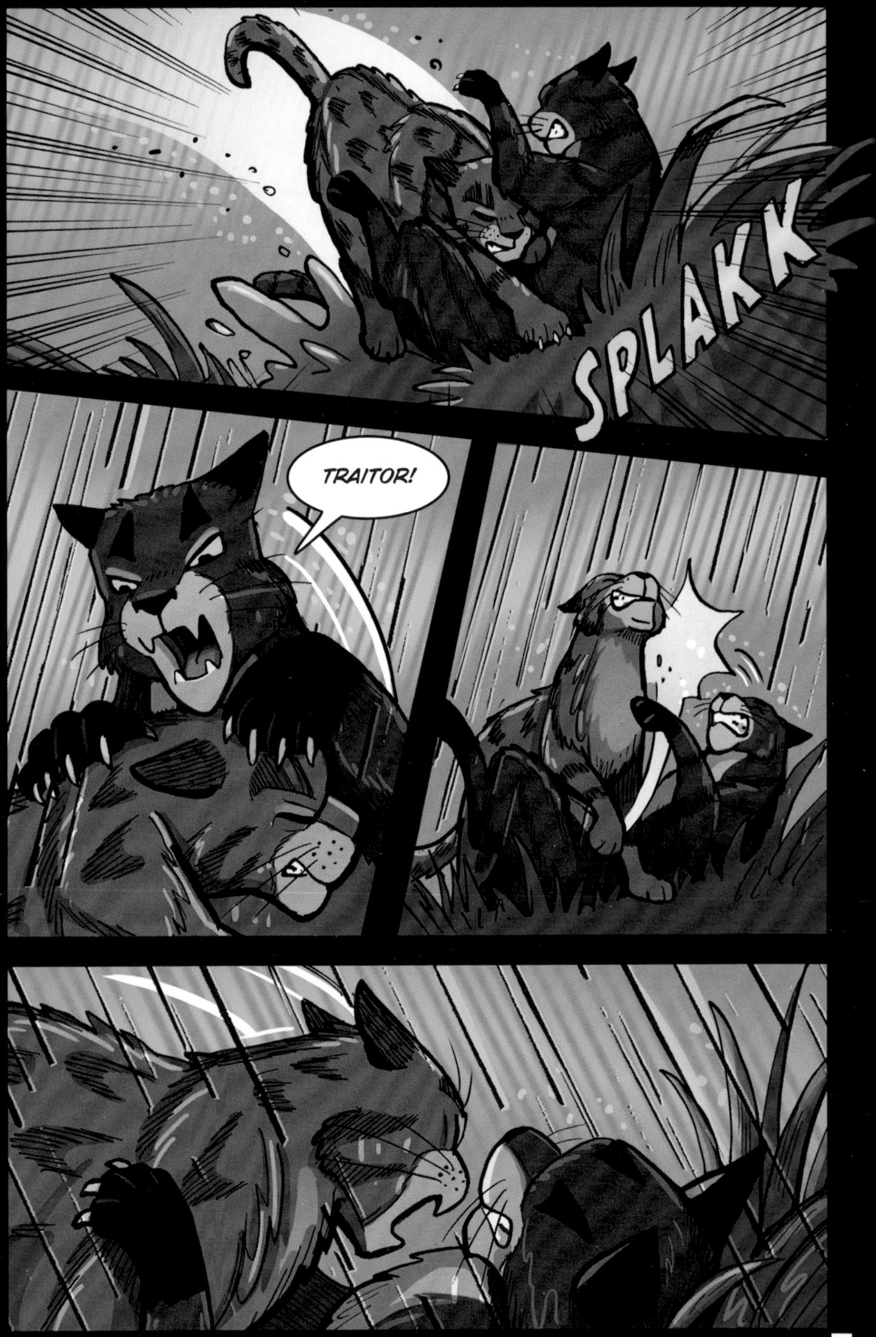
SPLAKK
TRAITOR!

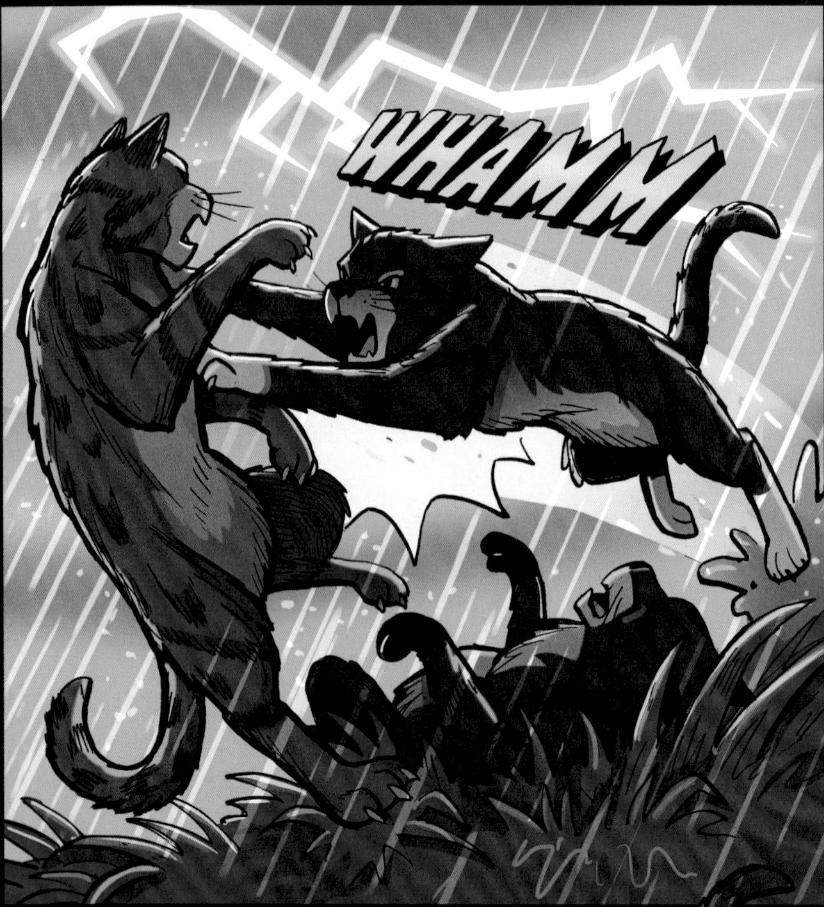
WHAMM
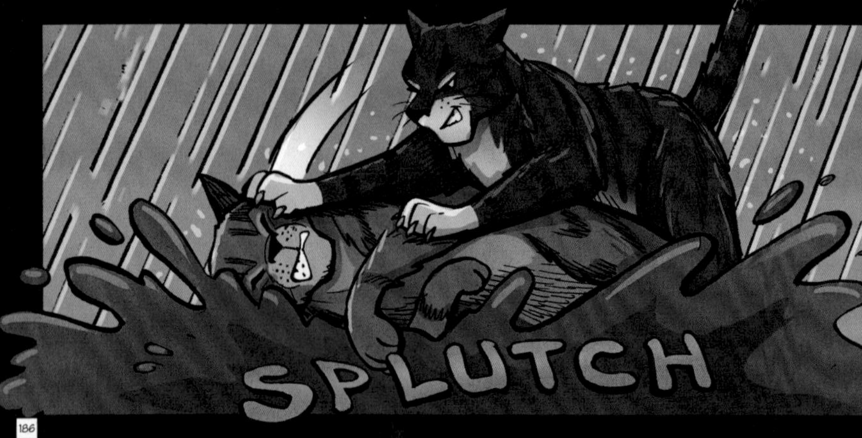
SPLUTCH

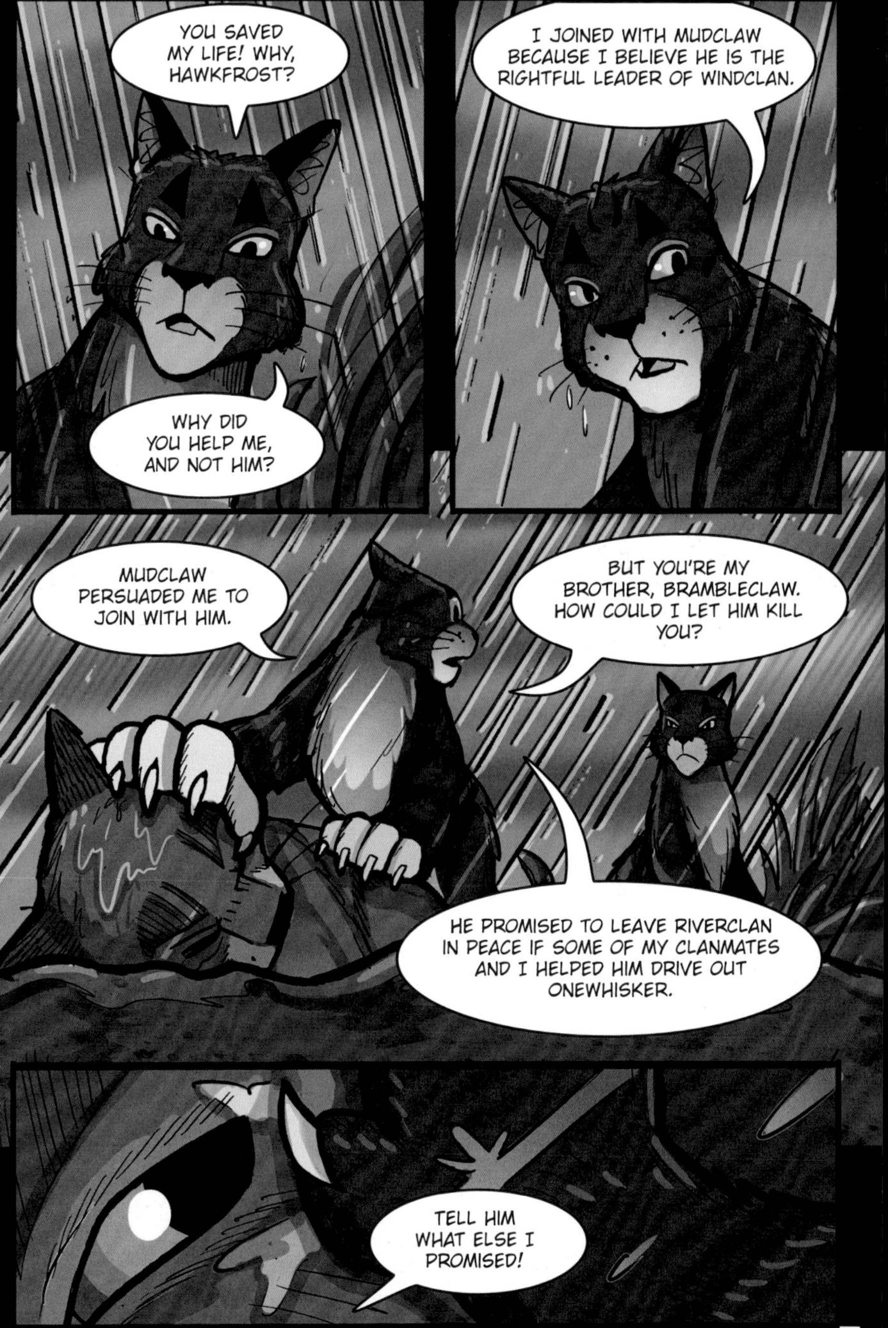
YOU SAVED MY LIFE! WHY, HAWKFROST?
WHY DID YOU HELP ME, AND NOT HIM?
I JOINED WITH MUDCLAW BECAUSE I BELIEVE HE IS THE RIGHTFUL LEADER OF WINDCLAN.
MUDCLAW PERSUADED ME TO JOIN WITH HIM.
BUT YOU'RE MY BROTHER, BRAMBLECLAW. HOW COULD I LET HIM KILL YOU?
HE PROMISED TO LEAVE RIVERCLAN IN PEACE IF SOME OF MY CLANMATES AND I HELPED HIM DRIVE OUT ONEWHISKER.
TELL HIM WHAT ELSE I PROMISED!

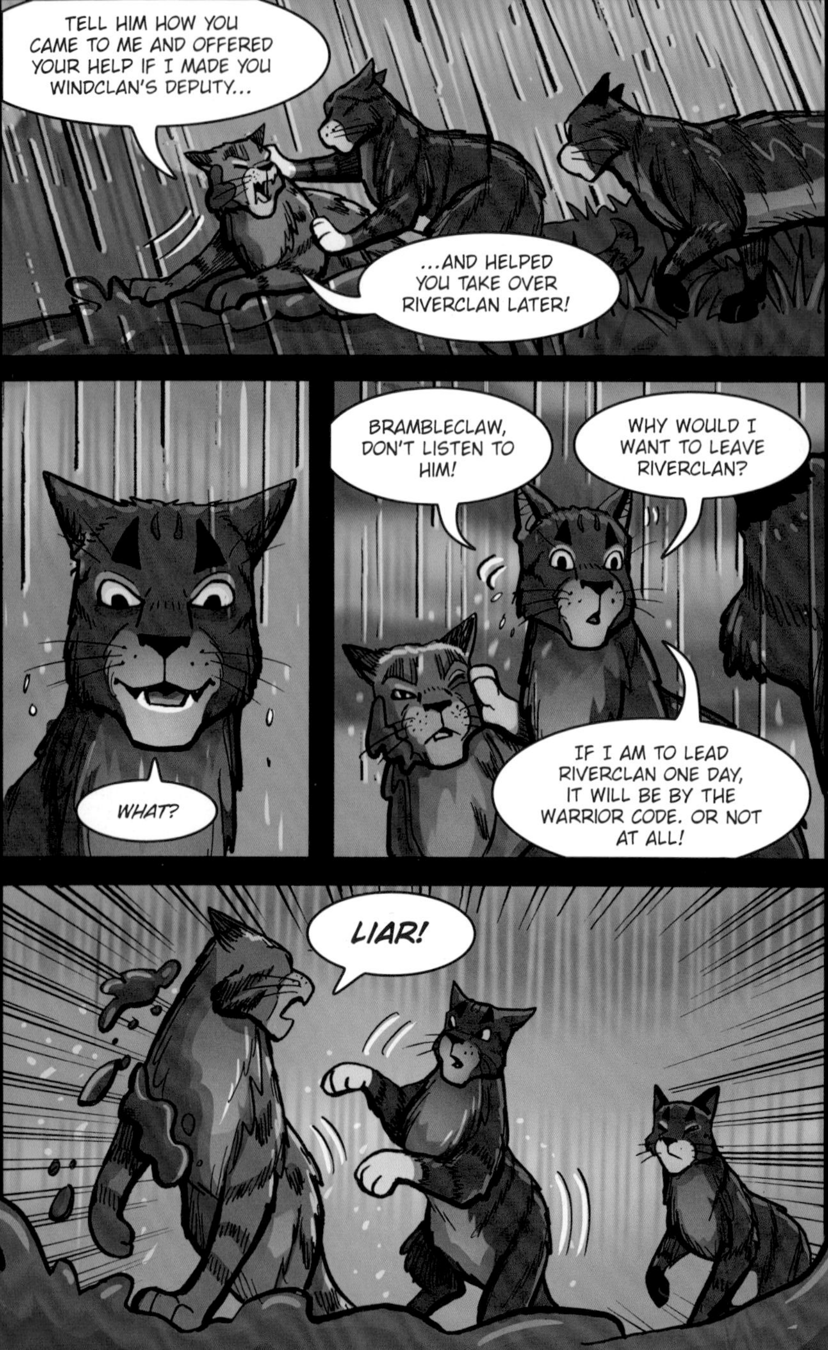
TELL HIM HOW YOU CAME TO ME AND OFFERED YOUR HELP IF I MADE YOU WINDCLAN'S DEPUTY...
...AND HELPED YOU TAKE OVER RIVERCLAN LATER!
WHAT?
BRAMBLECLAW, DON'T LISTEN TO HIM!
WHY WOULD I WANT TO LEAVE RIVERCLAN?
IF I AM TO LEAD RIVERCLAN ONE DAY, IT WILL BE BY THE WARRIOR CODE. OR NOT AT ALL!
LIAR!

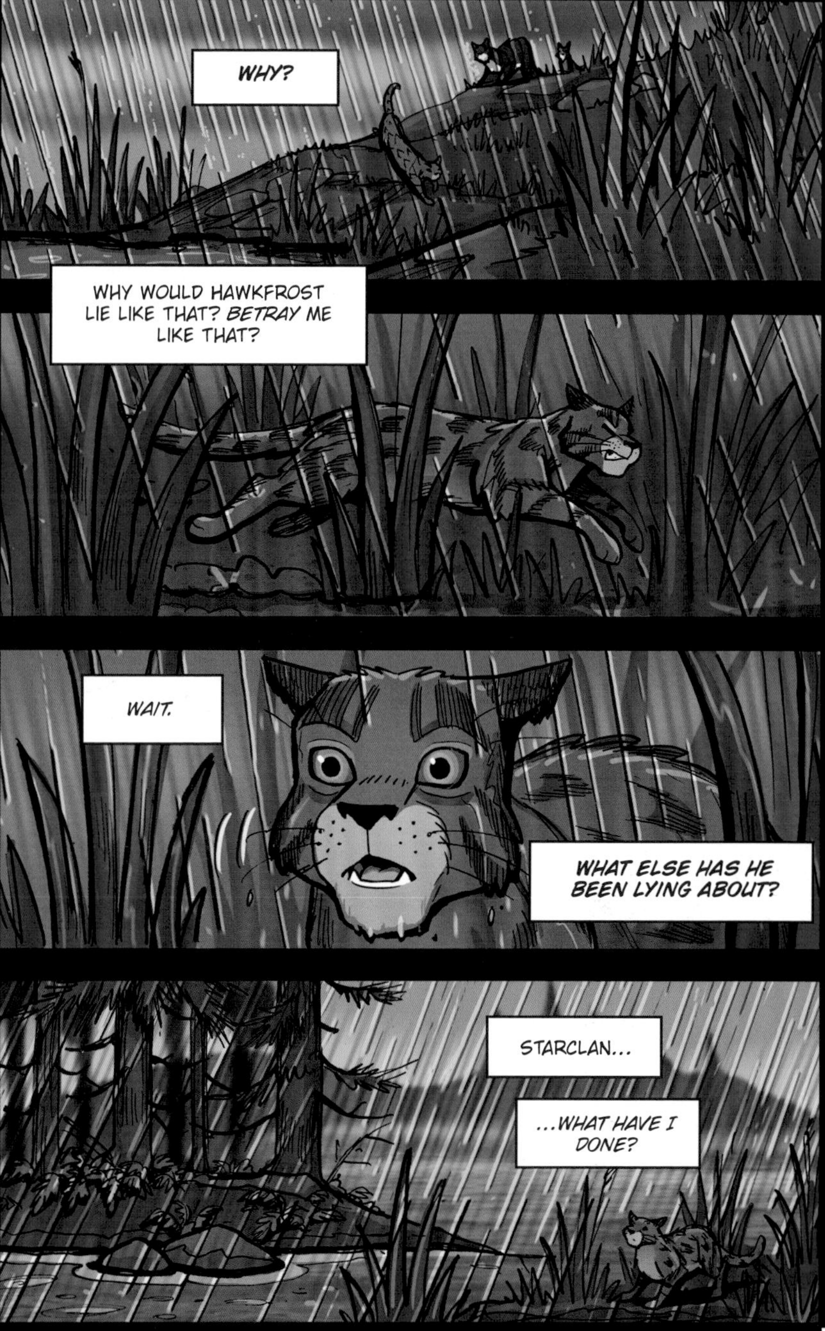
WHY?
WHY WOULD HAWKFROST LIE LIKE THAT? BETRAY ME LIKE THAT?
WAIT.
WHAT ELSE HAS HE BEEN LYING ABOUT?
STARCLAN...
...WHAT HAVE I DONE?

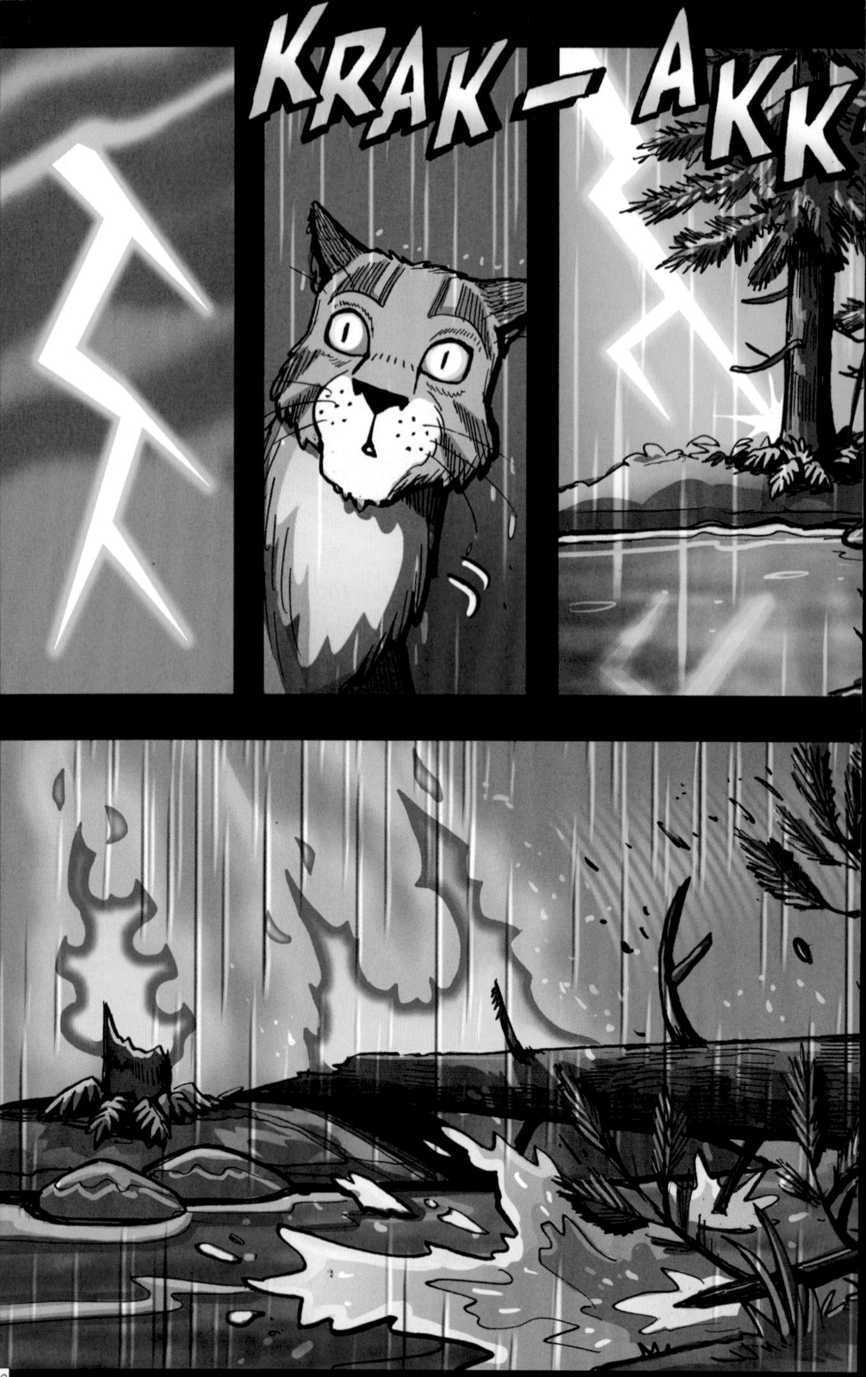
KRAK-AKK

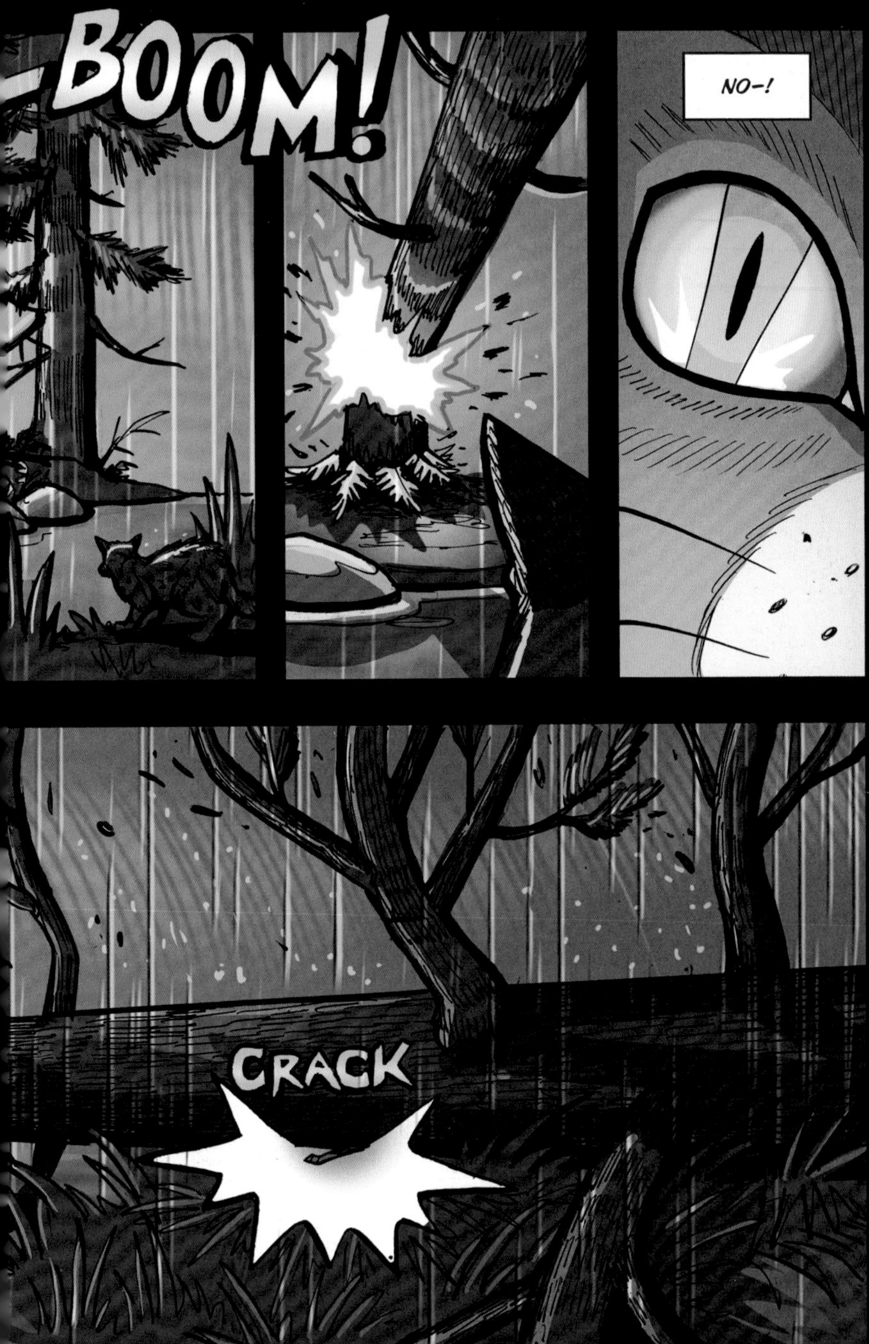
BOOM!
NO–!
CRACK

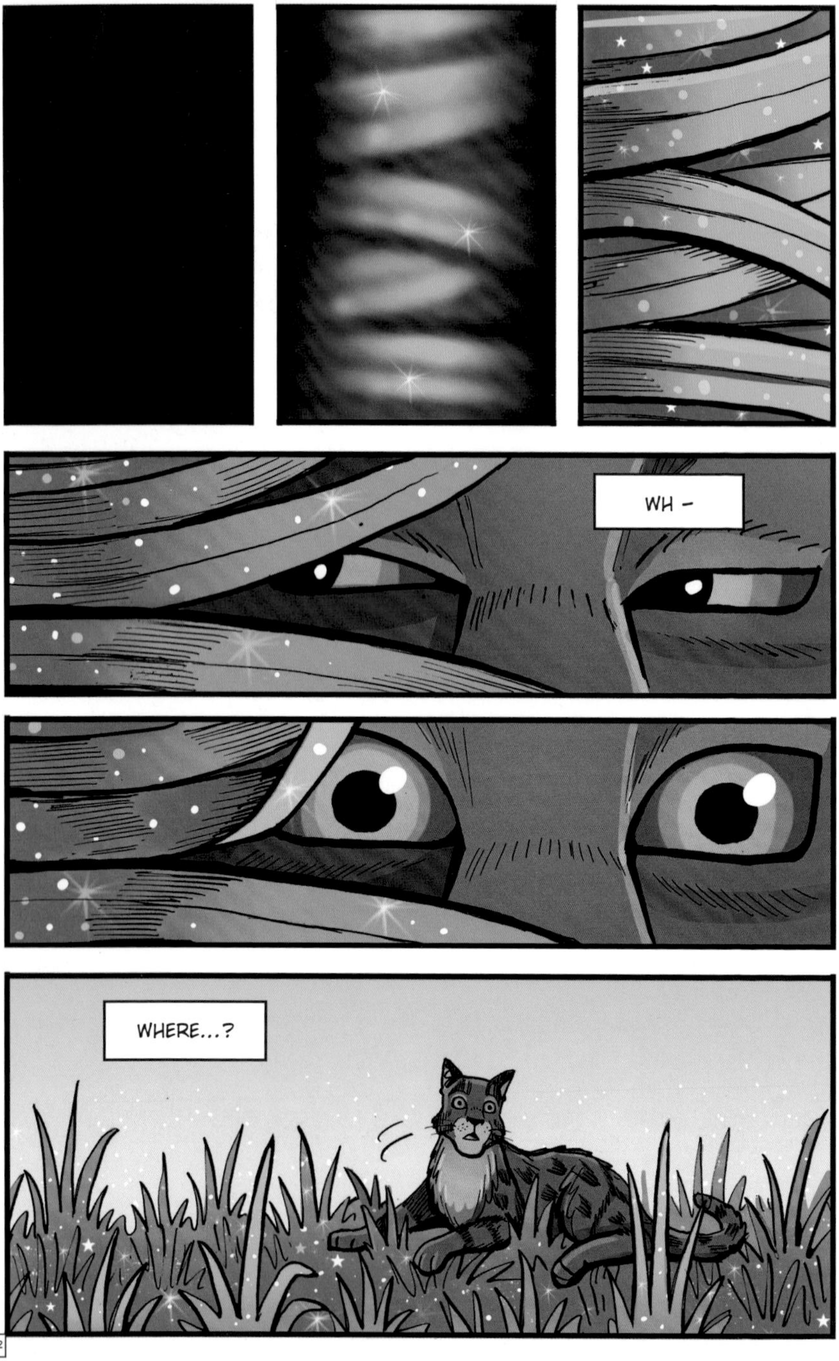
WH –
WHERE...?

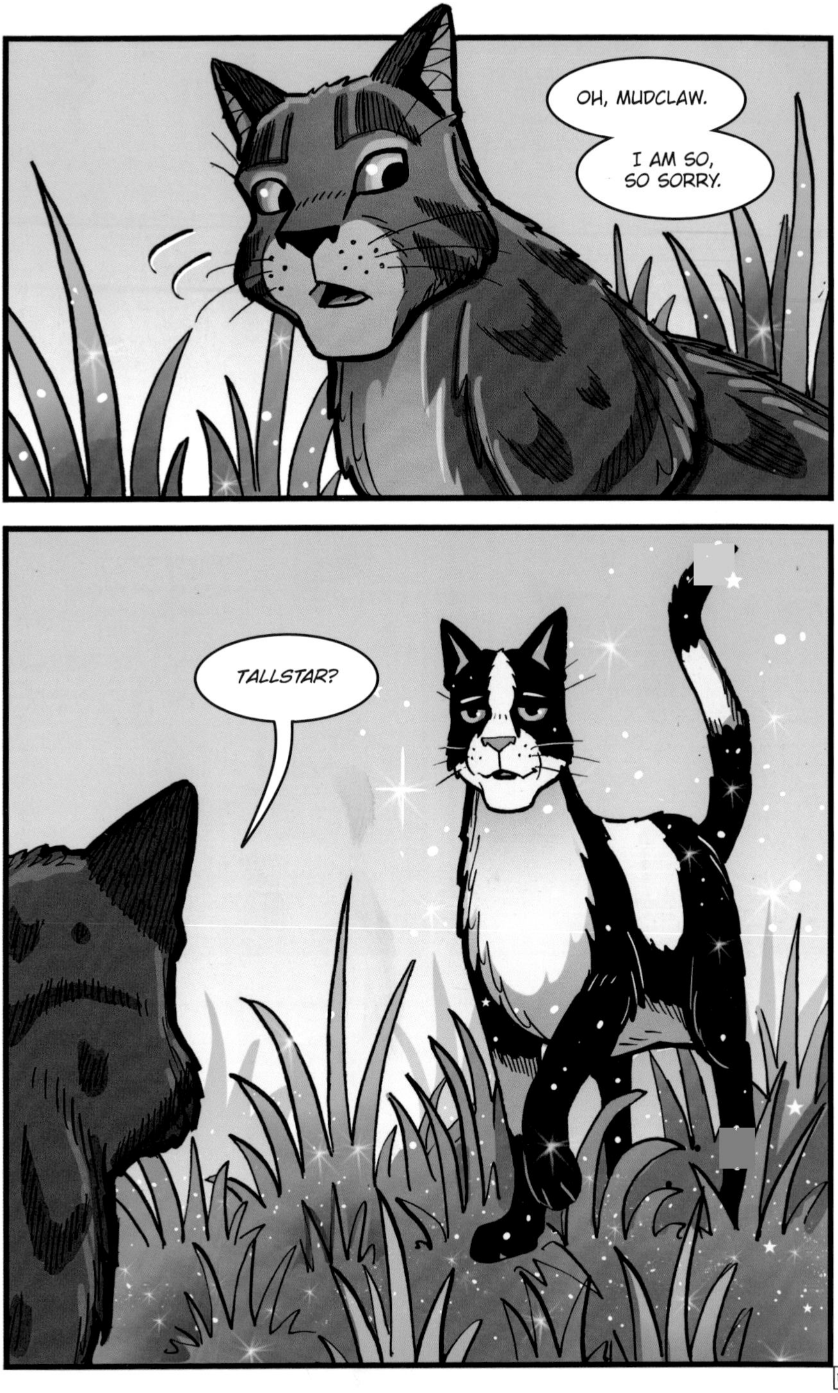
OH, MUDCLAW.
I AM SO, SO SORRY.
TALLSTAR?

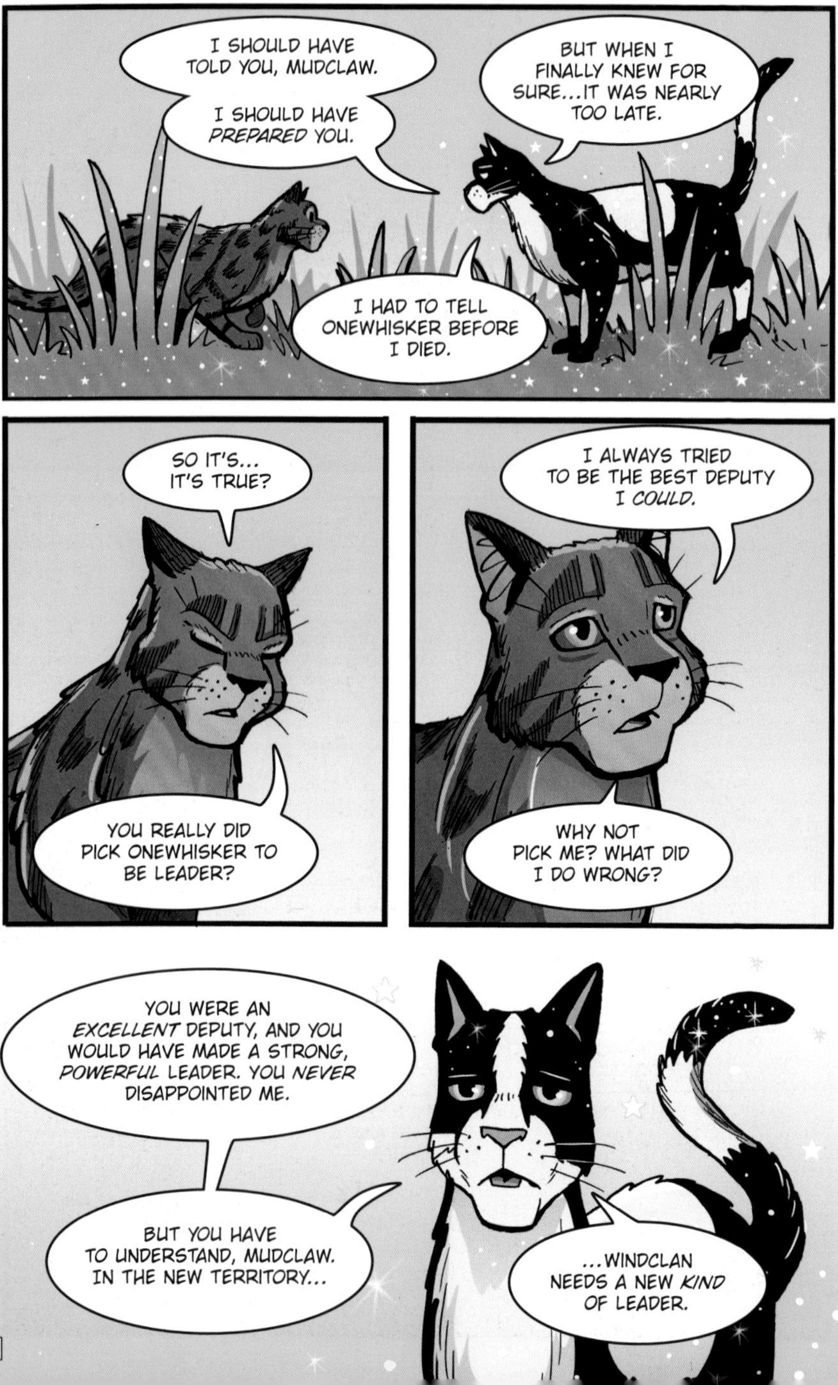
I SHOULD HAVE TOLD YOU, MUDCLAW.
I SHOULD HAVE *PREPARED* YOU.
BUT WHEN I FINALLY KNEW FOR SURE...IT WAS NEARLY TOO LATE.
I HAD TO TELL ONEWHISKER BEFORE I DIED.
SO IT'S... IT'S TRUE?
YOU REALLY DID PICK ONEWHISKER TO BE LEADER?
I ALWAYS TRIED TO BE THE BEST DEPUTY I *COULD.*
WHY NOT PICK ME? WHAT DID I DO WRONG?
YOU WERE AN *EXCELLENT* DEPUTY, AND YOU WOULD HAVE MADE A STRONG, *POWERFUL* LEADER. YOU *NEVER* DISAPPOINTED ME.
BUT YOU HAVE TO UNDERSTAND, MUDCLAW. IN THE NEW TERRITORY...
...WINDCLAN NEEDS A NEW *KIND* OF LEADER.

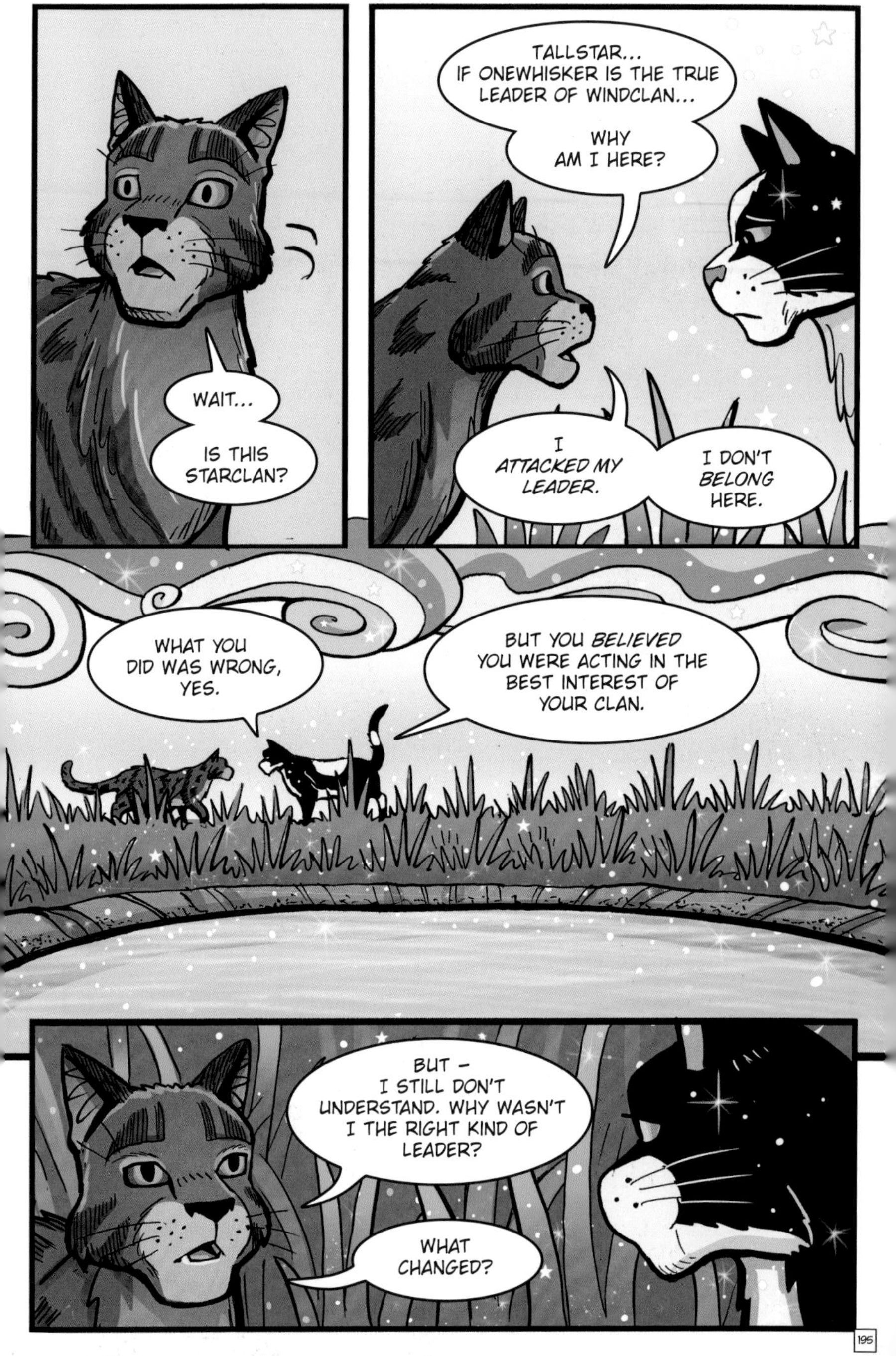
WAIT...
IS THIS STARCLAN?
TALLSTAR... IF ONEWHISKER IS THE TRUE LEADER OF WINDCLAN...
WHY AM I HERE?
I *ATTACKED* MY LEADER.
I DON'T *BELONG* HERE.
WHAT YOU DID WAS WRONG, YES.
BUT YOU *BELIEVED* YOU WERE ACTING IN THE BEST INTEREST OF YOUR CLAN.
BUT – I STILL DON'T UNDERSTAND. WHY WASN'T I THE RIGHT KIND OF LEADER?
WHAT CHANGED?

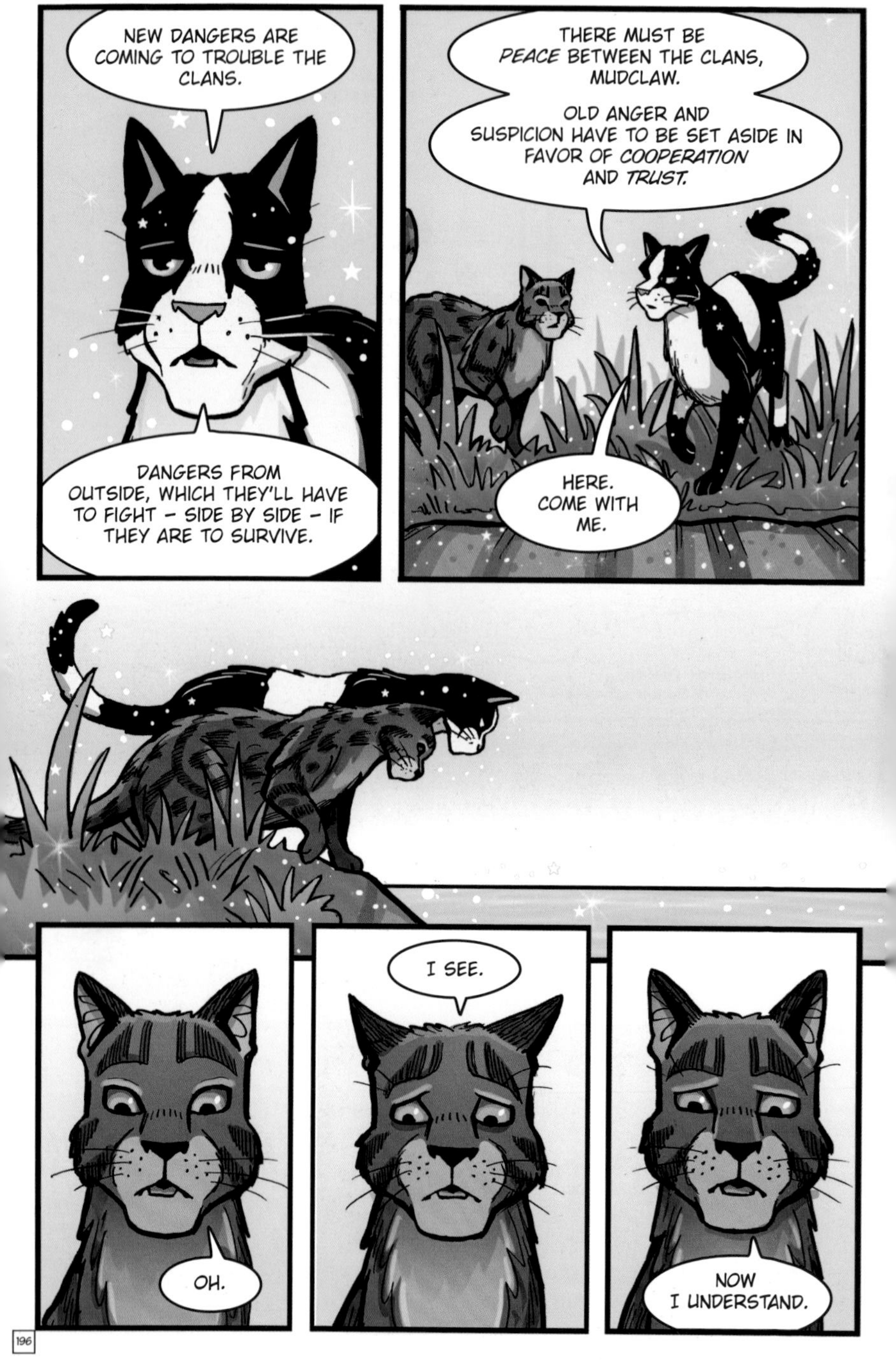
NEW DANGERS ARE COMING TO TROUBLE THE CLANS.
DANGERS FROM OUTSIDE, WHICH THEY'LL HAVE TO FIGHT – SIDE BY SIDE – IF THEY ARE TO SURVIVE.
THERE MUST BE *PEACE* BETWEEN THE CLANS, MUDCLAW.
OLD ANGER AND SUSPICION HAVE TO BE SET ASIDE IN FAVOR OF *COOPERATION* AND *TRUST.*
HERE. COME WITH ME.
OH.
I SEE.
NOW I UNDERSTAND.

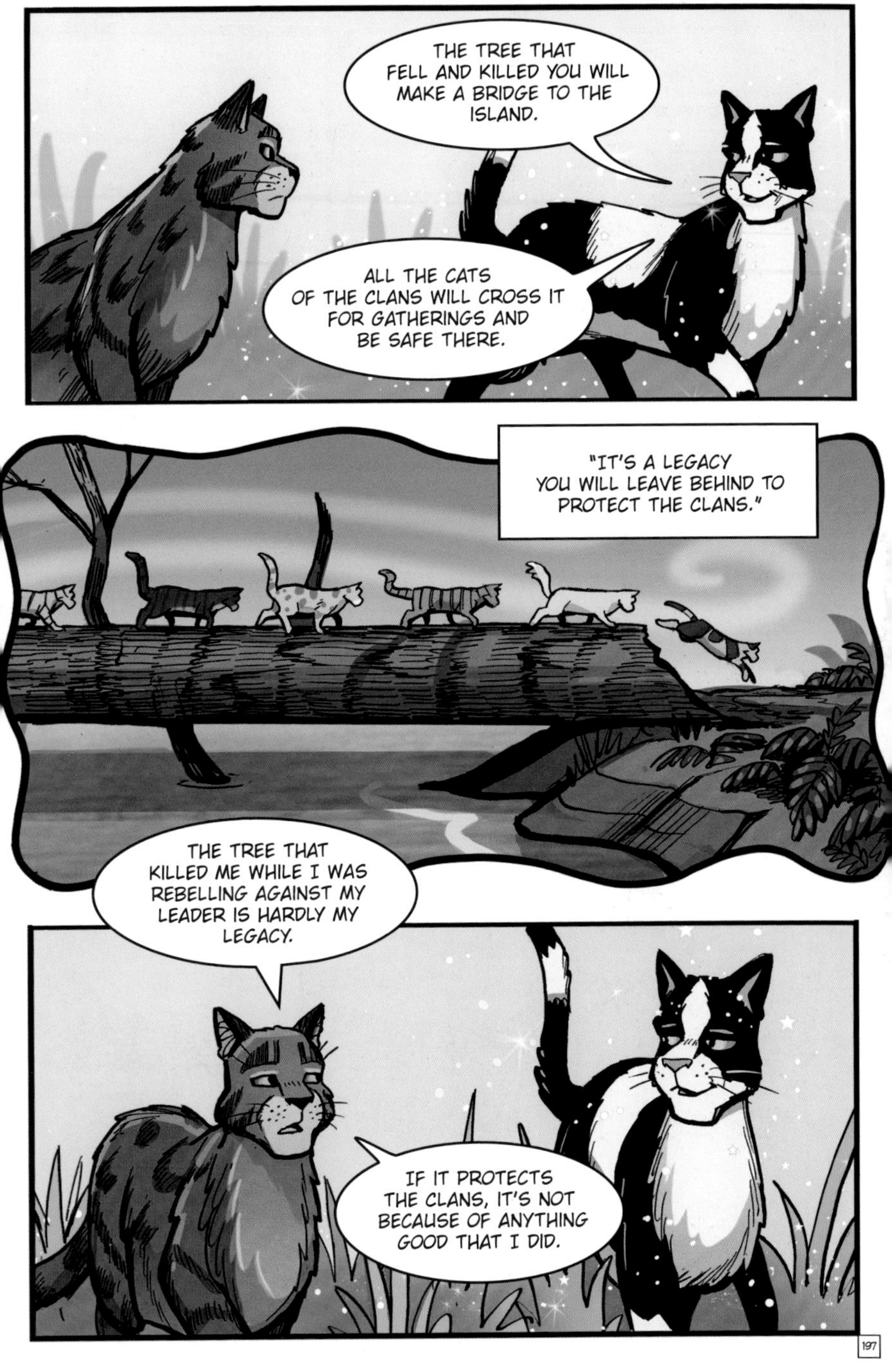

THE TREE THAT FELL AND KILLED YOU WILL MAKE A BRIDGE TO THE ISLAND.
ALL THE CATS OF THE CLANS WILL CROSS IT FOR GATHERINGS AND BE SAFE THERE.
"IT'S A LEGACY YOU WILL LEAVE BEHIND TO PROTECT THE CLANS."
THE TREE THAT KILLED ME WHILE I WAS REBELLING AGAINST MY LEADER IS HARDLY MY LEGACY.
IF IT PROTECTS THE CLANS, IT'S NOT BECAUSE OF ANYTHING GOOD THAT I DID.

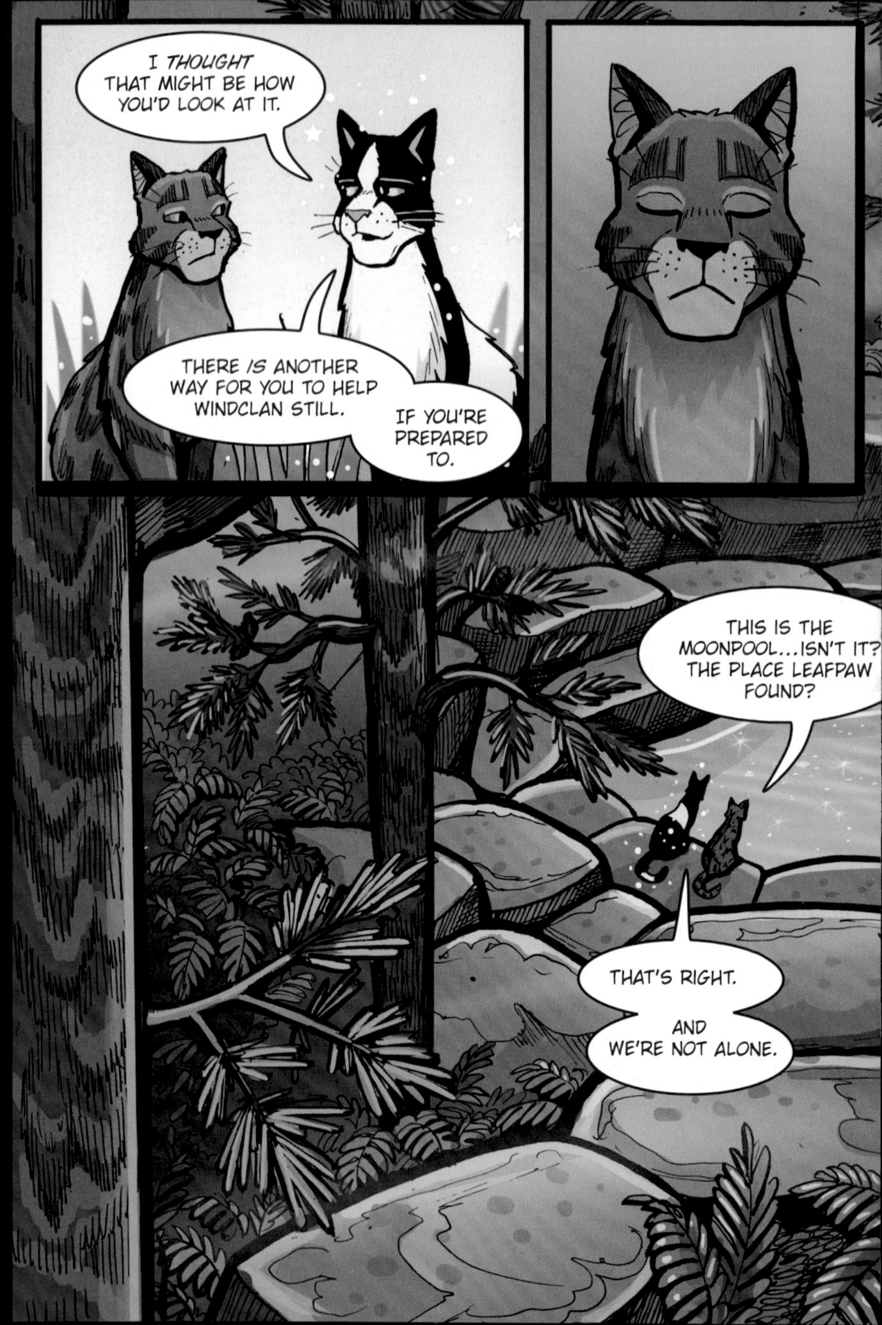
I *THOUGHT* THAT MIGHT BE HOW YOU'D LOOK AT IT.
THERE *IS* ANOTHER WAY FOR YOU TO HELP WINDCLAN STILL.
IF YOU'RE PREPARED TO.
THIS IS THE MOONPOOL...ISN'T IT? THE PLACE LEAFPAW FOUND?
THAT'S RIGHT.
AND WE'RE NOT ALONE.

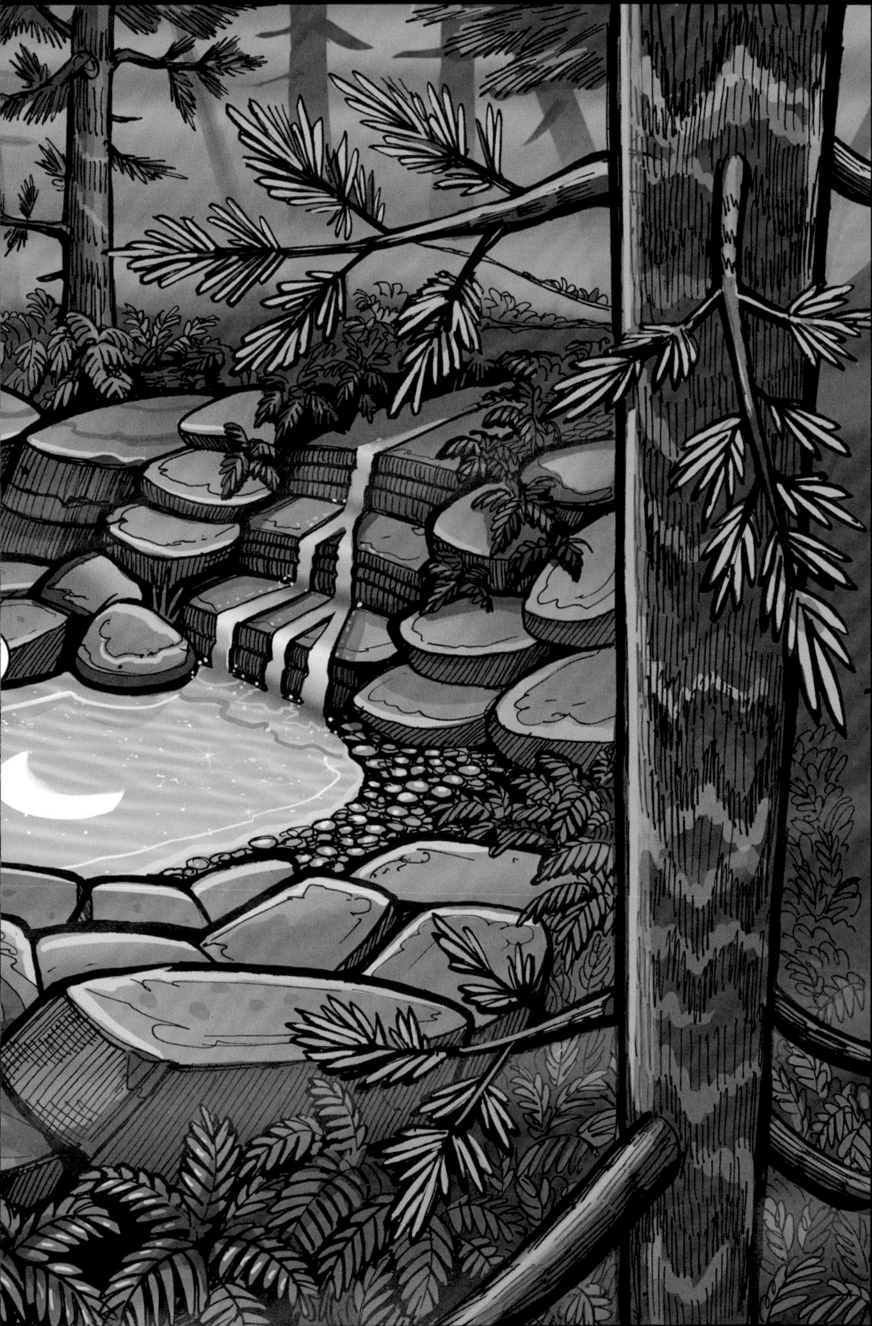

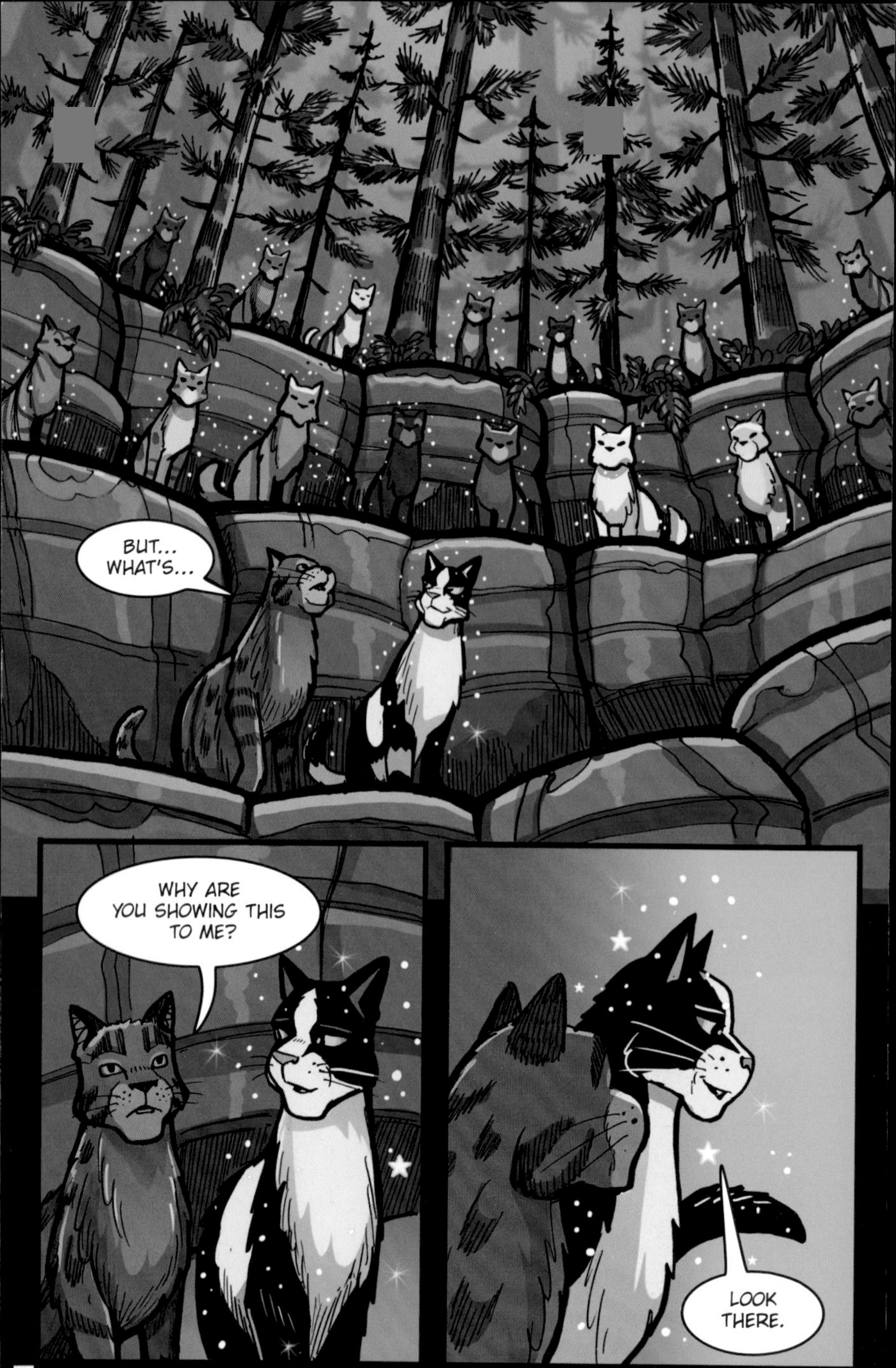
BUT... WHAT'S...
WHY ARE YOU SHOWING THIS TO ME?
LOOK THERE.

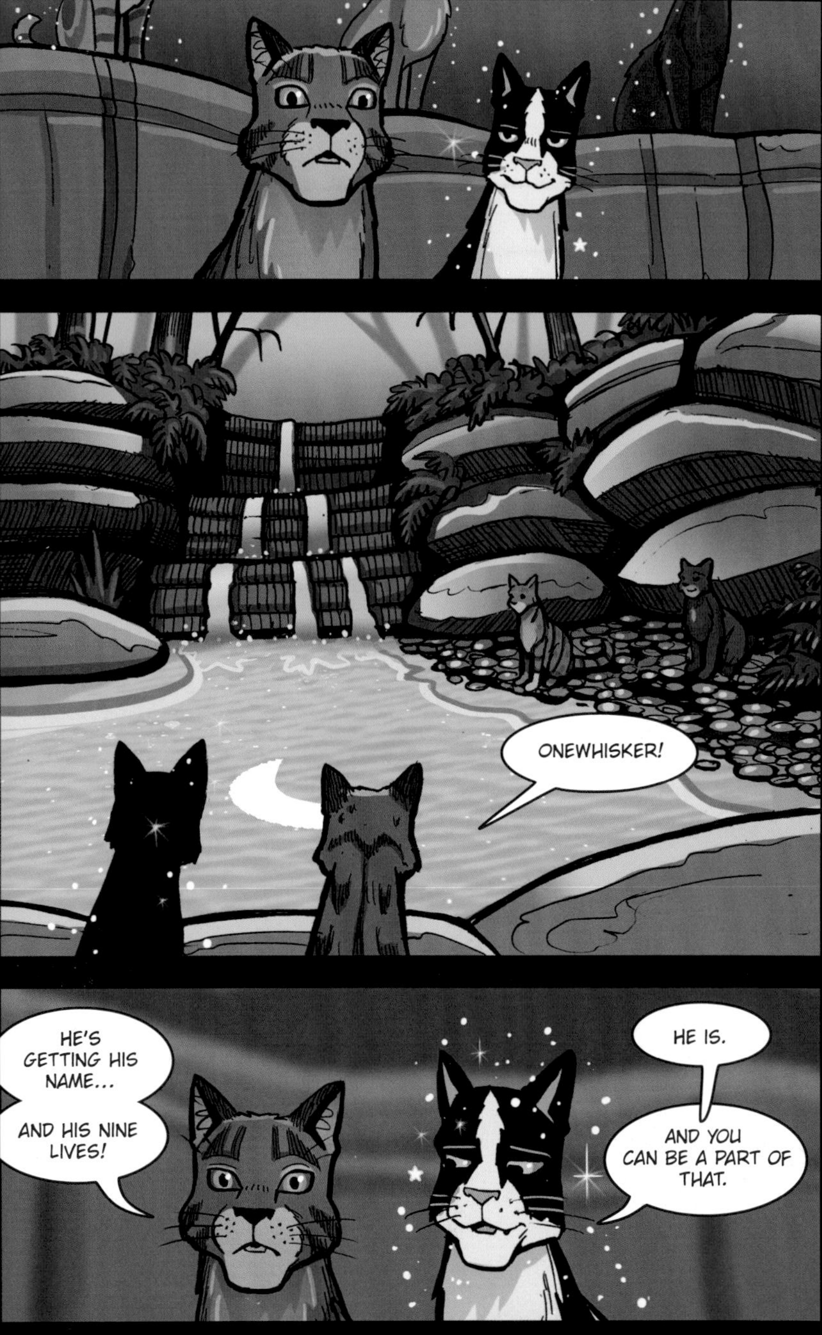
ONEWHISKER!
HE'S GETTING HIS NAME...
AND HIS NINE LIVES!
HE IS.
AND YOU CAN BE A PART OF THAT.

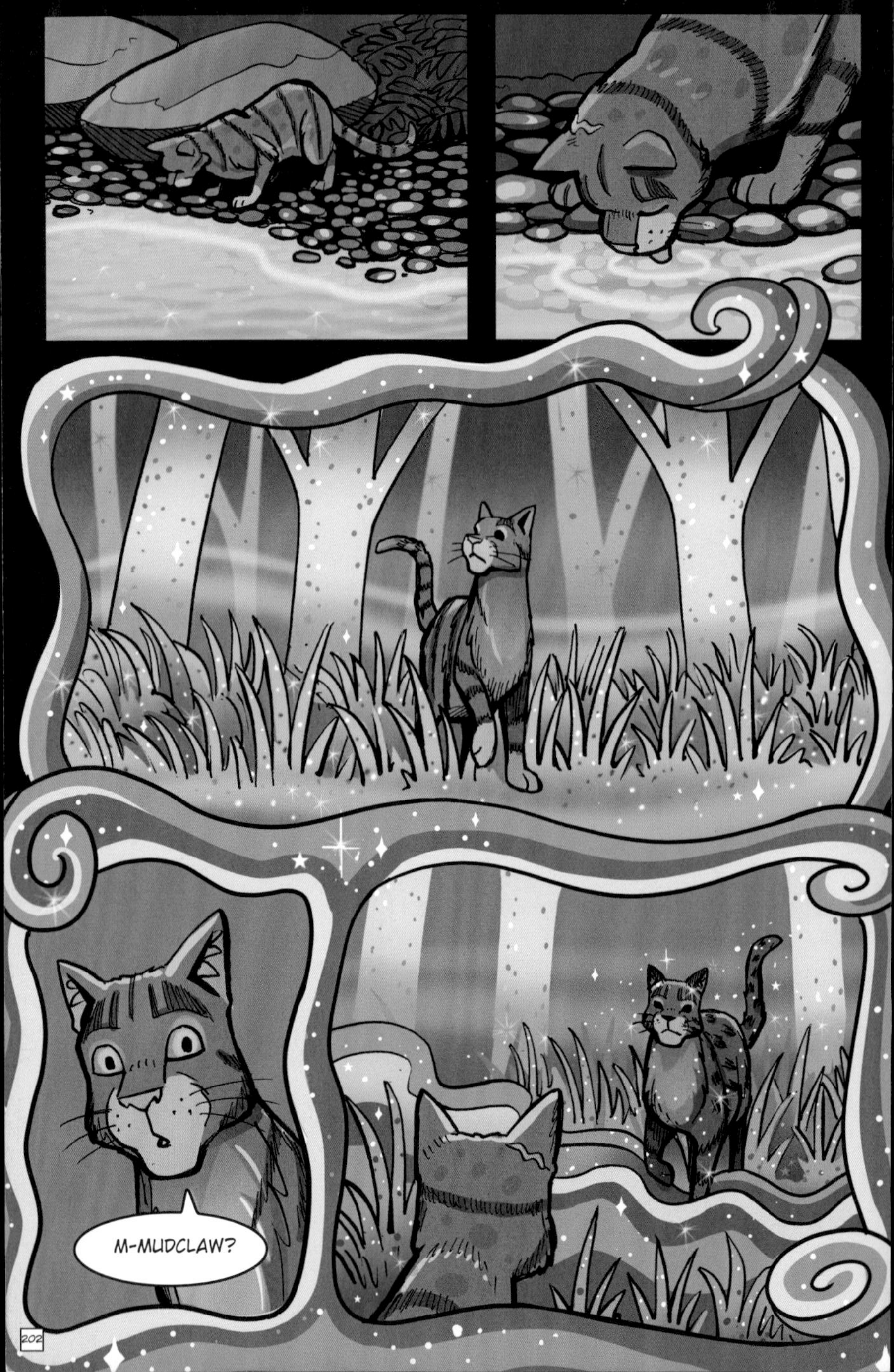
M-MUDCLAW?

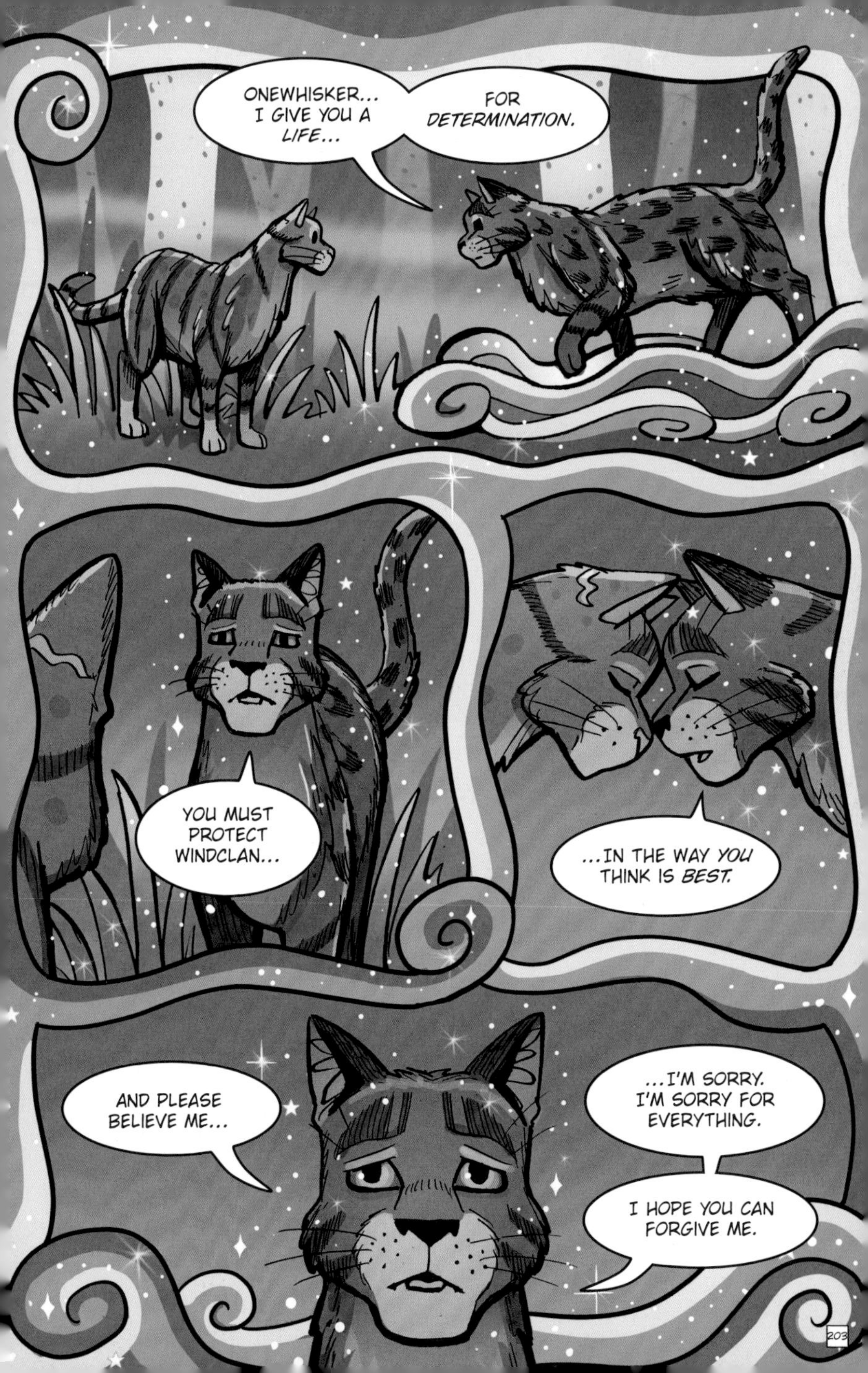
ONEWHISKER... I GIVE YOU A *LIFE*...
FOR *DETERMINATION.*
YOU MUST PROTECT WINDCLAN...
...IN THE WAY *YOU* THINK IS *BEST.*
AND PLEASE BELIEVE ME...
...I'M SORRY. I'M SORRY FOR EVERYTHING.
I HOPE YOU CAN FORGIVE ME.

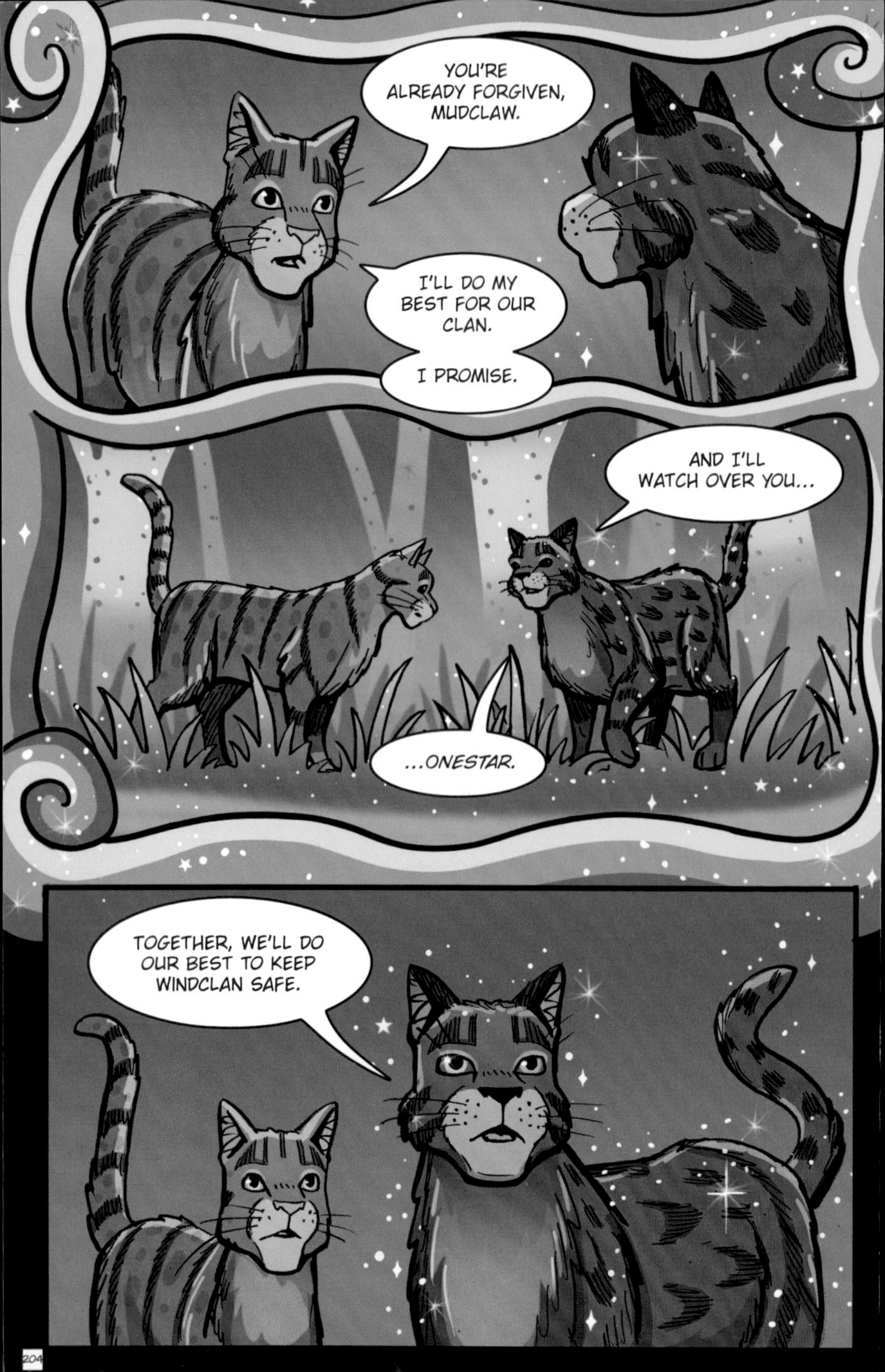
YOU'RE ALREADY FORGIVEN, MUDCLAW.
I'LL DO MY BEST FOR OUR CLAN.
I PROMISE.
AND I'LL WATCH OVER YOU...
...ONESTAR.
TOGETHER, WE'LL DO OUR BEST TO KEEP WINDCLAN SAFE.

A NEW **WARRIORS** ADVENTURE BEGINS!

DON'T MISS

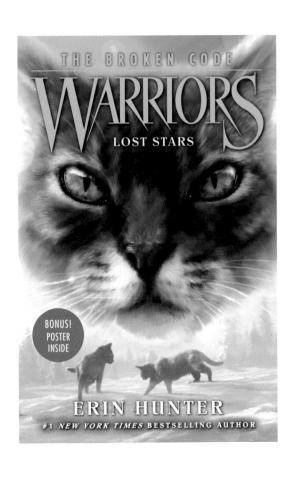

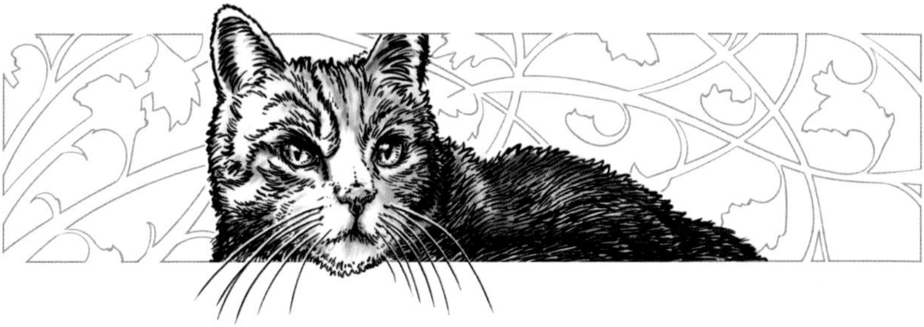

Chapter 1

Shadowpaw craned his neck over his back, straining to groom the hard-to-reach spot at the base of his tail. He had just managed to give his fur a few vigorous licks when he heard paw steps approaching. He looked up to see his father, Tigerstar, and his mother, Dovewing, their pelts brushing as they gazed down at him with pride and joy shining in their eyes.

"What is it?" he asked, sitting up and giving his pelt a shake.

"We just came to see you off," Tigerstar responded, while Dovewing gave her son's ears a quick, affectionate lick.

Shadowpaw's fur prickled with embarrassment. *Like I haven't been to the Moonpool before,* he thought. *They're still treating me as if I'm a kit in the nursery!*

He was sure that his parents hadn't made such a fuss when his littermates, Pouncestep and Lightleap, had been warrior apprentices. *I guess it's because I'm going to be a medicine cat. . . .* Or maybe because of the seizures he'd had since he was a kit. He knew his parents still worried about him, even though it had been a while since his last upsetting vision. *They're probably hoping that with some training from the other medicine cats, I'll learn to control my visions once and for all . . . and I can be normal.*

Shadowpaw wanted that, too.

"The snow must be really deep up on the moors," Dovewing mewed. "Make sure you watch where you're putting your paws."

Shadowpaw wriggled his shoulders, praying that none of his Clanmates were listening. "I will," he promised, glancing toward the medicine cats' den in the hope of seeing his mentor, Puddleshine, emerge. But there was no sign of him yet.

To his relief, Tigerstar gave Dovewing a nudge and they both moved off toward the Clan leader's den. Shadowpaw rubbed one paw hastily across his face and bounded across the camp to see what was keeping Puddleshine.

Intent on finding his mentor, Shadowpaw barely noticed the patrol trekking toward the fresh-kill pile, prey dangling from their jaws. He skidded to a halt just in time to avoid colliding with Cloverfoot, the Clan deputy.

"Shadowpaw!" she exclaimed around the shrew she was carrying. "You nearly knocked me off my paws."

"Sorry, Cloverfoot," Shadowpaw meowed, dipping his head respectfully.

Cloverfoot let out a snort, half annoyed, half amused. "Apprentices!"

Shadowpaw tried to hide his irritation. He was an apprentice, yes, but an old one—medicine cat apprentices' training lasted longer than warriors'. His littermates were full warriors already. But he knew his parents would want him to respect the deputy.

Cloverfoot padded on, followed by Strikestone, Yarrowleaf, and Blazefire. Though they were all carrying prey, they had only one or two pieces each, and what little they had managed to catch was undersized and scrawny.

"I can't remember a leaf-bare as cold as this," Yarrowleaf complained as she dropped a blackbird on the fresh-kill pile.

Strikestone nodded, shivering as he fluffed out his brown tabby pelt. "No wonder there's no prey. They're all hiding down their holes, and I can't blame them."

As Shadowpaw moved on, out of earshot, he couldn't help noticing how pitifully small the fresh-kill pile was, and he tried to ignore his own growling belly. He could hardly remember his first leaf-bare, when he'd been a tiny kit, so he didn't know if the older cats were right and the weather was unusually cold.

I only know I don't like it, he grumbled to himself as he picked his way through the icy slush that covered the ground of the camp. *My paws are so cold I think they'll drop off. I can't wait for newleaf!*

Puddleshine ducked out of the entrance to the medicine

cats' den as Shadowpaw approached. "Good, you're ready," he meowed. "We'd better hurry, or we'll be late." As he led the way toward the camp entrance, he added, "I've been checking our herb stores, and they're getting dangerously low."

"We could search for more on the way back," Shadow-paw suggested, his medicine-cat duties driving out his thoughts of cold and hunger. He always enjoyed working with Puddleshine to find, sort, and store the herbs. Treating cats with herbs made him feel calm and in control . . . the opposite of how he felt during his seizures and upsetting visions.

"We can try," Puddleshine sighed. "But what isn't frostbitten will be covered with snow." He glanced over his shoulder at Shadowpaw as the two cats headed out into the forest. "This is turning out to be a really bad leaf-bare. And it isn't over yet, not by a long way."

Excitement tingled through Shadowpaw from ears to tail-tip as he scrambled up the rocky slope toward the line of bushes that surrounded the Moonpool hollow. His worries over his seizures and the bitter leaf-bare faded; every hair on his pelt was bristling with anticipation of his meeting with the other medicine cats, and most of all with StarClan.

He might not be a full medicine cat yet, and he might not be fully in control of his visions . . . but he would still get to meet with his warrior ancestors. And from the rest of the medicine cats he would find out what was going on in the other Clans.

Standing at the top of the slope, waiting for Puddle-shine to push his way through the bushes, Shadowpaw reflected on the last few moons. Things had been tense in ShadowClan as every cat settled into their new boundaries and grew used to sharing a border with SkyClan. Not long ago, SkyClan had lived separately from the other Clans, in a far-flung territory in a gorge. But StarClan had called SkyClan back to join the other Clans by the lake, because the Clans were stronger when all five were united. Still, SkyClan had needed its own territory, which had meant new borders for everyone, and it had taken time for the other Clans to accept them. Shadowpaw was relieved that things seemed more peaceful now; the brutally cold leaf-bare had given all the Clans more to worry about than quarreling with one another. They were even beginning to rely on one another, especially in sharing herbs when the cold weather had damaged so many of the plants they needed. Shadowpaw felt proud that they were all getting along, instead of battling one another for every piece of prey.

That wasn't a great start to Tigerstar's leadership. . . . I'm glad it's over now!

"Are you going to stand out there all night?"

At the sound of Puddleshine's voice from the other side of the bushes, Shadowpaw dived in among the branches, wincing as sharp twigs scraped along his pelt, and thrust himself out onto the ledge above the Moonpool. Opposite him, halfway up the rocky wall of the hollow, a trickle of water bubbled out from between two moss-covered boulders. The water fell down into the pool below, with a fitful glimmer as if the stars themselves were trapped inside it. The rippling surface of the pool shone silver with reflected moonlight.

Shadowpaw wanted to leap into the air with excitement at being back at the Moonpool, but he fought to hold on to some self-control, and padded down the spiral path to the water's edge with all the dignity expected of a medicine cat. Awe welled up inside him as he felt his paws slip into the hollows made by cats countless seasons before.

Who were they? Where did they go? he wondered.

The two ThunderClan medicine cats were already sitting beside the pool. Shadowpaw guessed it was too cold to wait outside for everyone to arrive, as the medicine cats usually did. Alderheart was thoughtfully grooming his chest fur, while Jayfeather's tail-tip twitched back and forth in irritation. He turned his blind blue gaze on Puddleshine and Shadowpaw as they reached the bottom of the hollow.

"You took your time," he snapped. "We're wasting moonlight."

Shadowpaw realized that Kestrelflight of WindClan and Mothwing and Willowshine, the two RiverClan medicine cats, were sitting just beyond the two from ThunderClan. The shadow of a rock had hidden them from him until now.

"Nice to see you, too, Jayfeather," Puddleshine responded mildly. "I'm sorry if we're late, but I don't see Frecklewish or Fidgetflake, either."

Jayfeather gave a disdainful sniff. "If they're not here soon, we'll start without them."

Would Jayfeather really do that? Shadowpaw was still staring at the ThunderClan medicine cat, wondering, when a rustling from the top of the slope put him on alert. Looking up, he saw Frecklewish pushing her way through the bushes, followed closely by Fidgetflake.

"At last!" Jayfeather hissed.

He's in a mood, Shadowpaw thought, then added to himself with a flicker of amusement, *Nothing new there, then.*

As the two SkyClan medicine cats padded down the slope, Shadowpaw noticed how thin and weary they both looked. For a heartbeat he wondered if there was anything wrong in SkyClan. Then he realized that he and the rest of the medicine cats looked just as skinny, just as worn out by the trials of leaf-bare.

Frecklewish dipped her head to her fellow medicine cats as she joined them beside the pool. "Greetings," she mewed, her fatigue clear in her voice. "How is the prey running in your Clans?"

For a moment no cat replied, and Shadowpaw could sense their uneasiness. *None of them wants to admit that their Clan is having problems.*

Shadowpaw was surprised when Puddleshine, who was

normally so pensive, was the first to speak up. Maybe the cold had banished his mentor's reserve and enabled him to be honest.

"The hunting is very poor in ShadowClan," he replied; Shadowpaw felt a twinge of alarm at how discouraged his mentor sounded. "If this freezing cold goes on much longer, I don't know what we'll do."

The remaining medicine cats exchanged glances of relief, as if they were glad to learn their Clan wasn't the only one suffering.

Willowshine nodded agreement. "Many RiverClan cats are getting sick because it's so cold."

"In ThunderClan too," Alderheart murmured.

"We're running out of herbs," Fidgetflake added with a twitch of his whiskers. "And the few we have left are shriveled and useless."

Frecklewish gave her Clanmate a sympathetic glance. "I've heard some of the younger warriors joking about running off to be kittypets," she meowed.

"No cat had better say that in my hearing." Jayfeather drew his lips back in the beginning of a snarl. "Or they'll wish they hadn't."

"Keep your fur on, Jayfeather," Frecklewish responded. "It was only a joke. All SkyClan cats are loyal to their Clan."

Jayfeather's only reply was an irritated flick of his ears.

"I don't suppose any of you have spare supplies of catmint?" Kestrelflight asked hesitantly. "The clumps that grow in WindClan are all blackened by frost. We won't have any more until newleaf."

Most of the cats shook their heads, except for Willowshine, who rested her tail encouragingly on Kestrelflight's shoulder. "RiverClan can help," she promised. "There's catmint growing in the Twoleg gardens near our border. It's more sheltered there."

"Thanks, Willowshine." Kestrelflight's voice was unsteady. "There's whitecough in the WindClan camp, and without catmint I'm terrified it will turn to greencough."

"Meet me by the border tomorrow at sunhigh," Willowshine mewed. "I'll show you where the catmint grows."

"This is all well and good," Jayfeather snorted, "every cat getting along, but let's not forget why we're here. I'm much more interested in what StarClan has to say. Shall we begin?" He paced to the edge of the Moonpool and stretched out one forepaw to touch the surface, only to draw his paw back with a gasp of surprise.

ERIN HUNTER

is inspired by a fascination with the ferocity of the natural world. As well as having great respect for nature in all its forms, Erin enjoys creating rich, mythical explanations for animal behavior. She is also the author of the Survivors, Seekers, and Bravelands series.

Find out more online at
WarriorCats.com.